HURRICANE MOON

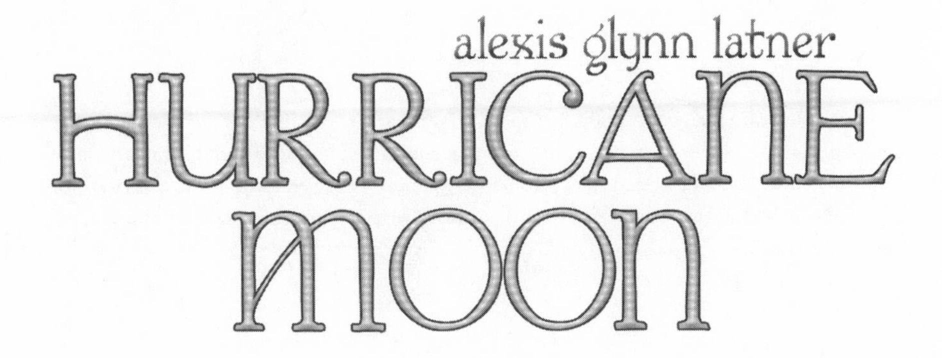

an imprint of Prometheus Books
Amherst, NY

Published 2007 by Pyr®, an imprint of Prometheus Books

Inquiries should be addressed to
Pyr
59 John Glenn Drive
Amherst, New York 14228–2197
VOICE: 716–691–0133, ext. 210
FAX: 716–564–2711
WWW.PYRSF.COM

11 10 09 08 07 5 4 3 2 1

Library of Congress Cataloging-in-Publication Data

Latner, Alexis Glynn.
Hurricane moon / by Alexis Glynn Latner.
p. cm.
ISBN 978–1–59102–545–0
1. Regression (Civilization)—Fiction. 2. Outer space—Exploration—Fiction.
I. Title.

PS3612.A9H87 2007
813'.6—dc22

2007011071

Printed in the United States on acid-free paper

To Elizabeth N. Moon

AD MAIOREM DEI GLORIAM

ACKNOWLEDGMENTS

This book could not have been created without the expert and lively advice of space physicists, biomedical researchers, engineers, social scientists, and astronaut candidates. My most profound thanks go to Paula Burch, Kristin Farry, Marc Hairston, Valerie Olson, Sedge Simons, and Eileen Stansbery, all of whom are PhD graduates of Rice University in Houston, Texas.

In the long adventure of writing and revising this book, I had invaluable encouragement and guidance from many wonderful people. I especially thank Kristin again, and Margaret Ball, Jennifer Juday, Laurie May, Dan Perez, Matt Reiten, Mary Rosenblum, Stanley Schmidt, and above all my agent, Joshua Bilmes.

CONTENTS

Chapter One

JUDGMENT DAY

Earth and the Moon looked the same size from here. Catharin Gault hovered close to the glass in the middle of the long window that framed Earth in one end, the Moon in the other. The angular docks and cranes of the L5 shipyard slid into the scene. The blue planet slipped toward the edge of the frame. The new starship was yawing, window and all. She had to make her way to the fourth briefing so far today on as many urgent issues, but for a few stolen moments she marveled at the double planet half-lit by the Sun. Earth's night side coruscated with the lights of vast cities. The Moon's pale face was marked by faint spider-lines of settlement. Very soon, human civilization would reach toward a better world than the Moon, across a vastly greater, purifying, distance. And she would have a role in that. Her breath caught in her throat at the familiar but never comfortable thought.

As Earth touched the edge of the frame, movement in her peripheral vision attracted her attention. She recognized the stocky form of Bix—Captain Hubert Bixby—floating her way. His grizzled hair stuck out in the microgravity. "Cat, something's come up. The Chicago Assessment office wants you to interview a last-minute prospect and tell them if we want him."

"Why me? It's their job."

"Apparently, this guy's got max qualifications of a sort you're suited to judge, but he's got one or two max disqualifications too. The assessor on duty kicked the problem to his higher-ups, and somebody routed it to you. The nearest telcon is the Test and Checkout chief's. Let's go borrow it."

Taking the quickest cut, they cruised across the transport level bay. The bay bustled with activity. White-suited technicians dodged around them. Inspectors checked each shuttlecraft's retaining rigs and braces. Other personnel darted in with replacement parts or revised checklists.

Catharin and Bix wore blue coveralls with red armbands that meant primary crew. The garb cleared a path for them. Even when they encountered five workers steering a heavy piece of equipment that outmassed the team, they managed to shove it out of the way for Bix and Catharin. "I've never felt so important," Catharin murmured.

"Me either," Bix said. "And I've never left on a mission knowing we wouldn't come back."

Catharin took a deep breath to damp down the dread and excitement that surged up at those words.

Bix made for the far wall of the open bay. GERALD DONOVAN, TEST AND CHECKOUT SUPERVISOR TRANSPORT LEVEL was lettered on a door that stood ajar. "Gerry?" Bix called. "Can you spare your telcon for a minor emergency?"

"Surely, and I'll get out of the way," said the white-haired man in the office.

"Chief Gerry Donovan. One of the best in the space construction business. Gerry, this is Catharin, our doctor. Her call won't take long."

"Take your time, Doctor. I've a pair of shuttles to see about. I don't want them slipping as much as a centimeter when this ship decelerates at the end of the trip." A pen floated in the corner of his office. Chief Donovan snared the pen with the bare toes of his right foot. With his left foot, he caught the jamb of the door to swing himself out of the office. His arms were shiny and artificial. Bilateral upper-limb deficiency, Catharin realized. Probably congenital. Trauma amputees never got that good using their feet as substitute hands.

Bix told Catharin, "Join the Transport briefing soon as you can." He left with Donovan.

Catharin contacted the Chicago Assessment office. The back wall of the narrow office shimmered, then imaged a sparse Earthside room and a man slouching in a chair. The assessor was absent: this would be a private interview. The man wore expensive, stylish clothing. Dark hair curled over his suit collar and over the edges of a long, strong-boned face. The build matched the face, tall and lean, spilling out of the functional little chair.

Catharin said, "Good day. Let me apologize in advance for the fact that this will have to be quick. I've not much time. I'm Dr. Gault, the starship's medical officer—"

He interrupted. "You're the gatekeeper. So what do you need to know?"

"To begin with, who are you?"

She expected a verbal resume. But he just said, "Joseph Devreze."

And that, she realized with a jolt, told her what she needed to know. "You recently won the Nobel Prize?"

"You're not too busy to keep up with the news, eh?"

Catharin bit back a retort. She located Chief Donovan's telcon touchpad below the surface of the desk and touched in a request for Devreze's medical file. The file appeared in a window on the wall.

Devreze shifted in the chair. "I watch the news too, including coverage of the starship. I gather that alien conditions on some other world might call for organisms to be invented, tailor-made for whatever the strange environment is." He had a clipped baritone voice with a clear timbre that Catharin would have liked in other circumstances. "I'm eminently qualified to do that."

She had parked herself behind Chief Donovan's desk with a leg hooked around the knee bar below the desk. Placing her elbows on the desk and folding her hands under her chin to make herself look grounded and secure, she said, "Yes, your qualifications do make you irresistible—almost."

"*Almost*?" He sounded startled. "Who do you want? God?"

"That would depend on His motives. Your participation in this mission depends on yours," she said pleasantly.

"Why the hell do you care why I want to come?"

"Some people want to go to the stars to escape personal problems." Glancing at the medical file, Catharin found the usual childhood illnesses, a high level of cardiovascular fitness, no present disorder, terminal or otherwise. "Do you have enemies?"

Devreze shrugged. "Only every scientist I ever trounced in professional journals." He shifted in the chair.

Height six feet, four inches, said the medical file. Catharin preferred men at least as tall as she, and she was tall for a woman. Her sexual self, not aware of her fate in the near future, found this man interesting. She maintained a professional tone. "This trip will be final. Very final. The starship will not come back. Once the colony is founded, we hope to communicate with Earth, but it will take fifty years for such communication—one way."

"I know. I told you I keep up with the news."

"It's my job today to make sure that you realize this is not just a concept. It's your future. Do you have family?"

"Not really."

The file concurred: unmarried, no siblings or living parents. "I see. You have fewer reasons than many people to stay. But why do you want to go? You do have to answer that."

He crossed his arms. "You could say I've done it all here."

"Done it all?" she echoed, too floored for a more original remark.

"I've made it to the top in my field. Which happens to be one where people get rich and famous."

"I'm aware of that. Novel organisms are very profitable. And people pay outrageous sums for cosmetic genetic alterations, such as calico hair."

He looked directly at her for the first time in the interview. "Good thing you didn't. You look better as a Nordic blonde." Catharin restrained an inexplicable impulse to smile. Devreze rose and paced around the chair. He moved the way he talked, with abruptness, nervous energy. She scrolled to the top of the medical file to verify that he had blue eyes naturally, not courtesy of cosmetic alterations.

"The upshot is, what I've haven't had, or done, or at least had offered to me, isn't worth having," Devreze concluded.

Catharin saw what the lower levels of Assessment had meant by, in Bix's words, max disqualifications. Commitment to the starship mission—or close relatives so committed—constituted a believable, solid reason for people to leave Earth forever. Ennui was not a good reason. "Surely you could find another innovation to make."

"Not legally."

Catharin frowned. "Altering the human germ line is tightly regulated. Is that what you mean?"

"It's the last biggest challenge I haven't met," he said.

"In other words, you find your playground too confining," she said, her tone biting.

Devreze sat down. "I fear stagnation. When you're a scientist and peak early, sometimes you never do anything wonderful ever again." He steepled his hands and gazed into the space between them. He had long, sculpted fingers. His hands should have belonged to a surgeon. "Altering terrestrial animals for alien conditions—that's a challenge I've not had. And won't, unless I go with the starship. I could live for that."

"Could you die for that? The journey will last almost three centuries. Colonists and crew will be in stasis, which is a cold suspended animation. It is not a kind of sleep. There is a small but significant chance of dying in stasis. Never coming out alive."

"So, it's a risk. So's staying here and being put in the science hero's trophy case."

She had to be relentless at this point in the interview. But the job of making people realize what the mission entailed was easier for assessors who were not going themselves. She had to name the same truths that haunted her every night at 3 AM. "Everyone you've ever known on Earth will be gone when you are revived. They won't be just too far away to talk to. Died, buried, and disintegrated back into the molecules they were made of." She paused, pressing her lips together.

He bowed his head, forefinger and thumb clamped to the bridge of his nose. "I'm not much of a social animal. But there are people who mean something to me. I understand you."

"And every home you've ever known . . ." Her voice was rough; her own raw emotion showed. But all that mattered now was that he understand the enormity of what he wanted to do. "Everything will be gone."

He nodded.

"Even the grass and the trees. After several more centuries of ecological disaster on Earth, the planet will be different."

"That's not a reason to stay," he said.

"I know." After moments of silence, she went on, "As for the new world, astronomers have located a planet much like Earth, orbiting a star fifty light-years from here." She found it easier to talk about the new world than the old one. "The chances that it has a large moon are more than ninety percent—so far so good—the chance of at least a primitive ecosphere, more than fifty percent. That means seasons, blue-green algae, and a nitrogen-oxygen atmosphere are probable. It does *not* mean we can expect trees, birds, flowers—that kind of ecosystem has a very low probability." *But oh, how we hope for it!* "The likelihood of intelligent life is less than a millionth of one percent."

Devreze shrugged. "Fine. Nobody to argue with us about our right to invade them."

"What I'm saying is, it won't be paradise. Only after generations of terraforming will it be pretty. You won't live long enough to see forests in the open air."

"I can live without trees." Then he gave her another direct blue gaze. "What about you? Are you tired of crowded cities and dying forests?"

"That's one reason for people to leave Earth. But it's not mine."

"Then . . . ?" His smile was surprisingly winsome. "I told you the truth, even though it's not what you wanted to hear."

Catharin said, "Civilization is diseased, and the diseases are very advanced. War, pollution, and oppression are the kind of things I mean. Overpopulation is another."

"I can't help that," he said offhandedly, "legally."

"Nor I, nor anyone else. We can't save the world. But if we start afresh on a new world—with the all of the lessons we've learned here, and science, but without the bloody history that keeps repeating itself—we can make a better civilization."

Joseph Devreze laughed suddenly and sharply, an outburst of either scorn or pain. "I hope you have better medical judgment than philosophical, Doctor!"

"What?"

"Civilization *is* the disease."

Catharin felt her face heat with a flush. "I think not. I do not regard a patient with cancer as disease itself. And I don't see the blight of cities as anything more—or less—than disease. It may not be curable at this stage. But it's preventable in a different future."

He tilted his head, listening with an intensity that gave her a quick thrill of satisfaction. Then he countered, "If you'd ever seen the black hearts of the big cities under the power towers, you'd know it's not the moral equivalent of heartworm. It's the heart of darkness."

She wanted to retort, *How do you know, you sheltered scientist?* But she just held up her hand. "We'll continue this discussion later. Much later."

"What do you mean?"

"You're in. But you were almost too late, as today is the last day for colonists to report to the ship. Take the next shuttle up." She shut the visuals off.

He'd drawn out of her the ideals that she usually kept to herself. And he'd attacked them. Fight-or-flight adrenaline coursed through her system. She would have preferred to fight. It was an act of will for her to assign Devreze to the appropriate place in the colonial force. Tier One.

According to the plans in the Mission Book, she would be revived as soon as the ship found its star. Only later, after the colony was founded, would the people in Tier One be revived. So Devreze would come out of cryostasis ten years later than she.

Catharin tried to remember when she had ever found a total stranger—much less an objectionably arrogant one—so attractive. She drew a blank. Maybe never. She shook her head, baffled by the coils of coincidence and necessity.

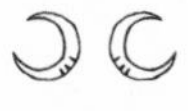

Catharin's days had been getting longer and harder, and this was the worst yet. From 0600 until 1700 hours, Catharin worked in the hospital in the starship as most of the starship's crew were initiated into stasis. All the while, the distinctive smell of a brand-new spacecraft—pristine plastic and fresh paint and sealants breezed by the circulating air system—reminded Catharin that this was no ordinary hospital, or day.

And then the hospital had been shut down, until it would be needed again to populate a colony on the other side of the stars. Catharin said good-bye to the team of medical personnel who had put all of the colonists and most of the crew into stasis. Most of the medics left on shuttles that would take them home to Earth.

As a primary crewmember, Catharin possessed the keys to the kingdom of the starship. In the lowest level of the deserted hospital, she let herself into the maintenance passageways. In a longitudinal passageway, she started to run.

The passageway seemed to curve upward, reflecting the curvature of the spherical starship. The ship was spinning now, which created artificial gravity, and Catharin quickly tired, but she kept running—toward something scheduled for twenty minutes from now, and into the exhaustion that would let her tolerate that event.

Smooth and well lighted, the passageway had system control panels at fifty-meter intervals, and the new-spaceship smell. This ship's name was *Aeon*. A Greek word; a reminder of the bright beginning of civilization when frail sailing craft sailed on the Aegean Sea, in the light of an impossibly distant moon. *Aeon* was made of that very moon—most of the ship's structural materials had been mined on the Moon and ferried to the shipyard here at L5. This was the greatest machine ever built. But not the most sophisticated. In the larger scheme of things, *Aeon* was nothing more than a sturdy packing crate, meant to carry the powers of terraforming—genetic and environmental engineering, nanoscale biological and material science, the seeds of ecosystem, and human beings—to the stars. It would be a very rough and perilous trip. *Just get us there safe*, Catharin repeated, like a mantra as she ran. *Just get us there safe.*

The gravity lessened as she ran out of the ship's equatorial region, toward the north pole. Panting, Catharin checked her watch. She would not make it to the crew level in time. She was still breathing hard as she emerged from the chase network near a transport level window. Now that the ship had spin-gravity, she could not simply float close to the middle of the window to look out at a wide swath of space. There was down now. The transport level window reminded her of church architecture. A window that made you see out and up.

Visible upward was the enormous bulk of the star shield at the north end of the ship and a rectangle of space. The regular spin of the starship took the window past the gleaming, angular shipyards at L5. Catharin sat down. She bowed her head, not wanting to cross gazes with the personnel congregating near the window.

A cool, stiff hand touched her shoulder. "May I join you?" Chief Donovan asked. He settled down, cross-legged and still barefoot. "I hope your call the other day went well."

"Yes, thank you."

"Look now, there's the Moon in our window." Luna arched across the view, its apparent speed reflecting the brisk rotation of the starship. "You expect to see one like it, I understand, when the journey's done."

Catharin nodded. "It's vital that the new world have a moon."

"Our own surely has an ugly face." He spoke with a quiet intensity that was more than conversational. "Sometimes, Doctor, Nature throws problems at you, out of the blue—or out of the black, as the case may be, like the meteors that smashed into the Moon and the Earth, early on." He waved toward the window with one artificial hand.

"Short-term exposure to environmental toxins, in utero?" she asked.

"Yes. It affected only my arms, not my legs or my brain. But I've found that doctors aren't as uneasy about me as most other folks. A bit more likely to listen to what I have to say, rather than just stare at what they see."

With white hair that gleamed in the starlight, he was too old to go to the stars. And so he was sending his thoughts instead. Catharin asked, "Is there something I should hear from you?"

He made a small satisfied movement. "My dear mother always told me, 'You must embrace what God gives you, even if you're given no arms.'"

Catharin tilted her chin up. Even as a child, she'd always reacted with that gesture, silently objecting, at what sounded unreasonable. Today, adult, she said, "I don't believe that."

"Well and good, but in my own experience, Doctor, the Universe, or God, or Nature, name it what you will, does throw problems at you, and she doesn't seem to care who you are, or how many she strikes down. But what happens after that, depends."

"On what?"

He flexed his hairless hands, deliberately. "Attitude, Doctor. Looking for the blessing behind the curse. Feet as dexterous as hands are an asset in space, and I've had a long and fine career up here. Only, you must remember that you just can't say to the meteor, begone. Or wish arms where there are none. I've decided that was what my mother really meant for me to hear. Some things will never be the way they might have been, so you must accept them the way they are. Plans are good, training better yet, but not if they blind you and bind you in the face of the unexpected."

Numb, Catharin nodded.

A pleasant, androgynous voice resonated through the level. "*Attention, please. The shutters will close in ten minutes.*"

Most of the murmuring crowd here were Transport workers, wearing sturdy coveralls. Self-conscious in her thin blue shorts and shirt piped in telltale red, Catharin felt grateful for Chief Donovan's company. The starship would have to leave the Donovans behind. And take an arrogant Devreze. It was grossly unfair. But stasis would have deleterious effects on the human body, worse with increased age of the subject. A strict age cutoff had been imposed on colonists and crew alike.

"*The shutters are closing.*"

Catharin shivered. She had been dreading this moment for days. Of all final preparations, this one bespoke finality most clearly for her.

Massive shutters crept from each side toward the middle to mesh together, to shield the window from the hazards of the interstellar medium. There was a subaudible sound, or vibration, that propagated through the superstructure. Catharin felt light-headed, caught herself hyperventilating. *No*, she thought, *I can't afford claustrophobia. Not now. It's not being trapped.* She stared at the black window that now had only a jagged thread of stars running down the middle of it. *It's protection against what the universe might throw at us.* She fought for calm and for some kind of proactive stance, not just sitting here being afraid. She heard herself say, "Thank you for your advice. I'm going to take it right away."

"I beg your pardon? I thought it was the sort of advice to keep on hand for a rainy day."

"We've been doing simulations of different planetfall scenarios. But we haven't had one where the universe throws such a curve at us that we can't save the mission in its nominal form. And we need that kind of attitude check. The Sim Supervisor is a friend of mine. I'm going to ask him to arrange something." Catharin added, "Talk about rainy days—the Sim Supe can make it pour."

☽☾

As often as she sat at the Life Systems station, and as intently as she played her part in the simulations, Catharin had never felt jaded in the control center, never failed to be awed. The control center of *Aeon* was a vast, vaulted room with massively scaled elements. The primary crew stations rimmed a large, elevated platform, behind which one high wall was taken up by a visual screen. Nicknamed the Big Picture, the main screen showed pictures and diagrams of the ship and its situation in vast scope and detail. Subsidiary stations were serried in rows along the length of the center, and screens filled the walls beside them with floor-to-ceiling information visuals.

A window in the Big Picture showed a small pair of points of light, blue and white, representing a new planet with its moon. What dominated the Big Picture was the Sun—close up, brilliant, with turbulent chromosphere and several sunspots.

Not the Sun, Catharin corrected her thinking. A strange star that looks and behaves like the Sun, so far. In simulation, *Aeon* at perihelion was swinging around the new sun on its way to rendezvous with the new world. Primary and secondary crew were on station. In the gallery, a dozen or so observers took copious notes for the debriefing later. Catharin noticed the white hair of Gerry Donovan in the top row of the gallery.

Captain Bixby paced between the Command and Flight stations. He called to Catharin, "Medical, how's stasis?"

"Stasis systems are solidly cold, no hot spots," Catharin reported. Her workstation screen was crammed with simulated reports from the stasis vaults in the bowels of the ship.

"Life support?"

Miguel Torres-Mendoza, who shared the Life Systems station with Catharin, said calmly, "All is well."

"Not for long," came a whisper over the medical link. Catharin recognized the voice of the Sim Supervisor, audible only in her headset. "Ready for the show, Dr. Gault?"

She double-clicked her microphone back and looked up at the image of the sun in the Big Picture as the Sim Supervisor altered it. On the limb of the sun, the edge of the lake of fire, sunspots multiplied in number. An incalescent ribbon—brilliantly hot—wound among the dark, cool spots like a snake.

The ship had autonomous, watchful instruments and an Intelligence to run them. But the ship did not sound an alarm. No one in the control center remarked on the altered sun either. The Sim Supe's whisper told her, "Oh, thank you. You've helped me catch everybody off guard."

Bix turned toward the Engineering station. "Any heat and tidal effects registering on the ship, Orlov?"

"Nominal," said the chief engineer, a square-jawed man with thick eyebrows and hair going gray around the edges.

Behind the spots and the bright ribbon, a spike of sun-stuff stood out against the edge of black space. The Sim Supe morphed the rim of the sun into a solar prominence. As the ship hurtled around the sun, the prominence grew more conspicuous. *The flare ribbon didn't get your attention, so look at me*, it said.

Bix turned on his heels, casually glanced up at the Big Picture, and did a double take. "*Omigod!*" Other people made puzzled noises, but the gears in Bix's head were ratcheting to high, Catharin thought, observing his body language. "All stations! Power down all systems down to minimum. Shut whatever you can all the way off! Pilot! Turn us so the star shield is facing the far limb of the sun!"

"Uh, Roger!" replied Joel Foster at Flight station. A window materialized in the Big Picture to show *Aeon* superimposed on a coordinate grid. "Twenty-six point five minutes." *Aeon* was not a nimble spacecraft. You might as readily turn a small mountain.

Bix growled, "Make it under twenty."

"Captain? That solar prominence is only a hundred thousand kilometers high, or so," someone on a subsidiary station said. "We won't run into it."

"It's not just a prominence. It's a solar flare," Bix retorted. "Dead ahead."

A murmur of consternation swept through the control center. The observers in the gallery leaned closer, intent.

"The guardian code didn't know to look out for this kind of event either!" Bix bent over the Command station interface—a rugged but failsafe keyboard. He hammered it with his fingers, overriding the ship's programming. Alarm lights and signals sounded all over the control center.

The image of the sun crescendoed into false-color mappings of radio, ultraviolet, gamma ray, particle, and magnetic field emissions. A storm of color boiled off the surface of the sun. *Aeon* would be a mote caught in the maelstrom.

"Shielding sufficient to protect us from cosmic radiation is sufficient to protect us from solar events," said a woman at the Astro/Survey station, quoting the Mission Book word for word. But she sounded worried.

"Yeah, but does it say that holds true when we're this close to a sun? Look it up," Bix snapped.

Bix paced toward Life Support. He covered the mike of his headset to address Catharin only. "Is this what you meant when you said we should run an attitude check?"

Catharin nodded.

"Good idea, damn it. Life Support, how fluid is the water?"

Miguel answered, "It was not supposed to freeze in starflight, and with the exception of some incidental ice, it—"

Bix cut him off. "Good. Dump the reservoirs into circulation."

"That's a good call," Miguel remarked to Catharin as he keyed in commands to move the water. "Water is a radiation buffer. Circulating it in the pipes will help protect us."

"Program the ship announcer for an evacuation order," Bix ordered.

"Where?" asked Miguel.

Bix stalked back toward the Flight station. "Joel, can we keep the star shield turned into the brunt of the storm all the way through it?"

"The attitude thrusters'll go haywire in the storm unless they're shut down," Joel answered. "It's an electromagnetic pulse situation—right, Orlov?"

The chief engineer spoke slowly. "Expect voltage surges in circuits throughout the ship as a result of the sunstorm, and incident gamma radiation causing random bit errors in the control circuits."

"Random bit errors?" echoed somebody at a subsidiary station. "There are always those."

"Not like this," Bix answered. Catharin had never seen him so galvanized. "Hordes of errors. Some'll do mischief. Remember, this ship is a distributed computer with machinery stuck on the ends."

Orlov said, "Under these circumstances, attitude thruster malfunction is probable. I recommend against using them."

"Then I can't guarantee our backside won't catch hell from the sunstorm," Joel said.

"The stasis vaults, in the very middle of the ship, are the best place for people to be," Catharin said. "The deeper into the stasis vaults the better."

Bix said, "Life Support, announce a general evacuation to the central ranks of the stasis vaults."

Joel looked over at Catharin with a lifted eyebrow. "The more frozen people between us and radiation, the more cover?"

"They've got stasis containers around them. We don't," she said.

Bix said, "Also announce that the ship's elevators are not to be used. It's ladders all the way. In a sunstorm the 'vators might stop working—or go the wrong way."

Joel groaned. "Exercise, here we come!"

Bix turned toward Engineering. "Orlov, we've got to have the engine on to keep up the ship's magnetic field. That field will shield us from ionized particle radiation. But it'll also get a helluva twang. What do you advise? Turn off the engine and the field and let the material shielding handle the radiation—or keep the engine on and put up with massive induced voltages in the engines?"

Orlov protested. "Main engine damage would leave us unable to make planetfall!"

"Dead in the water," Bix agreed.

Joel said tersely, "We've started running into radiation effects. I've got static in the thruster control circuits."

The control center hummed with the signal lights and chimes of dozens of ship systems being shut down. Catharin took the stasis control substations on every level offline, so that no concatenation of random bit errors in computer chips would accidentally revive someone from stasis. Beside her, Miguel muttered in Spanish. On the Big Picture, the sunstorm lifted into the chromosphere like an ominous, gaudy banner.

"Man, look at all those sunspots. This star is sick!" Joel said.

Bix said, "Ours gets that way. I rode out the solar storm of seventy-three on the *Regina*. We turned around at Venus and limped home. Almost didn't make it." He scowled at the memory. "*Aeon*'s closer to the event than we were then, but better shielded against cosmic rays, and this is just a solar flare, so—"

"Captain?" said the woman at Astro/Survey. "It's bigger. If this were our sun, it'd be a ten-thousand-year event."

Joel whistled. "Sounds like Sim Supe ran out of likely possibilities and started in on unlikely ones."

Miguel spoke up. "Without the ship's magnetic field to deflect ions around the ship, many more particles from the sun will stream through the ship. There will be secondary radiation when those particles strike the hull and the corridor walls and—" he shot Catharin a dark, serious glance "—the stasis container walls. The people in the containers will experience damaging secondary radiation."

"Damn," Catharin whispered. "We have to save them from that."

"Right. We keep up the magnetic field and risk damaging the engines," Bix said, grim and terse. "I figure one hour to max trouble. Then two or three hours of transit through the storm and what can go wrong, will," he said.

Orlov said, "Does that mean we've got four or more hours of this charade left?"

"Damn right." Sweat beaded across Bix's forehead. "And it may turn out to be Judgment Day."

"I object!" Orlov's words sounded so out of place that Catharin broke off what she was doing to stare at the engineer. Other faces turned toward Orlov in equal surprise. He slammed his hand on the console and continued, "We need to practice doing this part of the mission right. Instead, what we have here is so unrealistic that it's absurd!"

"No," said the voice of the Sim Supervisor, on the common link, audible to everyone. "Not unrealistic. Merely unlikely. There's a big difference. Proceed, ladies and gentlemen."

☽☾

The narrow pallet extended out from an opening in the wall in the small, barren white room. The pallet's medical chart bore only a name: CATHARIN FIRENZE GAULT. The chart was blank because it hadn't been activated yet, Catharin reminded herself. Not because she was dead. At least not yet.

Catharin gingerly seated herself on the pallet to wait. It was cold in here. Her clothing was no help. The close-fitting underwear, patterned with small tubes woven throughout like lace, would cool her body in stasis, and the tubing already felt chilly to her skin.

She stared at the square opening in the wall. When she reached the first unconscious stage of stasis, the pallet would slide into the wall—carrying her into the stasis container, which stood open, waiting like a crypt.

Two more containers in this vault waited for Bix and Joel. Their time would come a few days from now.

Shivering, Catharin felt vulnerable, anticipating the arrival of the medic who would put her into stasis. Would the medic be aloof? Skittish? Or absurdly reverent, as though embalming her for the hero's grave? She had seen all of those attitudes in medics putting people into stasis.

The chamber door swung open. A silver-haired old woman entered the room, moving with the hesitancy of somebody unaccustomed to anything but Earth gravity. Astounded, Catharin said, "Miranda?"

Miranda Blum, the chief assessor, and long before that, Catharin's favorite professor from medical school, and now the last face Catharin would see before the stars, hugged her. Catharin felt Miranda's embrace through the stiff lacy tubes of the cryogenic underwear. Then Miranda attached an intravenous line to Catharin's arm. Stasis chemicals began trickling through the tube into Catharin's body.

"Are you frightened?" Miranda asked.

"Very," Catharin said in a low voice.

"Good. Otherwise I'd assess you abnormal. Think of it as death."

"That's what I'm trying not to think."

"Give up. Relax." Miranda sounded calm. "We all leave this world sooner or later."

"You took a chance, Miranda, coming into space. Your time could have come sooner."

Miranda shrugged. "Not much sooner." She was 112 years old, nearing the longest life span that modern medicine had enabled people to attain. "I wanted to apologize to you."

"For preparing me for this?" Catharin remembered hours of lectures and grueling tests in the medical field of cryostasis. At dinners and teas in Miranda's home, the professor had shared her fears about the future of civilization on Earth and her dreams about the stars, and helped Catharin form her own.

"For your career choice, I congratulate myself. The apology is a different matter. Do you remember Joseph Devreze? I reviewed your interview with him, afterwards."

"He's not easy to forget. Miranda, did I make the right decision about him?"

"Quite. It was the decision I'd have made, had I wanted to live with the consequences. Which I most definitely did not."

"What do you mean?"

"Devreze lied to you, my dear. He had antagonized someone with inordinate political influence. Never mind the details—the matter will be of no relevance on the other end of your trip. To put it briefly, it was made clear to me that if I let Devreze escape to the stars, both my reputation and my finances would be ruined in retaliation. I must say, Devreze picked no ordinary enemy."

Catharin felt her face flush with anger. "That bastard."

Miranda chuckled. "Yes, but an invaluable bastard. Officially, I left the office on urgent business, and a resourceful staffer passed the case on to you. I orchestrated it so that the person accountable for admitting Devreze into the starship—you—won't be coming back either."

Catharin vented her consternation in a long sharp breath. "And he lied through his teeth. It's a good thing I'll have ten years awake to cool off before I see him again."

Miranda checked her watch. "What do you think of *my* choices, especially the rest of the crew?"

There was a taste on Catharin's tongue now, like a laboratory chemical or bad white wine. Catharin heard herself say, "Since you ask, I'm not sure that Orlov is the right chief engineer."

Miranda's elegantly thin eyebrows arched up. "He was the best qualified inside the age limits. Credentials, psychological stability, motivation—Orlov has it all."

"He's barely inside the age limits. Just like Bix," Catharin said. "But unlike Bix, he can be too rigid. We had one simulation that was the kind called Judgment Day, where everything goes wrong. It was grueling. And he was uncooperative. He demanded that things go right, not wrong. I think his stability can manifest itself as rigidity under certain kinds of stress."

"Oh, I don't think you should worry about him."

"I'm not worried." That was true. The beginning of stasis involved anesthesia that felt somewhat like inebriation. Catharin felt her worries trickling away.

"Remember that the gate has two sides. It's more of an airlock, really."

"Airlock?"

"When the ship reaches the new world, someone will have to decide who to let out of stasis, and when. For a while, you will be the gatekeeper. If Orlov really is unsuitable, revive his backup."

"That's tempting," Catharin murmured. She felt relaxed, almost woozy. "His backup is a good friend of mine."

"Do you have a personal-effects locker?"

Catharin twisted around to reach a latch beside the vault. A small locker door hinged down.

Miranda took something out of her pocket and showed it to Catharin: a man's heavy, plain wedding band. "I would have given this to my own child, if I had children. It's an heirloom from my husband's family. May I give it to you, instead?"

Feeling light-headed, Catharin lay back on the pallet. "That would mean so much to me that I don't know what to say, except thank you."

Miranda Blum added the ring to Catharin's jewelry bag and snapped the locker door shut. "It belonged to my husband's great-grandfather, who fled from Europe to America in the mid-twentieth century as a refugee. He left behind his house, his homeland, wearing the clothes on his back and the ring on his finger. But he took his violin, of all things to drag around the world when his life was in danger! He was a classical violinist, you see. Culture was as important to him as life itself."

"We have music. To help wake up, we've prerecorded instructions to ourselves with music." The white ceiling swam in Catharin's sight. She closed her eyes.

"You have everything," Miranda said. "Never before have people been able to take everything at once, to a truly new world."

Dark light swirled behind her eyelids as Catharin murmured, "Books. Music. Science. Medicine . . ."

She felt Miranda's hand pressing hers, and heard Miranda say in a voice choked with feeling, "And all my love."

Catharin sank into a brightly dark oblivion.

Chapter Two

GLASS TIME

She dreamed of herself as a pane of glass, a window fixed between a winter night and a dimly lit dining room with table and china place settings, empty. Congealed motionless, colder than cold, she did not freeze. Frozen water crystallizes into ice or snow. Glass does not.

A voice told her to wake up. *The star flight is over, wake up*, urged the voice, contralto—Catharin's own. She willed her eyelids to open, and saw a blurred whiteness, a ceiling above her. *I am in the starship, and the journey is over*, said the voice. Music percolated into Catharin's mind with the voice, and the bright notes helped Catharin comprehend the words.

The starship had left Earth centuries ago. Never to return to the home world. The ship had crossed star space to terraform a new planet: still nothing but the future's plan. For her, now, reality was only a sliver of possibility, so narrow that it constricted her heart, which could find no space to make a beat. Her blood stagnated. The edges of the ceiling frayed to blackness.

The music—a simple, strong, lilting melody—moved her out of paralysis. She bent her arms. That hurt but gave sudden depth and breadth to her reality. Her heart pounded; her blood coursed, free fluid. She sobbed in relief.

Catharin felt cold from the inside out. A draft felt warm on her face and blew strands of hair into her eyes. The draft came from the wall behind, from her niche in the stasis vault. The stasis machinery had extended her pallet out of the vault and into the room. For another minute she just listened to Copland's *Appalachian Spring.* The voice speaking over the music in her ears said,

"This is all about people building a new life in a new world, and that's exactly what I'm here for, and it's time to get up now."

Flexing her hands felt like finding shards of glass in every joint. But she knew what had to be done. She had practiced often enough. Methodically she disconnected the stasis tubes from her body. She took out the earplug, still playing her prerecorded voice and music. Pushing back the stasis shroud, she sat up. She gasped as pain flared through her torso like a firecracker burst.

She looked around for Bix and Joel. They lay on their own pallets, all but motionless. Despite the ministrations of the stasis machinery, which for nine hours had slowly warmed and detoxified the blood and given patterned electrical stimulation to their muscles, the male astronauts had not completely revived.

Everyone you've ever known on Earth will be gone. She remembered explaining that to someone else. Now it hit her. Faces swam in her mind's eye. People she'd loved, liked, hated. All of them were dead.

Miranda Blum had stood beside her before stasis.

Miranda had been dead for centuries.

Alive, awake, utterly alone, Catharin swayed on the brink of panic. Friends and colleagues and thousands of colonists lay in the vaults. Cryostasis was an unnatural condition closer to death than to life. At worst something went wrong and it destroyed its subjects. Had everything gone wrong? she wondered frantically.

Then she remembered the Book. Mission rules, the Book, specified what the first crewmember revived from stasis had to do with total concentration. Help the other two up.

Standing, Catharin found her flight coveralls where she had left them, folded and clamped in a rack on the wall, but a strange silver dust rimed them now. She shook off the dust and painfully climbed in. A weird tang coated her tongue, the aftertaste of stasis chemicals in her bloodstream.

As she fumbled with the coveralls, the bold shoulder patch caught her eye. Over the letters AEON 2093, it depicted something like a Christmas tree ornament, a ball with a tapering spike on one end and a knob on the other. Catharin traced the edges of the shiny silver design with her finger. Like an ornament onto a tree, the starship had to be hooked onto a new planet. It was up to the crew to do it. She managed to zip up her coveralls, then turned to her colleagues.

She switched on the medical chart labeled HUBERT "BIX" BIXBY. Bix was very much alive, vital signs excellent, hovering just below the threshold of consciousness. Catharin expelled a shaky sigh, disconnected his tubes, and removed his earplug. The voice-and-music cue had not been enough to wake him. Taking his hand, she talked about the ship having made its voyage, and work needing to be done, until his eyes snapped open. "Ship okay?" His voice was a sandpapery rasp.

"If you'll get up, we can find out," she answered. He moved, giving an explosive groan.

The other medical chart said JOEL JOHN ATLANTA. His color was good—the rich, chocolate skin color of the healthy Joel. His shroud looked ruffled, so he had stirred without rousing. "Joel. Good morning. Time to rise and shine." As she disconnected him from the stasis machines, he moaned. Catharin touched his hand. Her pale fingers contrasted with his dark skin. "Joel, we're here. Wake up—" with deliberate significance, she added, "—star voyager," and gently moved his arm back and forth.

He smiled faintly. "Cat. Hi. Ouch."

The men donned their flights coveralls with pained groans and expletives. Then Joel laughed. "We're *here*!"

"We hope," Catharin said.

"Let's go find out," Bix grunted. The three of them stumbled out of the stasis room. "What's this gravity?" Bix asked.

"A sixth g or so," said Joel. "Which means we're still accelerating."

The starship had slowly, steadily accelerated ever since it left Earth, and must have reached a velocity of—the numbers slipped from the grasp of Catharin's mind. What mattered was to start the countdown to braking, when the Ship would let the new sun claim it.

They staggered around the Axis, the huge column that ran down into the heart of the Ship. Bix led the way through the hatch into the flight deck. He and Joel began activating the flight control stations. Hundreds of informative little lights came on.

"Wanna view, Cat?" Joel flipped a switch.

Bix growled, "I want coffee."

"The first thing you'll get is destasis medicine," Catharin said.

On the far wall, a string of stars appeared. The string broadened as the shield-shutter rolled back. Catharin approached the window, a deep-walled slit in the Ship's hull.

The starship *Aeon* was a sphere with a great spike of an engine driving it. Opposite the engine, *Aeon* had a wide, convex shield that the hurtling ship presented to the hazards of deep space. The crew level lay in the valley between the star shield and the orb where ten thousand colonists lay in stasis. Catharin itched to know how the colonists had fared. But it was too early to check. The Book said: first, ascertain that the Starship has reached its destination. Joel and Bix were tasked with that.

At present, up—toward the star shield and the Ship's north pole—was the direction of the Ship's ongoing acceleration. Looking down through the flight deck window, Catharin saw *Aeon*'s bulk as a wide horizon against the drifting stars. *Aeon* did not shine like its depiction on the coverall shoulder patches. It looked tarnished, not new anymore.

"Chronometer on," Bix said.

"Twenty-three seventy-two," Joel said. "About right." Nearly three centuries of star flight had aged the skin of *Aeon*.

A chill clung to the window's glass and made the nearby air feel cold. The Ship's hull had cold-soaked in the sunless spaces between the stars. Three days ago, the machinery had automatically begun warming up only the crew level. Pumping livable heat into all of the environs of *Aeon* would take a full year and a sun.

"Time for the auto-observatory's report," Bix said. The three of them exchanged tense glances.

A new sun flooded into the window with light that flashed across the flight deck. Eyes watering from the glare, Catharin dimly saw Bix switch on the auto-observatory interface.

Then Bix swore. The silence cracked like shattered glass. "*It isn't here.*"

"What! It is the wrong star?!" Joel demanded.

Catharin asked, "The planet isn't here?"

"Right star. Planet, too. It's the moon," Bix said. "The goddamned moon's not here."

Catharin's mind skidded on slick, hard incomprehension. *There won't be any music here*—No. Music had nothing to do with it. Without a moon, there would never be seasons here. There would be no Spring.

"We better defrost reinforcements," Joel said. He sounded shaken.

☽☾

The galley smelled of coffee. The two mission specialists did not partake; they had to drink their destasis medicine first. Joel summarized the situation for them. "Repeat. No moon, much less a good-sized one," he concluded, and glowered into his coffee.

The planetologist's name was Lary Siroky-Scheidt. Lary's sour face showed that he found the destasis medicine, the situation, or both, unpalatable.

Nguyen El Ae, the other specialist, said weakly, "That is very bad."

Bix said, "Remember, the Book *does not assume* that we have no choice but to stay here. It has several fallback options. We can select from those if we have to, and go back into stasis while the Ship goes on."

Joel relaxed a bit. "Yeah."

Catharin almost objected immediately. Instead, she glanced around the small group. Nguyen had youth in his favor. So did Catharin herself. Not so Joel with his salt-and-pepper hair. Lary had salt-and-cayenne, and Bix's years had made his hair solidly gray. The dangers of stasis increased with the subject's age.

"The options are why we thawed you out, Nguyen," Bix said. "You're the right man to evaluate three centuries of auto-astronomy, and tell us which direction looks the best these days."

PhD in astrophysics, PhD in computer science, genuine genius: Nguyen was the right man for that job. At that moment he looked more like a boy: young, slight, rumpled, and plainly feeling ill.

Catharin protested, "But we came so far, to this one place, because we thought there'd be a moon. It took us so long to get here!"

"Not in astronomical time," Joel said, and asked Lary, "What could happen to a moon in just a few centuries?"

"Well. Something could. Happen, I mean." Clutching his drink, Lary took a swig. "Yech! Collision with something big. Or close encounter with a stray black hole, tidal forces breaking up the moon. Or tearing it out of its orbit. That sort of thing's not likely, but possible."

But unfair! Catharin had to bite back an outburst of protest. They had come so far, so successfully; they had known what to expect as no explorers ever before. *How dare the universe do this to us?*

Lary said, "No moon means the planet has an unstable axis of rotation. And that in turn means no regular, predictable seasons in the temperate zones, plus a catastrophically erratic climate across time." He sounded alert and coherent. But too chipper, as though he were talking about a hypothetical world, and not their lost future.

Joel drained his coffee cup and hurled it toward the used-dish receptacle. "It *was* here."

Bix nodded. "But the moon was right at the resolution limit of the visual interferometry."

"Before we left, the astronomers observed this planet and said the orbital perturbations verified the planet had a moon. They were sure the moon was here. Instead, we get nothing!"

"Not nothing," Bix corrected him. "The planet is in the habitable zone, though toward the outer edge of it. Bigger than Mars and warmer too."

"That's hopeful," Lary said.

Joel shook his head. "We can't come this far and settle on something not much better than Mars."

"Apart from Earth, Mars was more habitable than any other body in the Solar System," Lary said testily. "I should know. I was born and raised there."

"Not good enough," Joel said. "We've got to push on."

Nguyen drained his glass, put it down, and closed his eyes, evidently fighting queasiness. Catharin watched him with concern. Then the empty glass distracted her. It crept across the table on its own, like a snail, on a trail of condensation.

Joel noticed her consternation. He pushed the glass back. "Ship spins—gyroscopic stabilization." That was right, Catharin remembered now, and loose objects would migrate outward. She wondered if other knowledge that should have been immediate and obvious was no longer so, in her mind, or in the minds of her colleagues, after the long stasis.

Bix said, "All right. Given that none of us have gotten our hands dirty with the up-to-the-minute facts in our areas—how do we feel about what to do? Cat?"

"The bottom line in my field is, first, do no harm," she replied. "I've got to be sure that more time in stasis won't damage everyone."

"Joel, I take it you'd want to go on."

Lary burst out at Joel, "Be realistic! The best we can expect to find is a barren world that won't be greened up until long after we're deceased."

"Maybe, but I want my great-grandkids to have woods," Joel said. "And seasons. Not just altiplano grass and twenty kinds of sand."

Lary snapped, "People on Mars don't feel deprived!"

"I wonder . . . ," Nguyen ventured. "Was it meant to happen this way?"

"How so?" asked Bix.

"They sent us here, but there's nothing but further possibilities. But the auto-observatory is very good. Maybe the Aeon Foundation meant for us to look at the stars here and figure out the next move for ourselves—"

Lary snorted. "This is not a guessing game!"

"Okay, Lary wants to stay. I take it you're inclined to go on, Nguyen," Bix said.

Nguyen nodded with stiff dignity.

Catharin said, "Bix?"

He sighed. "I'd like to keep going. But we've got ten thousand passengers down there. Your point about the stasis doing harm is well taken." Then he said, "Two to go and two to stay."

According to the Book, the primary crew, Bix and Joel and Catharin, could revive any or all of the mission specialists, if necessary. But they were obligated to keep the total number of voices, besides that of the Captain, even. In the event that the crew found itself evenly split on a crucial decision, the Captain would cast the deciding vote. Catharin did not envy Bix if it came to that.

"When's our best window for braking?" Bix asked Joel.

Joel relocated to the galley's workstation. "Fifth day from today."

"All right, that's our deadline. We've got to decide what to do by then. Cat, have we been up long enough to tackle the stasis status report? Five days could be a tight deadline, and the sooner we get moving the better," he added.

"Yes, I think we can handle it now—or a least, I think we must," she replied.

Joel pulled the report up and scanned the workstation screen. He said, "*Damn*. Cat—"

The hair on the back of Catharin's neck prickled with dread.

"We may have a problem. If this report is true—I mean, if there's not a data error—there's a hot spot in the passenger decks."

The Axis contained an elevator shaft. After centuries unused, its door opened and closed with a fine whisper. "Level Eighteen—about a third of the way to the south pole," Catharin murmured, and punched a button. The 'vator shivered. It started downward. "Brr."

"Crank up to medium-high," Bix suggested.

Catharin adjusted her coldsuit's temperature control upward. The 'vator was dimly lit. Bars of light marched up the wall, indicating vertical motion. Reflections fluttered on Bix's faceplate.

"I hope the hot spot isn't real," Catharin said.

"One way to find out." Bix leaned at ease against the 'vator wall. "Anything you need to tell me that you didn't in the galley?"

"No, Bix. I am worried about the consequences of the stasis. Any physician would be. It's never been done for this long before. In observing us, though," she added, "I haven't seen signs of deterioration, physical or psychological."

He gave a short laugh. "Since I may be the canary in the mine shaft, I'm glad to hear it." Older than the rest of them by a decade, he knew all too well that ill effects of stasis would probably show up in him first.

Catharin felt mild queasiness in her stomach, and it had been there since she woke up, but it did not qualify as a serious symptom. She stopped the 'vator at Stasis Level 11. "This is well removed from the hot spot. Let's see how things are going here."

The sensors said that the air on the other side of the 'vator door was good—pressure and composition normal, no contaminants. The door opened into a long dim corridor. Near the door, a medical station waited for them. She turned it on. Hundreds of pinpoint lights appeared, nearly all of them green. "This agrees with what the status report said about this level."

"Nominal isn't news," Bix grunted.

"There's a casualty." A point of red glinted among the green. She displayed the dead passenger's stasis history in detail. "We expected a very low, but real, casualty rate, because of unforeseeable problems in how some people's bodies are affected by stasis. It's much like the risk of someone dying under general anesthesia—a very low risk but a certain one."

Catharin bit her lip to hold in her anger at the implacable odds. She remembered her hospital internship in Baltimore. She had hated losing patients, no matter how normal, or inevitable, the processes that led to death. No matter how negligible the death toll in the greater scheme of things.

"Think the rest of 'em are good for the whole millennium?"

"I can't answer that yet. Besides, the whole hypothesis that stasis should be good for a thousand years before deterioration gets serious—may be wrong. It's never been tested. And it may be colored by romantic millennialism. I don't trust it." She ran her hand over the board with its emerald points of light and the single, accusatory red one.

"They all knew the risk. And for it they expect something better than a bigger, warmer edition of Mars." Bix sighed.

They reentered the 'vator to go deeper into the Ship. The 'vator coasted into Stasis Level 17. This time they hesitated when the door opened for them.

Catharin became aware of something different in the air, a frigid foul odor of decay. She caught herself stepping not out, but closer to Bix. "Do you smell it?"

"Something stinks." He strode out of the 'vator to confront the med station. The problem indicator had come on. Bix activated the board. It lit up green with an awful red wound. Red pinpoints, a mass of them, haloed with amber, glared on the green field.

Shocked, Catharin blurted, "Almost all of Wedge T!" Her voice shook.

"Outside of T?"

"Showing green." Swiftly she read the status of some of the green points. "I can't be sure the rest are okay until I check more closely."

Bix glared at the board. "If this icebox is faulty, then that's it," he said abruptly. "We stay."

Feeling sick and cold, Catharin nodded.

Chapter Three

VANDAL STARS

Compared to the depths of the Ship, the flight deck looked brilliantly busy. Catharin and Bix took off their helmets, unsealed and unzipped their coldsuits. "Seventeen Wedge T's dead, more or less," Bix announced.

Lary and Nguyen dropped what they were doing, stunned. Catharin groaned privately. *Too harsh, Bix!* Somebody might have had a relative there.

"Med log, Cat," said the Captain.

She took a seat at her station. Her fingers trembled, uncooperative, as she opened the automatic medical log.

"Lary. How's it look?" Bix sounded gruff.

"The planet's orbit is quite elliptical, and that means we'd have seasons of a sort, a range from something like summer on Mars to winter in Anchorage."

"Nguyen?" Bix meant to nail them all to their jobs to keep them from dwelling on thoughts about a dead Wedge. Catharin would rather have talked about the loss, openly and now.

Nguyen answered, "The auto-observatory shows a binary star very nearby."

"So?" said Joel, entering the flight deck. With a little salute, he acknowledged the return of Catharin and Bix from their expedition to the passenger decks.

Nguyen explained, "It is a tightly bound pair of white dwarfs—very dense, very faint stars. They were observed from Earth, just under a light-year away from this star at that time, but no one bothered to measure their velocity vector. And no one noticed that they were Population Two stars, not in a planar orbit like most other stars here, but in a halo orbit. They were moving almost perpendicular to the plane of the Milky Way's disk. Toward this solar system."

A frown carved deep furrows on Bix's forehead.

"In fact, they were diving toward this system with a velocity of seven hundred and fifty kilometers per second, and the relative velocity was closer to one thousand kilometers per second. That's fast enough to cover a light-year in three hundred years. While *Aeon* was on its journey from Earth, these stars moved through this system and caused the moon to be kicked out of its orbit. That was less than fifty years ago. The binary dwarf is not far away. It is leaving very rapidly."

Catharin sat back, pressing her lips together. So. That was what Nature had thrown at them. That and the hot spot in Wedge T.

For a long moment, there was a thick, brittle silence on the flight deck. Bix rubbed the frown furrows on his forehead as if physically erasing them. "Anything to report?" he asked Joel.

"Main engine works fine. Feel it?" The Ship shivered slightly, steadily. The engine had been designed to operate when the Ship found dust and gas for fuel. Now, having come to a planetary system, it fed and burned vigorously, and would do so until Bix ordered engine shutdown. "The one-sixth g of acceleration right now is the most we've had since we left our solar system." Joel flopped into a seat at the Command station, loose-limbed in the low gravity. "The flight deck WC works fine, too."

Seeing a good opening, Catharin spoke quickly. "Do you have anyone in Seventeen Wedge T?"

"No, why?"

"That was our hot spot. There are casualties."

"Whew! Just there?"

"Yes."

"They didn't feel anything, did they?"

"I very much doubt it."

Shaking his head, Joel turned his attention to the screen at his station.

"Before I stepped out I was looking at the attitude thrusters, Bix. We may have a problem. Looks like their thrust has been more or less erratic over the years. The Z-pos and X-pos arrays less erratic. Y-neg more so. Nothing that the Ship hasn't been able to compensate for—so far."

All attention, Bix leaned over Joel's shoulder. Joel pointed to information on the screen. "Look. About fifty years ago the Ship shut down the most of the Y-neg thruster array. Been making do without ever since."

"Don't we need those thrusters before we brake?" Lary said edgily.

"Need 'em for everything," Joel replied.

"Just great!" Lary sounded upset. "What'll go wrong next? At this rate—"

Bix interrupted him. "Nothing about the Ship is wrong. Not yet. Some casualties were expected. So were a few mechanical problems. Let's all get on with the job."

They were skirting panic like a basketball rimming the hoop. Years of training and simulations, the ingrained reflexes of space work, kept them from falling into that panic.

The med log chronicled thousands of fluctuations in the temperature of the stasis vaults over the years. As with the attitude thrusters, however, the Ship corrected most temperature problems before they got out of hand. No dangerous hot spots cropped up in the first century of star flight. For that Catharin thanked the Ship and the designers who had made it to be self-regulating, self-repairing, intelligent.

Nguyen spoke. "Captain, I've made a preliminary evaluation of our choices for going on. One of the options specified in the Book looks very good."

"The Eta Sagittarii option?" Joel said

"Yes."

"What makes that star so good?" Lary asked.

"Nothing by itself. But from the vantage point of Eta Sagittarii we can take a good look at three more stars, each of which is known to have a planetary system, probably with large moons at the habitable planets. That is, the auto-observatory can look for us. Then the Ship can choose the best of those three and use Eta Sagittarii to change our course in that direction."

Joel stepped over to look at Nguyen's screen. "Piece of cake to change course here and head for Eta Sagittarii! Just swing toward this sun and back out again." He added, "It'd be a pity to waste the speed we've built up so far. Remember, until we brake the Ship, we're still accelerating. That's why our feet are on the floor."

"Sounds like you want to play rocket jockey," Lary said.

"Damn right!" Joel shot back. "It means getting to someplace worth going to."

Catharin listened intently. Lary sounded nervous and irritable, which was normal for him, stasis or not. Nguyen had been acting quiet and serious—again, in character. And Bix and Joel sounded like their old selves. But if Bix felt ill, he would conceal it and carry on.

She had to ask the most vital question. "What's the time frame for a planet search?"

"A few decades to Eta Sagittarii," said Nguyen, "thanks to our present speed. Then, depending on which tangent the Ship takes, as much as a century more."

Joel said, "We won't know the difference. We'll be asleep."

"Don't ever call stasis sleep!" Catharin said sharply. "It isn't sleep. It isn't natural. If it goes on too long it will destroy you, cell by cell." The med logs told Catharin that the real trouble had begun in the second century of travel, when the global cooling system developed a slight but definite imbalance. The fatal hot spot made a brief appearance, but the stasis program corrected it. Had the journey ended before the third century began, Seventeen Wedge T would have lived. At worst, thirty or forty individuals might have suffered frostbite.

"We don't know if the Eta Sagittarii tangents will pan out," said Lary.

"Eta Sagittarii is the prime option in the Book," Bix said.

"Quoth the Captain," Lary muttered with a trace of insolence.

Catharin fretted. Bix was a man of action, not words. He said what a commanding officer was expected to say whether it sounded wooden or not. Frequently it did. Which would cost Bix some respect on the part of cynical, articulate Lary Siroky-Scheidt.

Catharin resumed reading the med log. The fatal hot spot reappeared in the third century, this time persistent. It took an unacceptable fraction of the

Ship's energy reserves to counter that intractable entropy. So, with the same remorseless reasoning that led it to shut down the Y-neg thruster, the Ship's Intelligence abandoned the hot spot. It confined the stasis system's temperature problems in one place. But the triumph came at a high price: 107 human lives.

"Bix. That hot spot . . ." There was no point in sharing this, knowledge as useless as it was horrid. But Catharin could not stand being the only one to know. "It persisted over the last eighty years. The whole wedge. Off and on. I'm sure the people didn't feel anything. But everyone in there is goo by now. There aren't any bones or organs any more. Just—"

Struggling to hold back tears, she felt Joel's comforting hand on her shoulder.

☽☾

Night fell with automatic dimming of the lights in *Aeon*'s crew level. The Axis illuminated the core of the level with a thin ring of red light.

Six wedge-shaped rooms surrounded the Axis. The day had begun in the recovery room, the galley, and the flight deck. It ended in the break room and the bunk room. The sixth wedge was the flight lab, which Catharin had not yet opened up. It could wait until the morning.

Another of the tall slit windows loomed in the break room. Leaving the lights off, she stretched out on a couch to watch the stars spin by. Her head spun too, with the events of the first day, facts, and discoveries too recent and uncomfortable to sleep on. She sighed and took down her hair, stowing the clips in a pocket. The bedtime ritual might make her feel sleepier. She kept her long blonde hair braided and clipped up, except at night. The single braid fell down on her shoulder. Stroking it, she wondered about herself. The others seemed to have come through in decent emotional shape. And she? She had always had abundant emotions, braided: woven together to stay under control, but never repressed, never cut off, passions flexible enough to be intelligently shaped. But today she felt brittle as never before. She remembered waking up and the desolation of being alone, and the cold glass dream before that. Undoing the braid, she combed her hair with her fingers, then buried her face in it.

Someone else came in. He was darker than the rest of the break room. "Cat?"

"I'm awake, Joel. Unfortunately."

"I can't sleep either."

"What about Bix?"

"Out like a light."

"That man could sleep through the end of a world." She smiled in the darkness.

"Lary, however, is pacing in the bunk room, and Nguyen's in there meditating, which seems to be how they deal with insomnia."

"What do you do?" she asked him.

"Find somebody to talk to."

Talking would do both of them good. "Insomnia doesn't surprise me," she said. "In the stasis experiments on Earth, it affected one person out of three. On top of that, we're under terrible stress. We're the only people awake in this gigantic icebox, which for some is already a morgue, and we're responsible for the whole damned thing."

"Yeah—stressful setup!" He settled down on a chair, rubbing his neck. "You know, while I should have been sleeping and was wide awake instead, I started to dream."

She had been reclining on the couch. She sat up straight. "Hallucinations?"

"No, Doc," he laughed. "Dreams, like in my namesake's book, the book of Joel in the Bible. There's a verse that says 'Your old men shall dream dreams.'"

She collapsed back. "Oh."

His teeth flashed in a grin. "More than three hundred years qualifies as old."

"Do you feel old?"

"No. Hell, for a starship pilot, I'm young. For a starship's physician, you are very young."

"The Foundation wanted us that way as a hedge against the effects of stasis."

"But Bix is fine. Stasis works great in practice, just like the Ship," he said with confidence that Catharin could not share.

"Tell me about your dream."

"Ever heard of the Ramamirtham Maneuver?"

She shook her head.

"It's the Apocrypha in the Mission Book," he said mysteriously.

"Whatever do you mean?"

"*Aeon* scoops up interstellar matter for fuel to burn by hydrogen fusion and mass to expel. We spent most of the three centuries coasting, and the rest of the time accelerating by degrees as the Ship found hydrogen and dust between the stars to burn. Slow way to go—but we've been at it for a while. We're up to a fair fraction of the speed of light." He had an expressive baritone voice that sounded like a storyteller's, Catharin thought. "But the Ram Maneuver is a way to get a lot more speed in a hurry. And we've got what it would take. A good strong ship and lots—" He broke off, struck by a flood of golden light that lasted for a minute or two as the new sun crossed the window. It gilded his dark-skinned, handsome face. He resumed, "Lots of initial speed, and a handy binary star."

"Eta Sagittarii?"

"No, the A star is an orange giant, a huge bag of hot gas. It would fry us if we tried to loop around at Ram distance. But Nguyen's Vandals, that's a different story. *That's* an ideal binary star for the Ram Maneuver."

"Why?"

"The Vandals are two white dwarf stars whirling around a common center. Basically the Ship does figure eights around them. The Ship loops around one star, accelerated by the star's gravity. Comes around and shifts course to fall around the second star. Back and forth. Ten or a hundred times or more. Faster and faster. Relativistic effects lead to diminishing returns, though, because the faster the Ship goes, the more massive it is, and harder to speed up. At some point you declare victory and the Ship breaks away and shoots out of the binary dwarf system going more than half the speed of light, maybe a lot more."

"Without having been fried?"

"No. They built *Aeon*'s hull like a thermos, with one helluva a layer of insulation between the outer and inner hulls, both of which are incredibly hard and strong. *Aeon* could take the Ram Maneuver."

Interested, she curled up on her side and propped her head on a hand. "Are you suggesting we go to Nguyen's Vandals and accelerate like that? That would cut down our travel time to a new destination, so we could be there in only a few decades, wouldn't it?"

"*Aeon* could loop around the Vandals in only a few years, since they're small and close together, and repeat the Maneuver as many times as it took to build up enough speed."

"Enough?"

"To go to where there are lots of stars, stars and planets like a grains of sand in a sand bar in a river."

"Where, Joel?"

"Look out the window and wait. . . . There." Through the window the stars were thick as diamond dust. "We're looking at a spiral arm of the galaxy, the next one inward from the Sun's. On Earth it was known as the Milky Way in Sagittarius. Look at the stars and the dust. Planet stuff."

"It is beautiful."

"Between the galactic arm where we are now and that one, space is relatively empty. So why not go ahead and cross the desert? And go toward the heart of the Milky Way!"

"It's far, isn't it?"

"Two thousand light-years."

"How soon could we get there?"

"Earth year 5000."

"Then you are making up a story to tell me. It's a wonderful one, though. Thank you."

He looked at her, his expression intense, then said, "I'm talking relativistic speed, Cat. For the Ship and us, the trip would be more like seven hundred. We've only gone three centuries so far. Seven more is still inside the stasis limit."

Catharin sat bolt upright. "One thousand years is the hypothetical maximum for stasis before irreversible organic damage occurs. We can't commit to pushing the limit like that!"

"Yes we can. The stasis is just as good as it was cracked up to be."

She retorted, "I'm the physician. I'll decide that."

"We could look for planets as we go. Modify the Moonseeker code to account for a lot more speed. A planet with a big moon might turn up between here and there."

"Forget the Book's options? Just like that?"

"It's in the back of the Book," he answered. "Just not the prime option, not one of the easy, incremental options. I don't think the Foundation meant us to be slaves to the Book. They meant us to go find a future."

The Book had been written by the Aeon Foundation. Behind it there had been wealthy and powerful men and women—mostly old people. Too old to go to the stars: stasis would have killed them outright. But they had been convinced that a starship and a new world meant the future of human civilization. "The Book is all that we have to go by."

He shook his head. "No. We've got ourselves—education and dreams and all."

Amazed by him, she replied, "To say the least, we've got to correct the stasis. There can't be any more hot spots. And I have to determine just what the stasis has done to us so far."

"So put that education of yours to work," he said, and smiled.

"Besides, it can't be that easy to do your maneuver. Can it?"

"It's like a billiard ball shot. The Ship has to roll in on the perfect course at the perfect speed. But we've got Nguyen to figure it out for us." He gazed at the stars beyond the window. "The other problem is the interstellar medium. It'll help that the space between the spiral arms is emptier than most. Still, at most of the speed of light, the wind from the stars is nothing less than violent. But we're shielded, insulated and otherwise protected far more than we had to be just for the little trip here. The Ship's magnetosphere is our friend. Instead of the Ship colliding with all of the interstellar matter, it deflects ions and channels 'em around to the matter scoop for fuel. And the magnetic field gets stronger the faster we go.

"We could do it, Cat. All the way to the Sagittarius arm. We'd find lots of planets there, maybe even green ones. Planets with moons. With rivers and seas. Maybe even trees."

Catharin said slowly, "I believe you. But I'm not ready to agree to go anywhere."

He crossed his arms. "Remember Starlink? And how they were going to transmit messages to us, and news?"

"Of course I remember Starlink." The huge radio telescope stood on the far side, the star side, of Earth's Moon. It could send radio signals as well as receive them. In all of the Solar System, only Starlink had the power to send messages to *Aeon* as the starship journeyed farther and farther away; only Starlink had the sensitivity to detect the ever fainter whispers of reply.

"Well, maybe they listened to the automatic reports from *Aeon* the whole time. We only got sixty-nine years' worth of messages from *them*. Then the signal stopped coming."

"Stopped?" she repeated, incredulous. "Why? Did something happen to the machine, or to the Moon?"

Joel shrugged. "The last twenty or so years of messages was just media news. Hard for me to understand. Words I wasn't sure about the meaning of. But I get the idea bad things happened—greenhouse floods, religious wars. The colonies on the Moon and Mars may not have fared too well either. I think the Aeon Foundation was right. Earth was going to hell in a handbasket. And we just got out in time. Anyway, the signal stopped, and I didn't find a good-bye, either."

"But Starlink—," she began, and broke off, unable to say her thoughts.

The Starlink telescope had been constructed on the Moon six decades before *Aeon* left Earth. The hardworking radio astronomer who supervised the project happened to have been Catharin's great-grandfather. That coincidence had encouraged her profoundly. She knew that the ephemeral train of radio signals between *Aeon* and Earth would also be hers, a slight but very real link to her own origin.

The link was shattered on the end that had been home.

Chapter Four

VALLEY OF DILEMMA

The selection process for starship astronaut culminated in a three-day interview at the Aeon Foundation's biosphere in the California desert. The process left all of the candidates exhausted and some with minds changed about going to the stars. Dr. Catharin Gault did not change her mind. But she was forced to clarify it to an uncomfortable degree.

After the interview, Catharin accepted the offer of a ride into LA from Rebecca Fisher, one of the other candidates. Becca's jet, a small but capable Kestrel, made short work of the runway at Unity Habitat, soaring into the sky like its namesake falcon. Exhilarated, Catharin momentarily forgot the ache of exhaustion and the pain of self-knowledge.

As Becca turned the jet westward, Catharin looked down at the huge biosphere called Habitat. The astronaut candidates had toured the facility the first day here, trouping through walkways and stairs built on the outside to observe the ecological test bed for a new world. Under midmorning desert sun, Habitat's rain forest flourished inside a pyramidal greenhouse. A miniature ocean made waves behind the glass bastion of Habitat. Catharin thought she could see the sun glint on the little ocean's surface.

Gaining altitude, the Kestrel skirted the Chocolate Mountains—corrugated landforms, more beige than brown in color, dotted with stunted trees and slashed with canyons. "I grew up on a farm in Tennessee," Becca remarked. "But I've come to love desert. Good thing, because that's what the new world will be at first."

Becca was off the Air Traffic Control Net and expertly doing her own flying. If the Aeon Foundation wanted experienced astronauts with additional skills needed by a young colony—such as piloting and farming—then Becca Fisher was almost certain to be chosen, Catharin reflected. Her own chances seemed uncertain. Much depended on whether the selection board had liked her answers to the Big Questions.

The Kestrel arrowed through a wispy cloud. Becca laughed. "I love cloud bashing. There aren't many places to do this anymore, fly on your very own."

"Is that what you told them?" asked Catharin. The first Big Question posed to a candidate was *Why do you want to do this?*

"No. I said that to explore is to discover the human spirit. When we reach far from home is when we meet ourselves, personally and as a race. That's why I'm an astronaut."

"That must have been a good answer. You were only in there for an hour."

"Well, a short interview by the board either meant you gave them good easy answers or bad easy answers."

"I tried an easy answer," Catharin said. "I said I want to help build a better world on a new, Earthlike planet."

"Lots of people sang that tune. Rumor had it that's what the board wanted to hear."

"Not from me. They ruthlessly dissected my motives."

"Oh. Did your motivation end up with its guts spread all over the table? Or put back together again?"

"Together."

Miranda Blum was on the board, but Miranda was only one out of twelve. And *Who do you know?* was definitely not one of the questions. Miranda had nodded slightly at several points in the interview. But Catharin had no idea what the board thought about what they had heard.

"Care to tell me more about it?"

"To make a long story short, I believe the social, political, and environmental ills of Earth are like a disease. Medically, if a deadly virus reaches a certain point of proliferation, or a cancer metastasizes, you treat symptoms only. The disease will win in the end. That's where we are with Earth." Feeling her fatigue, and the larger dismay of the twenty-first century,

Catharin settled into the seat and rested her eyes on the cool blue of the sky. "We have to start over again."

"Making a new start on a new world has been tried before. That's where we are now—in the New World—but it has as many problems as the Old World. It's the Same World. Why do you think a new world on the other side of the stars will be better?"

Catharin gave the explanation that had taken her two torturous hours in front of eleven strangers to compile. "If you know what to do when a disease is small, you can cure it. Like antibiotics administered early in the course of an infection, or surgery for a localized tumor. This is an opportunity to do just that for civilization. For the first time in history, we know enough science, sociology, history, and psychology to understand what constitutes a healthy civilization. A new one might be started small and cured of diseases when they first appear, before they're out of control."

"Things like toxic pollutants or antibiotic-resistant plague? Or war and violence?"

"Those things are functionally the same. Epidemics of antibiotic-resistant bacteria and of urban drug abuse and violence have very similar results. Civil war that ends in a nuclear explosion leads to radiation sickness. That's an example of disease beyond cure."

"That hurts you," Becca said, so quietly that her voice was almost lost in the engine's soft roar. "Mind if I ask why?"

"No. The board did. My mother was a diplomat. She was involved in diplomatic negotiations in Turk-Kyrgyzstan ten years ago, trying to establish peace."

"*Ten* years ago? Where was she when the bomb went off?"

"Too close to ground zero. She died."

The coast of California lay ahead, fronting the wide blue Pacific. Catharin let the view absorb her, blunting the old pain that the board had, very systematically, stirred up.

"What about your father?" The second Big Question for starship astronaut candidates was *What does your family think?*

"Mother's death left him so alone—they had been such a perfectly matched pair—that he's been married to his work ever since. He's the surgical chief of staff at Johns Hopkins. We don't have the closeness that would make permanent separation unthinkable. We don't have the bitter estrangement that makes the board suspect unexploded psychological baggage, either. What about yours?"

"My parents have been accepted into the Tiers."

Catharin had no easy answers. Just a multifaceted idea that felt more compelling ever since the board had forced her to clarify the feelings and experiences behind it. "Modern medicine made possible a lifespan of a hundred and twenty vigorous years. My father is an excellent physician. But he can't save people from old diseases that they weren't vaccinated for because the medical infrastructure is breaking down. No one in Turk-Kyrgyzstan will have a hundred-and-twenty-year life expectancy. There's too much residual radiation. In a way, both of my parents gave their lives to futile work." She closed her eyes, feeling raw around the edges.

"Ultimate futility is hard to judge," said Becca.

"Not for me. When gains in knowledge lag behind the best time to apply it, when disease is caught too late to cure, that's futility. The starship is an opportunity to get ahead of that process for once in history." It was far easier to talk to Becca than to the board. But once again, as then, she felt frightened. If the board bought it—still a big if, she reminded herself—this idea could compel her to surrender everything else.

In the distance, north of their course, LA Hightower sparkled, a giant skyscraper erected above the murk and sprawl of the huge city like a lotus growing out of a swamp. She liked the vitality and culture of great cities. It wasn't that she loved nature above all else, hated cities, or had nothing to lose. Nothing as easy as that.

Becca seemed to devote her total attention to flying, checking her instruments and the landmarks below to make sure of the Kestrel's location. But Becca said, "I like your thinking. I want you to be selected."

"But it scares me," Catharin blurted.

"It should. But we need you."

Instead of angling toward LA, the Kestrel continued westward, its nose pointed toward the Pacific Ocean. Becca explained, "I need to touch base with Catalina Island. It's my way of digesting what's happened the last few days. Okay?"

"Sure. My flight back to Baltimore doesn't leave until evening. And I'm enjoying this."

The island was an oceanic mountain with a cliff face rising out of a mix of small clouds and sea. Becca seemed to aim the jet directly at the cliff. Catharin was only partly relieved to see a runway carved on the top of the Mountain; the runway looked impossible to land on at this angle of approach. Gripping the edge of her seat hard enough to hurt her hands, Catharin wondered how wise it had been to fly with someone she'd only known for three days, all of it safely on the ground.

"This can unnerve even experienced pilots," Becca told her. "You have to come in just above the cliff. Part of your mind thinks you're way too high, because it's so far straight down to the water. But the other part thinks you're too low, with that cliff staring you in the face. We really will make the runway, regardless of what it looks like!"

"Oh." Catharin wondered who had come up with the idea of putting an airport here. The island had very little flat terrain at any elevation. The ground for the runway had obviously been prepared by shearing off the top of the Mountain.

Just as Becca promised, the Kestrel cleared the cliff to promptly touch down on the runway. But the runway looked as though it lacked the length for a jet and ended in the sky. Catharin gasped loudly enough to activate the intercom.

Becca used thrust reverse and brakes; the deceleration forced them both forward against their seat harnesses. Somehow, against Catharin's alarmed expectation, the Kestrel ended up with runway to spare. As she taxied toward a parking spot, Becca explained, "That was another optical illusion. The runway's got a hill in the middle, and if you put your plane down on the numbers, you can't see to the end and think you're going to be run off into the blue." She grinned. "Welcome to the Airport in the Sky!"

"It's amazing how compelling a mere optical illusion can be," Catharin said. Her body felt awash in adrenaline.

Becca parked the jet and jumped out, gesturing for Catharin to follow. She was a smaller woman than Catharin, a petite redhead who moved with an air of purpose. Becca waved an arm across the island, which tumbled northward down to the sea. "The first foothold could be a lot like this. They expect to find a rudimentary ecology and an oxygen atmosphere. On an island like this, people could plant grass and scrub oak and build the first ecosystem on the new world."

The sunlight glazed one tidy town nestled in a bay. Otherwise, a haze on the coast of the island hid most of the evidence of habitation. It could have been a new land on the other side of the stars. Catharin's heart pounded with strange excitement. Becca's words were putting flesh on the bones of Catharin's own idea. Catharin drew in a breath. "I could live that way. Especially if you're there too."

Becca replied with a bright grin. Catharin knew they would be become good friends.

"How about lunch?" Becca asked.

The airport cafe had a lovely view of the picturesque town on the bay. Laughing, they ordered things that would be unavailable on the other side of the stars. Catharin lunched on grilled salmon and chardonnay. Becca downed a steak.

☽☾

Catharin lay motionless in her small cubicle in *Aeon*, too insomniac to sleep, too demoralized to toss and turn. She wept, missing Becca, who was still in stasis, missing Earth and the Moon, the Pacific Ocean, cities. The tears were oddly empty. She could recognize her homesickness but not really feel it. It surged like the miniature ocean in Habitat, waves behind a glass wall.

☽☾

The next day went as routinely as possible for the second day after eternity. Catharin opened the flight lab and spent the day there. Nguyen studied his astronomical data; Lary made virtual models of the planet and applied hypothetical terraforming to the models. "It greens up in about a thousand years," Lary said smugly at lunch. Joel worked out the orbital mechanics of braking and of changing course around the golden sun, the mutually exclusive and final options.

Bix decided that the attitude thrusters had to be fixed. Whether the Ship braked or changed course, they needed more reliable control of its orientation. Bix scheduled a repair mission for the following morning.

During the night, insomnia cropped up all around—sick, tired sleeplessness. Catharin dispensed sleeping pills and antinauseants and grimly waited for the third morning.

Even Bix had had a bad night, but he did not mention it while he armed himself and Joel with tools and thruster parts. Catharin took a medical bag and followed them. Before leaving the crew level, they shut down the main engine rather than attempt to repair thrusters on the outer hull of an accelerating ship. The sense of weight faded away. No one talked about the possibility of a failure in restarting the main engine as they glided into the 'vator that took them into the depths of the Ship, no longer necessarily "down." Lary and Nguyen were left to chase the inevitable items that had been overlooked in securing the crew level for weightlessness.

At the center of the Ship, Bix changed the 'vator's course. Vertical bands of light marched across a channel near the top of the 'vator's front wall, marking the Ship's shells the 'vator transited until it reached the outermost, the service shell.

In the thruster access bay, a small square room with an airlock on the far end, Catharin powered up the medical EVA-monitor. The men packed each other into spacesuits while she tested the monitor. Joel brandished his tool bag, and his voice came over the radio as he entered the airlock with Bix. "Just making a little house call." The airlock door closed. "Do you, Cat?"

"Make house calls? Sometimes. I hear you loud and clear."

A few minutes later Bix's voice came over the radio. "We're on the outside of *Aeon* now. How's your reception?"

"Fine."

The hull here had no windows. Bix planted a video camera on the far side of the outer door. "Got pix, Cat?"

"The thruster housing looks like a metal hill."

With dual tethers holding him to *Aeon*'s skin, Joel ascended the thruster housing. It was slow going, as he had to move one tether attachment at a time. The thruster's mouth pointed away from the airlock, frozen in that position. Joel leaned into its maw. "Knew we'd have problems with these thrusters."

"Why?" Catharin asked.

"Weathering. They're the most exposed part of the Ship, plus the fact that their guts are too sophisticated for their own good." Joel vanished over the top of the hill. Catharin listened to a discussion of replacing valve seats and solenoids.

Joel emerged from the thruster's mouth. Arms akimbo, he looked up at the stars. His slightly elevated vital signs let Catharin guess that he was taking time out to rejoice.

In the corner of the television picture, Catharin saw Bix tossing a replacement part to Joel on a thin tether. His heart beat slowly and rock-steadily: the Bixby signature heartbeat that stayed the same under circumstances that would send anyone else's heart pounding wildly. Joel caught the part. "Take the line back, Bix, I detached the friend."

Catharin asked, "The what?"

"The hook at the end of the tether," said Bix. "Out in the Asteroid Belt they called it the spaceminer's best friend. A tether hook that's both failsafe and easy to operate, even when your hand is in one of these bulky spacesuit gloves, is one of the most damn helpful pieces of space technology there is."

"Well, obviously," said Catharin.

Clipping the part onto his short belt tether, then releasing the longer line for Bix to reel in, Joel laughed. "No gadget, including the Trevino Hook, is obvious until somebody imagines it. No plan is, either," he added.

Joel pushed himself hard. Finally Catharin said, "Joel, take five." His tether, snaked over the hill, stopped twitching.

"How do you feel?"

"Whew. Okay. Well, better! Mama always said, if you're half sick, work it off."

"You mean you feel better than earlier?"

"Yeah, I've been kinda sick ever since day before yesterday."

"We all have. I may prescribe calisthenics all around."

Joel went back to work. Soon he told Catharin to look for a dial near the airlock. She turned it for him. The housing hill slowly wheeled around. The thruster's mouth was a cave high on the hillside, with Joel standing in it. His helmet was briefly crowned with bright lights as the beams of built-in flashlights passed across the camera's lens. He waved.

"Now we go for the bad valve," Bix said. Alternating safety tethers and bristling with equipment, he joined Joel in the thruster. After that Catharin saw little more than dim motion in the cave. Suit-booted feet emerged at odd angles, sunlight flashing on the white soles.

Relaxing, she thought about less immediate concerns. Bix was so much better at doing than talking, better at judging than explaining his judgment. Not a charismatic Captain, yet a good one: she trusted him enough to follow his lead into anything up to and including the Ramamirtham Maneuver. But Lary and Nguyen did not know him so well.

A microburst of static came over the radio. "Flight deck to Captain!" The voice was Nguyen's, and he sounded alarmed.

"I hear you. What's up?"

"Eta Sagittarii isn't double, it's triple. The A star has a white dwarf companion, very close, so we didn't detect it earlier."

Joel hissed, "Damn! Three's a crowd!"

"Is the dwarf stable?" Bix asked.

"So far."

"Check it out, but good!"

Joel asked, "How do the other options look now?"

"Not good for planets with moons. And Catharin wouldn't like the time frames."

Catharin found herself shaking. "What's the matter with Eta Sagittarii?"

Joel said, "A white dwarf star hiding in the skirts of an orange giant is how you get novas. But this probably won't blow in the century it'd take us to get by."

Bix growled, "Let's get this thruster fixed."

☽☾

The flight laboratory now looked and smelled used, more natural than the incredibly perfect little facility that Catharin had opened up on the second morning. She glanced at the chronometer. The fourth day's noon had just gone by. A crew conference was scheduled for 1400 hours. Wearily she finished dissecting a piglet, made notes, and began to clean up. This one had been difficult. Emotional strain and a lack of good sleep had affected her performance. And zero gravity made a routine dissection problematic. Organs did not stay where put.

With the place cleaned and instruments packed up, she lingered by the vault wall. The vault held a variety of animals, mostly dead. Not rotten like the casualties of Seventeen Wedge T: the stasis had never broken here.

Little bodies that had been pumped full of exotic chemicals had turned into glass, not ice, when they were frozen. Their cells remained intact instead of rupturing with ice crystals. In the vault, the animals looked unchanged, like glass figurines. But their vitreous tissues had deteriorated. The figurines disintegrated when they thawed.

The laboratory stasis log and the dissections told the story. Stasis had destroyed the small rodents first; mice live thirty times faster than humans. The flesh of the cats and dogs began to deteriorate in the second century. They too were dead by now. Two of the four piglets had been alive until she killed them to dissect, mercifully, because they had been decrepit.

The indicators told a different and more hopeful story about a glass parrot. Catharin had no intentions of dissecting him. She was already sure of her results. She turned off the lights and went to the galley.

She met a fork, a used one, tumbling toward the outer wall of the room. Catharin felt too tired to catch the fork and put it away. She anchored herself at the table beside Joel.

Lary bustled in. "Hey, who left a fork adrift?"

Joel said wearily, "Might have been me."

"You really shouldn't leave things floating around like that. They can get into our instruments."

"I know! I know!" Joel stretched to snag the fork, pitching it into the dirty dish bin.

"Yesterday you let that blob of toothpaste get loose in the bathroom," Lary accused. Joel looked ready to bite Lary's head off in reply. But Bix arrived just then, with the bad-news glower on his face. Nguyen slipped in behind Bix.

"Crew conference is now," said Bix. "Nguyen."

The astrophysicist looked pinched and unhappy. "Eta Sagittarii is too dangerous. Material from the orange giant is building up on the surface of the white dwarf. It could turn into a nova engulfing all three stars."

"And us," said Bix.

"Like Judgment Day?" Catharin asked in a low voice.

"Yeah. But more so."

Lary did not wait to announce his opinion. "And the Book's other options aren't worth two bytes each. So we stay here."

"Hold it!" Joel protested. "You ready to tell me that the planet here is stable? Terraformable?"

"I most certainly am. Settlements will be in domes for the indefinite future, but—"

"*Domes!*" Joel sounded aghast.

"Nguyen has more to say," said Bix.

"The Vandals are leaving. Their trajectory is away from this star." The young astrophysicist fidgeted. "I haven't found any other danger. The sun is stable and its output steady, for example. It may be too dangerous not to stay here."

So Nguyen had oscillated to the conservative position, joining Lary. Catharin guessed that, probably for the first time in his life, the universe had frightened Nguyen.

"That your official recommendation?"

Nguyen nodded.

Joel protested, "We came to find a world with a moon—maybe even a world with green stuff and an atmosphere that we can breathe, dammit!"

"I'm not sure we can," Nguyen replied.

"Did you unpack all of the options or did you just get scared?"

Nguyen stiffened.

In a self-righteous tone, Lary told Joel, "You, my friend, ought to study the risk-benefit tables. You'll see that—"

"The tables made up three hundred years ago by fat old bureaucrats?" Cursing, Joel hit the table with the palm of his hand. "Has everyone forgotten why we came here?"

Nguyen tried to protest, and Lary sputtered, "I resent—"

Joel shouted them down. "For a green planet! How can we settle for one that'll never be good and green?!"

"And you'll hold out for that even if it gets all of us and all ten thousand passengers killed!" Lary shrilled.

Bix finally spoke. "Cool jets all around and that's an order!" No one dared argue with him. "Cat?"

He had given her a clear window in an atmosphere clouded with frustration, crackling with hostility. "My concern is the stasis, its consequences for us. And not incidentally what it does to our livestock. It would not be desirable to terraform a planet and have nothing but people with which to populate it."

"Get to your point," Lary muttered.

She ignored him. "As to animals, most can't survive stasis this long. Fortunately, their embryos can. Clumps of cells, tissues, certain organs, and simple organisms are good for centuries. With higher creatures, it's a function of life span. The longer the natural life span, the longer the duration of stasis before tissue deterioration sets in. When it does set in, things go downhill rapidly. Exponential decay.

"Thaw it out—what used to be a creature—and it falls apart. Bones aren't connected, even though the heart beats briefly. You have a pulsing bag of flesh. The maximum safe duration of stasis is a reality to be respected."

"Seems the big question is, what's the limit given the human life span," Bix said deliberately.

She nodded. "Yes. We have a green parrot in the laboratory stasis vault and some porpoises in the main vaults downstairs. My readouts indicate that they're all intact, alive, unlike the shorter-lived species. The pattern is clear. Stasis can last as long as ten times a species' maximum lifespan. Which means that human stasis is good for a millennium."

Joel grinned. "That's a change of tune."

"Recommendation?" Bix asked.

"I now believe that our course of action depends on the existence of another option. No, not option, I'd like to go on record saying that it depends on an alternative to remaining here." She caught Joel's eye. He nodded thanks. "If there's a reasonable alternative, I recommend that we take it."

"What makes you so bold all of a sudden?" Lary asked.

"Facts."

Lary threw up his hands. "Four days later we've still got a split right down the middle!"

"Looks that way," said Bix.

"We ought to wake up more people," said Lary. Startled, none of his listeners replied to that. They still had eight mission specialists as well as the rest of the primary and backup astronaut crew tucked away in the stasis vaults. "People who know what they're talking about. Scientists!"

Not, presumably, astronauts and doctors. Joel scowled. "There's no point in adding legs to a committee."

"I'm referring to the addition of brains."

"You're—We are forgetting something," Catharin said, holding in her temper. "The Book says those awake vote. Period. The responsibility for this decision rests with us."

She refrained from pointing out that the mission specialists had been picked for their credentials, not their personalities. Lary was evidence enough of that. More scientific talent would not help. They needed leadership.

With analytical clarity, yet feeling disloyal, Catharin wondered whether Bix could resolve this conference by saying the right thing. But Bix did not have Joel's gift for words.

Bix said, "The Book also says the Commander breaks a tied vote. But it's still early for that. The key to the whole business is 'reasonable alternative.' Cat's just given us all the time we need for any option in the Book. Joel and I've made certain that this ship can hold up through any of 'em. We've got about one more day before the window for braking opens and we have to act one way or another. One more day to dig for that reasonable alternative."

Catharin glanced at Joel, who remained silent. Perhaps the Ramamirtham Maneuver did not qualify as reasonable.

"We've done enough jawing," Bix said. "Nguyen and Lary, I want you, with Joel, to run through our options. By tomorrow morning. The Book's specified options."

Joel asked sharply, "You trust the options in the Book that much?"

"As of yet, there's no good reason not to go by the Book."

You mean no defensible reason, Catharin thought suddenly. *No reason to give to the ten thousand colonists when we revive them, or to give to your conscience if more of them die.*

"The reason is the moon that wasn't there," Joel said in a harsh voice.

"I have to go by the Book," Bix said heavily. His shoulders drooped as if the lifelong military starch had worn out. "I have to assume that the Aeon Foundation knew what it was doing and that it sent us here with reliable instructions."

Joel turned away from the Captain.

☽☾

Late in the Ship's night, Bix decided to go on an inspection tour. To her surprise, he asked Catharin rather than Joel to come along. "I don't need his expertise. I need yours."

The 'vator took them a short way down the Axis and out toward the hull. They emerged at a tunneltrain station.

Compared to any of the 'vator's other landings, the station seemed enormous. The 'vator had been designed for the crew's exclusive use. The train was mass transit. But the weightlessness, the dark, and the cold made the station as strange as though a dream had conjured it up, a cavern of the subconscious mind.

Using the banister of a stairway to pull herself along, she followed Bix toward the platform. Bix parked himself on the platform's guardrail and stared into the tunnel on his right.

A breeze wafted out of the dark tube. Light gleamed on the tunnel's curved walls. Headlight dazzling to the eye, serpentine bulk flowing from the tunnel, the train came on wings of wind like a dark angel of the psyche. Catharin's heart pounded in ridiculous alarm. *It's just a vehicle*, she told herself.

The train slowed to a stop beside the platform, and all of its doors hissed open. Bix gestured toward the conductor's cabin at the head of the train. They pulled themselves in.

Doors closing, the train accelerated. The tracks ran on the outside of Outtown. Just the right size for two people, the little cabin had a large front windshield and a console from which the automatic route programming could be overridden. The cabin's roof pointed toward the center of the Ship. As soon as the train moved, a slight centrifugal force set in, sufficient to make sitting down feasible. Catharin felt herself pressed into the seat, feather-lightly.

Here the train ran below Outtown, close to the hull. After a mile or two the tunnel angled upward. The train emerged into Outtown in the North Industrial region. It climbed to an elevated way between deserted buildings.

Bix took in the scene: factories, warehouses, a sewage treatment plant, revealed by sparse nightlights. "I forgot how big Outtown is. A damned city."

"It doesn't look used enough to be a city," Catharin replied.

"Will be if we stay here." He put his feet up on the console, careful, in the slight gravity, not to dislodge himself from his seat in the process. "You wanna be my sounding board?"

"That's part of my job."

"My circuit boards all clear?"

"Unqualified yes."

"Rest of us?"

"Yes. Those of us who are exhibiting difficult personalities are normally that way."

Bix grunted unhappily.

The tunneltrain ran south toward the residential zone of *Aeon*'s Outtown, where people would live while remaking a new planet. Catharin identified holes and bare architectural rims meant to be filled later with landscaping plants.

"Are you physically well?" asked Catharin.

"I don't look off, do I?"

"Remember how you got your nickname, 'Old Ironsides'? You cracked two ribs and finished your mission without revealing the fact. That's why I'm asking."

With a short laugh, he said, "I'm queasy around the edges. And I feel old. Little aches and pains. Maybe I've always had 'em, but I never thought about it before."

In the distance, a building loomed above the rest, recognizable as the hospital. "There's the Doc Shop, let's hear what it has to say." Bix hailed the hospital on the radio, and a string of information came back in response. The hospital stood ready to receive the thousands of people from the stasis vaults.

At intervals they came to train stations. In the midst of the residential zone they reached the station called Celestis. Bix had the train stop there. The station lay in the bottom of a valley made of glass, thick and strong with arching braces, part of the inner hull itself. One day the Ship's outer hull and insulating layer would be used up in the making of a new world, and the station would lie in a trough full of stars. Now, insulation lay on the other side of the glass: doubly useful materials that were needed for the Ship's future life as a terraforming satellite-city and presently stowed between the inner and the outer hulls for the duration of the star flight, more protection from the elements of interstellar space.

"This ship's the real Old Ironsides," said Bix. "Hide's in fine shape. All three layers of it."

"Could it withstand the Ramamirtham Maneuver?"

He raised his eyebrows. "So he brought that up with you, too, huh. Hell, yes. The double hull's *hard*, fantastic engineering. Plus the star shield. Whatever hits the star shield glances off and is deflected so it doesn't collide with the rest of the body of the Ship. Plus the magnetosphere has a shielding effect where it comes to charged particles. Plus we've got the automatic guns to ionize rocks that are in our way. *Aeon* was designed for the Ram Maneuver."

"I didn't know that."

The train purred away from the glass valley Celestis. "*Aeon* was overdesigned deliberately, to make sure it was up to the rigors of the stars. And the Ram Maneuver was the benchmark, up to which the design criteria were elevated." Bix looked her in the eye and asked abruptly, "Would you agree to it?"

"The Ramamirtham Maneuver? Yes. I would."

"Got any justification in mind?"

"One has occurred to me. I'm not an astronautical engineer—"

"Good thing, too."

"Thanks, I think. At any rate, I've studied how the global cryostasis settled down and why. It's a big system, the vaults, the medical machines, the cooling lines, the Intelligence. Factoring in the complexity of it, it's a *vast* system."

"Damn complicated big," he agreed.

"It was modeled exhaustively. The model couldn't possibly predict everything. Too many details had to be left out, too many small factors added up in unexpected ways. Synergies that no one could have anticipated cropped up."

"Roger that."

"Now that things have settled down, the stasis has a great deal of inertia, so to speak, and barring really strong disruptive forces it will stay as it is for hundreds of years."

"Luck?"

"Yes, Bix. We were lucky. The stasis could have lost its balance at some point early on and run away. Since planets are even bigger systems, I should think similar principles apply."

He listened closely, content to hear her thoughts unfolded at her own rate.

"We never modeled Earth's weather or its ecology accurately enough to predict what civilization would do to the planet. Mars was being terraformed with uncertain results," she said. "Terraforming was failing on Venus, theoretical models to the contrary. Planets—even ones that we have studied for centuries—are too big and too complex. If you try to change them, they may rock back to their original equilibrium. Or the change may run away from you."

"You're right," he replied. "Lary's good at what he does, though. I'd trust his models of the new planet's future before I'd trust what most planetologists said about its present."

"Still, planetary modeling is not a sure thing."

"No. It's not."

"The planet we have here is already teetering on the edge of even hypothetical habitability. For one thing, it has an elliptical orbit and wide climate swings, and for another, it has no moon. Its axis could wander and turn a pole toward the sun, putting the equator into the icebox while melting the polar ice. Terraforming might fail. Our descendants would live in domes forever."

He rubbed his chin. "That's so bad? Folks on Luna do. Did at the time we left. Whatever."

"They had the Earth in their sky, always. I'm afraid that if we stay here, a day will come when people have forgotten green land and blue seas."

"It's possible," Bix admitted.

"That is a risk too. Not a medical one but spiritual. I truly believe that it's more grave than the risks of the Ramamirtham Maneuver."

He looked through the windshield into the distance. They had reached the equatorial region. Here farms and gardens would be planted in the future.

"Bix? Would you do it?"

"Would I take the stars by the tail to fly to a better world in the Sagittarius arm of the galaxy? You bet I would—if I weren't in command." He brooded now as he watched the terrain go by, blank square plots separated by wide bands meant to be future windrows of trees. Dotting the sterile plains were geodesic domes designed to serve as barns. "We got horses?"

"Embryonic ones, yes, lots."

"I grew up on a farm," he said. "In upstate New York. That was before your time, before the land there died. I am old. I'll never see the green of a world that we terraform from rock-bottom scratch. I wanted that. I'm afraid it's affecting my judgment."

"It could. You're wise to realize that. Remember also that you might overcompensate."

"Am I overcompensating?"

"I don't know. It's possible, that's all."

"Goddamn Eta Sagittarii C." Hearing the bitter tone of his voice, Catharin's heart sank. She feared that she knew what his decision would be. At the station on the equator, Bix stopped the tunneltrain and headed it back toward the north pole, the crew level, and the final day of star flight.

Chapter Five

HALO

In the morning they assembled on the flight deck. "Eta Sagittarii is out," Bix said bluntly. "Other options fall below the threshold of acceptability when updated astronomy is factored into the Book's risk/benefit tables. In short, I don't see a reasonable alternative. We stay." He ordered braking. Made, the decision did nothing to ease the tension.

Joel took his place at the Flight station. For once his face was impossible to read. He started the countdown.

Catharin, at the Medical station, did not expect the impact of braking to disrupt the huge stasis system, though she would monitor it closely. She also watched the physiological states of the flight crew. Joel's blood pressure read high, driven up by anger. From Bix came the signal of the signature heartbeat. Durable, dutiful Bix: had he gotten command of *Aeon* by virtue of sheer durability? A more charismatic commander, a man with a gift for words, might have turned the vote toward moving on. Catharin's own distress level ran high. She disagreed with Bix's decision. She felt as though a part of her were dying. She wondered what she would say to the people she brought out of stasis here, days and months and years from now.

"Fifteen hundred A.C.," Lary announced. He had won. To his credit, he refrained from gloating and instead modeled away at their future world more energetically than ever. "The greenery has stabilized and diversified into altiplano grasslands and snow forests."

"Everybody lives in greenhouses?" Joel asked, with acid around the edges of his voice.

"That's where the houses are, and people stay indoors in the extremes of winter. But they can go outside in summer. And the sky is blue over the glass," Lary said defensively. Silent, Nguyen watched Lary. Neither specialist had an assigned role in the braking maneuver.

Catharin thought about Joseph Devreze, revived from stasis ten years in the future, asked to genetically engineer better altiplano grass or perhaps algae. How would he fare, arrogant and restless spirit that he was? It would be his purgatory, if not his hell.

Bix gave the order to turn on the thrusters. The stars in the flight deck window swayed. "Little rough," Joel murmured, hovering over the thruster controls.

"Definitely rough," said the Captain. "Try to clear Z's throat there."

"Z's choked—it just shut down on us."

"Keep the others steady."

The burn lasted for several minutes, making the Ship yaw, swinging the engine's spike around to point in the direction of their forward motion. The quality of the yawing burn dissatisfied Bix. He held a muttered discussion with Joel about the problem.

"Can you make it go faster?" said Nguyen.

Lary answered, "Well, yes, there's a way to project the terraforming on a time scale ten times faster. But with less detail."

"Would you do that, please? I'm curious."

From the flight station, Catharin heard the countdown to the second and final thruster burn. This one would fix the engine in position, pointing at Sagittarius, the Ship turning its back on the farther stars. Suddenly she remembered what Chief Donovan's mother had said: *Embrace what God gives you, even if you're given no arms to embrace with.* A spasm of bitter recognition shook her. That kind of fatalism was exemplified by what they were doing now, here.

"Firing!" Joel said. "X-pos, X-neg, Y—Hey! Z-neg just fizzled out."

"Up the thrust on the rest!"

"Too late!" Aware of the eyes of the others on him, Joel explained. "One thruster array largely failed, its partner never even came on. We didn't quite stop the yaw. Should be able to manage a stop on the next revolution, though."

"Y's?" Bix asked.

"Did just fine. Y-neg appreciated the attention we gave it the other day."

Unwillingly, Catharin wondered if Joel had deliberately misfired the thrusters. He hated the idea of stopping here. But what would such an act accomplish, except to protract a painful hour? More slowly now, the Ship revolved around its *x*-axis, drifting back toward its original position as Bix and Joel ran test patterns on the thruster control circuits.

Nguyen and Lary returned to the planetary model.

"We've got seas with coral reefs and old-growth forests," crowed Lary. "Ten thousand A.C."

"That is very beautiful," said Nguyen, longing and sadness in his voice. Then, "What happens when the planet's axis tilts?"

"I don't know when that will be."

"I do. I worked it out just today. Eighty-three thousand years after colonization. Can we see what happens then?"

"If you insist. You're aware that that's longer than modern humans existed on Earth? It's hard to imagine our descendants on this planet not coping." Clicks and beeps came from their station as Lary busied himself with Nguyen's request.

Lary, even Lary, had said "this planet." Not even he had bothered to give it a name. That was a bad sign, evidence of a lack of emotional bonding to the new world. Yet they were in the very act of committing themselves to make it their home.

"Begin the main engine countdown at T-10 minutes," Bix ordered.

"T-okay," Joel said.

"Thruster burn countdown at T-3 minutes."

"T-okay."

"Get it right this time. The window won't stay open forever."

"We're good for five to six revs, even at this rate," Joel replied evenly. "And this isn't the only window."

"I want to get it over with now."

At least Lary and Nguyen had found a distraction for themselves. But

Catharin had nothing to do but watch. Her own pulse and respiration rate soared.

At forty-six seconds before the thruster burn, Lary let out a yelp.

Bix glowered.

"Look, everybody, look!" Lary sounded choked.

"Now?!"

Nguyen said, "It is sad!"

"Hold the counts." Dead calm, Bix said, "What is it?"

"It had seas," Nguyen said, "but they will freeze."

"Glaciation of an unprecedented order of magnitude," said Lary. He sounded stunned. "And the glaciers flow. It's awful."

"Awful?" Bix repeated. "Scrape the domes off the land?"

"That's not the point," said Lary. "It had seas, grasslands, rain forests, living deserts, a diversity of ecosystems. But the world turns on its side because there's no moon to stabilize the tilt of its axis, and then the equatorial seas ice over. The species die-offs in seas and on land are phenomenal. Nine-tenths of all species gone. Glaciers overrun the forests and grasslands and estuaries alike. It's like scraping a painting off a canvas, almost back to where it is now."

Joel stirred. Fearing that he might want to jump in with a rash remark that would antagonize Lary, Catharin shot him a warning look with a slight shake of her head.

"So far in the future, humans might not exist there anymore," Nguyen murmured.

"That's not the point. I can't agree to stay here."

All of a sudden, Catharin understood Lary. He was Martian, and it did not matter to him whether his remotest descendants had to live in domes forever, or whether they finally went off to another new world. But the beauty of the future terraformed world had entranced him, and he could not stand to see its eventual doom, so graphically illustrated by the virtual model.

The Ship continued to revolve, passing its original position. Bix glanced at the chronometer.

Nguyen said in a plaintive tone, "What else can we do?"

Bix replied, "Something called the Ramamirtham Maneuver." He rapidly explained the maneuver and how it might bring the Ship to the spiral arm in Sagittarius. "The really tricky part is the fancy footwork around those dwarf stars," he concluded. "It'll take a couple of years. Too long to stay awake, and manual piloting would be pointless anyway. It's got to be a billiard ball shot, a damn near perfect one, out of interstellar space into the dwarf system that we've been calling Nguyen's Vandals. If we didn't have an Intelligent autopilot as good as this one, and if we didn't have Nguyen to program it, there's no way I'd attempt the maneuver. But Nguyen can do it."

Nguyen stared at the window, at the untwinkling stars, troubled. "If we make for Sagittarius, can we bias the Moonseeker code toward more desirable planets?"

"Definitely," said Bix. "At least till time gets short, say in the last ship-century. Which gives us two thousand of the stars' years for browsing."

"All right." Lary turned the screen off.

"Nguyen?"

Trepidation in his voice, Nguyen answered, "We would be entering the leading edge of the Sagittarius arm, where stars are still forming in clouds of gas and dust. Terrestrial planets might be very abundant there, though not all of them old enough to have evolved life. But it's dangerous." Nguyen floated to Catharin's side. "What do you say?"

"This isn't the first I've heard about the maneuver. I've had time to think about it," she replied. "It is dangerous. It is also the bravest and best choice for us."

"But reasonable?"

"Reason includes a certain amount of daring, doesn't it?"

"How can it be reasonable to throw away the Book?" he pleaded.

"It would not be reasonable to throw the Book away, but no one has proposed doing that." She said gently, "We may just outgrow the need to adhere to every letter of it. We can think for ourselves, which is eminently reasonable."

He floated there, thinking hard. Then his face cleared. "Yes."

"Unanimous." Bix heaved a sigh. "No braking. We accelerate instead. A hyperbolic pass by this sun, such that we leave on course toward Nguyen's Vandals. Joel and Nguyen, you two calculate the course."

Joel started out of what seemed to have been a daze. "Yes, sir!"

Aeon revolved around until the engine pointed toward Earth and streams of thruster fire stopped the yawing. The main engine flared on, the shock of it taking long seconds to communicate through the Ship's bulk to the crew level. Pouring out a cataract of plasma, the Ship accelerated.

Mild gravity pushed Catharin down into her seat. It felt good, like certainty.

"Open the matter scoop full," said Bix. "On our way through this system, we'll pick up some fuel for the trip to Nguyen's Vandals."

"We'll let this old beast feed," Joel replied, grinning.

Bix crossed his arms decisively. "Before we leave this sun, we're gonna have the thrusters working right, even if Cat and Lary have to learn to turn a zero-g wrench!"

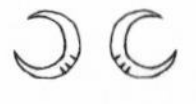

For the last meal this side of stasis, they forsook the drab little pigeonhole galley on the crew level. Instead, forks, plates, food, and all, they carried the meal down-Axis, to Level Seven and the Ship's prime dining hall.

The Ship's acceleration away from the vandalized yellow sun created enough inertial gravity to keep food on the plates. The inertia also kept the astronauts in place. They seated themselves on what would be the south wall of the dining hall when the Ship reached its final destination and spun around its axis to create a full g of artificial gravity for its populace.

The hall's other wall, above their heads, had another of the Ship's tall, narrow, deep-sided windows embedded in it. During star flight, the window was protected by its location deep in the shadow of the star shield and by the shutter, which had been rolled back for this special occasion, and the window overhead was full of stars.

Catharin said, "Lary, this beef Wellington of yours is delicious."

"'Tisn't quite the real thing," he replied. "When you're stuck with a space galley, you learn the art of food fakery."

"Where'd you learn to fake food so good?" asked Joel.

Lary laughed. "Triton Station, also known as the tail end of nowhere."

Galleyware clinked all around. With four to six weeks of wakefulness, appetites for food as well as for sleep had returned to their owners. Stasis effects simply wore off.

Joel waved his fork. "Nguyen's code is beautiful, just beautiful. We'll really waltz with the Vandals."

"It was just a kind of degenerate three-body problem," Nguyen said.

"I'd say it was more than that, son," said Bix.

Catharin noticed how deep the silences in the conversation sounded. The dining hall was huge and shadowy. Over their heads the hall's window faced the stars in front of *Aeon*. The Ship rotated very slowly in its gyroscopic stabilization. Stars arced from side to side across the window with almost imperceptible motion. The size and gloom of the dining hall and the appearance of the window reminded Catharin of early medieval architecture. In old Europe on Earth, she had seen Romanesque churches and castles, massive walls with narrow wary windows, erected against an outside world of darkness and danger.

When the last bits of the meal had been polished off, Lary produced a pitcher. He poured green liquid into glasses for everyone. "This concoction is brought to you by myself and Catharin. It contains the first round of go-to-sleep drugs, camouflaged by synthetic crème de menthe."

Bix eyed his drink. "To the future!" he said finally.

At last there was time to sit still and think about that. Taken in small sips, the drink tasted sweet and wildly minty. Catharin remembered the casualties below, the few who had died because of the vagaries of physiology, and the many who had been assigned to Seventeen Wedge T. No more, she hoped and prayed; no more accidents like that. A hundred in one place had been too terrible a tragedy. At least their dream was alive, the dream of all of the voyagers of *Aeon*, as the Ship hurtled toward its rendezvous with the dwarf binary star and toward their hope of a good green planet.

Joel said, "Here's another toast. To the Milky Way."

"That is my sister's name," said Nguyen softly. "Ha Minh. In Vietnamese it means River of Light. She's down there in the passenger vaults."

"That's a good sign," said Joel. "How about turning off the rest of the lights so we can see it?"

With the hall in darkness, the stars in the high window blazed. "See the brightest blue star? It's called Nunki," said Nguyen. "It's one of our navigating reference points for the next leg of the trip."

As Catharin sipped the drink, her eyes adjusted to the darkness. The River of Light eddied near the blue star Nunki. Her glass felt smooth and cool to the touch. Tonight they would return to the glass time of stasis.

"My eyes must be adjusting to the dark," said Joel. "Anybody else see what I see?"

"I didn't know it would do that," Nguyen whispered.

Lary said, "What? I only see stars."

"The Ship's magnetosphere is in high gear," said Bix, "and we're plowing through a solar system. So particles hit the magnetosphere and get channeled to the south pole. Into the matter scoop. We get more fuel for the trip and a light show to boot."

Almost invisible against the Milky Way in Sagittarius, a pale pink light glimmered in front of the stars. "It looks like the Northern Lights," Catharin whispered.

"There's no atmosphere outside the Ship, so it's not a true aurora," Bix answered. "It's kin to the charged-particle shuttle-glow around spacecraft in low Earth orbit."

"Starship-glow." Joel turned on the small communication console in the nearest table—which, attached to the dining room floor, was vertical with respect to Joel. The screen illuminated with a picture of *Aeon* as the Ship would look from the outside now. And Catharin saw that the glow circled the Ship's north pole. The light made a flickering halo around the starship's new course.

Chapter Six

AEON

"We made it. We went light-years farther than any ship sent out from Earth before us," Catharin said.

Becca listened intently, but her eyes flicked around the small, spare cubicle, furnished only with medical equipment. Cross-legged on her pallet, Becca sat very straight. Catharin knew why: just out of cryostasis, it hurt to flex the backbone, hurt to move at all, as though one's whole body had fallen asleep, with a needly numbness in every part. Including the tongue. "So's everyt'ing okay?"

"After almost three centuries, we reached the star that was our destination."

"Ship?" There were several urgent queries packed into the one-word question. Is the Ship damaged in any way? Is it heading for planetfall? What's my job going to be like?

"There's something more I must tell you."

Becca's attention riveted to Catharin. "Whassat?"

Catharin took a deep breath to steady her voice and explained the Vandal stars, the missing moon.

Becca's blue eyes widened. "Are we there? Or *where*?"

One white wall featured a large rendition of the mission logo: the Ship on a black field of stars. The star field represented a couple of constellations, the names of which were now irrelevant. *Aeon* had traveled so far that the constellations of Earth were gone. And that was what Catharin had to explain to Becca. "We sent the Ship toward the binary dwarf."

"But no planets there."

"The Ship used the stars to accelerate."

Catharin could visualize how it had been, the white stars, small and dim and dense, whirling around their common center of gravity. And then the starship fell into the picture, on a precise trajectory: a path that let the Ship fall around one dwarf, picking up speed—and then be wrenched away by the gravity of the second dwarf to whip around that one, before returning to the gravity of the first one. And so on: the Ship used the dynamo of the paired, dense stars to accelerate. Faster and faster. Finally the starship broke away from the whirling white dwarfs, accelerated to relativistic speed. "Becca, the Ship did the Ramamirtham Maneuver."

Becca gaped. "That's not what the B-Book said to do!"

"It wasn't our first choice. It was our last. We told the Ship to use the dwarf stars to accelerate, to go farther than ever, and faster, and find a green world for us."

"How'd the structure take the Ram maneuver?"

"As far as we can tell, it did no damage to the Ship."

Becca frowned, struggling to rev her mind up to its usual running speed, to comprehend what Catharin was telling her. "Did the Ship find a green world?"

"Yes."

Becca heaved a sigh, one with a wheezing edge. Not congestion: a stiff, sore diaphragm. Becca seemed healthy—a miracle that Catharin did not yet dare believe in because she wanted it so much. Becca started moving her arms, doing the isometric exercises to rehabilitate muscle function. "Ouch—! Tell me more."

"The planet has an oxygen-nitrogen atmosphere, seas, and continents. And one more thing. The landmasses have green markings detectable even at this distance. That means abundant plants of some kind."

Becca unfurled a grin, then clapped her hands to her mouth with a muffled, "*Ouch!*"

"I know, it feels like knitting needles in your arms and legs, and sewing needles in the facial muscles. Keep using them and the pains will diminish."

"Keep talking to me."

"The Ship is approaching the new sun in a highly eccentric elliptical orbit like a comet's. After a rather close approach, the Ship will swing out to the planet."

Becca started rotating her shoulders. Her movements were becoming more supple. "Does it have a moon? Tides and good stuff like that?"

"It's a double planet, with approximately the separation of Earth and Luna. *Both* are approximately Earth's size."

Becca's blue eyes sparkled. "Two for the price of one?"

"You might say that." A corollary came unbidden to Catharin's mind: *we don't know yet what the price is*. "The one that we're calling the moon is covered with seas."

"I get it. We'll settle on the one that isn't all wet, since we're not equipped to terraform a planet-sized ocean." Becca clambered off the pallet. "Why didn't you tell me the good news right off the bat?" But she cheerfully supplied an answer herself, sparing Catharin. "You're so methodical—you never do tell the end before you tell the story, Cat!" She started into torso rotation. "So is Orlov up and running?"

"No. He's still in stasis. Not many people are up as of yet." Catharin named them: Captain Bixby, Joel, environmental engineer Miguel Torres-Mendoza, and Lary Siroky-Scheidt. "You may not know Lary. The original schedule didn't call for getting a planetologist up before planetfall, but then the double planet wasn't what we had in mind."

Becca stopped the isometrics. She ran a hand through her hair: her I'm-thinking-about-this gesture that kept the flaming red hair perpetually tousled. "Why isn't Orlov up?"

"I told the guys I wanted to see the male-female ratio around here improved," answered Catharin. "Which was just a joke, not a very good one. The truth is that the trip took far longer than planned, counting the second leg of it. Cryostasis affected our bodies. Those of us who are younger and female seem to be less affected and recuperate faster. We need an engineer now, not next week or next month. So I urged in no uncertain terms that Orlov be passed over in favor of the alternate. And you got the job. I'm sorry."

Becca exhaled. That wasn't part of the isometric sequence. "I'm not," she said.

"Do you feel like walking to the flight deck?"

"You bet."

Becca did not lean on Catharin's offered arm. She steadied herself on the wall of the connecting corridor a few times as Catharin continued the briefing. "Joel and Bix want to aerobrake when we get to the double planet, provided that the planetfall checklist is done by that time. Otherwise we swing back out and try again in the next orbit."

"Why aerobraking? That's an emergency measure in case of engine trouble or low fuel supply."

"The Ship almost exhausted its fuel slowing down enough to stop here."

Becca's mind was now clicking along at nearly its usual operating speed. "If the Ram Maneuver didn't damage the Ship, looping around a binary dwarf star, we ought to think about doing it in reverse around the double planet. Aerobraking is not the best way to slow down. It'd cause problems like heat stress on the structure. By the way, how many g's did we pull decelerating from star flight?"

"Three for one hundred and thirty-two days."

"What! That was pushing some safety margins! Just what speed was that decelerating *from?*"

"Nine-tenths of the speed of light."

Startled, Becca stumbled against the wall. "That's—faster than any spacecraft ever went." She reflected. "I guess the Ram Maneuver worked. But I wish you had consulted a structural engineer before you committed the Ship to it."

The flight deck was deserted, dark apart from scores of small monitor lights. Stars shone through one slanting deep window. Becca approached the window and stood so close to it that she must have felt the cold from deep space seeping in. Outside and, relative to the artificial gravity, down, the bulk of *Aeon* curved against the stars. The Ship's northern hemisphere was aimed at its new sun and brightly illuminated.

The starship's hull looked like a battlefield, gouged and scarred with craters. Streaks radiated from some of the craters where the outer shell had been vaporized.

Becca gasped. "Oh my God! Is any of that damage structural?"

"Not as far as we know."

"Okay. Okay. I take it no thermal leaks and no pressure drops detected by the sensors," Becca muttered, visibly upset. She crowded against the corners of the window to see a wider portion of the star-blasted hull. "Looks like the hull's discolored even where it's not damaged. We knew exposure to interstellar radiation would stain it in time, but that's so much discoloration that—" Then she asked, "Just how long did we go?"

Stars wheeled by, and the craters' faint sun shadows shifted before Catharin found her voice to answer. "We didn't think it would take so long to keep looking. Becca, the Ship lived up to its name."

"Huh? *Aeon . . . A thousand years?!* Oh, no! That's why it looks like that!" Shaken, Becca folded her arms across her chest to hug herself. "You just said young female people came out in better shape. But I feel sick around the edges."

"Right out of stasis, that's normal."

Becca's mouth leveled to a straight line, determination, the slight change in expression almost imperceptible in the faint reflected light from the distant sun. "Okay. The only thing to do now is go ahead and get the job done. We've got to make planetfall. You were right."

"I hope so. What about?"

"Orlov. He's by-the-book all the way. That's a problem when somebody threw the Mission Book out the airlock."

"We didn't throw the Book away," Catharin said. She sounded defensive to herself. "It's still what we have to go by."

"So where are we in the Checklist?"

"Day Five. Remember the reservations you had about whether the Checklist could be accomplished in the time frame specified by the Book? Well, it's been six days since we started on the Checklist. We're already a day behind."

Becca nodded. Arms crossed, feet apart, her stance projected an unlikely sturdiness for such a small and fine-boned woman. It was her willpower showing. "I've got to go get something. Then I'll head for the control center and look for the afterburner button on the Checklist."

☽☾

In a grave mood, Catharin climbed up to the Axis, where with the Ship spinning around her, there was no artificial gravity. She pointed her feet at the north end of the elevator. The elevator picked up speed, gliding southward, and its north end touched her slippers, a tenuous facsimile of gravity.

A light on the elevator wall signaled passing the transport level, where stored space shuttles awaited call into action. The transport level also had facilities to fabricate aircraft tailored for whatever conditions the new colony planet might present. Reminded of Becca, Catharin felt a fresh pang of anxiety, wondering how their friendship would fare now.

Catharin exited the 'vator several signals farther down, on Level Seven. She wheeled into the blue well. Blue was the color code for flight operations. The gravity increased. Catharin compensated without thinking about it, shifted from slithering down the blue well's ladder to aiming her feet at the rungs and making sure not to let go with both hands at once. At the bottom she stepped off into most of a g.

The north polar crew level from which she had just descended could have belonged to any ordinary spaceship, with pigeonhole flight deck, galley, bunk room, and so forth. The control center was something else. With its high, curved Big Picture wall above the wide primary stations dais, with the ranks of subsidiary stations under the auxiliary screens, and the two-story observers' gallery on the farther end, the control center was the theater for a huge drama. Here, one guessed the true size and bulk of *Aeon*; one sensed the colossal magnitude of the duty of bringing *Aeon* to a safe future. The gravity weighed on Catharin. She felt slight vertigo.

Miguel Torres-Mendoza looked up from the Life Systems station that he shared with Catharin. She met his worried, dark eyes with a nod, and waved the A-OK sign to Joel at the Flight station. Joel replied with a wide grin. Lary, hunched over his own work at Astro/Survey, did not look up. Catharin decided to take a seat beside Bix at the Command station until her dizziness went away.

"She okay?" asked the Captain.

"Alarmed, but in good shape both mentally and physically. She's the most resilient human being I've ever known."

As her dizziness faded, Catharin checked herself for other malaise. Slight queasiness in the recesses of her stomach—more like a disinclination to eat or drink than real illness. This was a distinct improvement over her condition as of one week ago. When she had first come out of stasis, after the Ship found the double planet, she had been too sick to work. So had Bix and Joel. But the three of them had been in stasis twice. Double stasis was double jeopardy.

So they had lost a day of work. With reinforcements in the form of Miguel Torres-Mendoza, they had managed to keep up with the Checklist since then. The Ship's Intelligence represented the Checklist as a branching diagram, a tree. The tree's branches represented the Ship's systems, its twigs the many subsystems. Each twig could be unpacked to a schematic of the detail behind it. From root to twigs, the tree had to turn from red (needing checking) to amber (check in progress) to green (systems operational) before they entered orbit around the new world.

Miguel signaled Catharin over to Life Systems. He had pulled up on the screen a schematic of the Ship's water lines. "I'm concerned about the effects of deceleration on these ancient lines. Debris may have settled somewhere, causing blockages."

Nodding, Catharin pulled up the stasis schematic, ordered a similar check there. The pipes and lines that carried stasis cooling liquid would be equally susceptible to blockage.

Becca arrived. With hair combed and the flaps and pockets of her flight-suit zipped up, she looked as crisp as ever before. She held a large object, around the sides of which the edges of paper showed: an old-fashioned binder, crammed full.

Captain Bixby stood. "Welcome up, Engineer. What's that?"

"My notes and printouts on the design decisions and stress tests during the Ship's construction, sir."

"Does it also contain information about unapproved procedures and the like?"

"Yes, sir."

"A Goodie Book, huh. And it must weigh seven pounds if it weighs an ounce. Did it get put in with crew cargo?" Bix asked, his tone severe.

"No. It was in among my personal effects. And my effects totaled under the weight allotment."

Bix cleared his throat. "You had an assigned file in the Ship's Intelligence. Why did you find it necessary to pack that?"

Catharin felt distressed at Bix's severity until she realized that Bix was running a little stress test on Becca.

Becca replied, "I decided I needed my own backup. I didn't completely trust large electronic systems over centuries of cold storage."

Bix rocked back on his heels in his own version of I'm-thinking-about-this body language. "As a matter of fact, I brought my Goodie Book too." A smile livened his craggy features. "I'd say you're well equipped for your job." Changing gears, Bix said, "You know our pilot, medical officer, and environmental engineer. I don't believe you've met our planetologist. Dr. Lary Siroky-Scheidt."

Becca extended a hand to Lary with a smile. "Hi. Becca Fisher."

Lary shook her hand, frowning. Without a word, he turned his attention back to whatever he was doing at his console. Ignoring the discourtesy, Becca settled into the Engineering console, turning it on sequence by sequence.

"Are you still calling yourself Fisher?" inquired Joel, whose last name was now Atlanta, from his place at Flight station.

"The way I understood it, you changed your last name to commemorate your metropolis of origin, as in Earth's great cities," Becca answered. "Which Brightwood, Tennessee, wasn't."

That prompted laughter from Joel and Bix. "You are a long way from the old hometown now, Becca," said Joel.

Catharin felt relieved. Joel had found a way to say the truth that needed to be acknowledged—but casually, so that it did not overwhelm them all. *We are a long way from home.*

Miguel indicated a window on his half of the workstation that detailed system purging in progress. "If this fails, someone must go to clean the sewer," he told Catharin.

A fraction of Catharin's attention followed the livelier conference between Engineering and Flight. "Did we get a log of impacts? At point-nine *c*, even a dust grain could have made some of the craters I saw on the leading hemisphere."

"Complete log. Let me feed it to you."

"Hang on while I crank this up. Okay."

Then Joel said, "You better have a look at one of the periscopic views of the hull." He rattled out a code number.

"That one correlates with an identifiable hit in the log," Captain Bixby informed Becca. "I think you ought to worry about it."

After a pause, Becca said, "You're right. Captain. I'd like to send out the inspection robots *soon*."

"At your discretion."

"Joel, let's have a look at that activation list," Becca said. A few minutes later: "Oh, darn. This robot act list has more steps than a hound dog has fleas. Hey, while I digest this, can we see the Big Picture?"

"Put it on for her," Bix said.

One high wall of the control center flickered like a curtain and faded to black. There was space, starrier than any nights of Earth, backdrop for a chip of brilliant orange—the K-class star that was the new sun. And there were the new planets, twin dots, one ice blue, the other a greener blue, like turquoise.

"Thanks," said Becca. "I like to see where I'm going."

In addition to the astronomical picture, the Ship's Intelligence had illustrated the double planet's dance around a common center of gravity. The tandem dots trailed braided threads. The twin planets fascinated Catharin. Not the solitary, barren globe they had found in the last place: here were two worlds for one price.

Eager, Becca asked, "What's the axis inclination? Do we know what we're getting by way of years and days and seasons and if Earth plants and animals will like it?"

Joel instructed the Intelligence to show more information. Now the green dot bisected a thin line: the planet's axis of rotation, not quite perpendicular to the plane of the ecliptic. "The ocean moon stabilizes the tilt of the green planet's axis," said Joel. He sounded reverent. "That the axis doesn't drastically tilt back and forth means that the world has had moderate temperatures, conducive to life. And, with a constant, moderate tilt, there are seasonal variations in climate. Winter and summer and spring and fall."

Bix said, "Even if the original target, moon and all, had panned out, it was supposed to be a sketchy biosphere that needed work. But with this one, we may be in luck." There was something almost plaintive in his gravelly voice. He yearned for luck. "We may just be able to drop into a livable world."

Catharin felt the yearning too. This green dot meant more than she had dared hope for. Had evolution on that still-distant planet produced flowers yet?

"The green planet has a fifty-hour day," Lary announced.

Startled, Catharin groped for comprehension, and imagined a tropical place with very long, very still, hot middays. She tried to quell a sharp, knife-edged pang of anxiety.

"But we'll stay here and make the best of it," Lary went on, a harsh edge to his voice, "because we're at the end of our rope. If we go any farther, we'll all end up like Seventeen Wedge T!"

"What?" Becca asked.

"Freezer mush," Lary said.

"What? Everybody?" The tone of Becca's voice made Catharin move to intervene, too late. Becca had paled. The freckles across her nose and cheekbones stood out in vivid contrast.

Lary started, "It seems that the cooler—"

Catharin interrupted him. "Shut up, that's enough." She went to Becca's side. "Did you know somebody in Seventeen T?"

"A family. A family of four. All gone?"

As gently as she could, Catharin explained, "A machine malfunction caused temperature fluctuations across the entire compartment. Everyone in that compartment died. They didn't suffer." Catharin put an arm around Becca's shoulders, furious at Lary. This bombshell of bad news should not have been dropped on anybody just out of overlong stasis—much less the engineer whose judgment could make or break the Ship.

In a deathly silence in the control center, Becca swallowed hard. She wiped a tear off her cheek with the back of her hand.

Nobody turned off the Big Picture. The blue planet and the green one waltzed on. The Ship was a tiny mote on the tip of a vectorial line that pointed toward the bright orange sun.

Aeon hurtled toward planetfall. Drawn on the Big Picture, the Ship's vector was like a javelin. That represented only a fraction of the velocity at which the Ship had left the dwarf stars on the way out of the Ramamirtham Maneuver.

Chapter Seven

DAMAGES

New stars appeared, shifted out of infrared into the visible spectrum. Stars already visible coruscated toward blue. Bluing stars crowded ahead, toward the Ship's line of travel, until half the universe of stars compacted into one mass of brilliance. The unearthly image did not change, but a shimmer cycled around the edges of it.

"How eerie," Catharin murmured. She had come to the Captain's office to ask for a blood sample, but he had wanted her to see this first: a replay of the acceleration to relativistic speed. The Ship's Intelligence had compiled this sequence, based on the observations of the auto-observatory, but presented it as if the Ship had accelerated in a simple straight line rather than executing the complicated loops around the binary dwarf star.

"That shimmer's an artifact of the intensity of the light, not a function of the relativistic effect," said Bix. "Anyway, that's what it looked like to the Ship at point-nine *c*. Why's it seem so familiar to me?"

"Because you read somewhere what the universe would look like at most of the speed of light?"

He grunted, not in the way that meant affirmative. "It's more like déjà vu, something I've seen before. But how the hell could I have seen it? I was frozen tight. Do people dream in stasis?"

"No. The brain activity isn't there. People do dream on the way in and out, in the twilight stages."

That shimmer gave the relativistic universe the illusory look of a tunnel of light. It suddenly struck Catharin as familiar to her, too. Before she could guess why, Bix said, "Forward to deceleration."

The mass of light exploded. Stars cascaded from massed brilliance to their natural colors, spacings and luminosity. Bix said, "The Ship tweaked data out of that mass of light. Deciphered the mess into this double planet when we were a sixth of a light-year out—barely in time to decelerate. I'd sure as hell like to know why it took so long to find a tweak good enough to stop for! Wasn't there a planet with a moon before now? Go ahead," he sighed, "take my blood."

Catharin drew a vial of blood from his hairy, sinewy arm.

Bix continued to brood. "Back there at that sorry excuse for a terraformable planet with the moon that wasn't there, when we twiddled with the parameters, we thought we were just asking the Ship to look for a slightly greener world. I think we were messing in territory inside the damn computer brain that we didn't understand. The Ship concluded it had to hold out for green with a capital G."

One star shone brighter than the rest, because now it was close enough to be a sun slightly more orange than Earth's Sol. The Intelligence depicted concentric circles around it, representing a solar system. One of the circles, drawn in green, flashed. That meant *terrestrial planet in the habitable zone*: the aim and the end of the odyssey of *Aeon.*

☽☾

After the house call on Bix, Catharin returned to her medical laboratory. Miguel Torres-Mendoza arrived on schedule. Perched on the examining table, he dutifully rolled up his sleeve and extended his arm. He had a wide, sturdy hand and forearm, well-defined musculature on strong ulna and radius bones. "Make a fist," she told him. As his blood spurted into her vial, the muscle groups in his arm stood out so clearly that she could have named them by sight. His whole body was like that arm: "stocky" did not do justice to his solid bone structure and well-defined musculature.

Miguel scanned the furnishings of the infirmary. Fold-down cots, medic machines with arms neatly folded, floor-to-ceiling supply cabinets. Walls and equipment and cabinets were accented with the color gold. When Catharin was done, Miguel departed without small talk, disinclined to linger in the medical area with or without its attractive gold-color-coded edges.

Catharin went to supper. She reached the dining hall as Joel and Becca were departing from it. Tall black man and small fair woman, the two seemed engrossed in a discussion. Becca was unself-consciously grubby. They had planned to inspect the engine today, and she, being very much the smaller of the two, had evidently been the one to visit the narrowest of the chases in the engine room. She animatedly described something mechanical to Joel, her hands making a sketch in the air. Catharin's glance lingered on Joel as he laughed and replied. Even he, twice frozen and a decade older than Becca, looked vigorous. His dark skin seemed to have the undertone of health. His black hair was only lightly touched with frost.

The dining hall was huge and shadowy except for a few lights illuminating the corner where the mess machines were. In a few more weeks, there would be more people revived—if all went by the Checklist—and the dining hall would fill up at mealtimes. At present, Catharin would have liked a smaller, cozier place to eat. She would have also liked better food. For the first time since coming out of stasis, Catharin cared what kind of food ended up in front of her. It was long-frozen, reconstituted, basic rations. People in the Space Force hadn't called the feeding equipment "mess machines" for nothing, she thought in disgust, spooning up so-called beef stew that had the consistency of oatmeal. Lary knew how to coax good-tasting food out of the mess machines. Catharin wished he felt well enough, secure enough, or whatever it took, to put him in the mood for preparing baked goods. She would have liked chocolate cake. Catharin left the dining hall full but dissatisfied.

Under her feet the mauve (for Food/Housing) striping on the floor turned into Medical gold. Weary, she returned to her laboratory with reluctance. It was Checklist, Day Ten. They had kept up with the Checklist only by dint of working ungodly long days. Neither she nor the others could keep up that pace until planetfall, some ninety days from now.

Catharin pressed on. She had enough data points, medical samples from different people over a span of days, for the Ship's Intelligence to model the medical situation and its possible outcomes. The Intelligence had a template for the model. But the template wasn't good enough for her needs, so

Catharin tailored it. She made mistakes in her haze of pained tiredness, biting her lip in frustration as she fixed them.

She broke off to visit the lab's restroom. Lacking the color-coded gold edges, it looked like an ordinary restroom in any hospital.

Suddenly Catharin realized why the relativistic image on Bix's workstation had looked so familiar to her as well. She shared a stricken look with herself in the little room's mirror.

It was the iconography of near-death experience. Patients who nearly died in the hospital sometimes reported having been suspended in a black or blank void, having seen a tunnel of light. She had always been skeptical about such accounts. And yet for *Aeon* it was utterly true. All of the starship's living survivors, the revived as much as those still in stasis, had been near death, skirting death's brink for a long, long time.

☽☾

A light, inquiring knock sounded on the laboratory door. Catharin checked the chronometer, which read nearly midnight, before she looked around to see Becca letting herself in. "You ought to be in bed. Do you feel well?"

Becca noticed the medical model displayed by the medical Intelligence. The central image was a human body, crammed with colored icon codes. Parts of the screen showed graphs, charts, and, in one window, the atom-studded twists of a big molecule. "What's that?"

"Hemoglobin."

Becca said, "You've been watching us to see how we're doing, but I'm pretty good at not letting feeling sick slow me down. Just in case you didn't notice—I still don't feel so great. Not quite myself."

"What are the symptoms?" Catharin asked quickly.

Becca shrugged. "Nothing to put a name to. Vague aches, malaise or whatnot, changes from day to day. If you put a medical textbook in front of me, I could convince myself that I had anything in there."

"Vague malaise isn't abnormal, this soon after the stasis we've been through," Catharin said. "Tell me if you start feeling worse, but probably you'll gradually feel better."

"Yeah, like you said on my first day, I am young and female. Where does that leave old guys like Bixby?" Becca asked.

Catharin glanced toward the hemoglobin. The molecule was deformed. Becca did not have enough knowledge of molecular biology to read the evidence of damaged DNA in a stem cell in bone marrow from its result—that mutated and poorly functioning hemoglobin. "Just feeling better more slowly than he'd like." Catharin changed the subject. "How's Engineering?"

"Busy! Joel and I checked out the main engine. Then after supper we finished the activation list for the inspection robots."

"I'd like to know more." She offered Becca a chair, and water in lieu of a more interesting beverage. Becca accepted both. It was late. Catharin should have been asleep, or attempting to be. But Catharin needed this—the chance to talk to Becca at the end of a long day, like so many late nights during training.

Becca said, "We've got flying eyes and the walking robots that we call spiders. They have sticky feet for where there's no atmosphere—meaning, the appendages extrude a quasi-adhesive that works in hard vacuum. So they can traipse around on the hull of the Ship." Her hand scurried across the arm of the chair, demonstrating. "I tell you, Cat, the darn activation list for those spiders nearly drove me bonkers. I kept wishing we could just wind 'em up and let 'em go."

Catharin smiled, imagining Becca sitting on a floor, like a kid under a Christmas tree, surrounded by toys, winding them up and releasing them one by one to prance around her.

"But we've got to be sure everything works. In theory the Ship can check itself, but if there's something wrong with *its* brain, so much for that. So we've got all these cross checks, not to mention site checks to make sure the remote reports match what the instruments on location say. And act lists by the bucketsful. I wonder if we could abbreviate the planetfall Checklist."

Catharin could have called it up on her workstation here in the laboratory, the Checklist in its nominal representation, the branching-tree diagram. She wondered what medical checks and sublists she could dare omit. *None.*

"Heard the latest about Planet Green? Lary thinks we can plant grass, crops, and trees right away."

That set off a cascade of associations in Catharin's mind. Tears started in her eyes. "I've wondered what Planet Green will be like. That the day is so long made me fear that there might be nothing but plankton and lichen, or that our seeds would never grow. . . . Did you bring your flute?"

"Have flute, will travel. I played it a few times the past week. And I was incredibly rusty." Becca made an exasperated face. "It seems like only days ago that I went into stasis, but my body doesn't see it that way. At least not for playing music."

Catharin filed the data point away in her professional mind. And closed that file for the time being. She asked, "Do you know 'Simple Gifts'?"

"Sure, the old Quaker hymn. I'll play it for you if you're forgiving. Not tonight, though. It's too late to root around in the storage drawer in my cubicle. Every time I open the drawer door, it's audible to Lary on the other side of the wall, so he tells me in no uncertain terms."

"I like the tune because Aaron Copland used it in *Appalachian Spring*," Catharin explained. "The whole symphony is about a new life in a new world."

"Spring is right," said Becca. "The green color on Planet Green covers a significant portion of the dry land, according to Lary. I pestered him to tell me more about it. I don't think Lary likes me, or likes me being the chief engineer, or something." Becca made a face. "And the feeling is getting to where it's mutual, but anyway, he dropped a hint that it's the kind of green that looks in infrared a whole lot like leafy plants, chlorophyll and all. He thinks it may compare to the Devonian period in Earth's prehistory. Plants on the land, but no animals yet, except maybe some primitive insects and a few fish crawling on the shores of the seas. Anyway, an atmosphere and all such that our plants will do fine—and, wherever we put them, easily outcompete the natives, because ours are more highly evolved. So, in just a few years," concluded Becca, as optimistic as ever, "we'll be growing corn and daffodils, and grazing sheep down there in pastures! How'd our livestock fare?"

"Those who were frozen as individuals perished," Catharin said bluntly. "Their life spans are too short. But they were experimental subjects anyway. On the other hand, the colony material, the eggs and sperm cells in stasis, fared well. After planetfall, I'm going to fertilize some eggs in vitro and implant the results in the artificial gestation chambers. Want a pet?"

"Pet?"

"If the embryos are viable and turn into baby animals, someone other than me will have to take care of most of them. I hope to get a kitten and a puppy, a chick, and a miniature pig—a potbellied piglet." Catharin was surprised to discover a sense of relaxation in herself. She felt tired, but not racked with tension. Crossing her legs, she twined them, tucked one foot behind the other ankle, and sipped flat, pure water from her glass, wishing it could have been white wine. "I want the kitten."

Becca relaxed too, draped over the chair in what would have been an untidy sprawl had she been a gangly male. Being neither gangly nor male, on her it looked winsome. She said brightly, "How about a horse?"

"I could produce one. But on a starship, the upkeep might be rather awkward."

"So when are you gonna defrost some good-looking guys?"

Catharin raised her eyebrows. "Did anyone ever tell you that you come up with unusual psychological associations?"

With a self-conscious air, Becca replied, "Yeah, well, my sex drive seems to have thawed out. I didn't notice it wasn't there until it was."

"That sounds normal. The same thing happens with appetite for food." Catharin frowned. "I noticed my lack of interest in meals. But, since you mention it, I haven't felt any sexual interest since stasis."

"It'll show back up when it's ready to," Becca assured her.

"How about Miguel Torres?"

Becca shook her head. "Mike's as square as a building brick. No small talk. And no more large talk than necessary."

Becca was right. Torres was like that, now. Before the star flight, he had been a quiet but pleasant man. Not fixedly serious and silent, like now. Catharin wondered whether stasis could change personality traits permanently. She did not want to think about that. She said, "Well, the two of you might average out to a normal amount of conversation."

Becca responded with a good-natured laugh that shifted into a yawn.

Catharin said, "It's late, and you need your rest to activate your robots. Go."

"You need sleep too," Becca commented as she departed. "Physician, heed thyself!"

☽ ☾

Hurled out and away by the spin of the Ship, the flying eye ascended along the Ship's equator. Blasts of nitrogen released through tiny directional nozzles countered its radial velocity until its motion followed the curve of the starship, but more slowly than the Ship's turning.

A periscope housing ponderously came by. The flying eye traded a solemn gaze with the monocle of the periscope before it resumed collecting data, scanning with its camera. Craters pocked the arc of the Ship's horizon, a bright imperfect curve against the star field.

Advancing, the horizon revealed an even more irregular terrain. Rumpled folds like a miniature mountain range stood on the Ship's horizon. The camera locked onto this irregularity.

Because the Ship was spinning under it, the mountains marched toward the flying eye. It circled the seeming mountains and the fringe of foothills—pressure ridges radiating out across the skin of the starship. The illuminated contours were bright in the sun's glare, the shadowed folds deep black.

Under the crown of the mountains lay a semicircular ravine. It was a gash in the starship's outer hull. The flying eye came in low over the area. The severe contrast between light and shadow made the inner depths of the damage impossible to discern. The eye dove toward the black valley, pulled up again—but not before it jettisoned an object smaller than itself. Carried by the momentum of the eye's dive, the object tumbled once on its way into the ravine. It extended six pairs of jointed legs, alighted on the wall of the ravine, and stuck.

The robotic spider called Tango 21 briefly conferred with the flying eye—an automatic check sequence. Function thus proved nominal, the spider began to climb the disrupted hull material. One delicate, lightly adhesive footfall after the next, the spider proceeded into the deeply ripped hull, going upward against the force of centrifugal gravity.

The flying eye hovered above and behind the spider. It let out flash bursts of light that enabled Tango 21 to gather optical data. The spider's antenna transmitted a video stream back to the flying eye, which relayed it to the control center of *Aeon*.

The spider's forefeet went over an edge, where the disrupted ceramic stuff had fractured. Tango 21 tipped its body over the edge of the fracture to continue its trek.

The contours of the fracture interrupted its link with the flying eye. It halted. It retraced its steps until the telemetry was restored. The spider angled a different course, its antenna pointing out behind it like a bristle.

The little robot switched from optical to infrared observation, and what it saw, it transmitted, a ghostly picture from inside the gouged hull of *Aeon*. What had been a featureless dark recess optically was a terrain in infrared: irregular and jumbled as a canyon land, deeply fractured. And in infrared, the deepest part glowed, warm relative to the extreme cold of space.

Tango 21 trekked up to the root of the gouge in *Aeon*'s hull. There, it confirmed the infrared reading. Its thermal sensors picked up heat. The bright roof of the damaged area was a pool of heat leaking out of the starship.

Instructed to explore, the spider unfurled sensor arrays like long feelers. Mechanically shuffling its jointed legs, it moved sideways, brushing the bottom of the gouge with its sensor-feelers. The spider was making contact with the naked pressure hull of the starship.

The spider registered a change in its surroundings and froze in its adhesive tracks. The damaged material around it shifted, closing down on the spider. Before its distress signal could bring a command back from the control center, telling it what to do, the spider was trapped between the ruptured insulation and the pressure hull. It reeled its feelers back into the protection of its carapace just before it found itself flattened to the maximum flexion its jointed legs could withstand.

☽☾

Flat video screens dominated the walls of the conference room. Each screen featured an image of the damage to the hull—outside, inside, infrared, and the global view—the damage overlaid on a skeletal white diagram of the Ship's interior structure. Color rendering of the infrared picture—a telltale blob of orange—told of the heat leak through the exposed part of the pressure hull. There was a pinpoint of purple too: the location of the trapped robot.

Bix, Becca, Catharin, Joel, Miguel, and Lary sat around the conference room table, absorbing the imagery and its implications. Catharin noticed how discouraged the men looked—slumped shoulders, heads propped on hands. But Becca sat up straight, braced with determination.

Joel said, "Toldja it's too complicated of a critter to be reliable."

"No," Becca answered quickly. "The gouge goes so far into the ceramic insulating layer of the hull that it's like a flap, and the flap oscillates. You see, the ceramic is a rigid material, but not one homogenous piece. The oscillation is happening along one or more of the seams. It's slow and slight, but enough to get my spider wedged in! That was at 0943 this morning. I sent commands for creative little calisthenics, but it couldn't extricate itself. So now it's in lockdown mode." Her Goodie Book lay open in front of her, fatter than ever and dog-eared around the edges. She added, "Sorry, Captain."

"Don't be. Letting a spider hitchhike in on the flying eye was a damn good idea. Now we know the worst."

"What happened to the Ship?" Miguel asked.

Becca answered. "An impact that the star shield deflected almost successfully. It was a small, hard object, maybe a nickel-iron meteoroid. The object grazed the star shield, then bounced off the hull at the equator at a very shallow angle—I mean, as much of it as didn't vaporize bounced off. The ceramic was shocked by impact and heat. Probably the properties of the ceramic are locally changed for the worse. Anyway, the encounter gouged us all the way down to the surface that the spider found just before it got wedged in. And that's the real hull, as in, the last thing between us and space. We've got to find out if it's damaged. We've also got to mend the insulation."

Bix nodded. "What do you need?"

"A repair crew. I'd like five fresh space-able bodies, including somebody who knows how to do large-scale ceramic bonding in zero gravity."

"See who we've got, Cat," said Bix.

Even as she called up the list, Catharin objected. "There are good reasons not to wake up a whole repair crew unless you're sure they can do the job—and the whole Checklist can be completed—on time." It was day sixty-three. The Checklist languished in the upper fifties.

Becca asked levelly, "Reasons like what?"

"Those remaining in stasis are safer."

Bix said, "That's not a good enough reason."

Reluctant, Catharin explained more of the medical situation than she would have wanted to. "Revived from stasis, the body goes back to biological time, meaning that the consequences of damage at the molecular level unfold at the normal, biochemical rate. And damage there is. Medical modeling predicts an elevated incidence of cancers and of multisystemic diseases in which the autoimmune system malfunctions. Blood disorders as well." Sensing ripples of disquiet in her colleagues, she continued, "We can combat such illnesses with the medical science we brought with us. But that means reviving medical specialists, who will be at risk for the same problems they're needed to cure. The medical problems might even outpace our human resources to deal with them."

"But without more people, we won't be ready to make planetfall." Becca ran a hand through her hair.

Bix said, "I'll take what you're saying under advisement." Then, "Torres, are we ready for more people?"

"Only if some of them are plumbers," Miguel replied glumly. "If we put a load on the life-support systems, including plumbing, problems will crop up. Not dangerous problems, but people will be needed to fix them."

Bix said to Becca, "Can you pare down the list and make do with a skeleton crew to repair the hull—like three?"

Becca nodded. "That makes sense, I guess. But I'll be darned if I can see any sense in plowing on like this with too few people for the job! We're like an egg, sealed up with all our nutrients, which are finite. It doesn't do a chick any good to stay in the egg too long. It'll die if it doesn't get out of there."

Joel chimed in, "We've got to go to the planet and hatch. Let's have some fresh reinforcements and get the job done!"

Becca said, "At least, I do need a ceramic technologist. Without that much, forget it."

Bix grunted assent. "Cat, who's the lucky guy?"

"One mission specialist is cross-trained. But to expect 'fresh' reinforcements may be too optimistic. I think that so far we've been luckier than the odds dictate. There's a note in this man's medical history about allergies.

Almost half of all people have identifiable allergies of some sort—it was impractical to disqualify people on those grounds—but my gut reaction in this case is that's a bad omen. I'm almost certain that if we revive him now he will be incapacitated."

In the act of running her hand through her hair, Becca clenched her fingers in frustration. "Isn't there somebody else?"

"Almost certainly. Among the passengers. Shall we breach the protocol to revive them?" Catharin looked at Bix.

Bix cursed. Then, "Around the table. I want to hear advice. . . ." He placed the stubby fingers of his hands against each other. "I want opinion *against* waving off. As in, tell me exactly why we have to break our necks in order to make planetfall the first time around?"

Joel, at Bix's right, said promptly, "Any solar system's a dangerous place. After we swing around the sun we're in the ecliptic, and speaking of collisions, the ecliptic's more hazardous than the whole rest of the trip. Besides planets and moons, this system has asteroids and interplanetary debris."

Becca nodded. "The Ship is as fragile as an egg in collisions with bodies like that."

Miguel chose his words with care. "This Ship is designed to be a starship with everyone in stasis, everything shut down, and a nitrogen atmosphere; or else, an orbiting city that provides an Earthlike environment for the population. In between shutdown and fully habitable modes, its operation is more problematic."

Lary said, "I think we ought to loop around for a while. Study what we've got here." There was a disapproving stir from Becca and Joel, and Lary insisted, "It is *asinine* for us to be in too much of a hurry to 'hatch' on Green. Green isn't isolated. It's got Blue, as close as Luna was to Earth. But Blue's six times the size of Luna, with a vigorous magnetosphere and God knows what other features—none of you realize how much we don't know about Blue! Believe me, we should be—"

"I see your point," said Bix. "Cat?"

Catharin answered, "'First, do no harm' is the rule of my profession. I do not want to harm an unwitting and innocent passenger."

In a sharp tone, Becca said, "The Ship is more important than individual people. Check the passenger lists for a ceramic technologist with experience handling Dup-Dow fourteen to thirty-five."

"I've found two," Catharin retorted. "One is over fifty and probably won't have the stamina to handle an outside repair anytime soon, given the effects of stasis on older men. The other is a much younger man, married, with wife and two children and a brother, all of whom—and these may be the only people he knows on the whole Ship and in the whole universe—are scheduled for revival in the third decade of the colony. Am I to tell him that he may not see them for thirty years?"

Sounding grim, Bix said, "Revive him anyway."

☽ ☾

Catharin felt drained. She could not face the stasis vaults yet. The scuff of her shoes on the corridor floors echoed. She climbed up the blue well toward the Axis, out of the sway of the Ship's artificial gravity. Zero gravity did not really ease her exhaustion, but rather masked it like a drug. She could still feel the exhaustion in her bones. Floating, she waited for the 'vator to come, not knowing where she would ask it to take her.

She was too tired and too strained to keep the truth out of her mind. The whole truth. *We went so fast that time dilated. One thousand years for the Ship took us almost two thousand light-years and three millennia from the Earth we knew.*

Catharin found that she had taken the 'vator to the flight deck. Through the window, she stared out at the star-blasted hull. They were almost at perihelion, nearest approach to this new sun. Vividly illuminated, the hull of the starship had turned into a savage chiaroscuro, black shadows in the craters, blinding light reflected from undamaged areas. Catharin was mesmerized by the sight of the hull. It told the predicament of *Aeon*: the brilliance of a civilization that could imagine crossing the stars—and succeed—juxtaposed with nature in its most final and uncompromising aspect: death.

Behind her, someone entered the flight deck with a faint scuff of shoes. "Can we talk?"

Catharin feared that Becca would ask about the ceramic technologist. "I'm not in the mood."

Becca moved between Catharin and the window. Silhouetted against the ruin of the hull, Becca said, "Then listen. I did not mean to hurt your feelings. If I did, I'm sorry." She added, "I'd be lying if I said I wasn't worried about the hull. It's my job. At the same time, I believe—"

The Ship's ongoing spinning suddenly framed the sun in the window. Near, redder than the sun of Earth, its fiery light poured over Becca and made her tousled red hair blaze. Becca quickly turned away from the glare. The blazing effect of the backlighting on Becca's hair underscored her words in a way that Catharin would never forget. Becca said, "We had the dreams and the technology and the courage to come this far. Now there's a good green world waiting for us. We'll make it. We're meant to. Go ahead and revive the passenger."

Miguel went with Catharin. Together they took the 'vator down-Axis, into the serried ranks of passenger stasis vaults.

Wearing a coldsuit, she heard only her own light breathing. The soundless stasis vaults offered nothing for her suit's external microphone to pick up. The intersuit two-way was voice activated, with nothing but silence there either, unless Miguel spoke.

Catharin verified that the remote assessment displayed at the Life Systems station matched what registered on the instruments here. Then she instructed the machinery to revive the ceramic technologist. Miguel stood by. His solid presence made Catharin profoundly grateful.

Initiating the revival sequence was a simple act. The machinery itself would deliver the passenger, inside a capsule and still in the limbo of cold semilife, to the recovery room up-Axis. She watched the instruments report the first stages of the procedure.

"Has any thought been given to funeral rites for those passengers who have already died? Will you revive a priest soon?" From Veracruz, Mexico, Miguel was Old Roman Catholic.

"There was that ceremony on Earth, before we left," she reminded him. However, it had been exceedingly ecumenical, designed to accommodate all religions as well as secularists and naturists at the same time.

"That was not a funeral." Miguel paused. "Or perhaps it was. But it was a funeral for the Earth."

Still waters run deep, Catharin thought. "For now, we have to keep the stasis unbroken. It has a great deal of stability that we can't afford to compromise. I think there will be an official mass funeral sometime after planetfall—when many more people, including clergy, are awake to mourn for the deceased."

"So we live with the dead for a while," said Miguel.

"Does that bother you?"

"In Mexico, one day a year is *El Día de Los Muertos*, the Day of the Dead." His Spanish accent blurred the edges of the words in a way that Catharin found pleasant to listen to, even through the two-way. He paused. Catharin had the impression that he was mentally shifting Spanish ideas into English words. "The Day of the Dead is done to make us remember, realize, that every day of life is lived in the company of the dead who used to walk and talk and work in the same places where we, the living, do now. No. I am not bothered."

Catharin turned off the instrument monitor. "That's all, let's go back."

Miguel asked, "Would you come with me to do a site check?" When she agreed, he went on, "Can we walk? I need exercise."

She reviewed the readings on the controls of her coldsuit. Oxygen and power packs showed solidly in the green—vital in a cold nitrogen atmosphere. Both suit two-ways checked out in good working condition. So also her electric undersuit and visor defogger. "Let's."

Here in the broad central levels of *Aeon*, ramps spiraled out from the zero-gravity Axis all the way to the full-gravity environs just inside the hull. They took a ramp instead of the quicker 'vator route down to the substation, in bounding strides, uncoupled: first Catharin found herself a bound or so ahead of Miguel, then a bound behind him. The gravity increased. They settled into a long-strided walk. Catharin's legs felt rubbery. Her muscles had not been prepared for this jaunt, and would be sore tomorrow. Miguel's breathing was harsh enough to activate the voice-sensing circuit of the two-way.

The ramp swooped down to the level of Outtown's tallest buildings. Outtown was an entire city, albeit a compact one compared to the urban sprawls in Earth's open air. It had been planned as the capital in orbit for the new colony, the vantage point for the terraforming of the new world.

Catharin and Miguel continued downward through an interstice between the crowded crowns of barren high-rise buildings. They stepped off the ramp at the bottom, plaza level.

One future day the plaza would be fully civic, with shrubbery, a row of flags, and fountains. Now it was empty, blank. Miguel set off down the main avenue and turned two corners. Catharin followed. She was lost here without a map. And without other human company, she would have been half out of her mind with the eerie, blank feel of this place. Only a dream, not a pleasant one, could have depopulated a city so thoroughly. But this compact city was not truly depopulated; it was unused.

A stairwell set into the sidewalk took them down to the undertown through which ran the Ship's circulatory system. Miguel slipped an electronic key into the slot by the door of an environment systems substation, which opened to reveal a control room. He activated the control Intelligence, evaluated its self-checks, and, satisfied that the Intelligence was in good order, used it to check the local subsystems.

Catharin wandered around the substation, finding it perfectly well appointed with instruments and bolted-down furniture but devoid of the usual workplace signs of human usage. There was no clutter or grime, nothing fastened askew to the walls, no coveralls hanging on the rack appointed for such. Lying solitary in a corner, a small box-end wrench caught Catharin's attention. She brought it back to show Miguel.

"Centuries ago, a workman must have forgotten to count his tools when his job was done." He had a masculine voice that sounded gentle even in this bare, clean place. "And that is the only thing amiss. So one more detail in the Checklist is accomplished. Thank you for coming with me."

One of the high-rises in Outtown had no apex. Instead, it extended all the way up to the Axis, this tower that one day would be called City Center and house the government of Outtown. Catharin and Miguel rode up the 'vator in the heart of the tower.

"Let us stop to admire this city." With a flick of his fingers on the control panel, Miguel stopped the elevator at the observation point, where just above the tallest of the other structures in Outtown, the sides of the tower and 'vator were glass. They surveyed the panorama of Outtown, its unoccupied skyscrapers, the blank streets far below, and the distant, surreal curves of the ramps to the Axis.

Miguel pointed to one sector below, not as geometric as the rest, with empty grooves and round depressions. The depressions puzzled Catharin until she remembered the pools and fountains in the planned city park. Miguel said, "Someday, and soon, those streets below will be alive with the people that you have brought out of stasis. And there will be air to breathe. Landscaping with plants absorbing carbon dioxide, emitting oxygen; and in the park, water, pools, a fountain, beautiful to see, and part of the closed loop of life support in this place. People inhabiting a small but hospitable world."

Catharin welcomed Miguel's reflective mood. Today he seemed more like himself, expressing thoughts beyond the work at hand. Miguel leaned on the railing inside the 'vator wall, an oddly ordinary pose for a man in a coldsuit. "When I went to the University in Mexico City, I studied, besides engineering, anthropology. It interested me—especially the cultures and religions of the many peoples who lived in Mexico in the old days." Through the faceplate of his suit, she discerned the convex bridge of his nose, and coal black fringes of hair. He had more than a drop of the blood of the ancient tribes. "Every culture, with its land, was its own world. And for every culture-world, there was an origin myth. This place needs one also. Would you like to hear it?"

Coldsuits did not lend themselves to subtlety of communication. Reflections on the faceplates made it hard to see expressions; the two-way tended to divest words of emotional overtones. One had to be verbally explicit. "I don't know what you mean, but tell me if you wish," said Catharin.

"It is a re-creation myth. A small world has been lost for ages in a winter colder than ice. The people are brought back to life by a lady, a goddess. It is another god's work to make the place for the people, to surround the people with air and water, green plants, and to bring food out of the metal flesh and bones of the world.

"These two deities. They make the world. She is called the Queen of Stars." Behind the reflections on his faceplate, Miguel seemed to smile. "His name is—" Miguel pondered. "God of Water's Course. Because a life-support system depends on the right circulation of water. Most creation myths start with a pair, male and female."

He was completely revived now, Catharin decided, sexual interest and all. "And in most creation myths, the two have children," she said. "What about this one?" It was a veiled challenge: would he presume to answer in the affirmative?

His somber reply surprised her. "Only the High God knows."

The 'vator resumed its ascent up to the Axis. Arms crossed, Miguel was not seeing the level indicator lights even though his gaze was fixed on them. "What of the molecules in our bodies, Catharin? Our stasis was terribly long, and it was known that stasis would result in some damage at the molecular level. But the longest and most fragile molecule is the DNA, such as that in our chromosomes. I have thought about this. It worries me on account of future generations here." He hesitated long enough for the 'vator to pass several levels and the reflections of the indicator lights to march upward on his faceplate. "You have not asked me for any sample of a certain kind."

"Others are at higher risk of cellular damage than you. You were only frozen once." In truth, she had not asked any of the men for sperm samples. But she could not put it off any longer.

Chapter Eight

PLANETFALL

The blue planet loomed in the Big Picture, but it was just a simulation. The Intelligence presented the sim imagery without regard to astronomical observations of the world, which in actuality was still distant, and presented it as a glazed blue ball.

Bix said, "Begin braking sequence. Attitude thrusters. Turn us around."

The thrusters fired to orient the Ship for its trial by atmospheric fire. The smoother, less scarred southern hemisphere had to hit the atmosphere first. "Firing, firing badly." Joel scowled. "I embedded real test-firing of the thrusters in the sim. And they're not doing so good!"

"All systems are ready for aerobrake, Captain." Becca was serious, all boisterousness ruled out of her even tone.

Joel shook his head. "Real bad firing."

Bix snapped, "Post-sim action item: schedule a detailed thruster check."

The Ship touched the blue ball's atmosphere. Still moving at star-speed, it plunged in. The Big Picture showed how a cocoon of friction fire enveloped *Aeon*.

"Sensors say excessive heat at the damage site!" Becca exclaimed, her voice high-pitched. "Aerodynamic drag on the irregularity of the hull there and it's tripped the boundary layer!"

All eyes turned toward the Big Picture. Unreal but convincing, the pale sheath of plasma knotted, glowing brighter and redder on the starship's side.

"Structural strain too! The damaged insulation may break—"

Letters and numbers flashed across the bottom of the Big Picture: STRUCTURAL FAILURE, and coordinates, those of the damaged, gouged-out place in the hull. Becca cried out, "*It broke off!*" Blazing, a chunk of the Ship's insulation arced away in the airflow around the starship. And at the damage site, red friction bloomed like a flower.

Joel swore. "That heat'll melt through the pressure hull!"

Alarm tones sounded all over the control center. Every workstation came alive with lights and messages, announcements of loss of structural integrity, loss or drop of atmospheric pressure, breaks in fluid lines. "Crit-one failure!" Becca announced.

"End simulation," said Bix. The alarms abruptly silenced.

Becca flung herself back in her chair, hands covering her face.

Bix turned to Catharin. He growled, "When are you going to let that ceramics expert out of the recovery room?"

"Today," Catharin replied. Her heart pounded. That had been a very convincing simulation. "There's a vid feed into the recovery room. He was watching, and now I imagine he understands the problems we're facing."

☽ ☾

Catharin felt adrenaline left over from the simulation, plus frustration, plus guilt stewing inside her as she entered the recovery room, next door to the medical laboratory. She concealed the stew, put on her medical manner like an overcoat. "Well, how are you doing?"

His name was Zak. "Fine!" He gestured toward the vid-feed. "That was very exciting. I understand why you need me." Dark-skinned and wiry, Zak looked like a racial amalgam, like someone from the underclass in a city of twenty-first-century Earth, polished by the intelligence and willpower to climb up and out and reach for the stars.

Zak was the only person from his background now awake. Catharin felt a pang of hopeless conscience for the unasked-for loneliness that she had brought him into. She directed him to the Engineering office with best wishes.

She had a headache. So she took aspirin and headed for the dining hall for what the mess machines served in lieu of good coffee: a bad substitute, freeze-dried and tasting almost as old as it was. In the dining hall's doorway she nearly bumped into Lary Siroky-Scheidt, on his way out. He bristled at her and charged off.

Joel was hunched over a plate in the corner of the hall, radiating anger. Catharin brought her coffee to sit beside him. "Don't tell me you just had a fight with Lary."

"Okay. I won't tell you." He speared a synthetic meatball and glowered at it.

"You shouldn't let him get to you! Don't hesitate to put him in his place. Joel, he's not sick, he's a hypochondriac."

Joel sighed bitterly. With a fork, he rearranged the flaccid spaghetti on his plate. "I hate those thrusters. I think we'll be asking for a propellant specialist next." He did not meet her eyes. "I'm sorry."

"For needing somebody else to help you? Joel, I don't blame you for that." Before she was more than half aware of it, a startling strong impulse came over her: to ask him to come to her tonight. She wanted to comfort him and for him to make love to her. She wanted to let cold shock waves of tension transmute into warm sexuality.

But Joel was married. His wife was in stasis, oblivious fidelity, on Level Twelve. High tension tends to arouse passion, Catharin thought, shaken by the intensity of her feelings, which only force of will restrained, and not completely. She reached out to massage the back of his neck. By the way his eyebrows and shoulders lifted, that came as a pleasant surprise to Joel. She marveled at the rich chocolate color of his skin.

A bustle of laughter spilled through the dining hall door. People trooped in, a group with Becca in its midst—her repair crew, now including Zak. Becca was introducing Zak all around, asking about his experience and opinions, and generally installing him in the crew. Catharin took her hand back from Joel's neck.

Dropping his head on a fist, Joel said in a rueful voice, "I feel old and creaky. But she's bright and bouncy as a kid who hasn't learned what it means to hit a limit."

"She's hardly a kid, she's a woman," Catharin retorted. In the same breath, a perception shift came to Catharin, and she saw Becca in a new light: the engineer of a damaged ship, with a repair crew in orbit around her like planets around their star. "Joel, you know, terraforming isn't the same issue that it would have been in the original plan. Lary's role has changed significantly, and not in a way that pleases him."

"Yeah, but how did we get back to Lary?"

"He expected—and reasonably so—to be called upon to mastermind the making of a new world, starting with a rudimentary ecosystem and a primeval atmosphere. Everyone and everything would have depended on his expertise. Instead, we'll accommodate ourselves to the green world that we've found."

"So he's a disappointed hypochondriac?"

Catharin had read Lary's biography in the records to which, as medical officer, she had access. He had been a precocious child: a genius, far ahead of his age group in school, a bright and busy, stellar, red-haired kid. "He's a jealous hypochondriac. Where do you suppose he went?"

Joel snorted. "Not where I wish he would! He holes up in his cubicle when he isn't making other people miserable."

"I'm going to go make a house call." Her prescription would be attention. It was worth a try.

At the door of Lary's cubicle, Catharin tapped without getting a response. "Lary, I need to talk with you."

He admitted her in with a sour and defensive expression. The workstation in the tiny, neat room displayed a blue sphere ringed with information icons. There were orange markings on the sphere, features of some special interest to Lary.

"Are you running a study of the blue planet on your own time?"

"No, I'm playing tic-tac-toe," he said with sarcasm.

Catharin said, "Your tests have been coming out in the normal range, but I realized I should give the results extra attention. That's because you are a Martian. There hasn't been genetic drift—Mars hasn't been colonized long enough for that—but there may be slight congenital effects that I should take into account," she improvised. "So come to the lab—tomorrow, oh-nine-hundred, would you?"

"You could have sent a message," Lary pointed out.

"I also wanted to ask you in private to cook something. I, for one, have had it with the mess machines. Can you make them do anything that tastes like chocolate?"

The edges of his face and of his stance softened. "I might."

☽☾

A circle of luminescence flickered in front of the star shield. As the starship's magnetosphere hit the charged particles in space, funneling the ions back into the engine's fuel reservoir, it created the starship-glow effect. Crowned with faint fire, spinning through space in stately silence, *Aeon* approached Planet Blue on a parabolic curve. Within there was frantic activity. Work crews hurried from place to place, banging out repairs, conferring in strained or tired, loud voices.

When the Ship was still hundreds of thousands of miles away from the double planet, a shuttle lifted out of the transport level lock near the north pole. The shuttle flew south toward the Ship's equator, high, so the Ship spun away beneath it. The shuttle veered toward the scar on the equator.

The Big Picture generated an image from the expedition for those in the control center. At the Life Systems station, Catharin watched intermittently. On her own screen she had a segment of the Checklist pulled up. With dogged determination, she was turning it green for go, one section at a time.

Catharin's nerves sang with tension. The repair was not an overtly dangerous job for Joel and Becca, who would stay in the relative safety of the shuttle. But things could go wrong. The way the Intelligence depicted it on the Big Picture, the shuttle looked improbable and frail against the strange stars.

One sidebar of her Intelligence screen displayed medical telemetry from the expedition. Becca and Joel both registered elevated heart rates—Becca's higher, a fugue to Joel's. She, not Joel, was sending two men and a woman into the depths of the ripped outer hull of the Ship. While Joel flew the shuttle, Becca reviewed the game plan with the repair crew, including Zak. Becca's motions were graceful and assured, and she sounded confident, Tennessee accent at a minimum. The rapid canter of her heart was not outwardly evident.

The repair crew suited up as they floated at various angles in the shuttle as it approached the damaged area, which bore an eerie resemblance to a small mountain range on the Ship's surface. The spacecraft descended sharply, and hovered—tricky piloting for Joel: he had to track the spin of the Ship exactly. As Becca and the repair crew viewed the on-the-spot visuals being gathered by the shuttle, the world called Blue inched up from the horizon of the Ship.

There had been no world like that one at home. Thousands of years and light-years from Earth and its familiar solar system, the Ship was the only known world left in the universe, and it was damaged. From the shuttle-borne camera's point of view, the stars and cloud-laced Planet Blue wheeled beyond the terrible scar on the Ship.

Catharin jumped at an unexpected loud comment. "I tell you, we're leaping before we look." At his station, Lary continued, "I admit that Green looks like an oasis. But nobody can be bothered to *think* about Blue!"

The repair team emerged from the shuttle's airlock into its cargo bay, exposed to space under wide-open clamshell doors. The team snapped on tethers that looked frail as spiderwebs. Maneuvering packs lined one side of the bay like a neat row of beetles, ready to go. Each team member wormed into a pack and tested its controls.

Becca's voice came on the link. "Catharin—I'm looking out through the cargo bay doors. Planet Blue's visible above the bay."

"We've got it on the Big Picture."

"The white clouds are hurricanes. Hurricanes like lace all over it! Isn't that a sight?"

Lary muttered, "Scenery! Is that all she thinks it is?"

Catharin let her temper vent in a long sigh. "Well, Lary—what do *you* think?"

"It has those pretty hurricanes because it rotates rapidly. The winds stay pumped up. Storms never cease. Do you realize the significance of that?"

Catharin had a distinct urge not to scratch Lary's itch for attention. But as attention was what she herself had prescribed for him, she found no good reason not to. "No, Lary, I do not."

The repair team released tethers and steered themselves, with jets from their maneuvering packs, away from the shuttle. Like small space tugs, two of the three pushed equipment that bulked larger than their packs. Crew and equipment disappeared into the depths of the damaged area. Inside the deep gouge, they secured themselves with pitons, like mountain climbers, against the centrifugal force that would have made them slide right back out again. Catharin was relieved to hear the all-secured report.

Unasked, Lary sent a transmission to Catharin's workstation. Imaging the worlds Green and Blue, it appeared in a window, which overlaid some of her Checklist data. "Look at those planets. They should tend toward spin-lock. Remember how Luna always kept the same face toward Earth? It was much smaller, so it got spin-locked first. Many more hundreds of millions of years and Earth will keep one face toward Luna too. But two planets of the same mass, like Blue and Green, should exert tidal effects on each other to an equal degree. Therefore, any initial difference in the rate they spin around their respective axes should tend to disappear over time. But the sea world rotates *six point five times* as fast as the other one. Blue has an eight-hour day, for God's sake, and Green a fifty-two-hour one."

The repair crew started to work. Catharin checked the sidebar. Zak had a nice steady heartbeat. He was a pro: doing his work, he didn't worry about where he was. "That's interesting, Lary."

"Interesting? It's impossible!"

A picture from the gouge came in, transmitted from the crewwoman's helmet-mounted camera. Her colleagues moved around in their bulky suits like spelunkers on the moons of Saturn. The beams from headlamps built into all three of the spacesuits splashed on the contours of the disruption in the thick ceramic hide of the starship. Distracted, Catharin snapped, "Lary, it doesn't matter if Blue ought to be impossible. It's right there!"

"It's not possible if the two planets formed at the same time and if there's been enough time for life to evolve on one," Lary amended. "If a double planet like this had this same separation at their formation, they should spin-lock in a few hundreds of millions of years at this separation. The tidal forces they exert on each other are huge. If, on the other hand, there's been time for life on one of them to evolve to the level of vascular plants like the trees we expect to find on Green, then that says the system has existed for a few billion years. It doesn't add up." He added, "Even a doctor ought to know that much planetary science."

Miguel was away from the Life Systems station. Of late he had been spending long hours at the yeast vats, which were the nucleus of the Ship's food-producing capability. Catharin suddenly missed Miguel: he was easy to work with, as unobtrusive as competent. And, she realized, Miguel had been serving as a buffer between herself and Lary. Unbuffered, Lary was every bit as irritating as Joel had been trying to tell her all along.

The repair crew's communications had static in them, but Becca's voice—high, sharp—pierced the fuzz. She made sure the crew knew exactly what she wanted—and what she would settle for if the ideal proved undoable. Catharin said, "Perhaps planetary science needs better theories."

Sounding scornful, Lary retorted, "Suppose you saw somebody, oh, start growing younger instead of older, sprout wings, or something equally ridiculous. Would you decide medicine was wrong? Or look for an answer?"

She turned toward him and used her coolest professional tone. "I've never seen anything like that in a patient, and I do not worry about the real or imagined conditions of people who are not my patients. I haven't the time and energy to waste on conditions that are no business of mine to understand, or heal."

They were spraying foam insulation, appearing as a white wiggling noodle in the picture. The mobile blob that was Zak wielded the stream of foam with quick, steady movements.

Lary fumed. Knowing how truly crucial this part of the expedition was, Catharin mentally told Lary and his worries to go jump into that worldwide ocean that was Blue.

Before she expected it, the audio link filled with directions for the shuttle's retrieval of the crew. Becca dictated a work log in a precise, decisive tone. "The repair crew flooded the deepest part of the breach in the Ship's ceramic insulating hull with insulating foam. It hardened in the vacuum and bonded to the ceramic satisfactorily. We've still got an irregularity in the Ship's surface where the meteoroid impact rumpled up the ceramic—there's no way to sand it down with the means at hand—but the inner pressure hull is no longer exposed to space. The ceramic layer is now reattached to the pressure hull, greatly reducing the chance that it will break off during final braking." She paraphrased for Catharin's benefit: "The patient's gonna live."

The crew reemerged from the now shallower, partially filled-in hole, rappelling out toward the shuttle's welcoming bay. The airlock cycling that brought everyone safe inside seemed interminable; Becca came in last. Joel lifted the shuttle up, swiftly curving toward rendezvous with the transport-level airlock. Catharin sagged slightly, sheer relief leaching out some of her posture.

Inside the shuttle, the backpacks of spacesuits popped open and swung wide like cabinet doors. The users of the suits emerged, a jumble of arms and legs and torsos.

"*Also*, though of course it isn't a discrepancy of the same order of magnitude, plate tectonic theory can't explain the orogeny. Mountains, that is."

"Blue has mountains?" Distracted, Catharin was confused.

"Chains of seamounts, some of which are taller than the ocean is deep. They're visible as barren islands."

"Lary, look. They got the spider back."

Lying in Becca's hand, it did look like a spider, a dead one, folded up. Becca produced a slim screwdriver, with which she aimed a tap at the tiny robot's abdomen. It unfolded its legs and beeped. Becca laughed in delight.

Catharin heard Lary mutter, "*What a ship of fools!*"

He was doing his level best to throw ice water on this moment, at least insofar as Catharin was concerned. She held her temper in by sheer force. "Really, Lary, how bad is it to colonize Planet Green without understanding just why Blue is exactly the way it is? At least it's a moon, for which we ought to be grateful."

Lary answered, "Sure. And our descendants can go for generations not understanding Blue. How about a nice myth to explain what it's doing up there in the sky? A colorful, unscientific myth. Is that what you want?"

"No," she admitted.

"Myth will be needed, to symbolize what Blue means to the human spirit," said a quiet voice, consonants blurred by a Spanish accent. Miguel had returned from the yeast vats. "It is a religious matter. But myth is not science." Miguel took the sharp look Catharin gave him for a question, and answered, "Yes, Catharin, I do feel that it is important to explain Blue scientifically." Lary, surprised at reinforcement for his position, opened his mouth and shut it again. Miguel looked over Catharin's shoulder. "Did the repair go well?"

"Outstanding. They even got the spider back." The shuttle's passengers had mobilized into a melee of talk and handshaking. Becca was lavishing congratulations on the repair crew, especially Zak, who basked.

"So *you* think it's important to study Blue," said Lary.

Calm and thoughtful, Miguel answered, "Blue stabilizes the axial tilt of Green, allowing life to evolve in peace without drastic climatic disruptions. Blue must also produce huge tides which propel life to evolve more rapidly than it would with only low sun tides." Lary nodded emphatic agreement. Miguel concluded, "Life as it is evolving on Green will concern us very much. So we should study Blue to understand why Green is green."

"The Ship has instrument packages designed to be dropped down into a planet's atmosphere," Lary said. "But Bixby insists that they're all dedicated to Green."

"Bix is operating by the Book, and any way you read the Book, we are in a critical situation, with no resources to spare for pure science," Catharin replied, careful to sound neutral—not defensive of Bix.

"One package would tell me a lot. Just *one*!" He sounded frustrated.

On the Big Picture, the hurricane-laced moon rose again over the horizon of *Aeon*, dramatically beautiful and alien. For the first time, it occurred to Catharin that this blue apparition would be the night sky's moon for colonists on Green. She found the idea startling and disquieting. Earth's moon, Luna, had affected evolution and human culture. This moon had a different character and much greater size. Lary might be right. Catharin said, "I can justify an investigation into the blue moon."

"Do what? You?" He sounded incredulous.

"On Earth, there were subtle but real medical, and psychological, concerns about the moon. Blue is bigger, brighter, and altogether unknown. Yes. In my official capacity, I can name concerns and I can justify some research. I don't think I can argue for a major research project, with lots of personnel and material, though." She raised her eyebrows at Lary. *Well?*

Then Lary proved to Catharin's satisfaction that he was basically a reasonable man. "Why, get me an instrument package or two, and I'll get you results!" He added, "Planetary science has a long tradition of operating on a shoestring." She could see the analytic gears meshing in his mind already.

☽ ☾

The patient's heart stopped.

Rare side effects of revival from stasis include cardiac arrest. Inject one milligram of atropine. Start CPR. Watch for signs the drug is acting. The room was strangely vague. It must have been the stasis recovery room. That didn't matter. The mental voice—as always, a calm contralto, her own—tightly focused her attention. Using the heels of both hands, stacked, Catharin repeatedly compressed the dark-haired man's sternum with almost mechanical regularity.

The atropine perfused through the patient's bloodstream. Soon it must restore the stasis-deadened cardiac nerve pathways. But something else was wrong. This man's rib cage did not have normal elasticity; his chest resisted compression. Catharin pushed harder.

A gray pallor of the skin spread from the artery where she had injected the atropine. Dulling and stiffening the living flesh, it invaded his neck, his torso. With horror, she realized that the atropine was having the wrong effect. Instead of regulating the nerves, the atropine was changing the man's flesh into old, dried wood.

The ribs under her hand shattered. The thin shroud of skin shredded. Her hands plunged into a ruined chest cavity and a nest of hissing snakes.

Catharin woke with a jerk that nearly sent her off her bed.

Her heart pounded. The room's darkness seemed thick with dread. Overcoming the dream's residue of paralysis, she reached out, swatted the bedside lamp to make it turn on, then collapsed back onto the bedclothes. Yellow light flooded her cubicle. All bare walls and no furniture except the bed and built-in desk, the lighted room was almost worse than the dark.

Catharin shivered. Post-stasis nightmares? Not a problem she'd had yet, herself, though others had reported such to her. She reviewed the bad dream, every offensive detail of it, as though examining a wound. Losing anyone is the physician's nightmare; here and now, losing *that* man would be catastrophic. For the stuff of nightmare, her dreaming mind could not have done better.

So. It had been a real nightmare, nothing worse. Unfortunately, after that blast of adrenaline in her system, she would not sleep soundly again. She checked the chronometer and groaned aloud at the reading of 4 AM.

She tossed. The barren cubicle was no comfort to her. She had not had time to personalize her private quarters. After planetfall she needed to do something about this. Such as, ask Miguel for a plant. Leaving the light on, Catharin drifted into a restless semiwakeful haze.

Wait.

Catharin's eyes snapped open, focused on the off-white ceiling above her. Her mind raced. No medicine would turn a man into dead wood. But it was altogether possible that someone—or everyone—might react differently to medicine now. The changes that stasis had wrought at the molecular level were so systemic and multifarious that the entire medical baseline might have changed.

Catharin rolled over abruptly, throwing herself and her bedclothes into a tangle. So. This was what her unconscious had been trying to warn her about: that even the most ancient and routine drugs—atropine, epinephrine, even penicillin—could have the wrong effects now, could kill someone.

She could not stand this barren little cubicle any longer. She got up and went for a walk, alone with her dreadful new knowledge.

☽☾

This early in the Ship's morning, nobody else was up and about, and it felt as it had weeks before—vast, empty, still. Not altogether quiet. The blowers of the air-conditioning system whirred. Water murmured in the wall, hinting at the presence of a plumbing line.

Catharin wondered why she had not noticed those sounds weeks ago. Perhaps some kinds of peripheral attentiveness came back late after revival from stasis. Conceivably, the nightmare's adrenaline overload had cleared the last residue of stasis out of some of her sensory pathways. Catharin followed the murmuring pipe behind the corridor wall. The trace of sound led her out of the mauve-striped Food/Housing part of Level Seven. The stripe on the floor changed to green, for Life Support Operations.

She detected a distinctive smell, sweet-sour and complicated—Miguel's yeast vats. A tandem lure, the sound of the pipe and the prickly aroma in the air led Catharin toward the work control center in Life Support Ops. At a workstation, Miguel brooded over a display of bar graphs with the slouch of someone who had not slept.

He had thick, powerful shoulders, matching the rest of his build. As a physician, Catharin admired his body. As a woman, she was attracted to men of a different type: slimmer than Miguel, and taller, and more high-strung. Not for the first time, Catharin wondered why sexual attraction could hold out for an ideal even when reality offered a man with a good physique and good character. She said, "Is the God of Water's Course brooding over his work?"

His brown eyes flicked her way, but Miguel only answered after a long intake of breath, translating English sentences out of a continuum of Spanish thinking. "An evil spirit has appeared in the new, small world."

Catharin was baffled. "Say again?"

"I am establishing yeast cultures in these vats, to be a substrate for manufactured food. There are problems with these yeasts. Some strains are dead, killed by the long stasis. Others have mutated. I get strange results, as well as unusual odors and other biochemical products."

"Make sure we don't get poisoned by our food!"

"I will. But these mutations worry me."

Catharin was not surprised. Her medical models had already told her what to expect, and not just in yeasts. She pulled out for herself another chair like his, stowed in the wall, attached with a swivel joint.

"Catharin, if these yeasts have mutated, what about all of the other useful microbes that we have brought? What about our plant seeds and animal germ cells . . . and what about us?"

"The microbes are more mutable than higher life-forms."

He gave her a dark look. Behind him was a wall full of glass boxes in which plant seedlings—the first plants for the Ship—had sprouted out of synthetic dirt under yellow lights, like frayed green threads. He gestured at them. "And some seeds are not germinating, while some seem to develop abnormally."

Instead of shallow reassurance, Catharin decided to share with him her best hope, so emotionally loaded that it could manifest itself in a nightmare. "Miguel, have you heard of Joseph Devreze, the theoretical molecular biologist?"

"I learned of his work in my postdoctoral studies at Cornell," Miguel answered immediately: the information was filed in his brain in English, not in Spanish. "He was a genius who did brilliant manipulation of genes to make new kinds of organisms. Why?"

"We've got him."

Miguel's black eyebrows shot up, an index of his astonishment.

"He joined us just before we left. Needless to say, we weren't about to turn down a passenger with his kind of credentials."

Miguel nodded vigorously.

Catharin sighed. "Unfortunately, I was not impressed with his commitment to human well-being."

Miguel's expression darkened. "A bad man?"

"Well, no. I don't think his motives are evil. But I don't think his motives are good either. He invented dogs who could breathe underwater—"

"The sea dogs. They were useful creatures."

"Some of his creations were just fashionable pets." Catharin did not manage to conceal her disgust. "He played games with genes to make fantastic creatures."

To Catharin's consternation, Miguel laughed like a carefree man. "Oh, but we need him. Most certainly, we need him. You see, the gods who are creator and creatrix, especially of small worlds, always take themselves too seriously, and they want their work to be perfect. But evil spirits appear and start spoiling things, and the gods would give up and throw the world away and start over, if they could. Fortunately, in almost every creation myth, soon there also comes the trickster god. His name is Coyote, or Pan, or Raven. He does absurd and mischievous things that annoy the creator gods. He saves the world, too."

☽☾

The huge main engine burned. *Aeon* changed its course to loop around the two worlds, third partner in a three-body dance that slowed the Ship down:

Ram Maneuver in reverse. Each loop was studded with braking simulations and with real, minor burns and position adjustments, and Checklist tests and clears like innumerable beads on a string. Early in the third loop, on the Blue end, that world dominated the Big Picture, centered in a rectangle of black space, like an azure sign on a sable heraldic flag.

Lary happily occupied himself with telemetry from an instrument package that had been dropped into Blue's maelstrom of winds. During one of the long waits between one burn and the next, he announced, "I think Blue's new."

"How so?" asked Joel, whose work, at the moment, consisted of waiting.

"Ejected from some other solar system and to arrive here long after Green already existed."

"Not new-made, new arrival?"

"Right! One piece of evidence is that Blue and Green orbit around each other in a plane tilted with respect to the solar system's ecliptic plane. Looks to me like Blue dropped in and was persuaded—by the gravitational influence of the sun here, and of Green—to stay. Mind you, I doubt that Green was green at the time. It may have been in a Cambrian stasis of sorts—life permeating the sea, but, in the absence of any but sun tides, not successfully encroaching on the land. Blue, arriving on the scene, would have created new high tides and stabilized the axis tilt of Green. Which would have started an evolutionary acceleration on Green."

"We should thank Blue for the other one being Green?" asked Joel.

"I believe so."

Sitting next to Catharin, Miguel looked thoughtful. She wondered if he was making up a myth.

"Your instrument package got ripped to shreds before it reached sea level," said Becca. Evidently tired of sitting, she was standing, elbows propped on the top of Engineering station.

"I can't help that! It's what happens to instrument bundles dropped into strange worlds with bad weather!"

"It happens to dumb bundles. I think you ought to try a smart one."

"There won't be a drone allotted to the study of Blue," Lary replied, testy. "I'm told that they're to be used exclusively for Green."

"I've got an idea," said Becca. "We could fab a special exploration drone out of spare and out-of-spec parts in Transport, like a hobby. How about if we plan to come back someday after planetfall and send that custom-made hobby drone down through the eye of a hurricane? I'll fly it for you."

Lary looked surprised and interested. "That would be a way to collect data that I can't get otherwise."

"Deal!" said Becca.

Miguel listened intently. It was work for him to identify the emotional nuances in an English conversation. He digested the exchange that had just unfolded. Finally, he said softly to Catharin, "What you started, letting Lary start investigating Blue, was well done, Doctor. For one thing, he is in a much better mood."

She answered, "Everybody needs to be understood. And that reminds me, I have a new laboratory technician. She hasn't been revived very long, but she's very bright and expert. She's Spanish-speaking Filipino. I have the impression that she would feel more comfortable—more at home—in Spanish than in English." *And so are you.* "Would you mind meeting her, when you have a chance, and talking to her a bit? I think that would ease her adjustment to the situation here. Her name is Evangelina."

Chivalrous as always, Miguel said, "Of course."

Catharin did not add that Evangelina was quite attractive, in a delicate, golden, Eurasian way. Miguel would discover that on his own.

Planet Blue dwindled in the Big Picture for the last time. The starship fell past the point where Blue and Green were equidistant. And that marked the start of the countdown for final burn and orbital insertion. *Aeon* approached Planet Green for the third, the nearest, and the final time before planetfall, preparing to brake, the final challenge for the ancient ship.

☽☾

The green planet dominated the Big Picture. Verdant, temperate-zone landmasses flanked an equator girdled by ocean. Vegetation reached deep into the river-cloven hearts of the continents and high up into the polar latitudes. The wide, warm, equatorial sea reflected the world's sun in a disk of shimmer.

Miguel, normally unflappable, excitedly called out to Lary, at Astro/Survey, "See how green it is!"

Lary bobbed his head. "Gorgeous!" he agreed.

Letters on the Big Picture read TERRAFORMING TIME. There were fields for millennia, centuries, and years. And the fields were filled with zeroes. This world was terrestrial already.

One by one the last few twigs of the Checklist tree turned green. Joel, Becca, and Bix called out subsystem checks and clears. The Ship's anatomy was like medical jargon, though the words for its parts and functions were not Greek and Latin, but were more clipped, more irreverent and Anglo-Saxon, and considerably more arbitrary than medical terms. Catharin's thoughts skittered on the slick ice of her tension.

Becca called out, "*Last* check: sequence."

Catharin felt a mounting excitement, almost a physical throb, but it was outside of her too, an electric expectancy in the control center. A rapt silence filled the gallery, overflowing with onlookers—Becca's hull repair crew, Joel's thruster mechanics, Catharin's nurses and lab technicians, and Miguel's plumbers.

Suddenly Catharin understood the Checklist. It was like the medical rote in her own head when she had a patient in critical condition. It made detachment conceivable. Except this one hadn't lasted for only the critical seconds of a medical emergency or the hours of a surgery. For one hundred days, it had kept them from reacting to the ultimacy of this moment, from being swept away by despair or excitement.

"*It's clear!*" Becca called out. With that, the one remaining tip of the tree greened. The audience broke into jubilant applause, which even Lary, at Astro/Survey, joined. Excitement surged—as irresistible as a river's current.

Bix kept his footing in the surge of excitement. "Go for planetfall. Six minutes, twenty-two seconds until attitude adjustment."

Catharin anchored herself on Miguel's methodical calm. He pulled up a life-support systems schematic on his half of the screen. She followed suit with a parallel schematic of the stasis lines. Neither system should prove oversensitive to a braking burn—not unless a bit of pipe lining was ready to tumble and clog a line, or a weakened line ready to break.

"Approaching perigee."

The Big Picture showed the dark side of the green new world. Like Earth from orbit, it gleamed faintly. But unlike Earth, there were no striations of yellow power grid. Lightning flickered on the fringe of one nameless continent, the sole illumination across the whole dark extent of it. Catharin's throat constricted. After a lifetime of hopes and fears, five years of training on Earth, a journey an eon long; after one hundred days of Checklist and simulations here, this was not at all what they'd expected, but was altogether real. Catharin could hardly breathe.

"Structural readiness?" Bix demanded.

"Ninety-nine percent nominal, one percent—that's the damaged part—tolerable. Ready." Becca's voice squeaked with excitement.

"Burn readiness?"

"Nominal. Two minutes, twenty-three seconds to the braking burn," said Joel, his voice rough with feeling. The excitement ran swifter and more turbulent than ever, like a river about to turn into a cataract.

"Stations—stay on your duty," Bix ordered. No wonder Hubert Bixby was the Captain. Space veteran, grizzled, imperturbable, Bix of the signature rock-steady heartbeat, only he could have kept his emotional footing in the flood. "Attitude adjustment, go ahead."

Easier said than done: spinning like a gyroscope the size of a small mountain, the massive starship wanted to stay pointed the same way.

Joel crowed, "Ninety-five percent across the board!" Coordinated blasts of energy rotated the Ship around until the main engine pointed in the direction of the Ship's motion.

Becca trilled, "Let's hear it for the thruster mechanics!" Applause came from the gallery.

The big new world swelled even bigger in the Picture. If the main engine failed, it was going to be a pass. A *close* pass.

"Go for main engine burn," said Bix, matter-of-factly.

Joel announced, "If there are any eyes to see down there, we are gonna write 'hi' across the night sky."

"Maybe some spiny fish are looking up," said Lary.

The engine poured out a cataract of plasma. Joel burst out, "Burn, baby, burn!" As the plasma exhaust interacted with the tenuous upper atmosphere, pale fire rippled back across the thick hide of the decelerating starship.

"Feel that shiver?" Becca called out. "That was the vibration of the engine. It took that long to travel through the structure to reach us."

The force of the deceleration was almost unnoticeable. Miguel produced a small plumb on a long line, which he held up with a solemn air. The line tilted a few degrees off vertical, responding to the building force of the engine.

The Big Picture depicted the Ship as a bright ball on a trail of fire. From down below it would have looked like a swift comet flying across the sky. Catharin felt like letting her feelings go, cheering the engine on as the crowd in the gallery had begun to do. But red flecks materialized on Miguel's half of the workstation window, flutters in the life-support system piping. Catharin's stasis-system sensors reported perturbations in the supercold fluid flowing in the line, but none of significance, not so far.

"Throttle down!" Joel announced.

Miguel's plumb drifted back toward vertical.

Wild applause erupted in the gallery, with whoops and cries of joy. Bix ignored it all. "Flight status!" he barked.

Joel sang out, "Engine shutdown nominal! Position—a slightly elliptical polar orbit."

"Structure! Report!"

Becca's voice was high, clear, her words rapid-fire. "Sensors indicate hull holding and no damage! No strain outside limits!"

"Life Support?"

"Minor problems, but the trunk lines check—clear!" said Miguel, whose voice broke.

"Astro/Survey!"

Lary responded, "All in working order! —But what's all that??" He waved toward the Big Picture. Particles surrounded the starship, a cloud, spreading out in front of the Ship in its orbit and behind it.

Becca said, "That's starship dander. Bits of insulation that came loose during braking."

The Ship arced across the terminator into its first sunrise. Ahead of the Ship, the swath of particles, sunlit, coruscated, a glittering host.

Bix said, "We're here, and you can start the calendar, Lary, with Year One, Day One."

Joel gave a great shout. Becca bounded over to him. "You did it, star pilot!" she announced, her voice high and ringing. Joel caught her up in his arms in a swinging bear hug. Bix contributed an open-handed whack to Joel's shoulder. Excitement eddied like the pool under the cataract, clear and bubbling.

The green bulk of the new world rolled by beneath the Ship. In its morning, it was blue and brown and green, with traces of white snow and expanses of silver cloud. Catharin discovered tears of gladness on her face just before Joel pulled her up into an embrace, which she returned with all of her strength. Joel said into Catharin's ear, "We did it, lady."

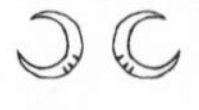

The mess machines, expertly coached by Lary, with some raw material provided by Miguel, were capable of conjuring up a facsimile of champagne. An inferior champagne, to be sure, but good enough for a party. And all twelve dozen of the revived persons in *Aeon* celebrated in the dining hall. For the first time since the starflight had begun, there were enough people to fill the space provided.

Lary's reedy voice carried over the general hubbub as he described a newly hatched pet project: to send a football-sized instrument package through the eye of a hurricane down to a soft landing on one of the mountaintop islands on the surface of Planet Blue. "A dumb bundle, but a well-aimed one." He chortled.

Catharin could hear Becca loud and clear too. Nearby, in an animated one-on-two with Bix and Joel, she tilted her chin toward them, saying, "I can't carry a tune in a bucket with my own voice. I chose an instrument that I could travel with, something that packs small." She described the size of her flute case by sketching the parcel in the air.

Joel suggested, "Go get it so you can make us some music."

Catharin located Miguel, engaged in conversation with Evangelina, who, dressed up for this occasion, looked prettier than ever. Miguel bubbled brightly in Spanish.

Zak the ceramic technologist turned up at Catharin's side. "I wanted to thank you for reviving me. I wouldn't have missed it for the world." His brown eyes burned with warm intensity in a thin, dark face. "The Captain says we can advance the schedule for my family, and I'll see them in a few years, not a few decades."

"I'm glad to hear that," she said, and meant it with all her heart.

Planet Blue appeared in the dining hall's tall window. A moon, but a huge, blue one, its surface covered with a skein of hurricanes.

Somebody started to sing. Catharin recognized the tune. "*Par le clair de lune argent* . . ." By the light of the silvery moon . . .

"'Watery'! It ought to be 'watery'!" someone else called out. There was laughter. "What's 'watery' in French?"

Lary piped up, "*Aqueux!*" So a dissonant chorus sang it that way.

The blue light outlined the contours of Lary's face. He grinned, pleased with his little contribution to the impromptu sing-along. The light had the effect of highlighting the bone structure of Lary's head, the shape of his skull.

Catharin was suddenly, joltingly, reminded of a death's head. She felt a stab of alarm, almost panic. It might be a mild allergic reaction to the *faux* champagne, she thought, and put her glass down. Even so, she decided that she would run more medical tests on Lary.

Halfway through the second and even more enthusiastic performance of the song, Becca returned with flute in hand. The silvery tones of the flute joined the melody.

Catharin stopped singing. Her adrenaline had flamed out. She felt herself sinking into a terrible exhaustion. For her best friends—Captain and Pilot and Engineer—the great deed was done, the grand dream had come to life and fulfillment. Even Lary had ended up with a windfall of opportunity to continue his life's work.

Her work was only beginning and might not end until her life did. She had bargained for as much: something to live for. But the work that faced her here was not what she'd foreseen. Pure survival, simply saving humanity from rampant illness and genetic disorder, might be the issue from now into the indefinite future. *That* was the price of the two new worlds. Catharin crossed her arms, holding herself together.

Becca approached Catharin. Perching on the edge of Catharin's chair, Becca lifted the flute to her lips, and resumed. This time the notes that sounded were the melody of "Simple Gifts."

Joel came too. He placed his hand on the nape of Catharin's neck, warm and firm. Tears trickled onto Catharin's cheeks. She became aware that Bix and Lary, Miguel and Evangelina were standing around her too.

"This is Cat's favorite song," said Joel, to everybody else. "Becca's been rehearsing all week," Lary informed Catharin cheerfully. "I could hear it through my wall."

The corners of Becca's lips quirked as she wrapped a smile around the lip plate of the flute. The blue moon's light reflected on the silver flute like water.

☽ ☾

The space-to-ground shuttle swooped down toward the colors of Planet Green. Streams of telemetry flowed back to *Aeon*.

Landscape unfurled below the shuttleplane, a panoply of greens, blues, and earth tones. Startling spots of more unexpected color, like puddles of tempera paint, were splashed across the land: lakes tinted purple, orange, and yellow by high concentrations of anaerobic bacteria.

It was late, and Catharin had the screening room to herself. She relaxed, watching the replay. The atmosphere down there was breathable: Earthlike in temperature, pressure, and composition, though slightly more oxygen-rich, on account of the abundance of vegetation. They *would* make it, build a colony and a future on Planet Green. Someone had already flown down and back up safely: the first of many steps into their future on that gentle green world.

The shuttleplane entered a canyon land of tall white clouds and cloud shadows. The craft punched into a wall of cumulus and the picture went streaming gray. Complex arrow symbols scrolled across the bottom of screen: wind speeds and directions inside the cloud. Then the shuttleplane broke into clear air with tremendous visibility, a late-morning desert, flat tapestry of browns and tans. A river crossed the desert. With a network of fine green tracery—confluent tributaries—the river and its watershed looked like a fern, or like a two-dimensional cross section of a lung.

At last the shuttleplane's big engines kicked in. One, two, three. That had been tricky. The shuttleplane could have limped back to the Ship on two engines, but not just one.

The door of the screening room opened. Becca peered in. "Did I miss the whole thing? Darn! And I haven't seen it but twice already!" She slipped into a chair beside Catharin.

The shuttleplane thundered back up toward orbit, the planet's land falling away below it, lakes and hills blurring into a flatter, mottled picture like camouflage cloth. Blue atmosphere thinned to space black.

"You know, Cat, back in the twentieth century, it took decades and it cost human lives to do that." Becca sounded reverent. "To make machines that could fly up out of the clouds into space, just like that."

The starship rolled up out of the blackness of space, battered and big. Its transport level lock opened, a slit of yellow light warmer than the stars, to admit the returning shuttleplane.

The women left the screening room together, walking along a corridor piped in the gray color signifying the transport level. "Did you know they're about to start fabbing a plane for downside?" Becca asked. "It needs long wings, on account of the slightly lower gravity that makes the atmosphere just a little thinner than on Earth." Definitely in her piloting mood, Becca's eyes shone, cloud blue. Her hands illustrated the long profile of the new airplane's wings. Then she asked, "How was your day?"

"I defrosted a good-looking guy. He's not awake—he's in the second day of revival, which means, still pretty far under." On impulse, Catharin added, "Would you like to see him?"

It must have sounded like an odd suggestion. A puzzled twist appeared at the edges of Becca's lips. "You know I never pass up the chance to see a good-looking guy."

Catharin led the way to the recovery room on Level Seven. She ignored the red-lettered sign that said MEDICAL PERSONNEL ONLY. Opening shutters on the window, Catharin gestured the invitation for Becca to look into the room.

Motionless except for slow breathing, the man lay on his back. He was tall. His long-fingered hands rested outside the sheet draped over him. His face was beardless—depilated—with sharply defined masculine angles.

Becca said, "That's the good-lookingest guy I've laid eyes on since we got here. Who is he and do I get to work with him?"

"His name is Joseph Devreze. He is a theoretical molecular biologist."

"Scientists don't look that good, as a rule!"

"He is a bona fide genius, which may be why he breaks rules."

"Brown eyes?"

"Get this: bluer than yours. Cobalt blue."

"All that and he's tall, too. And I know you go for tall, smart guys." Becca gave Catharin a mischievous grin. "Have you got designs on him?"

Catharin felt herself blush. "I know him very slightly. I interviewed him just before the Ship left."

"So what's he slightly like?"

Folding her arms, Catharin reviewed her memories. "The most arrogant bastard I've ever had the displeasure to meet."

Becca made a wry face. "Sounds like he made a great first impression."

There was a trace of a furrow across the man's brow, and a hint of frown lines engraved into his long face, like the signs of a medieval bishop's preoccupation with matters of his Church. The sculpted hands—with long, chiseled fingers—could have belonged to a modern surgeon. In truth, however, this man was at least as far from being a curer of bodily ills as from being a curate of souls. "There wasn't a Nobel Prize for biology, so biological breakthroughs were awarded the prize under the rubric of medicine whether appropriate or not, and in this case it was not. Medicine, indeed." Catharin did not bother to keep the acid out of her tone. "Genetic novelties is what he did, corporation-sponsored, for fame and fortune, and why he left Earth I don't know. He showed up at the last minute."

"Wait, whoa! You mean he's a passenger? And he's not expecting to be revived until the colony's all set up?"

Catharin leaned back against the wall, arms still folded. Becca was right. Devreze would think that he had been subjected to a most untimely resurrection. The millennium had come and gone in stasis, and there was no glory waiting for Joseph Devreze, no appreciative colony to seek his help with alienated organisms to conquer alien territory. Just a medical emergency like nothing his arrogant genius had ever met. "Our genes need fixing. Otherwise there will be no future," Catharin said flatly. "It's not just a matter of emergent illnesses caused by molecular damage. There are also double-strand breaks in the germ-line DNA. That means our ability to reproduce is questionable. I anticipate stillbirths and teratisms, or in another word, freaks. And more genetic diseases than I care to name, retardation being the most likely."

Visibly disturbed, Becca ran a hand through her hair. "That is one bad piece of news."

"I'm sorry—I needed to share it with somebody. I haven't told anyone else about the double-strand breaks. Please keep all that I'm telling you confidential, for now."

"I will," said Becca.

"I'm quite sure that he freely altered the human germ line, despite the fact that doing so was illegal. I also think he can restore the damages caused by stasis. Unfortunately, it's not clear to me what makes him tick. Altruism doesn't seem to be among his motivations. Becca, I do not want him to know how much we need him. Not yet."

Becca ran her hand through her hair again. "Understood," she said with a quick nod. "Well, things could get interesting with that guy up and about."

Catharin shot a misgiving glance at the motionless form of Joseph Devreze. "The phrase that occurs to me is 'loose cannon rolling around on deck.'"

Chapter Nine

LANDFALL

Three. Two. One. Zero. Earth dwindled to a gleaming disk, a silver coin in a well full of stars. Joseph Devreze wished for a new planet on the other side of stars and stasis.

Zero stayed. Cold and timeless zero—silent, insensate nothingness—went on and on.

Until now.

"One." The voice was hoarse, cracked, his. "Two. Three."

"Good," said the woman. "What comes after three?"

A hissing tinnitus in his ears sounded like a spring thaw, a rushing melt of blood in his brain. It distracted him.

"Count to ten. Please, Joe."

Joe. Rhymed with "go." Sounded basic, uncomplicated. He remembered somebody, somewhen, telling him to expect things to be pretty basic, no altitudinous technology, because black boxes stink in the middle of nowhere, and repairability was going to be more important than anything else. Joe sounded simple, repairable. That would be his name here. Joe.

The woman was tall and blonde, and she sounded worried. "*What comes after three?*"

"Four," said Joe. Behind the blonde woman, above a doorway, he saw the numbers *3, 2, 1, 0*. "Three, two, one, zero. Breakaway from Earth orbit. We there yet?"

She sighed. "Yes. How do you feel?"

Homesick. Sick, remembering that the home planet was as good as dead and gone for him. "Hung over." Joe made a weak attempt at a grin.

"That's the right idea. Your body is steeped in exotic chemicals that kept your body fluids from freezing—crystallizing and destroying your tissues—in stasis. Can you sit up?"

Joe grasped her hand. Her skin felt warmer than his. "Terraforming? What stage?"

"It hasn't begun. We woke you up early, because we need you now."

His mental image of the star-world future quivered and changed, like a telcon screen changing channels. That did not bother him. It had been a fuzzy, unclear, imaginary image to start with. He liked the sound of "we need you now." He sat up. "I'm ready. Where to?"

"How do you feel?"

Suddenly he remembered her from before. "I said, where to, Catharin?"

She gave him a level stare. "Let's see if you can walk, Joe, or if I'll have to call for a wheelchair." She helped him to stand up and put on a bathrobe made of soft paper over the pajamas of the same material. Joe steadied himself with one hand on her shoulder. His whole torso felt as though it were stuffed with cold, stiff cotton.

Catharin guided him into the corridor—it curved upward, making it seem that he was walking uphill—then into a room full of people, most of whom were milling around and talking. They seemed almost too active, too vivid for Joe to stand to watch. He let himself be helped into a chair beside a table. Then Catharin left him. He felt lost.

Another man sat at the table with him, also wearing a paper bathrobe. Somebody else resurrected from the dead. The other man had Asian features, and he was gently sipping from a cup of tea. He glanced at Joe. "Good morning, Mr. —?"

Joe went blank for the duration of three sips while he groped for an answer, his mind as dim and disordered as an abandoned warehouse, until he found what he wanted. "Toronto. Joe Toronto. First Tier."

The other man nodded. "You renamed, then. Lacking a home city that meant the world to me, I did not. My name is Carlton Wing. Sixth Tier."

The Sixth Tier was supposed to stay in stasis for a century longer than First. "Sixth?" Joe asked sharply. He felt confused. He hated feeling confused.

Wing pointed over Joe's shoulder to a wall that was a video screen. A new world slipped across the wall: a cloud-glazed, blue world with green-blotched tan continents. "I'm a field botanist. They revived me before my time because of all the plants down there."

Catharin returned with a glass of pinkish water for Joe. "That planet's too green to be new," he told her. Then he noticed that he was the center of attention in the room. People weren't crowding around him, but every one of them was watching him.

Before cold zero, he'd been the center of attention many times and in many places. It had felt good. It didn't feel good now. He was confused.

"It was green when we arrived here," said Catharin. "That's why we had to revive you, and others." Voices elsewhere in the rooms said, "It's a complex ecosystem." "—jungles—" "—megafauna!?" Catharin waved everyone else to be quiet and continued, "We soon realized just how lucky we are to have one of Earth's most distinguished biologists on the Ship."

Joe heard a murmur of assent, someone whispering about the Nobel Prize. Carlton Wing's eyebrows arched. "Now I recognize you."

"We revived you out of sequence," Catharin repeated. "We need your expertise as we evaluate the biological hazards involved in colonizing that planet."

Joe nodded before she finished speaking. "That's what we're here for," he said. "To do what's needed to colonize the destination."

Wing said softly, "This isn't the destination."

"Huh?"

Catharin grimaced. "We don't know all that went wrong. The Ship traveled to the destination star, and the stasis machines revived the astronaut crew—myself, Captain Bixby, and Commander Atlanta—as scheduled. The planet was there. But its moon was not. We reprogrammed the Ship, changed course, and put ourselves back into stasis. And the Ship went on and on until it came here." Before he could ask questions, she pushed the glass in his hands up to his lips. "Now drink."

Commander Atlanta—the Ship's pilot, a tall black man whom Joe recognized from newscasts on Earth—was leaning against a table behind the doctor. If he was going by Atlanta now, he'd renamed. The important point was that he was the starship's second-in-command. He told Joe, "We directed the Ship to search for a world with some green on it. Primitive plant life like the Cambrian time on earth, with plankton in the seas and oxygen in the atmosphere, was what we asked for." He glanced at the world now spinning out of sight on the wall-screen and shook his head amazedly. "The Ship overdid it."

Joe struggled to drink the pink, bitter medicine. The other people watched him. In the corner of the room, incongruous by its presence, a green parrot shifted its feet on a makeshift perch. Sulky and ruffled, the parrot watched Joe with one beady eye.

"He'll be all right," said Catharin.

"So will we," said Atlanta, with an authoritative ring to his voice. "This ship could have terraformed a desolate planet, to make it habitable. If we have to we can remake this one. Even sterilize parts of it, if the ecology's not good for us."

"Surely that won't be necessary!" Wing exclaimed. "What about our other options here?"

"Options?" Joe asked.

"Watch the picture," said Catharin. To Joe's astonishment, another planet rolled into sight. This one had just the water of a sea as wide as the globe, under swirling clouds. "Somebody turn off the lights." The artificial lighting flicked out. In its place, an eerie blue radiance flooded the room. "Sea-moonlight," said Catharin.

"It's pretty," said a reedy male voice, "but those clouds are hurricanes."

"But there's a third planet in this solar system's habitable zone," said Wing. "There, the red-brown star . . . this system's Mars, more or less."

"More sizable than Mars back home," Commander Atlanta said. "No moon."

"How far along is the exploration of the green one?" Joe asked, and was informed that an isolated, equatorial mountain had been selected for the first base camp downside. The peak had been flattened and sterilized with a single clean fusion bomb. The first landing by a manned shuttle had already been made there. The Base camp would soon be set up. . . .

Joe stopped listening, distracted by a distressing sensation that the pink medicine was burning out the cotton in his insides. No one bothered to turn the lights back on. In the huge picture, the stars wheeled by. Never in his life had Joe seen stars like that: shining shoals of them, laced with dark ropes of dust. Joe asked, "Catharin, what did you mean 'on and on'?"

Silence fell.

"What year is it?"

Atlanta said, "By the ship-clock, it's the year 3210."

Joe nearly fainted. He remembered the projected time limit for stasis, how fantastically overlong it had sounded, how absurdly millennial: one thousand years. But the flight had taken one hundred and seventeen years more than a millennium. They had gone a solid ten percent over the purported safe limit. By now, the cells in his body must have sustained irreversible damage. The molecules were hurt. With physiological consequences that might prove unpleasant. Or fatal.

Joe felt sick.

☽☾

The Ship shrank as Joe watched it through a viewport beside his seat on the shuttleplane. More and more of the Ship came into view. The few lights near the Ship's north pole represented the habitat of more than one thousand awakened people. Mostly dark and dormant, the Ship was an enormous Earth egg.

A month of labor lay between his wake-up day and the present moment. Never in his life on Earth had Joe struggled against a chronically unhealthy body. But the damned stasis fever refused to go away. His month's work now seemed as desperate and brief as a night full of bad dreams. He was on his way at last: one brief descent and he would arrive at Unity Base and the cusp of the future. Settling back into his seat, he glanced at his sole fellow passenger.

"Good to see you again, Dr. Toronto," said Wing. "Your health returned?"

"Not completely, but I need to be at the Base."

Wing continued, "I suppose that your research can't wait any longer, stasis fever or none."

It was Joe who couldn't wait. Once he had been fully revived from stasis, it had begun to sink in for him how much he'd lost: Earth with its great cities, civilization with all its energy and intricacy, the World Net with its power and subtlety. . . . Gone. Lost. He'd never felt so alone, stranded, and sick. He'd felt a riptide of despair pulling his brain back toward the cold zero. The only thing to do in a riptide is—don't fight it—swim parallel to shore. He had plunged into the research, assessing the biohazards of the green world.

From the cockpit, the shuttleplane's pilot chimed in, "We've all got a touch of stasis fever."

"Including you?" Joe asked.

"Yeah, but it's clearing up."

Joe said to Wing, "I thought you were down at the Base already."

"I was. But the protocol is never to have a shuttle flight without one biologist aboard, someone who knows something about the terrain and the vegetation, in the event of—" Wing gestured, delicately glossing over the concept of *emergency landing.*

The shuttle angled down from the Ship's orbit and streaked across the planet's nightside. With a blue splash of radiance, the hurricane moon rolled up from the horizon. Ironic, Joe thought, cosmically ironic that the diligent Ship had searched out a solar system where the habitable zone held not one but three planets. Joe turned toward Wing. "Haven't I heard your name in connection with the Third Planet Option?"

Wing nodded. "I'm no xenobiologist. My doctorate is in botany, and I did research in the fern family. But I think that this world is unsafe for us to colonize, even if we burn bare arenas in which to settle. The Third Planet, though, is barren and lifeless already. When we left the Solar System, Mars was being terraformed with success. This one would turn out better."

"That's not saying much," interjected the pilot. "Secure your belts, gentlemen."

The bulk of the planet swelled. The big hurricane moon's light stained the nightside, splashed vast splotches and streaks of cobalt across the topography.

With a tremor that offended Joe's stomach, the shuttleplane penetrated thicker atmosphere. Soon the shuttle shook. G-forces punched at his guts. Cursing the fever, he hoped that the antinausea drugs would do their job. A fiery friction mist swirled beyond his window.

Finally the ride smoothed, to Joe's relief. The window filled with the red light of a sun setting on the western horizon. Under that cataract of light, he could barely discern landscape hurtling by below. Eyes watering, he looked away. On the other side of the cabin, Wing sat glued to his window like a schoolboy on a field trip.

The pilot sang out, "Welcome to the World Wide Park."

"This world reminds some people of a park," Wing explained.

"Why?" said Joe, genuinely surprised.

"Because it seems to have mild weather, gentle topography, and no animals."

Joe had seen the reports that came up from Unity Base, but he had not paid attention to the emotional footnotes, the sentiments of the expedition team members. Now it might be useful to know how they felt about the planet. "No animals—how do people feel about that?"

"Disappointed, on the whole. Hopes are high for discovering large sea creatures."

It wasn't technically true that Green lacked animals. The world harbored plenty of animal biomass. Consisting, in the words of the microbiologist Srivastava, of "slugs, bugs, and crud." Crud meaning microbes. "Such lovely crud!" Srivastava exclaimed. The microbial ecology was as elaborate and extensive as Earth's, if not more so. Srivastava was the happiest scientist on the Ship.

"This world is not a park," Wing was saying. "There are no birds, no squirrels, no butterflies, and none of the flora which evolve together with the higher and more active animal life. Green has no flowers."

"S'okay," said the pilot. "We brought our own. Big turn coming up, fellas."

"What about those slugs?" Joe asked Wing.

Wing shrugged. "Large enough to have acquired a nickname. Zucchini slugs."

"Not anybody's idea of interesting animal life, eh?"

Adjusting its bite on the air around it, the shuttleplane turned back toward nightfall and moonlight. The red light of sunset in Joe's viewport faded. His stomach protested. He clenched his teeth, determined not to retch.

The pilot spoke, apparently addressing Unity Base. "Coming in on scenic route one. Over." To his passengers he said, "The Third Planet doesn't look very inviting compared to what's down there."

"We are not invited," Wing said with a sharp edge to his typically mild voice.

Joe had already seen the land around Unity Base, on television, and had listened to explanations of its every feature, to the point of surfeit. He half watched the expanding landscape as the shuttle descended. Shallow lakes were strewn across a plain. Anaerobic bacteria tinted the lakes red and purple and chartreuse, like puddles of tempera paint. World Wide Park. An asinine idea, but one that might militate against holocaust. Joe didn't want holocaustic site preparation to happen any more than Wing did, though probably for very different reasons.

East of the anaerobic lakes, the land got higher and drier, a rumpled rug, its dark green nap worn and barren in places. Rain showers dotted the slight hills in the distance ahead. Taller than the other hills, Unity Mountain lifted its head above the showery clouds.

"Look at the mountaintop," Wing said somberly. "Even from here, you can see the absence of vegetation where we blasted the peak flat."

Flying too high and fast for a landing, the shuttle banked instead. Joe gritted his teeth and told his stomach to lie still. He began to anticipate meeting the expedition team at Unity Base. Few in number, they included a good third of the colony's leaders—the most healthy and vigorous third. In the next hour or so, with his words and his science, he intended to chart the future of the colony. He folded his arms around his knotting and squirming stomach. His fingers found the smooth carbonglass shell of the notepad in the inner pocket of his jacket. His own notepad from Earth. It had made it across the stars too, with some electrons misplaced, so it had some odd bugs in it, but just as it had been his most prized possession on Earth, it was his only prized possession now.

Wing's voice interrupted his thoughts. "Look at the roots of the Mountain. I've been up to the Ship and back down again several times, but I've never seen that before—the vegetation looks maroon, like wine. That is the dusk. The red light of sunset and the blue light of the moon, making a wine-dark bath around the feet of the Mountain," he rhapsodized. "But the mountaintop—it is still sunlit. There is iron oxide in that bare soil. It looks red and raw."

"We'll make grass grow over that," the pilot said. "We haven't had time for landscaping."

"Why don't you shut up and fly?" Joe suggested.

"Okay, I've got to shed more speed before we land on the mountaintop, and I'm going to do it by making turns."

Wing said to Joe, "Even the park lovers only understand nature when it is remade by the human hand. Broken and butchered first, and then lovingly remade."

"This world, as is, appeals to you?" Joe asked.

"Yes. I don't see a park made for us to find. Its ecosystem is alien yet beautiful. Life is abundant here, and without animal violence, so far." He smiled. "Perhaps, if we leave this young world to itself, intelligence will arise by less bloody paths than on our world."

"Too late," said Joe.

Wing's eyebrows shot up. "What do you mean?"

With the toe of one long leg, Joe nudged the cockpit door. It clicked shut. The pilot did not need to hear this. "They've generated a hell of a lot of data down there at the Base, all telemetered to my lab on the Ship, so my research has been going at full tilt. I'm going down to Unity Base to deliver my recommendation in person and explain the findings that support that recommendation. The expedition team will be happy to hear what I have to say."

"May I ask what you recommend?"

"To colonize this world, without extraordinary precautions."

Wing looked appalled. "But you're a molecular biologist, who should know about invisible biological danger! What about microbes?"

The shuttle banked, high and hard. Joe swallowed the saliva of incipient airsickness. "The native microbes have two traits: specific adaptation to plants and slow activity including rates of mutation. On the molecular level, things happen slowly here compared with Earth. We, on the other hand, intruders that we are, have our own, exquisitely mutable terrestrial microbes. And razor-sharp immune systems compared to those of the native organisms. They can't hurt us."

"You're certain?"

"Believe me, the data are convincing. Then there's the fact that we brought science with us—in particular, a highly advanced level of molecular biology and genetic engineering. I guarantee you, we can outrun *and* outfight the native microorganisms."

Joe decided to let that sink in. Glancing out of the window, he saw clouds and one thunderhead in the sky around them as the shuttle turned again, circling Unity Mountain. The thunderhead, unlike the ominous anvils of Earth, looked pink and pudgy.

"How can you reach conclusions without having been down there?" Wing demanded. "You have no firsthand knowledge of the planet."

"Not necessary. I model the data. I'm a scientist, not a naturalist."

"Isn't it enough to conquer a lifeless world?" Wing flushed with anger. "Is it so much better to conquer a living one?"

"You'd rather see it burned? Your Third Planet movement doesn't stand a chance. But a lot of people—such as our pilot friend—will welcome my recommendation. If you pull with me, we may—barely—swing the balance away from local holocaust."

"If I didn't fear the unknown here quite so much, I think I'd wish a plague on both your houses," Wing said.

The shuttle curved around the side of the Mountain. In the dusky sky, the seamoon rolled by, shining blue and bright as a beacon. On the Mountain below, in the maroon dusk zone, Joe saw a river, a trace of water on the densely vegetated slope. An instant later, it looked like blood, a blood-red trickle from the blasted mountaintop. The brief vision jolted him.

The light did it. Light from a sun redder than Sol, setting, mixed with the big blue moon's light. Such a dusk the human eye had never known before. The eye did not know how to interpret it. That, plus the fever and the guilt that Wing was trying to disseminate, had made him see blood on the Mountain. He wiped clammy sweat from his forehead.

"I don't dispute your science," Wing said. "Maybe we have the knowledge and the might to make ourselves at home here. But we don't have the right."

"We reached the stars," Joe said shortly. "That gives us the right."

The last of the energy of dropping out of space had been burned off. Joe felt the engines kick in and the shuttle climb toward Unity Base, the scenic tour mercifully over.

"Open the cockpit door," said Wing urgently. "Tell this character to stop showing off. We're flying too close to the mountainside for safety."

Joe started to reach for the door, but glanced out through the viewport. He froze. The storm loomed over the shuttle now, a mass of cloud standing on a thick leg of precipitation. Lightning flickered in its belly.

They hit the fringes of the thunderhead's rains and winds. The shuttle quivered. Joe sagged back and pressed his arms against his quaking stomach. With sick fascination, he watched the storm. The cloud and its rain looked wrong, the thunderhead misshapen and too smooth, the rain that issued from it flushed with a maroon color. He stared, trying to convince himself of the simple meteorological nature of the phenomena.

Instead, in the alien light, Joe suddenly saw the clouds as a bleeding mass: vast flesh mangled beyond recognition. Vast wounds spurted blood. The rain looked like streaming blood. Raindrops spattered the shuttle's windows. Joe flinched.

Incredibly, so did the shuttle. It banked sharply away from the rain. The Mountain leaned over them. Wing cried, "No!"

Now the shuttle veered the other way. But a downdraft lowered on the shuttle like an invisible fist. The shuttle dropped abruptly.

The shuttle twitched as the pilot fought to regain altitude and control. The shuttle's wing grazed a treetop with a grinding scratch. The shuttle twisted, throwing Joe against the straps of his seat belt. Clear water streamed on the viewport glass. And then a hell of noise and violent motion broke loose. Cracking pain seized his left shoulder. In agony, he struggled, caught in a contorted position. Then he blacked out.

Chapter Ten

TWILIGHT

Curled up on sloping ground, Joe felt the roughness of dirt and duff under him. He began to notice a kind of vague light, a twilight. Propping up on his right elbow, he saw one, two, three dark blue tree trunks not far away. And then, downhill, a steaming, metallic ruin. He stared incredulously. Wing emerged from the ruined plane and hurried uphill. "How do you feel?" Wing crouched beside him.

"Something's fractured," Joe mumbled. "Can't use my left arm. Head hurts, too." With his right hand, he explored his scalp. His fingertips came away bloody. "What happened?"

"We crashed." Wing sounded shaken. "I managed to pull you out."

"The pilot?"

"The nose of the plane hit the Mountain first. He died." Wing bowed his head.

Rain began falling almost soundlessly. Water dripped off Joe's hair. Meanwhile, the pain in his shoulder eased to a tolerable level. Joe felt his left hand stinging. He discovered a nasty scratch on it. Both hands were streaked with soft black organic soil. He shuddered.

"I gave him last rites. Besides being a botanist, I am a priest, so—"

"If it comes to it, don't try that with me."

Wing stared him. "You are not a believer?"

"I'm an atheist."

"Given the straits we're in, perhaps you should reconsider," Wing said.

"Like hell!"

They heard an engine whirring. Both looked upward instantly. "That is the survey copter," Wing said. "Searching for us." The whir swelled. Then faded away. "They will not see a trace of us," Wing whispered. Slender tree trunks rose into the air all around them. High overhead, the trunks branched into massive crowns of fronds intermeshing with each other. The canopy showed no break, no sign that the shuttleplane had crashed through it.

"Voicelink?" Joe asked. "Locator beacon?"

"The crash destroyed the cockpit equipment, but I'm sure they'll come back," said Wing. But he absently wrung his hands. "Our colony cannot afford to lose you."

"Just so they don't waste time about it!"

Wing shook his head. "It may take time to decide how to search for us without exposing the search party to biological hazard."

"If the biohazard is all that serious, they might as well not bother," Joe gritted.

The raining wind breathed through the forest canopy. Finally Wing said, "If you are not going to die, then I must climb to the Base to get help."

"How far?"

"A few miles. You will be safe here. I think."

Stay here alone? Joe's notebook was in his pocket. But here there was no World Net for it to connect to. There was nothing. He felt the fingers of the riptide tugging on his mind, wanting to pull him toward cold zero. Shaking his head, Joe clumsily stood up. He twitched his shoulder. Now it didn't hurt, didn't feel at all. "Painkiller?"

"Yes. I salvaged a first aid kit." The rain soundlessly ceased. Cobalt silence surrounded them. Wing looked toward the wreckage. "I pulled a large broken frond over him. That's not a real burial, but—"

"It'll do. See if there's a sling in that first aid kit."

Wing obliged. With his useless arm secured in the sling, Joe felt marginally fit for a desperate hike. What choice did he have? If he stayed here alone, the riptide would get him.

The blue moon must have been high in the night sky above the forest. A viscous blue twilight filled the air under the trees. It made for uncertain visibility. Joe could discern the nearest few tree trunks. Everything beyond that melted into a murky sketch done in blue ink. His first few footfalls made sharp thin pains radiate through his body.

The first part of the climb seemed simple, a steady slope without much undergrowth. But slick moss coated the ground. Both of them slipped repeatedly.

Something glowed in the blue gloom. It was a dead tree. Some kind of fungus coated the tree in thick, dripping sheets like candle wax, emitting a faint yellow-green glow. Wing crept closer to investigate.

"Don't touch that!" Joe ordered. "No microbes here are specifically hostile to us—but chances are, some produce toxins. Metabolic by-products that happen to be toxic to us."

Wing stopped short. "It could be dangerous to touch anything."

"So could standing here breathing the air. Let's go."

The painkiller had made him light-headed. Between one footfall and the next, Joe was seized by the feeling that this place could be the bottom of the sea: liquidly shadowy, ultramarine, and silent. Following Wing, he moved in slow motion, like an ancient diver, his feet leaden, his head weightless.

With a startled cry, Wing pitched backward and started sliding away. Joe reacted just in time. Throwing himself to the ground, he grabbed Wing's wrist with his good right hand, saving Wing from disappearing into a deep darkness. The slope underfoot had taken a sudden, steep turn downward.

Joe swore at the unexpected ravine. With an effort, he hauled the smaller man back over the edge.

"Thank you," Wing said faintly.

Drug or no drug, the action had caused the pain in Joe's shoulder to flare up. He tried to rock the angry pain away.

Wing crept back to the edge of the ravine and peered into it. "I hear water rushing over rocks."

"You could have been killed."

"I was careless," Wing fumed. "Like our pilot, I just assumed that this is not a dangerous place."

The pilot had been too talkative, maybe careless, but not a bad guy, and he had died. Realization seeped in. Joe was walking away from a fatal crash. He could have been dead too. Rocking against the pain, he shivered.

After brooding at the ravine a while longer, Wing said, "I don't think that was what you meant by proceeding without extraordinary precaution on this world."

"No. Now what?"

"This ravine angles uphill. We should skirt it until we find a way across."

"Just watch your step."

"I think I'd better watch with my toes. My eyes are not at home here."

Wing edged along from tree to tree. The trees grew more slender, their foliage less dense; more moonlight filtered into the forest, improving visibility. The feathery crowns of the trees were silhouetted against the dim sky. "You're a fern specialist, eh? No wonder they defrosted you," Joe said. "These things look like prehistoric fern trees."

"So the Vanguard thought."

The ravine rapidly grew shallower, evolving into a tree-bordered depression that ran like a ribbon as far up and away as the eye could see. Illuminated by full moonlight, it glowed blue-green. "That damn moon puts out a lot of light," said Joe.

Wing halted at a narrow spot in the long depression.

"It looks boggy," Joe said dubiously. "And either I'm feeling my fever, or it's hot here."

"Hot and humid. And the air has a strange smell."

"Loaded with volatile organic molecules. Well, you're the field man. What do we do?"

"Cross here. I go first; you follow in my steps. Be ready to give me a hand if need be." Wing found firm footing in vegetation that came up to his shins. He paused. "These plants are odd! They shake even though there is no wind here." He bent over for a better look. "What do you say is the color?"

"Green but not green."

"Yes. I do not see any color either, yet the plants appear convincingly green. What strange light." He touched a leaf that resembled a fern, curled at the top, the rest wide with frilly edges that quivered for no apparent reason.

"This isn't a field trip," Joe reminded him. "And get your head up away from the muck." The strange organic smell nagged Joe's nostrils.

Wing straightened. "Colorless green ideas sleep furiously."

"What?"

"That is the textbook example of a perfectly grammatical but meaningless sentence in English. I never expected to see any."

"Why don't you keep your mind on getting across?"

Joe put his feet where Wing had stepped among the colorless greens. He heard faint crunching sounds from the underlying mat of vegetation saturated with water. Grimly he calculated that he outweighed Wing by fifty pounds at least.

"This is the center—solid enough," said Wing.

But it proved solid enough only for Wing. Joe's foot tore through the mat into mud beneath it. He lunged ahead. His other foot sank into the mat. The mud reeked of overripe bananas. An instant later, it smelled like a latrine.

"Can you pull out your feet?" Wing asked urgently.

"Ugh! Yeah—" Joe plowed through the mud. The smell wrapped itself around him, oscillating between fruit and sewage. Joe stumbled onto firm ground. He tasted the urge to vomit.

"That smell is strange," said Wing, leaning on a slender frond-tree. "Yet almost familiar . . ." Dumbfounded, Joe stared as Wing slid down the tree and sat down in a huddle, sobbing into his knees. "That smell!" Wing's words were muffled. "It is so very like—" He choked and sobbed.

Seizing Wing's collar, Joe dragged him uphill into fresher air. Joe breathed deeply to pull fresh air into his own lungs.

"That smell!" Wing said finally. "It reminded me of my grandmother's kitchen!"

"What?!"

"The fragrance of sesame oil heating in the wok," Wing said sorrowfully.

"Didn't strike me that way," said Joe.

"So real!" Wing murmured. "Many memories of home. Give me a few moments. I still feel overwhelmed. . . ." Wing trailed off.

With a grunt, Joe sat down to wait while Wing pulled himself together.

Getting himself out of the bog, he had ripped a visible trail through the plants. Never before on this world had that happened: plant life damaged by a large blundering animal. The semifloating vegetation seemed to be drifting back together, his trail closing up, jagged as a stitched wound.

Joe shifted his gaze to the sky. A dim yet intense blue, more than anything else it resembled a color of cyberspace. Which reminded Joe that he had not done any of his own work since he came out of the Ship's freezer. Modeling data; assessing other people's reports; politics; bossing technicians in the lab, yes. But not theoretical molecular biology. His genius was to lift up a great looming strand of DNA in cyberspace, and rearrange the bases, using the virtual manipulator that made it feel like physically handling the vast molecule. Until it felt right for what he wanted it to do that nature hadn't thought up on its own. Then, he would tell the hypercomputer to give the novel DNA a workout, model the expression of the new genes through messenger RNA, proteins, and organs into the final organism.

He had made manifold modifications to the canine double helix in cyberspace. His design had been executed by genetic engineers in Labrador retrievers. The result was a dog with gills, flippers, and other physiological modifications. By the time Joe left Earth, sea dogs were being used as helpers, messengers, sometimes bomb-carriers for undersea operations. Porpoises, useful in some of the same ways, were protected against being so used; they had para-human rights. The sea dogs retained the loyal and tractable temperament of Labs.

He had really wanted to design and develop a unicorn. But chimeras were expensive. They had to be practical and profitable.

The dark electric blue of the sky gave him ideas. Planet Green needed animals. They could be tailor-made. The Ship had brought a trove of germ cells from Earth. Here, there was a planetary pool of alien genetic material to investigate, exploit, and maybe recombine with genes from Earth. Why not? He took the notepad from his pocket and opened it. The flimsy screen unfurled and stiffened. Joe stroked hurried notes, squinting at the tiny bright characters on the display.

With a world full of plants, there was plenty of food for animals engineered to metabolize it. First, herbivores. Antelopes with appropriate digestive enzymes. Unicorns, even. Why not? Unicorns with silver manes and tails. Then predators that eat unicorns but find people distinctly unpalatable. Though it might do the human genome good to have man-eating predators on Green: keep the genes for survival honed sharp.

Unicorns with fluted horns to let them defend themselves against their predators. What kind of predators? Chimeras with horns and talons and serpentine tails. Staring into the moonlit sky, he imagined the coils of DNA, changes in the genetic code, transfiguration into breathing ornamented shapes, teratisms that would have been illegal, impractical, or both on Earth. His creativity had always been trammeled there. But here the possibilities were endless and compelling. One-handed, he frantically entered his ideas into the notepad.

Wing scrambled to his feet. "It is not good to sit and think in this twilight!" he announced, and dashed uphill.

Wing was right. Sit around in this twilight thinking, and colorless green ideas wake up furiously in your head. Tucking the notepad back into his pocket, Joe broke into a cold sweat. He did not know—would not know, until he got an uplink to the Ship's hypercomputer with its molecular biological database—whether what he had just dreamed up made any scientific sense, or was lunatic fantasy.

☽☾

They hiked directly uphill on a steep but not unmanageable slope. Joe's shoulder felt leadenly numb. Elsewhere on his anatomy, nerve endings complained loudly, claiming to be scraped. He did not dare to investigate with his good hand. By now, that damply dirty extremity must have collected a staggering number of microorganisms.

Wing pointed to a short tree draped with filmy stuff that shone slightly. "Shroud worms."

Bugs, slugs, crud. Srivastava, with his smile full of white teeth, had said cheerily, "The cake is much like Earth, you see, the layers of procaryotes and eucaryotes, single-celled and multicelled microbes, then plants and arthropods and invertebrates. Only there is no decoration on the icing of the cake—no large vertebrates running and flying around. The carbon cycle works quite well without them. The atmosphere down there is much like that of Earth. Richer in oxygen, but only somewhat."

On Earth, Joe thought, the primordial crud had enough imagination to evolve into large animals.

Looking back at the shroud, Wing said, "That tree is thought to be an analogue to Earth's ginkgo. The ginkgoes flourished with the great dinosaurs in Earth's Jurassic period. Yet here, nothing more complex than shroud worms eats that tree. The plant life and animal life are very far out of phase. Have you found an explanation for this?"

"Maybe. The native organisms have a kind of deoxyribonucleic acid for genetic material. Different from terrestrial DNA, and, it turns out, more stable. Too stable. My guess is that you need a certain mutation rate to make enough random experiments so that some of them go to the kind of nervous system complexity that makes for higher animals."

The pseudo-ginkgo trees were small, branchy, rooty, and close together. Joe fought his way through, while Wing slipped between the tangled trees like a cat. He paused to wait for Joe. "Could it not be that the pace on this world is simply slow and that animals will come about in time, if we let the world be?"

"I doubt it, because there's an incredible excess of genetic material in every organism we've studied. The ratio of genes that mean something to genes that mean nothing is absurdly low. A slug tissue sample collected near Unity Base had six million times more genetic material than it should need."

"I do not see how an apparent excess of noncoding DNA negates the further evolution of slugs," said Wing. "Of course, I am a botanist rather than a xenobiologist."

Joe detected a nettle. Joe was no xenobiologist either. His qualifications to assess the biohazards of Planet Green had been questioned by some of the scientists who were. To no avail: the reins had stayed in his hands. "Obsolete genetic baggage doesn't get selected out. Evolution here was never able to jack up to higher life-forms. And now it's too late," Joe said flatly. "From here on, we supply the higher life-forms."

Wing forged ahead in silence.

The bright blue gloom made it all but impossible to judge the position of obstacles. "Still think it's beautiful?" Joe snapped, after tripping over yet another root.

"Yes, I do," answered Wing, "philosophically. How I feel is another matter."

"You don't feel sick, do you?"

"No. But . . . I'm unnerved. Things here have no names. I might feel better if I expected a dinosaur—even a toothy one like an allosaur—to crash through the bushes." He ducked into a thick band of trees. Long, pliable branches with masses of round leaves hung in the way.

Wing seemed healthy enough. But Joe wondered morosely about his own weakened, fevered body. The ragged molecules and wounded cells of stasis fever—how vulnerable did that make him? "Ever read about the Black Death in medieval Europe? People literally dropped dead. I keep thinking about that," said Joe. "Irrationally expecting wild viruses to rustle in the air. And water. And goddamned dirt."

"That is more likely than allosaurs," Wing said in a low voice. He eased past a thick skein of branches. Joe followed more clumsily.

"More likely than allosaurs but still damn improbable," said Joe. "I'm no fool. I recommended colonizing without extraordinary precaution because the findings are straightforward." He patted the notepad, reassuring himself of its tangibility. "The idea of an alien virus scares the hell out of people who don't know better. But viruses are parasites fine-tuned to their hosts. No mammals here means no virus even remotely prepared to exploit the mammalian organism. No alien virus is going to ambush us."

"Most regrettable," said Wing, heading up a steep incline laced with roots and branches.

"You'd rather drop dead?"

"No. But if the prospect convinced the Vanguard not to colonize this world, I wouldn't be sorry." Wing emphatically pushed a fat leafy branch out of the way to climb past it. Joe failed to catch the branch before Wing released it, and it struck him in the face. Some kind of dust or pollen flew into his nose and mouth. Joe sneezed and coughed. "Keep your martyr complex to yourself!" he snarled.

"Sorry about that!" Wing said.

"How far do we still have to go?"

"Less than half of the way. This world's gravity is a bit less than that of Earth, and walking uphill is easier." Wing paused to examine a branch in his way, squinting in the uncertain light. "Tetrapterous!"

Joe asked, "How the hell can you be a field botanist and not want to live here?"

"Oh, I do. But if we colonize this world, we will eventually wreck it. Come on. Night is falling."

The leafy trees thinned out slightly. But the gloom turned darker and less useful for seeing. The ground roughened. Joe stumbled on big rocks, making clumsy missteps that caused the sling to chafe the back of his neck. In what was left of the light, the way up the Mountain looked steep and forbidding. Jagged stone outcrops slivered the starry sky.

"This mountain is openly rocky only at its crown." Wing sounded hopeful. "Our maps in Unity Base show quite a few dry streambeds running down the Mountain. They seem to be the courses where rain or melting snow runs off in some seasons. At this time of year, the streambeds are dry and full of low vegetation, and may be the easiest way up."

"What if the vegetation has thorns?"

"In the absence of animals here, that's unlikely."

Because Wing hoped to strike a streambed, he angled up the mountainside. That was fine with Joe. The going was difficult enough without trying to go straight up. After the jolts of slipping and stumbling repeatedly, Joe's shoulder began to ache again. And his good right hand accumulated still more scrapes. Blood, plant juice, dirt, water, and sweat mingled madly on his skin. He gritted his teeth and followed Wing.

To make matters worse, his earlier delusion of being in the depths of the sea returned. This time he found himself obsessed with the idea of climbing up from the still, safe blue deep into a tumultuous surf. It became an act of will to put one foot in front of another. Even while cursing his brain for its gullibility, he experienced the irrational sensation of wave action rocking his body. He was racked by the feeling that, if he climbed higher, the surf would fling him against murderous rocks. In desperation, he determined to master the delusion and all of its relatives: to figure out why they happened.

He went to work, attacked the facts with total intellectual concentration, made an all-or-nothing contest of it. And won—a more personal victory than usual: his mind made logical sense of the circumstances that had been toying with his brain. The sea-delusion dissolved.

Joe grinned, an invisible expression. Night had fallen. In nearly total darkness, they had to inch along by feel.

The land dipped, turning loose and pebbly as it did. "This is a nice wide dry waterway," Wing panted.

"Let's go." The climb uphill was hard, but it was getting them to the top of the Mountain. Joe liked it better than beating through the alien bushes.

Then Joe's heel struck something soft and slippery, causing him to crash down on one knee. Wing was by his side instantly, helping him up. Joe's knee hurt. He cursed furiously.

"You stepped on the highest life-form of Green," said Wing. "It was a zucchini slug."

Joe limped to a large rock and sat down on it to nurse his skinned knee. "Park, hell! This world's way too weird to call it a park!"

"I agree." Wing seated himself on a boulder nearby.

"You know, you really cracked up back there. In the bog. Anything like that ever happen to you before?"

"Never." Wing was a shadow with a rueful voice. "Smells often evoke nostalgia for me, but not as overwhelmingly as that."

"Did you see anything outside before we crashed that could have startled the pilot?"

"No. Did you?"

Joe described the delusion of mangled and bleeding clouds. "A sight like that, plus his 'touch of fever,' might explain his making a bad mistake."

"He was flying too close to the Mountain for safety. People in Unity Base have tended to become careless, as if this were a park and we all came here on vacation." Wing was silent for a moment. "What was it—the blood clouds?"

"Water, air, and light," said Joe. "And animal brains."

"We imagine violence when there isn't any?"

"No. Given hopelessly inconclusive data, our brains jump to conclusions." Joe shifted to a less uncomfortable place on his rock. "What happens when you look at a visual paradox—an illogical drawing? Your brain shuttles between alternative interpretations, rather than dismiss the thing as impossible."

"But such inventions are indeed impossible. Unnatural. This place is utterly natural."

"That"—Joe stabbed at the talking shadow with his forefinger—"is a philosophical premise, not an experiential one! As you are wont to point out, my friend, we did not evolve here. For us this place is *not* natural! Now, if a smell drifts into your olfactory receptors, and it consists of complicated organic molecules unlike any on Earth—what does the brain make of it? Dismiss it as nonsense, or jump to a conclusion?"

"Evidently the latter," Wing admitted. "But if so, my brain has jumped to astonishing conclusions this evening. At one point, I smelled wet dog. And again gasoline. Then there was the hot sesame oil."

"Your wok bog produced a complicated smell with God only knows how many different organic volatiles, how many coincidental similarities to terrestrial molecules. What we had there was the olfactory equivalent of 'Colorless green ideas sleep furiously.' Your brain was astonished. Jumped to a conclusion at random."

The shadow bobbed, Wing nodding. "But the blood clouds must have been a much simpler puzzle to the senses. How could that have so startled our pilot as to cause the crash?"

"Right then, he hadn't left himself much room for error," said Joe. "Now, think about blue moonlight. In the context of our evolutionary history that's unnatural. Bright blue moonlight—mixed with red sunlight—alien! And the clouds here look different—the gravity's different—hell, the bottom line is an alien gestalt. *Everything* is slightly different. Adds up to a global intuition of impossibility, eh?"

"Does that necessarily cause people to succumb to . . . ?"

"Let's say delusions. People go about their business, the sense of impossibility reaches critical mass, and then brains jump to deluded conclusions. Illogical ones, maybe disastrous ones."

The shadow moved as Wing went to stoop over the crushed slug. "I thought I saw the slug move and wondered if it was another illusion," said Wing. "It wasn't. Undertakers have arrived."

"Undertakers?"

"Insects—or insect analogues. The ground is alive with them. They are stirring and digging, and the slug is disappearing into the ground." Wing's voice sounded strangled.

"Let's get out of here," Joe said. Neither of them mentioned the dead pilot, lying under a broken frond on deep, rich, and possibly even more alive, squirming soil. Together they fled uphill.

Chapter Eleven

NIGHT

Loose rocks slid out from under Joe. He seized a bush. It doubled over like rubber, letting him fall flat and hard, which knocked the wind out of him. When Joe finished wheezing, Wing said, "Go by hand and foot. That way there is less far to fall."

The terrain got even worse. It turned into a jumble of rocks and plants. The stuff tended to slip, taking them with it in a shower of dirt and leaves. Joe's shoulder hurt savagely. His thin, strained grunts sounded almost like whimpers.

Wing paused. "Is the painkiller wearing off?" he asked, lightly touching Joe's shoulder. "There's another ampoule of it, if I can see to administer it in the dark."

"Do it after we're out of this."

They crawled farther. "This is debris!" Wing exclaimed. "We're near the top of the Mountain. Material from the blast fell here."

Minutes later, they emerged from the jumbled plants and ground. A sky full of stars hung above them, and the Mountain's bare crown loomed ahead. With a groan, Joe lay flat.

"Now for the medicine," Wing said, briskly unrolling the first aid kit. "I can see fairly well. There's so much starlight." He carefully injected the painkiller, which stung.

"Is that your Third Planet?" Joe pointed to an untwinkling, ruddy star.

Wing sighed. "Yes."

"You've got a religious affinity for it," Joe said. "Never mind the scientific camouflage, why are you convinced that we ought to start the colony there? Why shouldn't we have a second chance to cooperate with nature—here?"

"Since you ask," Wing said, "because God has not given this world to us."

"How do you know?"

"God gave us the Earth and its living things to name, to enjoy, to use. I cannot believe that the same rights extend to the universe and everything in it."

"So what are you doing here?"

"Believe me, I've been having my doubts about that," Wing replied ruefully. "I don't think we were supposed to stay on Earth forever, as fundamentalists of various faiths were insisting at the time we left. There was nothing morally wrong with making a journey to the stars, to terraform a barren land—working with sweat and sacrifice to build a good green home for our kind and the creatures that we brought with us in the Ship. It wasn't a luxurious prospect. It was what all of us expected when we left Earth."

"So God gives us a better option," said Joe. "Has the right to do that, eh?"

"True," Wing admitted. "But I believe that what we are given is not a better option, but a hard choice. To choose hard labor or sloth, humility or arrogance, sacrifice or greed. A wilderness or a park." Looking up at the ruddy spark in the night sky, he continued sadly. "Almost no one seems to think that the choice is hard at all. Everyone assumes that this Green is a gift from God or from the universe."

Mercifully, Joe's shoulder was going numb again. Three planets, he thought. The third was potentially habitable, provided that the present generation and a good many to come were willing to rough it. A second planet, the raw oceanic world: uninhabitable, so much so that no one except the planetary scientists had expressed any interest in ever going there. And then the first, this green world: immediately habitable, mild, tractable. Wing might be a religious unrealist, Joe reflected, but he had a good point. There would have been something ennobling about the challenge of molding a lonely globe in the wilderness of stars. Too bad that was unnecessary. Joe suspected that human nature would not be improved by the cosmic equivalent of a free lunch.

Three planets, two, and one. Then and still there was the zero. The planet with the moon that had failed to be there. The zero moon stretched from Earth to here, eleven centuries long and thin, a string of cold nothingness, attenuated death.

☽☾

"Joe. Joe Devreze—or Toronto. Wake up."

Joe started, surprised to be alive.

"Either the painkiller or my sermon put you to sleep. How do you feel?"

"The painkiller worked." He carefully climbed to his feet and took deep breaths. "You know, I can't feel the stasis fever anymore. Maybe the exercise burned it out."

"I hope so," Wing answered.

The last climb turned out to be strenuous, but safe and fast. They ascended from one terrace of the waterway to the next. The pure white light of the stars made it easy to find hand- and footholds. "Onward and upward!" said Joe, in a triumphant mood.

Trees of a new kind perched along the waterway: short, scrubby, and pungent. "Furry pines!" Wing said excitedly. "These are the dominant vegetation at the top of the Mountain. I have studied samples of them. But I did not know that they smelled so—like celery?"

"I get seashells. You know, used ones. Or else antiseptic. Contradictory as hell, eh?"

The waterway petered out. They pushed their way into a stand of furry pines. Some of the trees leaned outward at a twenty-degree angle, with broken branches and roots half pulled out of the ground. The damaged ones were resolutely thick with living needles.

Joe laughed. "Tough little beggars!"

Then they encountered scorched and shattered pines. Hurriedly they scrambled through, and over, those. A heavy smell hung in the air: the stink of combustion, Joe guessed, though his brain came up with several odors wildly unrelated to burned cellulose.

A ridge of dirt marked the edge of the mountaintop crater. Shallow and wide, it curved away into the distance on both sides. In the crater's center, a quarter of a mile away, stood the geodesic dome of Unity Base, an angular bubble lit from within by yellow light. No fencing surrounded the dome. No floodlights stood guard over it. None were needed on this world.

Wing slowly seated himself on a fallen pine's trunk, near the edge of the crater. After a few moments, Joe sat down beside him. Exhilaration had vanished. Joe felt drained.

"Haven't heard the copter since the first time," said Joe.

"I see it parked on its pad, almost behind the dome."

A few minutes later, Joe blurted, "They're clean in there."

"I know," Wing whispered.

"We ought to go knock on the door," said Joe, with a complete lack of conviction.

Neither of them moved. An idiotic thought popped into Joe's head. If they knocked on the dome, maybe the bubble would burst and disintegrate. He picked up a handful of small rocks and pitched them, one by one, back to the ground. Ejecta from the blast that flattened the Mountain's crown, these rocks had fresh sharp edges. Finally Joe said angrily, "Why aren't they looking? They ought to hope that we're still alive, and they know we're not necessarily sick!"

"They do?"

"Before I left the Ship, I transmitted my recommendation to the chief expedition scientist with an abstract of the findings that led to the recommendation. I'd have thought he'd send a search party out!"

"Maybe he didn't agree with your recommendation. Perhaps no one did and there were no volunteers."

"God-almighty-damn!" Joe exploded. "What time is it? I had a wristwatch. I lost it."

"No, I took it off, fearing that your arm might swell." Wing handed over the expedition-issue analogue wristwatch.

"Stopped. Reads two hours since we left the Ship!" Joe hurled the watch onto the ashy ground.

Wing went over and ferreted among the ashes to find the watch. "It's still running. I'm not sure we had so very far to come. If our other senses are disoriented, why not the sense of time as well?"

"Maybe, but we can't wait all—"

A brighter pane of yellow light fell out of the dome: a door had opened. A small group of people emerged. They wore landsuits, but no helmets, and they looked loaded with gear, ropes, flashlights, pickaxes, bags.

Joe leaped to his feet and whistled. Wing shouted, "This way!"

The search party hesitated, two of them pointed excitedly, and then they all came toward Joe and Wing at a run. The person in the lead looked familiar. Catharin. Joe was struck by her beauty. Wing could talk all night about Green being beautiful, but this planet was intolerably weird. Beauty was the tall, fair woman running toward him, with cold bright starlight glazing her hair and clothes.

About two yards away, Catharin stopped so abruptly that the other three in her group almost collided with her. In an awkward silence, Joe put his grubby free hand into his pocket. Then he cleared his throat and said, "Congratulations, we found you."

"Thank goodness." Her glance slid to Wing. "Carlton! I am so glad to see you! What about—"

"The pilot's dead," said Joe.

"Oh, dear God. We thought, we hoped, that it was just a forced landing, and all three of you were all right," Catharin said unevenly.

"It wasn't a forced landing. The plane crashed," Joe said.

"It had to do with freak meteorological conditions," Wing explained.

"You're going to have to settle for two out of three," Joe said curtly.

Catharin looked at him hard, taking in the sling around his arm, his torn and dirtied clothing, the scratches on his face.

The man's ego shrank. He felt like a little boy who had wandered away from home and found himself in some vaguely understood but awful trouble.

"Joe," she said, "I have to ask you this. Do you feel well?"

Catharin's search party paid close attention.

Joe nodded.

"Are you sure?"

"Apart from a fractured shoulder and being souped up on painkillers, yes!"

"I can't believe you, Joe," she said in a low voice. "You have stasis fever if nothing else. I want both of you to answer this question: Do you think that the other is well?—Carlton?"

Joe felt his heart drumming out anxiety.

"On the way down from the Ship, he looked haggard," Wing said. "The stasis fever look. Then the crash injured him. Afterwards, though, he's been alert and rational. He speculated that exercise had driven out the fever. That could be. He's had a sort of pained vigor this evening."

She sighed. "Joe?"

"He's seemed fit as a fiddle to me."

The doctor smiled slightly. "Now I believe you."

Catharin's people relaxed, whispered comments to one another. Joe was flooded with warm, giddy relief.

"We'll still have to take certain precautions with you two—," Catharin began.

"I know. We'll camp out for a few weeks."

"Oh, you won't have to camp out. They're setting up a medical isolation room right now, attached to the dome."

"No need to go to too much trouble," said Wing.

"He'd rather stay outside with the plants," Joe said. "Found lots of interesting ones tonight—he'd have been sorry if you'd interrupted us on the way up. Can't say I enjoyed the hike too much, though," Joe added pointedly.

"I'm sorry it took us so long to get organized," she answered. "Initially there was confusion and dismay. Then Aaron Manhattan read us your recommendation—about the safety factor for colonizing—and asked for volunteers for a search party to go out immediately. Captain Bixby vetoed that idea; he insisted on absolutely stringent precautions before a search attempt."

Joe cursed the Captain under his breath.

"He can't order people to take outrageous chances," Catharin said sharply.

"But people can take chances on their own," someone chimed in.

"And so," Catharin continued, "we took a vote on how to search. Not whether, how. It was decided about fifteen minutes ago."

"He's put the Base under quarantine," someone added. "But that won't last too long, if nothing happens."

"Nothing'll happen," said Joe.

And they took his word for it. Catharin's party began to stray. They moved in different directions, nudging the rocks with their toes, examining the wrecked pines, scratching the itch of curiosity about the place. Unconsciously, though, they fanned out in such a way as to keep their distance from Joe and Wing.

"So my recommendation struck you people at Unity Base as convincing enough to act on," said Joe, with satisfaction.

Catharin gave him a quizzical look. "Well, Aaron stood behind your scientific conclusions. But really . . ."

"Really what?"

"We tend to compare this world to a park. Most of us are city people with fond memories of our parks. Central Park. Golden Gate Park. Don't you have one too?"

"Centre Island," Joe said reluctantly.

"There you are. As far as I can tell, your scientific conclusions are perfectly sound. But the idea that this world is a park is what made us bolder."

Wing said quietly, "Parks do not have blood clouds."

"Or wok bogs." Joe exchanged a somber look with Wing.

"I beg your pardon?" said Catharin.

"Our pilot, may he rest in peace, taught us an important lesson," said Wing. "There's peril for us here, because this is not the world on which our senses and our minds evolved." He pointed to the golden dome of Unity Base. "That alone is Earth."

Catharin looked back at the dome. A wind from nameless latitudes blew some of the long strands of her hair across her face. "The dome is Earth for now, not forever," she said calmly. "We'll adapt to this world and adapt it to our needs. I agree, though, that the middle of the night isn't the best time to explore. Regroup, people," she ordered. "Let's go home."

Joe said, "Home nev—er looked so good." His voice betrayed him by breaking. Joe stood there as if rooted to the ground, incapable of taking steps toward the dome. He felt damnably grubby and ashamed to advance into the clear yellow light.

Catharin extended a gloved hand to Wing. "You can go back to study the plants you discovered tonight." Then she offered her other hand to Joe. Hers closed gingerly around his. Her glove felt dry and cool. She led them toward the dome, the yellow bubble under the strange dense stars.

Chapter Twelve

THE BRIGHTNESS BEFORE THE DAWN

Joel Atlanta, Starship's pilot, had taken the Captain's chair in the conference room. In one private corner of his mind, he marveled that he felt at ease in the Captain's place.

Across the table from Joel sat Kay Montana, newly revived from stasis, an ex-military space pilot who looked the part. Kay had short brown hair, a lanky build, and an alert bony face. "I'll be pilot in command of the interplanetary explorer *Lodestar*, as per the Mission Book. Roger that."

At Joel's left, Marie Mike Sisseton observed Kay closely. Joel did not take Sisseton's presence as reason for him not to evaluate Kay in his own fashion. Kay's psychology might be Sisseton's puzzle, but her flying was Joel's. He noted the clarity of Kay's grasp of what she had been told, and the satisfaction in her voice as she continued, "After the check flights, *Lodestar* will be commissioned to explore this solar system for resources, asteroids and such with minable minerals, and in addition, *Lodestar* will serve as a platform for scientific studies of the blue moon. Happy to be up, sir."

"There's one more job for you," said Joel. "You'll copilot our orbit-to-ground shuttleplane on every flight."

Kay's eyes narrowed. "I didn't train for that."

Catharin had once told Joel about the right way to break bad news in the doctor business: succinctly work up to the bad part, giving the patient and family a vital few moments to brace themselves. Joel figured the same approach would work in anybody's business. "Five days ago, our other shuttle was making an approach to Unity Base when it crashed on the mountainside." Kay stiffened. Joel continued, "It came down in dense forest. The machine was wrecked. Both passengers came out alive, though one was injured. Unfortunately, the shuttle pilot died. His name was Jason Scanlan, in case you knew him."

She was hardheaded, but not emotionless. Sorrow flickered across her face. "Slightly, sir. I'm sorry to hear that."

"Because of the crash, the passengers may have been exposed to alien microorganisms or toxins, but a rescue party from the Base brought them in anyway. So the whole Base is under quarantine for six weeks, while the two are kept in relative medical isolation." *Please God, nothing bad happens to anybody, especially not to Cat. . . .* "That crash is the reason we're never going to fly the shuttle again without a copilot. As you probably realize by now, this is what the Book called a poststarflight contingency briefing."

The Book also said the Captain would be the one to brief Kay in an event like this, so Joel added, "Captain Bixby's ill today. I believe you've been told how long stasis lasted on this trip. The fallout from that includes malaise and transient illnesses. How do you feel?"

"Fine." She sat up straighter. "Was the crash malaise-related?"

"Wind shear was probably the direct cause of the crash. But only after Scanlan was distracted by a weird cloud."

"Cloud?" Kay echoed in a disbelieving tone.

"The key word is 'distracted,'" Joel said grimly. "Everybody on flight status will soon be asked to submit to psychological tests. This is Dr. Marie Mike Sisseton. She's a human factors psychologist."

Dr. Sisseton nodded. Kay looked alarmed. "I passed a lot of psychological screening tests to get here."

"We all did," Joel answered. "But we don't know enough about how anybody reacts to an alien environment, because we've never had people in one."

"The reason for more testing goes beyond that," said Dr. Sisseton. A chunky woman with tawny skin and dark hair, she was what they'd have called a half-breed in the old days: half Caucasian and half Amerindian. She sounded like one hundred percent psychologist to Joel, with a jag that struck her as vitally important and Joel as nebulous at best. Altered human factors. Which she now brought up for Kay's benefit. "Your work as a space pilot takes place at the interface of a *machine cognizance*—your spaceship—and a *cognizant machine*—the human intellect. Due to the high intelligence of both, it is a very complicated interface." Sisseton shot Joel a significant look.

I know, I know, and you think it's more of the same between the Ship and the humans interfacing it, and I think you're chasing blue moonbeams. He couldn't argue with her in his capacity as Captain's proxy, but if she rambled on, he'd cut her short.

Sisseton did not, however, ramble. "If your intellect is subtly altered by biochemical changes induced by stasis, it introduces an element of unpredictability into an already complicated picture. This could adversely affect operations in space as well as on the planet."

Joel said, "The only problems we've had are Downstairs. The blood clouds were a wild card because we don't understand the meteorology on Green."

Sisseton said, "But sooner or later—and Kay, you need to be alert to this in your role as pilot-in-command of the interplanetary explorer—there will be a lapse in which the *predictable fails to be predicted*; something foreseeable goes unforeseen. The results could be consequential if not disastrous."

Detecting their discord, Kay looked from one to the other.

"We'll be careful, but we won't overanticipate imaginary trouble," said Joel, and he had the last word, because the telcon screen on the wall of the conference room jingled an alarm and turned itself on to reveal Lary Siroky-Scheidt's face, his bristly red eyebrows elevated in alarm. "We can't contact the Base!"

☽☾

Carlton Wing awoke with a start. His roommate in this makeshift observation facility attached to Unity Base was Joe Toronto, and Joe often tossed and muttered in his sleep. But Joe's fitfulness wasn't what woke Wing up this time. The shack had a plaxglass window set in its outside door. Green light poured through the window in waves, pulses of shocking illumination that fell onto the floor and Joe's form. Joe flung an arm over his eyes but did not rouse.

Groggy, Wing's mind fluttered around in English—*perilous alien world!* —and Cantonese—*demons?!*—and settled on Church Greek: *Kyrie eleison*, Lord have mercy. With that, he took a deep breath and crept to the window to look out.

The sky glared green. The light reminded him of fungi they'd seen coating a tree on the long night's walk up the mountainside. Wing felt the hair on the nape of his neck stand erect. Could it be a morbid hallucination, the first sign of the contagion the blond doctor had been watching for? But beneath sharp anxiety, Wing's mind felt ordered and logical, and he didn't think this was a hallucination. He braced his nerves, opened the door, and leaned outside.

The green light blotted out the northern half of the starry heavens. Brilliant in the center of its region, it faded to a gauzy glow toward east, west, and zenith.

Sunrise was not far off. But that light wasn't the sun, unless the world had spun madly off its axis, which seemed unlikelier than contagion in his brain. The furry pines at the rim of the mountaintop pointed toward the sky with the same erect poise as ever, needles remarkably distinct in the eerie illumination.

Noise reached Wing's ears. Unity Base was astir. The Base resounded with agitation. He waited. People emerged from the main door, a quarter of the way around the dome from where he stood. He could see their hands gesturing toward the sky.

The light slowly rippled as he watched. It began to look familiar to Wing. He began to think that he had seen pictures of such a phenomenon before.

Aurora.

It was natural light, not contagion in his own brain. Wing relaxed slightly. There was nothing wrong with him. In several more weeks, the doctor would release him from this peculiar observation situation, and he could resume doing the lesser part of that for which he had come to the stars.

His resume showed scientific credentials in botany with an emphasis on ferns with years of field work in China and Australia. The resume also listed ordination in the Reformed Evangelical Catholic—New Catholic—Church. Dr. Catharin Gault had taken the ecclesiastical part of his resume to be a sideline, and had revived him to study plants. So here he was, a botanist still, but a priest no longer, because a priest in his Church had neither ordination nor calling without a congregation. His congregation remained in stasis in the Ship. The several New Catholics in Unity Base were disinterested in practicing the faith.

He had almost, but not quite, forgiven the beautiful blonde doctor for waking him up so far out of his place.

A person approached. Wing recognized the stocky stature of Samantha Berry, the ecologist. She stopped when thirty feet of ground separated them. "Carl, what do you make it out to be?!" Samantha yelled, waving at the sky.

"An aurora," he called back.

"The hell you say!"

"It's a mighty aurora, to be visible so close to the world's equator."

"Well, hell, that explains the communications problem!"

"What problem?!"

"We can't get through to the Ship. The channels are full of static. We're on our own."

The aurora showed no sign of fading. And the Ship, source of all knowledge, could not tell them what the storm of light in the sky would do next. Or what safety precautions they should take now. As Berry turned away, Wing shivered, feeling threatened. And very alone.

His extended family was still in stasis too. His younger aunts and uncles, his cousins and nieces—two dozen descendants of the first Carlton Wing, an intrepid man who emigrated from Canton to San Francisco in the early twentieth century. His sons had prospered in San Francisco. His grandsons had been prominent people, some businessmen and others clergymen, the whole family pillars of the Chinatown Christian community. The great-grandsons and great-granddaughters had not made the decision to journey to the stars lightly—or individually, either. The Carlton Wing on Planet Green felt like a fish astray from its school, a minor flash in a wide and very dangerous sea. He wasn't one of the cohesive Vanguard—and thanks to the crash and exposure to the alien biota, he was consigned to medical observation. He was suspect.

The green aurora awoke every particle of his sense of lonely vulnerability and drove the feeling into the deepest recesses of his heart.

☽☾

Joel's first response to the Big Picture was "Lord almighty!" Fire crowned the green world—stupendous, lopsided ovals of auroral light surrounded both poles.

Bix charged into the control center right after him. Bix had dragged himself up out of sickbay at the emergency call.

"It's Blue's effect!" Lary explained excitedly. "The sun blows Blue's magnetosphere out on the side away from the solar wind. A magnetotail, that is, and it's long enough to reach Green when the orbital geometry is just right. Ions are flooding through the magnetotail into Green's magnetosphere and creating an auroral display."

"So there's a geomagnetic storm in progress," Joel said, glad to have solid technical words for it. "Which is why we can't contact the Base."

"There should be a usable wavelength somewhere. Get on it," Bix said, causing a scramble of activity at several stations. "Are the folks Downside in any danger?"

"The most pronounced auroras are in the four AM to noon section of the planet," Lary answered. "What time is it Downside? I see, it's before dawn down there. They're getting a light show, but everybody should be safe in bed. A lot of their instruments are useless right now, but they probably aren't turned on in the first place."

Bix sat down at the Command station. Bix never settled into a chair in an emergency. So he must really be feeling bad. "We're lucky it happened at night," Bix said. "If they'd had an aircraft up, it'd have mucked with the instruments."

"Lary," said Joel, "I want to ask you something. Don't take this the wrong way, like I'm jumping on you—I'm not. We've all got our hands more than full. This event is disruptive—and if they'd had planes aloft, it could have been really dangerous—but was it foreseeable?"

"Completely," Lary said. He was pinker than usual. Embarrassed. "I ought to have known this could happen and when."

"Who else should have foreseen it?" Joel asked. The control center became impressively quiet for a huge room with almost thirty people in it.

"I would have thought, um, the oversight teams—all three shifts of them—and the contingency planners, and even the Intelligence running the future planetary modeling. . . . I don't know why this fell into the cracks. Maybe because we think of Blue as a moon. Our own Moon didn't have a liquid core and magnetosphere."

Joel felt eyes boring into his back. He turned to meet Marie Mike Sisseton's somber gaze.

At least she didn't say "I told you so" out loud.

Chapter Thirteen

UNITY BASE

Gratitude, and the sheer relief of being alive, and the comfort of having his injuries tended by the doctor, had worn thin. Joe glared at the hut's inner door, the one leading to the bulk of the U-base bubble, to which this hut was attached like an excrescence. Initially he had called the makeshift quarantine facility the Outhouse. Wing had managed to substitute the word Penthouse.

For twenty of Green's long days the doctor had confined the two of them to the Penthouse as she waited for signs of infection from alien microbes: symptoms that would never materialize. The world's bland, green impression was misleading—accidents could happen!—but it was a safe enough place. Let them call it the World Wide Park, Joe thought. And let me out of here.

The other door of the Penthouse—the exit onto the outdoors of the mountaintop—opened with a brief cascade of orange sunset light and a gust of chilly air that brought Wing in with it. "I'm back!" He pushed the door shut against the wind.

Sitting cross-legged on the floor, Wing emptied his pockets of several handsful of colored pebbles. Singing to himself in Cantonese, he made neat piles of glossy pebbles—yellow, red, and other assorted colors—on the floor in front of him.

Wing was happy and busy. Joe felt a pall of corrosive boredom on his soul. They could have provided him with a telcon—a link to the Ship, to its Intelligence, and his laboratory up there. He could have worked here with a telcon. But none had been forthcoming. Catharin claimed that the Base had a limited number of those, all tied up. Joe had long since exhausted what he could do with his notebook.

Joe expected the doctor to check in on them right after sunset. A creature of habit, she arrived on time. She wore a disposable pair of gloves and a lab coat, but did not mind breathing their air: viruses that could be transmitted pneumatically had already been looked for and ruled out. Wing rolled up a sleeve for the doctor to take a blood sample.

When his turn came, Joe crossed his arms. "Still?"

"Take it easy, Joe. You earned a vacation."

"I was right. When do I get out?"

She gestured toward the outside door.

"No good."

With surprisingly strong fingers, she probed Joe's left shoulder. He grunted when she found a residue of pain deep inside. She asked, "You've crossed the stars to a strange world, then you don't care to wander around outside?"

She sounded casual. But her agenda wasn't casual at all. She sometimes probed his mind with words, in case an infection manifested itself by addling his brains. "Never been a nature lover."

"Try it sometime." To Wing, she said, "Find anything interesting today?"

Wing waved at his colorful pebbles. "Amber!"

"Isn't amber yellow?"

"On Earth, amber was the fossilized resin of coniferous trees, not always yellow," Wing explained. "These stones seem to be this world's amber, in even more colors than Earth's."

"Amber that's blue and violet and rose and green? How marvelous!" Real interest came across in her voice and expression. She had dropped the professional mask.

With reluctance Joe rolled up his sleeve for the bloodletting. "You damn well know you won't find any alien bugs. If my blood had chlorophyll instead of hemoglobin, then maybe."

"That would be an extraordinary human modification," she said pleasantly as his blood spurted into the vial. A green-eyed blonde, striking rather than pretty, she was tall and rangy and, in tan coveralls under the white coat, not quite flat-chested. She had her hair woven into braids and pinned up in a complicated, sculpted way—the professional woman's look on Earth in the late twenty-first century. And therefore, a millennium out of date. "Any pains, fever, flulike symptoms?" she asked.

"I got over stasis fever weeks ago."

"I'm aware of that. But there's a bug making the rounds."

"Bug?"

"Well, viral symptoms and epidemiology. We haven't pinned the virus down. It's mild, probably a variant of a virus we inadvertently brought with us. Your staff up on the Ship have been very helpful." With that, she slapped a small bandage on his arm.

"Damn it, I'm needed up there!"

Not his height but close to it, she stood in front of him with her hands on her hips. "Look, Joe, we're going to need you, all right. Not this minute and not for something this trivial. But fully recuperated. Which you are not."

"I'll decide when I'm ready to go back to work!"

"No. I will." She left, shutting the inner door. It locked with a snick.

Suddenly it occurred to Joe that Catharin was testing how he handled frustration. Keeping him away from a telcon to see how he reacted. And keeping him out of Unity Base to see how he held up in relative isolation. The idea infuriated him. "I'm taking a walk," he muttered. Putting on a jacket, Joe left the quarantine hut, walking away from the dome, between a purple dusk sky overhead and rough red dirt underfoot. And between two chalk lines drawn on the dirt. The lines marked out a slim wedge of the mountaintop as observation zone—off limits to everybody but Joe and Wing, while the rest of the mountaintop was off limits to the two of them. Within the lines, Joe could freely cross the dome's clearing and venture into the stand of conifers, as Wing had done today. But he could not step over the chalk lines. That would break the observation rules and give Catharin grounds to question his mental stability.

A volleyball game was in progress on the level dirt beside the dome. Since the crash and subsequent survival of Joe and Wing, the Base personnel had begun to make themselves at home outdoors—by way of team activities, exploring parties, and volleyball games. Team players. That was the Vanguard all over. Teamplay, teamtalk, teamthink.

Skewed off perfect vertical, two poles held the volleyball net against a garnet-colored sunset sky. Joe swung his arms as he walked just inside one of the chalk lines of Catharin's particular little game. She had found pain in the shoulder, but now he felt none. Wing came out into the evening too, and strolled behind him.

Joe glanced back at the domed frame of Unity Base. It exuded a yellow glow of confidence: internal lighting that showed through the thin skin. Portal doors punctuated the dome at exact intervals. Each door corresponded to a numbered and designated wedge of the dome, the nearest being Medical, Catharin's territory.

To the east, the Mountain sloped down precipitously, tumbled into lowlands of dark blue-green forest. The lowlands rolled toward a distant ocean that bowed with the horizon.

Out of the oceanic horizon rose Planet Blue. The sounds of volleyball continued, players managing to ignore the spectacle of the moon-lighted, incalescent bow of sea erupting, splitting off the equally vivid blue orb of moon. The two shapes parted, smooth and shimmering as icy blue superfluid. Joe let out the breath that he had been holding.

"'Once in a blue moon' means rarity," said Wing. "But here the moon is always blue."

"Puts me in mind of our first night down here."

"Yes. Blue was full then too."

Memory still shied away from the crash. But Joe vividly remembered the moonlit walk up the mountainside, odd plants and weird smells all in a bath of blue light the likes of which the human brain had never known in its evolutionary experience.

The yellow dome was a normal human environment, surrounded by simple dirt. But the dome amounted to one tiny blister on the skin of a strange planet, with a wilder world in the sky above. It struck Joe as absurd that Earth people should make themselves at home even here, on the tamer half of the double planet. No biological hazards, but it was a hell of a strange place. Joe picked up some stones, hurled them back into the red dirt.

"Listen!" Wing cocked his head toward the dome, from which Joe heard the muffled but unmistakable sounds of an argument with raised voices. Then came a crash and a yelp of pain.

The Medical portal flew open. A man bolted out and ran away from the dome, pounding across the open ground.

Catharin appeared in the portal. Catching sight of Joe and Wing, she yelled, "*Stop him! He's gone crazy!*"

Spring-loaded with the adrenaline of intense frustration, Joe sprinted to intercept the fugitive. The man did not see Joe in the dusk until Joe blocked his way. And then the man shied away from Joe, wild-eyed, as if the devil himself had stepped in front of him.

He was big and brawny but wide open. Joe poured all of his pent-up frustration into one blow to the jaw that spun the big man backwards. The man fell flat onto the dirt, out cold.

Joe's hand hurt, bone-bruised. But the adrenaline in his system sang victory.

"Good heavens," Wing said, bending over the unconscious man, who had close-cropped, sandy hair. "It's Fredrik Hoffmann."

Dashing up, Catharin crouched beside Hoffmann. "I didn't mean knock the daylights out of him!" she said sharply.

"So what did you mean?"

A stain that looked like wine in the twilight blotched the front of her coat. "That's blood!" Wing gasped. "Are you wounded?"

She shook her head. "It's yours and Joe's."

The volleyball game broke up and ran over, people animated by curiosity and consternation. A brown-haired young man emerged from the Med portal, carrying a stretcher. Hoffmann groaned.

"Some of you help me take him inside," Catharin said. "He's not badly hurt, but he's out of his mind."

A gasp ran through the crowd.

"And violent," added the brown-haired young man, and told Joe with frank admiration, "I'm glad you flattened him."

Joe's adrenaline hummed satisfaction.

Somebody asked. "Is it the new fever?"

Tight-lipped, Catharin shook her head. "No—Fredrik's got a problem of his own."

Hoffmann was rolled onto the stretcher. Two of the heftier volleyball players started toward the dome with the unconscious load. A breeze stirred across the mountaintop like a cold blue draft of misgiving. Catharin said, "Joe, I must ask you to cut your recuperation short. I need your help on this."

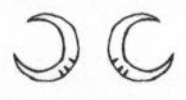

A ramp circled up to the apex of the dome, the conference room. Ironically aware that he had finally reached the destination of his flight down from the Ship, Joe noted the room's large oval table with a dozen chairs and half a dozen seated people. A telecommunications console—a compact one, only two feet across, with four windows smaller than dinner plates—sat on the table. Above the table, a skylight showed an octagon of purple sky, with a cirrus cloud like the tail of an ice blue mare.

The chief expedition scientist gravely shook Joe's hand. A bony, middle-aged man named Aaron Manhattan, his long face was crowned with dark hair going gray. Catharin showed Joe to a chair and selected one for herself, not adjacent to Joe's. The Captain attended in a telcon window, his image transmitted from the Ship. One final arrival took the form of a disembodied voice from the telcon. The voice belonged to Samantha Berry, the leader of a survey team out exploring the wilderness. The team had a two-way communicator, but its visual channels were tied up with images of native plants and visualizations of cellular analysis.

"I hear somebody cracked up!" the transmitted voice of Samantha Berry blared.

Manhattan adjusted the volume down. "What happened?" he asked Catharin.

The Captain said, "This is going in the official log."

Catharin nodded. "Fredrik Hoffmann was in the infirmary to have his temperature taken. I had just returned from the Pent—the observation facility—with blood samples from Carlton Wing and Joe Toronto, which I had placed in a rack on the infirmary counter. Out of the blue, Fredrik accused me of planning to infect him with a virus from outside—of intending to inject Joe's blood or Wing's into him to make him sick."

Manhattan's jaw dropped.

"Fredrik became very belligerent." Catharin's lips twisted in distaste—a crack in her cool mask of professionalism. "He snatched the blood sample vials from the counter, unstoppered them, and threw the blood at me. Eddy tried to intervene, but he shoved Eddy into a supply cabinet. Then he ran outside. Fortunately, Joe Toronto was able to stop him."

The woman to Joe's left, a small redhead, had crossed her arms as Catharin spoke, scowling. She said to Joe, "Thanks. He deserved it."

The preexisting worry lines in Manhattan's face deepened. "Hoffmann's actions and his accusations make no sense."

"Not a lick," commented Berry's voice. "Has a nasty ring to it, though."

"You mean the blood?"

"From two birds in quarantine. What if they had an evil virus in their blood?"

"They don't. They aren't sick," Manhattan protested.

"That's true," said Catharin. "But Samantha's right. That was a gesture with very negative symbolism. On the part of a sick man," she added, voice level, face pale.

"Sick how?" asked the little redhead next to Joe. "Better unpack it." Joe placed her voice, from his hours of listening to the Base communications while he convalesced in the Penthouse: she was Fisher, the pilot of the plane that had been mapping the land around Unity Base. She'd seemed talkative but interesting.

Catharin said, "Fredrik Hoffmann is hypochondriac, to start with. He's demanded that we check him for fever or infection almost every day for a week, when in fact he's not had a trace of either. Others did. We have a mild flulike sickness going around. But Hoffmann has yet to come down with it."

In the video window of the telcon, the Captain looked gravely attentive.

"We came as clean as possible, but some everyday viruses stowed away with us. They mutate readily, and this one seems to be the result of such a random change. We can deal with it. As I said, it's no worse than flu."

"Where does the mental breakdown fit in?" asked the Captain.

"There are two separate problems," Catharin countered. "The viral illness that's going around, and a problem peculiar to Fredrik. He passed the psychological screening tests to come in the Ship. Still, apparently mentally healthy people can break down."

Fisher said, "He's been hypochondriac to the point of paranoid. He vehemently objected to sending out a search party to look for you after the crash. He was full of scare talk—insisted that even if we found you," she informed Joe, "it would be too dangerous to bring you back to the dome. Alive or not, you might be infected with something and infect the whole expedition team, and we would all die a horrible death."

Joe rubbed his bruised hand with satisfaction. He had owed Hoffmann that knockout punch.

Catharin said, "He has a private psychiatric problem. There's been no mental disturbance on the part of anybody else."

Berry's voice crackled in again. "How about gross negligence? Happened earlier today. Haven't even told Manhattan about it. One of my team members out here wandered away."

"Wandered away?" Manhattan repeated.

"Over hill and dale, ridge and vale. Misplaced his two-way, so we couldn't use it to pinpoint his location. We lost half a day searching, and I gained gray hairs, I tell you."

"Weird," Fisher commented to Joe.

"Then there was the shuttle pilot." Manhattan frowned.

Maybe the shuttle pilot had been grossly negligent. Or suddenly slightly crazy. No one would know now. Joe remembered the sickening tilt of the shuttle plane, the crunch of metal and the crack of his bone. He shuddered. Fisher picked up on it and murmured, "Crashes take a while to get over even if you walk away."

The Captain said, "We haven't had any bad accidents or disturbing incidents on the Ship."

"Up there, nobody's ass is hanging out over strange terrain," Berry pointed out.

Evidently not offended, the Captain nodded. Under his visage the telcon clock read 1400 PM in angular red digits. 1400 PM? That made no sense, Joe thought. With a twenty-four-hour clock you don't need AM and PM. The Captain said, "I don't like the timing of all this. It's inside the quarantine period. Granted, neither virus nor mental imbalance cropped up where you expected—in the people who got dragged through the ecosystem. Still, I'm extending the quarantine indefinitely pending complete understanding of what's happened."

A middle-aged man at Manhattan's right spoke up. Joe knew that one's voice too: he was Wimm Tucker, the Base quartermaster, cook, and resident chess master. "We need supplies. All the greenhouse has produced is a few pecks of tomatoes and eggplants, and I've got twenty-one mouths to feed."

"Transmit a grocery list. We'll drop 'em to you from the Ship," the Captain assured him. "Aaron, you better bring in the survey team, at least until you know where your problems are coming from. Loss of signal coming. Captain out."

"Damn it all!" Berry exploded.

"He's right, Sam," Manhattan said. "I'll send the copter out for you first thing in the Green-morning."

Fisher asked, "Should I curtail my mapping flights, too?"

Manhattan handed the question off to Catharin.

"I don't think that's necessary," said Catharin. "But watch yourself, Becca." Catharin's professional mask was down. With warm concern, she told the other woman, "Disorientation, insomnia—be alert for *any* anomaly in yourself."

Fisher nodded. "Will do."

☽ ☾

The Medical section of Unity Base was a far cry from a world-class research laboratory—Joe's natural habitat on Earth and approximately what he had worked with up in the Ship. This place looked exactly like what it was—an abbreviated combination of infirmary and field laboratory.

Catharin replied to his tacit dismay. "Quarantine is making my work harder. The hospital's up there not here, and so is my research staff. To say nothing of yours."

"Telcons?"

"We have exactly one in here. You and I will have to share it. And there's loss of signal half the time, when the Ship's on the other side of its orbit. A communications satellite is scheduled to be deployed to remedy that."

The brown-haired young man who had brought the stretcher out for Hoffmann approached them. "Doctor, I disinfected the floor and your coat. Shall I make coffee?"

"Please. Joe, this is Eddy Pazmino, my nurse, lab tech, and office assistant all in one."

"You're the guy who got shoved into a cabinet?" Joe asked.

Eddy grinned. "I'm sure my backside hurts less than Fred's jaw."

Catharin handed a flash wand to Joe. "Here are the results of the fever study so far. See what you think."

Joe put the wand in his notebook's data port and scanned it. Offhand he would not have known a respiratory virus from tobacco mosaic. His specialty was retroviruses. But back in graduate school he'd chosen Epstein-Barr virus for a topic outside his own area for his qualifying exam, and recalled several single-base mutations involved in its virulence. "It's a variant of Epstein-Barr, less virulent than the original."

She gave him a surprised look. "That's what one of the researchers on the Ship thought. After studying it for hours."

"So name it after him. It's a nice little bug, nothing evil. Which is what you tried to tell the Captain. You didn't try too hard, though."

"The identification isn't conclusive."

"Hell, it's close enough."

"We need ironclad conclusions. Because when the Colonial Government is revived, they're going to second-guess our every move and look for someone to blame for everything that's gone wrong. Which is a lot." She frowned at that thought. "Write out your assessment of the virus and put some polish on it while the researchers Upside figure out the antiviral therapy. Then add your signature, and that should do it."

"That'll take tonight. So what do I do tomorrow?"

"I don't know," she said crossly. "You may be revving to go, but I've got to write up a report about today's incident."

"That's your problem. I can't do it for you," he pointed out.

Catharin regarded him with narrowed eyes. "You could take your plane ride."

"Huh?"

"That was originally planned. An aerial, VIP-tour survey with Becca Fisher in the mapping plane. Remember?"

Joe also remembered mentioning to the doctor that he'd had recurrent nightmares about the shuttleplane crash.

"She's a good pilot." Catharin sounded graciously encouraging, which had a highly irritating effect on Joe. "*She* won't crash through carelessness. And going up in the air again—or more to the point, coming down without incident—might do you good."

Joe was very unwilling to commit himself to another aircraft. And angry that the doctor had figured that out.

Eddy brought coffee in plain, white, expedition-issue cups. He was on the slender side, with a silky mane of brown hair that curled over the white collar of his lab coat, and a certain grace of movement, and he watched Joe with discreet interest. Joe recognized the pattern. "I think I know why it occurred to Hoffmann to throw blood. He had AIDS in mind, eh?"

"That was ancient history," Eddy objected.

"But memorable."

"You're right," said Catharin. "I'll add that. In addition to hypochondria, possible homophobia. Eddy, would you record your side of the incident? For the official log, so watch your words. What a warped bastard. That's unofficial." Coffee cup in hand, she went over to the telcon. "Joe, let me show you how to ring up the Ship." But instead of his lab up there, she addressed the control center.

"Hi, Cat!" said the man who answered. Joe recognized the Ship's pilot, Atlanta.

"Hi, Joel. How soon can you get that relay satellite deployed? I need it more than ever."

"Within the week."

"That's lovely." The mask was down again. Catharin clearly liked Joel Atlanta. Today Joe had seen her drop the mask for Wing, Fisher, Eddy, and Atlanta. She seemed to wear the mask just for Joe Toronto.

She transferred the link to the Ship's research center. "All yours. By the way," said Catharin, "do you still have any nightmares, anxieties, other disturbances?"

"No. Go diagnose somebody else," he said. "I'm no more vulnerable than the rest of 'em."

"And no less," she said.

Within an hour, Joe discovered that the telcon had only a rudimentary handwriting recognition function. The primary mode of data entry was a keyboard. He only had a vague idea of how to use it. "This technology was outdated a hundred years ago!"

"No, it was never totally superseded in the medical field, where the need for unambiguous data entry has always been paramount." Her fingers flew across the keyboard, demonstrating her expertise.

Joe felt one-upped, cut off from a machine he needed for his work and his happiness, and furious. But he didn't dare explode. Not to the doctor watching him for mental symptoms. "Voice recognition?" he asked gruffly.

"It does have that," she said, and activated it.

☽☾

The mess hall was a wedge of the dome, kitchen at the small end, tables at the large end, resounding with clatter proportional to the dozen or so people eating supper at present. They were a mixture of races and sorts, but uniformly healthy and energetic. And egalitarian, with duty insignia adorning the coverall sleeves, but no badges of rank.

One stood out in the crowd: a dark-skinned brunette who looked like a Euro–North Indian urban racial blend. She made a point of being introduced to Joe, following that up with the necessary maneuvers to gain a one-on-one conversation with him. Her name was Maya London. She was Manhattan's administrative assistant.

Maya was interested in Joe and less discreet about it than Eddy. She assumed that he was heterosexual and that she was the most beautiful woman in the hall. Both assumptions were reasonably accurate. Joe appreciated the dramatic curves of her body while answering her questions about his work. He registered the mesmerizing quality of her jade green eyes shuttered by dark lashes. There was one final assumption on her part, not intended to show, but it did: that she could have him if she tried hard enough. Maybe, Joe thought, but not tonight, because he wanted to use the telcon.

Joe gave Maya enough attention to indicate that he had nibbled the bait.

With a concluding pleasantry, she went away—like an angler careful not to frighten the fish, not let it know the bait had a hook embedded in it.

☽☾

The bulletin board in Medical bore numerous notices for meetings. There seemed to be some kind of meeting for some subset of the Base population scheduled for almost every hour of the day. Teamwork, teamthink, Joe thought.

More informative was the chart that correlated clock time with local sun time. Green's solar day was about fifty-two hours long: two terrestrial days plus a bit. Somebody had concocted a hybrid clock system, twenty-six hours plus AM and PM. Divide the hours after 1200 by two and note the AM or PM distinction to translate back to Earthlike times of day, the chart suggested. So the 1400 PM that Joe had seen earlier on the telcon was 7 PM—about right for the onset of midsummer, midlatitude twilight.

Reveling in the use of the telcon, Joe worked while the digits of the clock at the bottom of the screen flicked in the direction of midnight, 0000 AM. Suddenly Eddy rocketed in. "Where's the doctor?!"

"In her office."

Eddy raced out. Joe heard Eddy pounding on Catharin's office door down the hall. Joe caught the words, "Suicide attempt!" The doctor and her nurse left Medical in a hurry.

Joe signed off the telcon when people poured into Medical carrying in the victim, a small blonde woman with bloody wrists. Wing ushered a brown-skinned, Afro-Asian woman who seemed particularly agitated. Eddy informed Joe in passing, "They have a two-person bunk room, and it was her roommate who found her bleeding."

It took nearly an hour to settle things. Catharin bandaged and sedated the victim, settling her into the infirmary. Manhattan showed up for a while to look appropriately grave. Wing eased the shaken roommate out of Medical. Eddy cleaned up the floor. When calm finally prevailed, and only Joe was standing nearby, Catharin leaned against the wall, looking drained. "My God, what am I up against?"

"Think of it as job security," said Joe offhandedly.

She grabbed his sleeve and towed him around the corner into the privacy of the lab. Fiercely, she said, "You do not understand the situation. The stasis changed some viruses and microorganisms that came with us. We could experience virulence that's never been seen before, upon exposure to triggers that we can't predict!"

"You underestimate me, Doctor," said Joe, intrigued by her ferocity and intelligence. He removed her fingers from his sleeve and pushed her hand back against her ribs. "I do understand the situation. The genetic material in stowaway viruses was changed by the combination of radiation and dark reactions in the presence of stasis chemicals. Show me the gene map of the expected viruses and I can predict mutations and virulence."

Her eyes widened. "So easily?"

"Ease is relative. Viruses are simple. The human genome isn't. What I can't predict is how stasis changed *us*."

She winced as though he had hit a sore nerve. "That's what I'm afraid of. Aren't you?"

"Afraid of mutations in the human genome? Sure. Genetic change usually means death or ill-fitness in an organism. But there's a chance of something better. Transformation. Something new."

She was shaking her head. "Joe, the thought of something alien in our genes keeps me awake at night."

"It's not alien." Surprised that he felt inclined to explain the foundation of his scientific life to a woman he hardly knew and didn't like, he went on, "The terrestrial genome simmers with latent change. It always has. If the change confers any advantage that lasts until reproductive maturity, the genes will perpetuate themselves.

"Genes are still selfish. The genome is more like itself than ever. That's what the new virus has to teach us," he said emphatically, feeling the stirring of his oldest and surest, but long dormant, sense of wonder. "The genome still has imagination."

Chapter Fourteen

RAINING BLUE

Catharin had to get away from Joe Toronto, but retreating into her bunk room didn't work. Her thoughts bounced off the bare walls in distracting Brownian motion. Finally she resorted to the observation deck. Glad to find the deck deserted, she sat down beside the conference room's outer wall, huddled against the chill of the long summer night.

Today had made her feel as though she lived in a shaky house of cards that had fallen apart, knocked down by Fredrik Hoffmann. His illness troubled her. The man himself she hated, and found it cold comfort that the feeling was more than mutual. Then there was poor Sheryn: unhappy enough to make a bloody, botched attempt at suicide. Had Sheryn been the vulnerable flash point for the stresses that afflicted all of them? Catharin now had two unexpected new patients, while Joe Toronto wasn't just a patient anymore. He was loose, willful, and every bit as perversely attractive as in the interview light-years ago.

In her fallen house of cards, what kind of scattered card was Joe? Wild card or, as she had long hoped, her ace in the hole, her best chance for saving the bad genetic situation?

Pushed by the wind, clouds streamed across the night sky. The hurricane moon shone through thin spots in the cloud cover with a blue glare. The blue-tinged clouds changed shape as she watched, fluid as troubled water, chaotic.

Everything that had happened since *Aeon* left Earth bore the mark of chaos: disasters and opportunities that the exhaustive, all-encompassing training before the star flight had never anticipated. Vandal stars and double planet, illness and genetic damage. Now Hoffmann going berserk and Sheryn attempting suicide.

Joe had blithely informed her that the genome—the *human* genome—was shot through with chaos. Chaos reigns. And when it rains it pours. A shower spilled out of the clouds, brief rain splashing on the deck just beyond the sheltering overhang of the dome's roof. The radiance from the hurricane moon tinted the rain blue.

Catharin found herself feeling something she couldn't account for: *unfairness*. Joe had kick-started it, but not by doing anything unfair. So far, he was better behaved as a researcher than he had been as a patient. It was his commentary about the genome that obscurely outraged her.

The blue rain peppered the deck, making a scant sound in the overwhelming silence of the mountaintop. Once, in Earth's Africa, Catharin had listened to a jungle from the safety of the veranda of a guest lodge. There she'd heard mating frogs, a scavenger's howl, the shriek of a dying prey animal. This place was more silent than it was at peace. It knew no animal lust or violence. "Nature red in tooth and claw" did not apply here.

But genes were still savagely indifferent to human welfare. There lay the unfairness, Catharin thought with sudden harsh clarity. It was vastly unfair, a cosmic joke in wretched taste. After millennia of disease-ridden history, humanity had forged real understanding of the genetic and microbiological roots of illness. Medicine had attained a panoply of cures and preventions, even reining in the chaos of the genome and the selfishness of the genes.

And stasis pervasively hurt the human body at the molecular level. Stasis had disrupted humanity at the level of genes. It was as if *Aeon* had hurtled *back* in time to when illness was more universal and omnipotent.

The rain paled, became as colorless as ordinary water. Then it stopped. The clouds had lost their blue tinges, so thoroughly did they obscure the moon. Or else Blue's light had all rained down onto the face of Green. . . . Catharin entertained that speculation, with mild amusement, for just a moment too long. The irrational idea morphed into terror that Blue had turned into rain. She fled from the deck.

Bursting into Becca's office in the hangar behind Unity Base, Catharin smelled the aroma of Earl Grey tea. Becca looked up from a stack of small parts with a smile. "After the tough day you've had, I thought you might drop in. I made your favorite tea for you."

Catharin felt cold—unaccountably so from only a half hour's exposure to a mild night. Shivering, she explained Joe's view of the genome. Then she described the blue rain. "It spooked me. I don't know why. I'm not losing my mind too, am I?" She gulped the hot, fragrant tea.

Nothing ever left Becca at a loss for words or wits, not even this. "Have you ever heard of that ancient—really ancient, it was made before computer graphics—vid called *The Ten Commandments*? There's a part where the last of the twelve plagues, the angel of death, visits the land of Egypt. And there's no wings, no sword, no sickle—at the time, they couldn't do convincing special effects for something like that. So there's just a dark cloud in the sky. This cloud drifts down onto the land, into the city, and creeps through the streets as fog, and the firstborn children die. It's a scary scene."

Catharin slowly nodded. "That is what I fear the most. Plagues and death with no effective medical defenses, and genetic disorders killing our firstborn children. I don't think I can stand to think about it anymore."

"So how do you like working with Joe?" Becca asked.

"In a word, I don't. He's brilliant, egotistical, and cavalier." Catharin added ruefully, "But fascinating. If I'd met him on Earth, say, at a conference, I'd have considered skipping out so we could get to know each other socially."

"Would he play hooky? Or be too absorbed in the conference?" Becca asked. "For some scientists, personal relationships are strictly sideline stuff."

Catharin felt a welter of intuition crystallize into a startlingly certain answer. "I could convince him to play hooky."

Catharin was feeling better when they left the hangar together to return to the dome. The concrete apron around the hangar shone damp. The blue moon floated above the furry-pine fringe of the mountaintop. "It's still blue," Catharin said wryly. "I guess it really was my imagination, not the moon's blue raining down on us, and not a screw loose in my mind."

Becca chuckled. "Of course not. You're no lunatic."

Catharin mentally stumbled over the word Becca had used, deeply startled by it. "I just finally added two and two. Blue was full the night the shuttle crashed, and it's full again. And the word 'lunacy' meant the dire effect of Earth's Moon—"

The giant blue moon's light washed over them both, shining in Becca's widened eyes. "You think it might affect our minds? Let's get inside!" She led a dash to the nearest Base door and slammed it behind them, sealing out the moonlight. "I don't know if you're right, but I could believe it."

Catharin's heart pounded in fright. She felt safer in here than out in the open. But not much safer. "Months ago, I helped Lary justify doing research on Blue by emphasizing that Blue would affect people. But I hadn't connected that to the experience of being here. I've been too fixated on immediate medical problems."

Becca said emphatically, "Getting scared about it raining Blue was your unconscious saying you should recognize the danger right away, before anything else goes wrong."

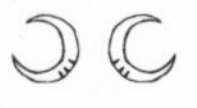

A thundering, mechanical noise jarred Joe awake.

For a disoriented few moments Joe stared at the ceiling of the Penthouse that slanted down toward his toes. Then he identified the racket as the helicopter circling Unity Base.

Wing sat up in his own bunk, looking rumpled but thrilled. "Since we're out of observation confinement, we can go meet the copter!"

Yawning, Joe followed Wing around the outside of the dome. The sun glanced across the world from behind the uplands east of Unity Base. A chill hung in the air after the long night.

The angular hangar flanked a concrete landing pad, where a gaggle of people watched the helicopter's final approach from the east. Long-bodied, robust, and military looking, the Starhawk slanted down toward its landing pad. The engines cut off, followed by the normal silence of Green, which sounded deafening in contrast to the machine.

Becca Fisher dashed up to the helicopter to greet the pilot as he emerged from the cockpit. The main cabin door opened, a ramp flopped down to the ground, and a short, plump, gray-headed woman marched out. "Well, here we are, damn it all!" she announced. So that was the redoubtable Samantha Berry, Joe thought. Berry was followed by her team: two women and three men with arms full of gear. Joe wondered which of the men had gone astray yesterday.

Fisher appeared at Joe's elbow. "Ready for your ride?"

Behind her, Joe could see a slender, long-winged aircraft parked inside the hangar. "No."

"You might want to think about it. You've got to get back upstairs one day." Becca Fisher pointed at the sky.

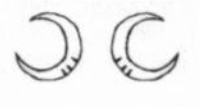

Joe handed the formal report on the new fever to Catharin. "You weren't kidding when you said tomorrow," was Catharin's response. Then she put the flash wand away. They sat in her small, sparse office, cups of expedition coffee in front of them.

Joe suddenly missed the taste and the quality of Kauai Blue Mountain coffee. Which was as gone as everything else on Earth.

"You can now forget about the flu," Catharin said. "And work on something more important. Broken molecules." She took another sip of her coffee. "Stasis weakened and broke protein molecules. I'm sure you understand why the stasis fever occurred later."

"Our immune systems got busy cleaning up the broken pieces."

"Right. They needed help, though, and got it."

"I remember being sauced with medicines after stasis."

She frowned. "You shouldn't be able to recall that. People are in the twilight phase, still deeply unconscious, during revival therapy."

But he did remember his body manipulated, sampled, and injected by machines. He had been utterly helpless to protest or move. All he could do was be mutely aware that change was being imposed on him without regard for his will, and he had hated it.

Something brushed Joe's leg, breaking his black reverie. To his surprise, he found a small calico cat twining around his ankles. It meowed up at him.

"You were treated with artificial clean-up enzymes and catalytic antibodies. Nunki!" She snapped her fingers. The cat leaped into her lap.

"Did it include skin rejuvenation therapy?"

"Yes. Without it we'd have woken up looking old."

Joe remembered his first morning after stasis. He'd looked at himself in the restroom mirror with trepidation. To his relief, his hair was still black, eyes clear, skin unravaged. At that moment, he had thought about women, lovers, with a cold shock, as he realized that all of the lovers he had ever known were dust now, scattered atoms on a distant Earth. Then, alone in the first hour of that first gray morning, he had cried.

"Besides collagen, the revival therapy cleaned up fragments of insulin and other vital proteins like hemoglobin." Catharin rattled on about the molecular specifics of the therapy.

Finally he interrupted. "No stone left unturned."

"We were prepared to clean up the organism at the molecular level, and tide it over until new intact molecules of these vital proteins could be manufactured in the cells. But we got heavy breakages where we weren't expecting it—weren't ready for it." She hugged the cat.

"Isn't it unsanitary to let that cat in Medical?"

"She isn't allowed in the infirmary or the lab, just the offices." In other words, the doctor made a loophole in the rules because she liked cats. "We need you to design additional clean-up molecules."

"I don't make molecules," he said. "I make life-forms."

"You should be bright enough to catch onto molecules, if you feel as well as you claim," she retorted.

"I feel fine. Give me a challenge."

"Catalytic antibodies for the damaged proteins of the muscles. Actin and myocin, the muscle globins. People are suffering from muscular pain and wasting. Study up on it. Make some catalytic antibodies and make them work," she said with finality. "That will demonstrate how fit you are, or are not."

Joe hadn't studied stasis since early in graduate school, hadn't worked on catalytic antibodies at all. But he had help in a big way.

For two decades of professional life, he had enjoyed, and taken for granted, unlimited access to electronically libraried information and human technical assistance, as well as supercomputing and artificial and virtual intelligence. The Ship had all of the above. Moreover, it was all startlingly responsive to his slightest analytic whim, like a tremendous genie hovering over his shoulder. Any factual observation or question on his part provoked a torrent of informed responses, relevant statistics, opinions from various specialists. The whole Ship, with its computing power, researchers, and all, was focused on the expedition Downside. It was the old Mission Control model of doing space business. It soon unnerved Joe. Earth's Net had been many orders of magnitude more complicated and rewarding, but the Net had been like an ocean Joe could jump into or step out of at his whim. The ship-genie in the sky tended to interrupt what he was doing.

The telcon said 2000 AM. Dividing by two put it at 10 AM—and except for the fact that he had been working for six solid hours, the day really did look like midmorning, with fresh sunlight filtering in through the translucent material of the dome overhead. Seized by restlessness, Joe dismissed the genie in the sky and left the dome.

Once outdoors, he realized how unquiet the Medical section had been. Machines continuously whispered and whirred, and Catharin or Eddy talked and handled laboratory instruments. Out here, there were no sounds. Not the commotion of a city, not the bird and bug noises of a park. Clouds dotted the eastern half of the sky. The cloudlets drifted westward, pushed by winds at a high altitude.

Then Joe heard a faint clamor. The knotted thread of sound led him toward the aircraft hangar. The hangar's roof doubled as the Base solar energy collector, with panes turned toward the ascendant sun. The hangar doors stood open, pushed to either side on their tracks.

Recorded music with a rapid percussive beat echoed off the hangar walls. The helicopter hunkered in one of two large bays, with the cowlings peeled off the engine under one rotor and the copter pilot balanced on a ladder as he operated on the engine. His tools made thunking and clinking noises. In the back of the hangar, a bright welding flare hissed, wielded by somebody in dark coveralls and a face mask that reflected the flame's glare.

The welder did not look up from his work, but the pilot noticed Joe, came down the ladder in one limber motion, and walked over to him. A compact man with brown hair and blue eyes, the copter pilot wiped his hand with a clean rag before extending it to Joe. "Domino Cady," he said.

"Joe Toronto." The surname still seemed strange to Joe, but at least he no longer caught himself halfway through "Devreze."

"*Bon jour, mon cousin!* I'm from Acadia, in Louisiana, where the French who were thrown out of Canada ended up." Cady had the regional accent, a slight lilt to his words. Plus an engaging smile and a casual, cocky manner.

Women would like Cady, Joe thought, with a flicker of competitive interest. "Cajun, eh? Any alligators in your personal effects?"

Cady laughed. "I didn't bring reptiles from home with me, just some spices and music. I ought to warn you, people who wander in here get an earful of Zydeco music and put to work on the copter."

Becca Fisher popped out of the helicopter's cockpit. "Worse than that, you might get taken up into the air. Not today. The weather's turning bad. But soon, right?" Grinning, she brandished a tool at Joe.

"It's nearly 2200 AM," Catharin said. "Why don't you quit for the day?"

"Don't feel like it."

The doctor sat down with a sigh. "I knew this would happen if I let you out. Don't you have anything between zero and full throttle?"

She'd been up and about since before he was. "Don't you?"

"I'm fit. You're not. Studying stasis therapy?" Over his shoulder, she looked at the screen. "You're a quick study, all right. But now's a good time to take a break."

"Why?"

The screen told him. It went blank. The Ship had gone behind the planet, and with that the telcon link was severed. "That's the third time today," Joe growled.

"Withdrawal failed to break the addiction?" she asked dryly.

"Here, the telcon's the lifeline of what's left of civilization."

"I thought you didn't approve of civilization." The corners of her lips quirked.

"Touché," said Joe.

At that point Eddy brought in a tray laden with cups and pale yellow cookies.

Catharin smiled at Eddy. "I thought we'd run out of cookies since the quarantine."

"The Ship dropped supplies. Including cookies. With the quartermaster's compliments," said Eddy.

Joe took a bite of cookie. Synthetic, from the Ship's food factories, approximate chocolate and nut. "Plants everywhere and you can't eat any of 'em," he said. "It'd be rough to get stuck down here without the Ship to drop supplies."

"It would be fatal," said Catharin. She asked Eddy, "How is the mood running today?"

"People have decided that Fredrik was cracked all along, and not a nice man, either. But three problems all in one day are too many to brush off, even if some of them happen to people who aren't well liked," Eddy said seriously. "People are nervous that it's catching."

"No," said Catharin. "Environmental agent."

"Such as?" said Joe. "My committee's report covered that ground. Not only are there no microbes that might get us, there's damn little in the way of chemicals, radioactivity, heavy metals."

"You missed one. It's the moon," said Catharin.

Eddy gave her a surprised look. She said, "On Earth, the moon had definite tidal effects, and was blamed for psychological ones. That's how we got the words 'lunatic' and 'moonstruck.'"

"Oh!"

"That's superstitious bilge," said Joe.

Catharin countered, "Emergency rooms beefed up their staff for the full moon even in the twenty-first century."

"And that's anecdotal. Let's talk science, shall we?"

"Sure. Blue's mass far exceeds that of Luna while the distance between Green and Blue is almost the same as that between Earth and Luna. Blue pulls the sea and other bodies of water. Our brains are bags of liquid, you know."

"A few ounces of water doesn't have tides. It takes a hell of a mass of water to register tidal effects. The moon raised the level of Lake Superior a whole three inches at high tide."

"Unlike Luna, Blue has a magnetosphere." She had her arms crossed. "Green actually runs through it sometimes. Thus the auroral display."

"Charged particles are funneled to the poles. They don't rain down on us here. No, if we've got psychological problems, they'll be in the nature of molecular psychology, and fixable, unlike the moon."

He had taken pains to trample her turf, and she was clearly vexed. "I didn't say the moon was an unfixable problem," she snapped. "It's there. We can cope with its effects."

"Which are negligible if they exist at all."

"That wasn't what you said about your walk up the Mountain. You reported major perceptual disorientation."

"I was sick. Sick people imagine things."

"Too true, and if I were you I'd rather it be the moon than stasis after-effects causing my mind to slip gears," she said curtly.

Joe bristled. "I thought you had stasis effects figured out. Not sure?"

"Its effects on the human body, yes, I can tell you that, in excruciating detail." She sounded cold. "Its consequences for the brain—that I do not know. Human beings have big, complicated brains that have been wavering on the brink of instability since Cro-Magnon times. The bigger, the brighter, the more complex, the more unstable. I advise you not to forget that."

Eddy seemed to be finding the exchange entertaining. Joe belatedly realized that he was not up to a prolonged fight. He felt tired, with a burning knot of pain in his neck. "When do we get the Ship back?" he asked, putting down his cup.

"Not for another two hours."

"I need a break."

☽☾

Joe retreated to the Penthouse, where Wing was relaxing on his cot. "That woman is an icicle," Joe announced. "Long, thin, and cold."

Wing chuckled. "If you want a warm reception, cultivate your acquaintance with Maya. She polished her wiles for a week before your arrival."

"Trophy hunter?"

"All the way."

Joe gritted his teeth. He wasn't anyone's trophy. "She's not my favorite woman around here."

"Ah. Who is?"

"Fisher. She's no beauty, but she's worth talking to."

"You might look more closely at her. She's made like porcelain. Fine and strong, like bone china that takes a great burden without cracking, a blow without breaking," Wing said.

Joe had to smile. "She's your favorite too?"

"Yes, but today, I am in love with Samantha Berry."

"The old warhorse? Why?"

"Sam feels inclined to let me join the survey team. I'm not really qualified, according to the high standards for that group, but Sam told Manhattan, 'I want somebody with less credentials and more common sense!'"

Joe remembered the walk up the Mountain. Wing had sense, all right, and didn't lose it in a strange natural environment. Joe nodded.

Joe's cot looked more inviting than it had for days. He really was tired, more so than he should have been after an easy day with a long night's sleep before that. While confined to the Penthouse, he and Wing had fallen into ragged sleeping patterns, sleeping a lot through the planet's twenty-six-hour night, relatively little through the equally long day. So he'd gotten plenty of rest. But he still felt achy. And pain deep in his shoulder reached all the way to his neck.

A strangely familiar sound impinged on Joe's awareness. Wing hopped up and opened the door. Outside it was raining. A gust of cold damp air brought in with it the smell of rain-damp dirt. Wing watched it rain for a while. "My grandmother said it's good luck if it rains when your life is changing. Maybe I'll get onto the team. I want to see more of this world for myself."

To Joe, looking past Wing, the ground looked bloody where the rain spattered it.

☽☾

The rain kept up, cold and heavy, turned the ground into red streams. Joe's nap turned into sleep—the night's sleep after the day's work, but this was Green with its long days, so it was light outside. When Joe got up, it felt like rising from a stultifying afternoon nap.

Catharin had set up a virtual lab notebook for their joint use. In it, he began to sketch novel molecules, seeking an antibody to bind with the wreckage of muscle myocin.

Joe stopped to rub the unwelcome stiffness in his neck. The more he thought about his discomfort, the odder it seemed—not just a pain, but a sense of localized fever running from his hurt shoulder up into his neck. Like a spreading fever sending tendrils up toward his brain. Joe felt a chill of alarm. He should ask Catharin about this.

But maybe he was hypochondriac. Like Hoffmann. And Hoffmann was not what Joe wanted to be like. Joe gritted his teeth. He wouldn't mention phantom pains after all.

But he could almost feel the tendrils of pain exploring for a way into his skull. Joe looked for and located a link to Catharin's medical records in the virtual lab notebook. The security was more elaborate than Joe would have expected in a lab populated by few and honest researchers—but it was nothing he couldn't outwit.

Entering Catharin's medical records database, Joe found the records that pertained to him. He took a morbid interest in the details of cracked bone, various contusions and abrasions that Catharin had found on his body. Then there were speculations about his psychological state: *The patient is uncooperative and irritable.* A not-so-clinical note: *He was like this during his assessment interview. Arrogance and irritability, however uncalled-for, are normal for him.* Joe stared at the words. As a matter of fact, he was feeling irritable right now.

Something rubbed against his ankles. Startled, he realized that the little cat had gotten into the lab. He reached down to offer it his fingertips to sniff. "You aren't supposed to be in here, you know." He patted the cat's back, prompting an audible purr. Joe invitingly scratched the fabric of his pants over his knee. The cat jumped into his lap.

Joe backed out of Catharin's records, using one hand to key in commands while he petted her cat with the other. Emitting a loud purr, the creature quivered with pleasure. It was a nice little cat, natural-acting, blithely unaware of its long journey in the form of a clump of eight cells vitrified and frozen. "Do you know your mama is a self-righteous witch?" he murmured.

Nunki kneaded her claws. Joe picked the cat up, detaching her claws from his clothes. He held her up to his face, putting the soft fur and purr against his cheek.

Then Joe noticed Catharin, in the doorway, silently watching him. She wasn't wearing the Mask—but her unguarded expression was hard to figure out, a downward curve of the edges of her mouth, maybe annoyance that he was making friends with her cat. "What do you want?"

"The telcon," she said. Joe reluctantly stood up, placing the cat in the chair. "*Nunki.*" Catharin pointed a finger at its nose. "You know you're not supposed to be in here." The cat skittered out.

Catharin and Eddy had apparently gotten some blood out of Hoffmann, against his objections. "We needed the help of several of the men in the Base," she explained with grim distaste. She wanted to transmit blood analysis data to the Ship.

Her plan was foiled by a telcon blackout. She had run just a little too late. She shook her head with a tight frown.

"What about the satellite?" Joe asked.

"Ejected today. It'll be positioned by tomorrow."

He didn't bother to ask if she meant tomorrow sun, or tomorrow by the clock. "Must be nice to have friends in high places."

She resorted to the lab's blood analysis program. Joe watched. He idly tried to calibrate her age, comparing her to researchers he'd known. He decided that she was closer to thirty than forty, younger than he'd thought: uncharacteristically unobservant of him to take so long figuring it out. "You must have been pretty young when you made the astronaut corps."

"Twenty-nine."

"That and what, PhD plus MD? Hyperachiever?"

"That could be said of most of us," she replied.

He casually leaned back in the chair. "Ever let your hair down, Doctor?"

"When it's appropriate to do so," she said absently.

"Inhibitions, eh?"

Wheeling around, she shot back, "Fine!" She took in a sharp breath. "Now what makes *you* tick?"

"Why do you ask?"

"Why did you come? Not for altruism. I know that. On Earth, you had everything. You were a crown prince of science. You had the world, not just a starship, for a showcase. Why leave? You don't make sense, and I don't like that."

She was hitting so close to home that it hurt. He grated, "I don't like *you*!"

"The feeling is mutual!"

Something thumped overhead and then made large scuffling sounds. Joe jumped, instantly aware of the alien world outside the dome.

Catharin shouted at the ceiling, "No! Over by the door!"

"What?"

"It's that damned leak."

"What leak?"

"Don't you notice anything that doesn't interest you?" she said with sizzling contempt.

A hatch in the ceiling swung open, and the bottom feet of a light ladder dropped to the floor. Down the ladder came a coveralled maintenance worker.

"Did you find it?" she asked.

He was the most unkempt Vanguarder Joe had seen yet, with a bad haircut and an ill-trimmed beard, and coveralls wet at the knees. "Yep, there's water in the crawlspace up there." Between two of the seams in the ceiling, a drop of water shivered and fell. It was a very inconspicuous leak. The maintenance worker stuck a hand out toward Joe. "Hi. Alvin Crawford—as in Crawford, Alabama. Nope, you've never heard of it."

"Did I see you earlier in the hangar, behind a welding torch?"

"Yep! I'm the resident welder. As well as plumber and handy man and expedition mechanic too."

Catharin asked impatiently, "Is it the plumbing, or what?"

"Oh, it's plumbing, all right. Just a pipe taking a leak." Crawford grinned at his own humor. "Not rainwater. Don't worry about that." He thoughtfully scratched his chin. "I might better shut the power down before getting in all that water. There's electrical works up there. I'll get to it tomorrow, and your people can take the day off."

Catharin said, "No, I don't want to jeopardize the equipment in here by waiting that long."

"I guess I can patch it up tonight." Crawford sounded exasperated.

"That will have to do until you can repair it properly."

It dripped again.

Joe enjoyed being a spectator for this little exchange.

Catharin folded her arms, visibly packing up her frustration. Then she turned on Joe and said, in a tone with a vicious edge, "This is a cold front. It's expected to blow through before sunrise, making tomorrow a lovely day for flying."

Chapter Fifteen

KITE

Silverware and plates clattered, and the mess hall smelled of synthetic bacon and coffee. Through vents to the outside flowed fresh air with a cool edge that felt like early autumn morning.

Plate in hand, Becca Fisher settled down across from Joe at the table. "Ready for your flight?"

Joe shook his head. "I'll pass."

"Last time around, you ended up as the filling in a titanium sandwich. But you can't stay glued to the ground. You'll want to go back to the Ship when quarantine ends."

"I thought you were the Ship's engineer. What are you doing piloting a plane down here?"

Fisher answered readily. "They revived the chief engineer. Orlov was originally supposed to bring the Ship in to planetfall, and he wasn't happy that the job had been given to me. He decided to make my life unpleasant. He stuck me with the most obnoxious work he could find, and then criticized every detail of what I did with it."

Joe took an instant dislike to Orlov. "Authoritarian bastard, eh?"

"I volunteered to do mapping duty down here. You know, in retrospect, I'm not too surprised that Chase got into trouble."

"Who?"

"Your shuttle pilot on the way down. Jason 'Chase' Scanlan." Twiddling her fork in synthetic scrambled eggs, she sounded sad. "His background was military, hot stuff jets that could power through most kinds of weather. It turns out that flying little stuff on Earth was better background for flying here. I'm used to tiptoeing around the weather, changing my plans, meeting nasty surprises in general. So I know how Chase could get into trouble like he did, and how I won't."

Joe looked into his cup, which contained one last slosh of brown beverage and no inspiration for how he could evade the proposed flight. The idea of flying made breakfast sit uncomfortably in his stomach.

"It's going to be a beautiful morning. Calm air and not a cloud in the sky. So here's my plan—"

"Good *morning*." Maya London claimed the place beside Joe. "How *is* your work? You've been frightfully busy for the last few days. We're so glad you're here working on our problems, aren't we, Becky?"

Distaste flickered across Fisher's face as she swallowed whatever she had meant to say next.

Maya fixed her whole attention on Joe as if Fisher had suddenly ceased to exist. "I've been hoping that you'd tell me all about what you do."

Fisher gathered her plate and utensils. "Bye."

Maya had glittering green eyes and long dark hair with auburn highlights, and a willful attractiveness that Joe sensed as tangibly as feeling wind or heat. The angler had gotten impatient, decided to set the hook in the fish's mouth, he thought. Careless of her.

"Later. I've got a date." Joe hurried by the kitchen window to toss his dishes in. He caught up with Fisher before she was out of the mess hall and clapped a hand on her shoulder.

After a startled moment, Fisher grinned brightly. "No time like the present, huh?"

Joe glanced back toward Maya, verifying that she had seen the interchange. Vexation was written across Maya's flawless features. Joe had successfully ruined Maya's trophy-hunting morning. There was only one problem. Now he had to fly, and his shoulder ached to remind him what had happened last time.

☽☾

Joe helped Fisher wheel the slender airplane out of the hangar. She jauntily circled around, inspecting the plane, flexing the control surfaces on the trailing edges of the long, flimsy wings. "You aren't talking much, but I can hear you thinking a mile a minute."

"No offense, but it doesn't look like much of an airplane."

"That's the beauty of it. The simpler a machine is, the less goes wrong with it. If making it back home is the most important thing, you don't go wrong with long wings."

Joe pointed to a black shape painted on the fuselage, the silhouette of a long-winged bird. "Seagull?"

"No. A kind of raptor called a kite. I call this plane *Tennessee Kite.* That's a joke—there was a species of bird called Mississippi kite. Very good fliers."

Joe was not reassured.

"Still want to go?"

"No." Joe was tense as an overwound spring. His shoulder hurt. "But I don't like not wanting to."

"If you think you'd panic, then I don't want you along. I couldn't handle a panicky person as big as you are."

That sounded like a way out, but not one that Joe was cowardly enough to take. "I won't panic. I'm a distance swimmer. I've swum in the open sea and Lake Superior. More than once, I came close to drowning in bad weather and rough waves. So I know what it feels like to be on the edge of panic. And how to pull back."

Satisfied, she lightly punched his upper arm. "That's the right attitude. Hop in."

He clambered onto the root of the wing to reach the rim of the cockpit. Stepping in with one leg, then the other, he had to fold himself to get into the seat. The canopy almost brushed his hair when Fisher pulled it shut. Fisher gave him an amused look as he struggled to fasten his seat belt in the cramped space. A shooting pain in his shoulder objected. *Go away*, he told the pain. *You aren't real.*

Then she showed him how to use the voice-activated headset. "How do you hear me?"

"Fine."

She started the propellers. The one on the plane's nose whirred up to speed, followed by the rear prop, which was located between twin tail booms. *Kite* rolled down the packed-earth runway. Tension knotted Joe's stomach so hard that it hurt.

At the end of the runway, Fisher wheeled the plane around to face the whole length of the runway and the open sky. She gave Joe a significant glance. He nodded with a lump the size of a baseball in his throat. This time *Kite* accelerated. Halfway to the other end, the vibration of contact with the runway let up. The ground below fell away, mountainside tumbling toward the lowlands. Joe gasped a curse.

"Don't look down."

Joe tore his eyes away from the falling green ground. Ahead of the plane, uplands rose on the horizon, beyond the front propeller, which had dematerialized to a mere shimmer.

Then the sound background changed. Joe twisted around to stare in horror at the back prop, which circled idly.

"I shut it down. The back prop's only for takeoffs, or when I need extra power. There's safety in redundancy," Fisher told him.

Beyond the bubble cockpit and the tail fins, the flat mountaintop tilted. "You're turning?"

"Only a little. We took off into the wind. Now I'm heading around toward the sea." Her fingers ran lightly over the instrument panel. "I'll be doing some photo-mapping. It's too good a morning not to. Later it'll be a different story. The days on Green are so long that heat and cloud buildup are pretty extreme in midday. By then, we'll be long since back in the Base."

"So you worry about weather?"

"I wouldn't say worry. I'm careful."

"Green has mild weather," Joe said. "Not my opinion. Chase's."

She shook her head sharply. "This is a dark world. Not just a dark *continent*, like Africa when the first pilots flew into it with a compass and a radio and that was it for instruments. Green is a whole dark *world*. Unknown to us. We can't afford to think we understand it." She looked out at the nameless hills and shore. "I grew up in the country. Land does have personality, it has temperament. And I'm telling you, I've never met any green land that feels remotely like this place does. Or *acts* like this ground does," she added in a low voice.

The day after the crash, a search party had found the battered body of Chase Scanlan. Wing had left Scanlan respectfully laid out under the ersatz pall of a fern frond. They found the body twenty feet away, sprawled like a discarded rag doll. After the initial shock, Wing had been able to explain what happened. Halfway up Unity Mountain, Joe and Wing had seen busy insectlike undertakers bury a crushed slug. Apparently the ground in the fern forest had similarly embraced Scanlan. And subsequently rejected him because his alien flesh tasted bad.

"The scenery starts changing about here."

☽ ☾

Hills and humps of the land flattened out. Featureless green was broken by sinuous channels and brief sheets of flat water. Nothing particularly upsetting had happened since takeoff, and Joe began to be interested in the land. "That looks like an antique map of Frisia I once studied. The water all the same shade of blue and the land all the same shade of green, interlaced with each other."

"Yeah, but what's Frisia?"

"The marshland sea coast of Holland and North Germany. My mother's parents were from Frisia. They named her Silke."

"Zeelkeh?"

"It's a Frisian name, and it means a Selkie. A mythical creature. A human who turns into a seal."

"Seal people? I think Ireland had that legend too. My ancestors came from Ireland, mostly." She had loosened up, but her hands did not leave the controls. "That's how I got my red hair and fair skin."

"I have Frisian looks. Black hair and blue eyes, like my mother's father."

Fisher gave him a sidewise look that appraised and, Joe thought, appreciated his appearance. "Dramatic combination."

He hadn't thought about Frisia, or his grandparents, or his mother, since he came out of stasis. Memories had been on ice.

"Joe?"

"Frisia drowned when the greenhouse effect raised the North Sea, so my mother's parents immigrated to Canada."

"My ancestors got out of Ireland in the Potato Famine. That's history, isn't it? From old worlds to new."

On the oceanic horizon toward the east, the rising sun lay in a bath of yellow brilliance. Channels and sheets of water in the marshes reflected gold. Joe shifted in his seat to better see the frilled and gilded edge of the sea, but *Kite*'s long wing was in his way.

"I can lower that wing," Becca offered.

"Ugh—go ahead." He braced himself.

The wing on his side dipped. The plane turned away from the sun. Marsh bunched up into lowlands with Unity Mountain off to the west, and then the plane's nose tracked the course of a river that flowed toward the sea and the gold-inlaid marsh. More than a full circle from where she'd started, Becca straightened the plane and flew northward toward the river.

"This is as far as we go. This is one kite that's definitely on a string." With a slight movement of Becca's hands on the control stick, the plane banked and *Kite* flew inland above the river.

Joe wanted to swim. The river below *Kite*'s wings was wide and would have been his kind of distance across, but God only knew what was in the water on this world.

Becca said, "Technically, I'm out of bounds, flying above the river. It's one of the limits of my mapping area. But I figure it's worth a mapping pass. And I have plenty of altitude. If we lost *both* engines and *Kite* turned into a glider, that'd be okay, because it has a high glide ratio, and I scoped out some nice flat emergency landing sites—and that's if I couldn't catch some thermal lift to make it back to Unity Base."

"So you don't mind breaking rules about how far to go."

"I don't blow the rules to bits. I bend 'em, when I know I know what I'm doing."

"Didn't you recently map the horizon?"

She laughed. "You saw that image? Oops. Yeah. I did a knife-edge turn just for fun. Without remembering to turn off the mapping cameras. And the moon happened to be in the sky."

"I like your style."

She smiled at him. Inside smile lines, the edges of her lips were as finely defined as the rim of a porcelain cup. "Hear that?" A soft, regular beeping sounded on the airplane's instrument panel. "It's the beacon at Unity Base. We're coming home."

Where a tributary from Unity Mountain met the river, Becca turned to follow the tributary. Unity Mountain lay dead ahead. "One more hurdle to go, Joe. Prepare for landing."

The reminder jarred Joe. In this morning sun, the Mountain's bare dirt crown looked like ordinary reddish dirt, not a wound. But Joe's shoulder hurt at the sight of it and the thought of the tangled fern forest on its flanks, and the dead man rejected by the soil. Joe sweated. He had a death grip with both hands on his belt's webbing.

Kite angled across the Mountain's flank, then banked back toward the runway. The plane descended with a slowness that made Joe's skin crawl. He could make out individual furry pines on the rim of the Mountain.

Kite fluttered in the air, slip-sliding left and right. Joe choked off a startled cry.

"Just a little air turbulence. It's *okay*, Joe!"

Joe felt the wheels touch the runway with an almost imperceptible bump. Becca steered the plane toward the hangar and brought it to a stop. She grinned brilliantly. "That was one of my better landings."

Joe's clothes were damp with cool sweat. "That was a hell of a lot better than my last landing. Thanks."

She extended her hand to shake Joe's with wiry fingers and a strong grip. "Congratulations!"

Joe felt the way he always had after a hard swim across a difficult body of water: victorious.

Chapter Sixteen

NEW MOON

GO NORTH ABOUT 70 METERS. FIND TREE MARKED WITH X.

Catharin took a compass heading and decided that the dimpled crown of a distant hill would serve as her guidepost. She walked that way, counting her steps. Seventy steps at an estimated meter per step, which for her at a brisk pace was reasonable, should get her to the marked tree. The fern trees grew widely spaced enough to make her trail veer only slightly from beeline-true.

The moon was invisible above the cloudy sky, in its new phase, throwing no reflected light on Green. But did Catharin's body nonetheless somehow know Blue was there? Did it still affect her brain? Because those questions had to be answered, she had the task of finding her way through the fern forest. It was an important test, because the team at Unity Base could avoid moonlight if it addled their brains. They could not avoid the moon's very existence.

With the solidly overcast sky, the sun offered no clues as to east and west. But the bulk of Unity Mountain, visible above the trees, was a very large and telltale clue. The land here gently sloped down from the direction of Unity Mountain.

An unusually large, multiple fern tree blocked her way, at least five stems growing up in one cluster. She stopped counting steps to work her way around the obstacle, called the diameter of the quintuplet tree ten steps, and double-checked the compass heading. Catharin looked up from the compass to see the dimpled hill in the distance and a purple pond right in front of her.

Purple pond? The instructions and sketched map indicated no ponds, purple or otherwise. She was lost. Feeling her face flush with dismay, she checked her watch. 1515 AM. She had a little time left before she would be late to the field camp. She sat down on a clean rock to review how she'd gotten here, desperate to understand what she'd done wrong.

The same test for a score of different people had been conducted across the long, cloudy Green-day. No one had flunked yet. Even Alvin Crawford, according to the report called into the Base by Sam, had sauntered out of the forest in good time.

But Alvin wasn't an astronaut who had been twice frozen in stasis.

When her turn came, Wing had driven Catharin along a rough track into the wilderness. Wing dropped her off equipped with canteen, two-way, compass, and instructions, which she'd followed to the letter: a series of compass bearings and distances.

Losing time by the minute, she sketched the sequence of directions and distances on the back of the instruction sheet. The resulting erratic path ought to end up not far from where it started. So why the purple pond? She hated being lost, not knowing which way to go and losing precious time by the second. Near despair, she wondered if the directions had been designed to fail, to test intelligence in a less than straightforward way.

But that would have been exceedingly unfair.

A flash of motion over the pond distracted her. Something winged and quick, the size of a small bird or a large butterfly, hovered over the pond, occasionally glancing the water's iridescent purple surface.

With her attention distracted by the flying thing, her subconscious succeeded in raising a pertinent question. *Isn't the sea east of the Mountain?*

Of course it was. But the Mountain itself lay to the east of this part of the fern forest. Catharin had grown up on the East Coast of North America, and had gone to Girl Scout camp where the hills sloped to the sea. That fact, engraved in her mind at an early age, must have been more indelible than she'd realized, and it took the not-always-helpful form of *east is down.* One of the today's instructions had said GO EAST. . . . And she'd automatically selected a tall fern directly downslope and walked toward it. That had happened just before she had more accurately turned northward to seek the X-marked tree.

Catharin sketched her real route on the back of the instructions. The X-marked tree could not be far away: 50 steps past the pond and then off to the right another 160 steps should put her there. She sprang up and circled the purple pond.

Something touched her shoulder. She turned her head to discover the thing that had hovered over the pond perched there. It clung to her shirt with at least six jointed legs.

"Ugh—go away!" She twitched her shoulder. The creature just flexed its fan-folded wings, one of which briefly brushed her neck, and hunkered down.

If it didn't take off on its own, she wasn't going to touch it, possibly prompting it to sting. Unwanted passenger and all, Catharin hurried along. She almost panicked when she did not see a mark on the likeliest ginkoid tree, then remembered to circle around its trunk. There the X-shaped mark waited to greet anyone who came the right way. Catharin vented a sharp sigh of relief. People made that kind of mistake all the time on Earth, swapping east for west or left for right. The human mind had always tripped over its own bright nimble feet.

The bug, still aboard, unfolded its wings into two fans. And then closed them again. "Big mistake," Catharin muttered. "Someone I know will just love to introduce you to her collection."

☽☾

Apart from the fact that several males lounged in the shade, the field camp definitely reminded Catharin of Girl Scout camp, complete with Samantha Berry playing scoutmaster. "Look, everybody, there's Catharin, just in time!" Sam announced.

"Sam, look at this thing on my shoulder."

Sam trotted over. "Where did you find that critter?"

Catharin decided not to mention her purple pond detour in public. She would tell Sam later and privately. "It found me, by landing on me while I was looking for the seventh checkpoint."

Eddy came over to have a look. Joe was stretched out in the shade, apparently napping, and Alvin had a two-way pressed against his ear, talking to Unity Base.

"Becca, hand me one of those screened collecting jars," said Sam. "It's the closest thing to a dragonfly I've seen so far, even with eight legs and purple feet."

Catharin tensed while Sam expertly flicked the thing into the collecting jar. Relieved, Catharin sat down in a folding chair in the fern tree shade with a cold, welcome, peach-flavored drink.

Becca sat down beside her. "You had us a little worried."

"This is the damnedest ecosphere," said Sam, studying the purple-footed bug. "If it is a dragonfly-analogue, I'd expect the things that Earth had at the same time. Amphibians and giant cockroaches. You didn't observe it eat anything, did you?"

"It didn't sample doctors," Catharin replied, peering under her shirt collar to check for broken skin on her shoulder. "Or textiles," she added, finding no holes in the shirt.

"So why no cockroaches?" Joe asked. He was awake after all.

"I'd guess it's the moon. Or the lack of one, before the seamoon eventually rolled out of the cosmic crapshoot and stayed here. My guess is that life has been trying to make a go of it on Green for billions of years. But seasonal irregularities and the occasional climatic upheaval set it back. Again and again and again, mass extinctions." Catharin remembered Lary's model, ages ago at the bright sun and world with no moon. *Like scraping a painting off a canvas.* "Every time around, a few more of the more highly evolved species manage to survive. But the upshot is impoverishment of animal life."

"But now the moon's here," said Joe.

"And so are we, and this is a perfect laboratory for planetology and evolutionary studies, and I want some more data," said Sam. "It's time to launch the boat. Everybody's passed our little field test. If we stay out of moonlight, we'll be safe. Right?"

Catharin compressed her lips, thinking about the purple pond. But she had quickly and accurately figured out her mistake, one that could have easily happened on Earth. "Yes—pending experience to the contrary."

"Ever christened a vessel?" Sam asked.

"Yes, as a matter of fact."

Joe sat up. "What, a sailboat?"

Aware that she hardly cut an elegant figure today, hot and sweaty in field clothing, Catharin corrected his misimpression. "US Navy destroyer."

"How'd you manage that?"

"The Navy always looks—looked—for the most noteworthy woman they can find who has any connection to the new ship. I'd just been tapped for the Astronaut Corps, and I'm related to Rear Admiral Hardin Tucker. So I was asked to christen the warship of that name."

"She had a flowing blue silk dress, and with her height, she was stunning," Becca informed Joe. "She fit right in with all the Navy crisp white cotton and gold braid."

"Do you want me to christen your boat, Sam?"

"Hang on. I've just about got the votes counted," said Alvin.

"Votes?"

Becca explained. "For the one who's going to christen Sam's boat, you're in a three-way race with Maya and Eddy—he was nominated by Joe and is getting the sympathy vote from people who want to break tradition and let it be a male."

Amazed, Catharin wondered if remote scientific bases on Earth had been like this, with enough monotony and free time for people to resort to such low-level amusements. Not so on space stations and ships, starting with ancient *Mir* and ending with *Aeon*. In space habitats, there was too much checking of equipment, changing of filters, cleaning mold out of the life-support system, ad infinitum, for idle hands to be much of a problem. In space, you had too much to do just keeping your environment glued together.

Alvin riffled a bunch of little slips of paper in his hand. "Aaron called in the count from the Base, and I've tabulated 'em with the ones here."

"Don't I get a vote?" Catharin asked.

"Yeah, but it doesn't matter. You're it by a good margin."

"Thank you, I think," said Catharin.

This wasn't such a bad deal, Catharin thought. She was getting a hop in Domino Cady's Starhawk in return for christening the boat. Headset on and sitting in the copilot's seat, she watched Unity Base diminish as the Starhawk lifted up from it. The rotors throbbed powerfully. With its heavy-duty hoist, the copter lugged the riverboat. The game plan was to put the boat in the river, and then christen it properly, with its keel wet.

Domino leveled the copter and made for Camp Darwin. Catharin relaxed. She had flown with Domino before, on Earth, when he was Becca's friend and aspiring Vanguarder, and he was a superb pilot. And a safety-minded one.

From the passenger cabin, Samantha Berry stuck her head into the cockpit. She pointed to the large brown bottle cradled in Catharin's lap. "So what is it? Water? I know we don't have that much drinkable alcohol, and if we did, I'd rather toast the boat with it than let it run into the river."

"I told you I'd do this right, and I will, and you'll see," said Catharin. "It's not alcohol, and it's not water."

Domino was concentrating on piloting the Starhawk, but he evidently had enough spare attention to follow the conversation. "But it's like baptizing. You can't just use anything!"

"You are aware that christening a vessel is an ancient offering to propitiate the gods?" Sam pointed out. "Or more to the point here, the goddess."

"What goddess?" Catharin asked.

"The moon. Haven't you ever heard of the moon goddess?"

Domino gave Sam a shocked look. He was Old Catholic. Sam was pagan. And they were quite welcome to sort through their theological differences without her, Catharin thought. She saw Camp Darwin ahead, where the river had hollowed a placid backwater out of the Mountain's heels. The surrounding land lay in gentle heights and valleys like a ruffled green rug.

A small crowd of people awaited the Starhawk and its burden. Hovering, the Starhawk lowered the boat into the tributary with a lively splash. "We want to baptize it, not drown it!" Sam yelled from the cabin, where she'd strapped herself back in for the landing.

Domino released the cable from the hoist and landed the Starhawk in a clearing beside Camp Darwin. He silenced the machine and quickly moved to the cabin door to let down the steps. Domino had old-fashioned religious ideas, but manners to match. He gallantly handed Catharin out with her brown bottle and its mystery contents.

Alvin had provided the baptismal liquid from his inventory of used and useless machine fluids. He grinned from his vantage point on the leading edge of the crowd that straggled after Catharin to the edge of the water, where some of Sam's team had secured the boat to a small metal dock.

"I christen thee—" Giving the bottle a wide swing, Catharin called out, "*Beagle!*" and smashed the bottle on the boat's prow. Rivulets of bright blue liquid ran down the hull into the water. After a moment of startled silence, everybody clapped.

"Antifreeze," Alvin explained smugly. "The doctor wanted something that wouldn't have a lot of Earth germs in it to contaminate the river." Thick blue rivulets streaked *Beagle*'s blunt bow. "Well, that should get the goddess' attention," said Sam.

Chapter Seventeen

FIELD DAY

Under gray skies, a trio of jeeps loaded with people and gear caravanned down Mount Unity for a workday at Camp Darwin. Feeling cooped up and restless, Joe went along.

The road ran arrow-straight to the edge of the Mountain and through the belt of furry pines. Gray skies made the trees' bluish tinge even more pronounced than usual. The furry pines looked unreal. Once out of the pines, the jeeps chugged along through bushy thickets, soft and rubbery, almost as blue as the furry pines. "All this greenery isn't the right shade of green," Joe told Wing.

"It's right for this world. The sun is slightly redder than Sol, so the leaves of all plants, not just the conifers, are bluish, to take best advantage of the light."

The driver struggled with shifting the vehicle's gears in a washout. The other passengers whooped. Joe crossed his arms, all the jollity getting on his nerves. Finally, the jeeps pulled up beside a wide gray stream. Three grubby tents comprised the satellite base, known as Camp Darwin.

The Vanguarders piled out and trooped to the metal dock and boat at the water's edge. *Beagle* was a short, stubby boat with an enclosed cabin and a thick glass window in the bottom, a portal onto a new world below the water. It reminded Joe of a child's bathtub toy.

The task of the day was to install instruments for an upcoming float test. Like a scout troop on an outing, everybody was orchestrated. Maya London took a few minutes to flirt with Joe, but she had her job too, and Joe didn't care to help her. When Maya wasn't looking, Joe walked away from the party.

The Vanguard had worked together for years before the Ship left Earth. Team players. A team used to winning. Here the team had no opposition. The world was soft and mild.

Joe walked downstream to the peninsula between tributary and river. The river wound out of the northwest, toward the sea, wide and shallow, water dark and gray as slate. Rains upstream had swollen the river. Joe scowled at the wide water. He felt a compelling need to swim, to work out the gloom that ate at his guts like acid. He picked up a stone out of the debris piled by the water.

Hurling sticks and stones, Joe found that the gravity of Green—marginally less than that of Earth—made it just possible for him to hit the far bank on his better throws. His misses splashed and bobbed away downstream.

Except for one. The stick splashed, bobbed as usual, and proceeded downstream. In front of it, then, the gray water crinkled: a tiny swell extended all the way across the river and even had a little fringe of foam on top. The stick spun and went under, to surface a good two meters upstream. And it continued to move in that direction: *up*stream. Crouched on the bank, Joe stared at the water. It looked a trifle higher on both banks, as if the river had risen a few inches, all at once and from downstream up. The rise had swept away one of his sticks lying just by the water.

Across the silent distance to Camp Darwin came a splash and burst of laughter. Joe glared back toward the camp, clapping a hand to his neck because of a twinge that made it hard to turn his head. The feelers of pain radiating from his shoulder felt hard and stiff, relentlessly pulling on his skull. Joe struck his forehead with his palm, wishing that he could knock the hypochondriac, brooding thoughts out of his mind. But exercise was the only way to do that.

Unity Mountain rose up over him, old, bare in places, not very high by Earth standards. He had walked up it once before. Starting farther up, but badly hurt at the time, he had still made it in a couple of hours.

Unnoticed, he followed the road back uphill.

In fifteen minutes, he worked up a sweat. Joe wondered about the season. The night they crashed had felt temperate, not too hot or cold. His memory went hazy for the weeks that followed, while he lay in the cot with his cracked shoulder bone and a serious relapse of stasis fever, a sick stupor. Later, there were long warm intervals that weren't fever but rather climatic heat, like a torrid afternoon, when air-conditioning blown in from the dome countered the heat but did not obliterate it. That must have been high summer.

Summer had now dissolved into rainy cold fronts. There had been no howling, crashing storms, just gray rain that fell and leached the green out of the frondy vegetation.

Maybe he hated this world. Hated the insipidness of it. No animals. Just soft blue-green plants. He scrambled cross-country between switchbacks, bruising blue-green leaves and trampling soft molds on the ground in the process, pushing a body that had gotten shockingly out of condition. When he reached the Base, his leg muscles quivered. But his mood had improved.

Entering the dome, the door of which stood wide open, Joe approved of the desertion of it. Almost everybody was at the river.

He entered the break room in Medical with no particular noise, and so did not disturb Catharin. Lying on the couch, prone, she had her head buried in her arms, with the little cat curled up on the small of her back asleep. Catharin seemed to be sleeping as well.

She wore the usual clothes, tan slacks and shirt, but they fit well over the long slight curves of her body. Joe restrained an urge to run his hand across her shoulder blades or her hips and find out if she felt as inviting as she looked. She would awaken as soon as he touched her. And likely slap him.

Joe opened the refrigerator and took out a can of kiwi-flavored beverage with a slight inadvertent rattle.

Even asleep, Catharin's nerves must have been strung tight. She jumped, which sent the cat bounding away. "*Where have you been?*"

"None of your business."

"They're looking for you at the river!"

"Won't find me there." He opened the beverage with a snap. "Walked back."

She gasped. "Are you out of your mind? It totally violates the rules for anyone to go off on their own!"

He cursed the rules with so much venom that she backed off. She held up her hands. "Okay. Just tell someone next time. And speaking of that, why don't *you* call Aaron at the river, and tell him he can call off the search for you?"

☽☾

It was Sunday on the Ship, and besides a skeleton crew of two lowly technicians, his staff in the research center up there had not reported for work, without asking for his permission. He managed to get a report out of the techs. A prototype bacterial factory had been set up, a clone to make the first of his molecules, and it seemed moderately successful. So Joe ordered the exhaustive analyses that would either prove the success or knock a hole in it.

Catharin showed up to use the telcon. She was making a report to the Ship on the deteriorating condition of Fredrik Hoffmann. Catharin advised transfer to the hospital on Ship. She emphasized Hoffmann's lack of infection by the newly discovered virus or any other. Even if it had gone quiescent, hidden in the nucleus of his cells, the diagnostic methods would have flushed a viral infection out. Organically, Hoffmann was clean.

"Got a video monitor in his room?" Joe asked. "Or did you get somebody to hold him down while you checked him out?"

"I just took him his lunch. At meal times he's at his most cooperative. He stands back at the other end of his room looking dejected. Not that it's any of your business."

Catharin's report went on to advance the possibility of brain damage from stasis and/or poststasis therapy. Possibly the stasis had damaged the neurotransmitting proteins of the brain in this patient and others as well. Hoffmann's case might be vitally informative if he was intensively evaluated and monitored in the Ship's hospital.

Ever vigilant and responsive, the Ship started sending down analytical responses to the hypothesis of brain-protein damage. Lights lit up all over the telcon. Catharin stabbed the FILE button in exasperation. "Why don't you stop looking over my shoulder?" she snapped at Joe. "I know that you have no use for medicine. Certainly not the part that says 'First do no harm.'"

"I never set out to do harm. But science comes first, not medicine."

"How did you get where you are without studying medicine?"

"I did study medicine. Check my molecules."

Having finished the transmission, she did, summoning the specifications of the biological activity of his newly minted molecules to the screen. "All right, I admit it. You seem to know what to do for therapeutic purposes. You have a better sense for the molecular level than I do." She faced him, crossing her arms. "Look, Joe, you happen to resemble a hero to some, and this kind of humanitarian work—however involuntary—will add to that impression. For God's sake, do try to act more like one."

"You're the one bucking for hero," he said, unmoved. "I don't care."

"At least act less like a willful child prodigy. You are too old for that."

"Keep your opinions to yourself. I don't want 'em. And get out of my way. I need to use the telcon."

She stayed put, thin-lipped, and said, "This is not your toy."

They locked eyes, locked wills, and neither one flinched.

Suddenly Eddy flung the door open so wildly that it banged against the wall. "Fredrik's gone! He's not in his quarters!"

"Damn!" Catharin gasped. "Go outside. Take a two-way. Look for him, for footprints. Call back if he's left the dome, or if you see him leaving. But don't get near him, Eddy."

Eddy stood rooted to the spot. "I can't leave you alone."

"I'll be with her," said Joe.

"Oh, thank you!" Eddy left at a run.

Catharin said to Joe in an intense voice, "You want a fight. Stay out of this. I can take care of myself."

"He's out of his mind and he hates you," Joe reminded her.

"He was calmer today." She hesitated, then nodded. "Let me go first; let me do the talking. Stay back unless you're needed. We'll start in the mess hall. Let's go."

The Base had corridors arrayed like spokes of a wheel along wedge-shaped sections. Joe stared up at one of the ceiling hatches above the corridor, uneasily guessing that the dome was laced with maintenance crawlspaces. Catharin followed Joe's gaze. "It's too tight a fit for him up there."

Finding no sign of Hoffmann in the mess hall, they hurried down a short flight of stairs, into a large basement section—the quartermaster's office and supply room—and back up to the sleeping quarters on the first floor. Hoffmann's bunk room door stood ajar. "Did you lock it after you took him lunch?"

Catharin checked the pocket of her lab coat, pulled out a small flat metal bar, and flushed bright pink. Joe took the bar from her and examined it. He fit it into aligned slots in the door and jamb. Once fitted in, the lock bar simply and effectively secured the door against being opened from the inside. Nor could it be shaken out. "Nice system if you remember to activate it."

"I've got too damn much on my mind," Catharin said bitterly.

They cut through the communal shower into another corridor. Catharin started opening doors. The small rooms held cots made and unmade, pictures tacked to the walls: Earth landscapes, smiling families. One of the rooms was a mess of jumbled clothes, dirty gear, shoes, used plates, and even machine parts strewn over the floor and both cots.

"Who's the pair of pigs?" Joe asked.

"Alvin made this mess single-handedly. Nobody else can stand to room with him."

Another room with two cots, one of which had a silver flute on the bedclothes and pictures of airplanes stuck on the cabinet doors on that side, had to be Becca Fisher's room.

The next door revealed a single immaculate cot with a mauve blanket. A distinctive fragrance hung on the air. As personal effects went, expensive perfume had been a good way to maximize value and minimize bulk, and this particular perfume was Maya London's. Trust Maya to have a private room. Joe remembered her overtures, designed to lead him to this very place. But he was having more fun hunting a schizophrenic with Catharin.

Catharin paused, shrugged, then opened the door of another single-occupant bunk room. The cot was made with a royal blue blanket. On a thin ledge in front of a small square window rested a small potted plant. She muttered, "I'm glad he wasn't hiding *here*." This was Catharin's own private room. Joe didn't blame her for not wanting to find that Hoffman had invaded it.

Catharin pulled a slim two-way out of her pocket and called Eddy. He'd seen so sign of Hoffmann outside of the dome or in the Penthouse.

The planetology lab in the dome's next wedge was crammed with looming equipment. A rustle made Joe and Catharin whirl to face a solitary female technician. "No, I haven't seen Fredrik. I thought he was locked up," Sheryn said. Her wrists bore bandages from the bungled suicide attempt.

"He got out. Go into Aaron's office." They'd just checked Manhattan's narrow, tidy office. Hoffmann hadn't been in there. "Bar the door," Catharin told Sheryn. "Stay until everyone comes back."

The girl hastily complied.

To Joe, Catharin said, "He's got a streak of misogyny. Not violent, not up to now. But she'd be no match for him."

"And you would?"

"Maybe I can talk to him. If not, my astronaut training included some hand-to-hand. But it would have been stupid for me to set out alone. Yes, I admit that."

As they went up the ramp to the conference room, Catharin said, "You had a big advantage in surprise the other day. He's paramilitary, and might be a match for both of us put together. Do *not* threaten him. Let me talk."

"Hold on. What do you mean paramilitary? I thought this guy was an electrical engineer."

"Yes, and a captain in the Home Guard."

"*What?*"

"Shhh!"

"Don't you know about the Guard? Did you ever see them in action?" Joe asked urgently.

"Of course not."

"Vigilantes. Christ almighty, that's bad."

Catharin raised an eyebrow. Then she buzzed Manhattan's office from the nearest intercom to verify that Sheryn was safe there.

Sheryn's voice sounded scared. "I saw him through the window in Aaron's office. I think he's following you."

Galvanized, Joe inspected the console by the head chair. "Here's a masterlock switch. Hit it and you lock all the doors electronically. You can let yourself out of any of the doors, but nobody gets in."

She frowned. "We can't just hole up."

"He's dangerous."

"He didn't seem volatile when I saw him earlier today, just miserable."

"Watch out the way we came. I'll be right back." Joe explored the short hallway on the far side of the conference room. The hall ended in yet another door of the generic type, barrable inside or out, that opened onto the observation deck, the other half of the apex of Unity Base. A breezeway with handrail went from the deck back to an outside door of the conference room.

Joe left the door to the observation deck ajar, the lock bar perched in the door slot, then circled back to Catharin via the breezeway. "I say we trap him."

She shook her head. "His calculating intelligence is unimpaired. He won't fall for it."

"You thought you could talk him into acting reasonable. Can you do the opposite?"

"Why?"

Joe outlined a plan. To his surprise, she agreed to it. Then Joe armed himself with the conference room's fire extinguisher and stationed himself outside of the breezeway door. They waited, not for long.

Hoffmann came with barely audible, slow steps.

Catharin was sitting at the conference room table, writing on a piece of paper they'd found there. The slight scratch of chair feet on the floor meant that she had stood up, with the table between her and Hoffmann. "Hello, Fredrik. What brings you here?"

"I'm looking for you."

Risking a peek into the room, Joe was appalled to see that Hoffmann held a long piece of pipe, a wicked weapon.

"Why are you looking for me, Fredrik?"

Hoffmann was only too willing to explain what was on his mind, with a speech so mumbled and bizarre that Joe strained to follow the words or the logic. Hoffmann thought the Base population had been wiped out by an alien virus. And that Catharin was responsible for it. Listening to the repetitious and badly connected words, Joe broke into a sweat. If Hoffmann threatened to attack Catharin, he'd intervene, and he'd be tackling a maniac.

Catharin went along with the flow of Hoffmann's demented ideas, in a calm and persuasive voice. "Of course the Base is empty. Everyone has gone up, one by one, to the Ship. The specialists on the Ship know how to cure the disease, and make everyone feel well again. How are you feeling, Fredrik? Would you like to go Upstairs too? The shuttle is coming right back down. You can see it land if you go out on the observation deck."

Joe started to edge quietly along the breezeway, in order to slam and bar the observation deck door in Hoffmann's face while Catharin hit the masterlock and shut the inner corridor door behind him.

But Hoffmann's warped reality was not quite plastic enough to be so susceptible to suggestion—or else he was too fixated on Catharin. His voice rose, and now Joe could make out the words all too clearly. "You were the astronaut, changed the Ship's course, brought us here, for a reason, to kill everybody!"

"No, I—"

"*Bitch, your plan worked! They're all dead!*"

Joe swallowed nervous bile and stepped into the room just as Catharin said, "You're imagining things, and you can join your fantasies in hell!" Reacting to the razory condescension in her voice, Hoffmann lunged at her. Catharin bolted with a clatter into the rigged hallway. Hoffmann pounded after her with the pipe poised for a blow.

Joe sprang to the head chair and hit the masterlock. The doors closed with a hiss behind Hoffmann's heels.

Joe heard the observation deck door slam. *Don't forget to bar that one!* he thought wildly. At a dead run, Joe circled to the observation deck. He found Catharin leaning against the deck door as if her strength could help the bar keep it shut. Hoffmann bellowed and pounded on the other side. Joe checked the lock bar. "It'll hold." The contents of the sealed corridor would stay there for a while. "You move fast."

"I've never moved so fast in my life. I just wanted to provoke him into coming after me. I think he meant to kill me." Her fair-skinned face had gone chalk-pale.

"You played him right," said Joe, making himself sound calm.

They ran back to the conference room via the breezeway. Catharin called Eddy and Sheryn, informing both that the coast was clear. Then she called the river party.

Feeling claustrophobic, Joe opened the room's window shutters while Catharin made her call. It was late in the day by the clock, but there was plenty of daylight, the cloud-hidden sun only halfway across the sky.

Catharin spoke to Manhattan, making a crisp report of what had happened with Hoffmann, without mentioning that she had let him escape from his room.

"Why didn't you call the river earlier?" Joe asked after she signed off.

"He seemed so tractable at lunch. Badly confused, but tractable. Besides, I didn't want to scare him off. I didn't think it would be this bad." The words came out short, sharp, defensive. "And I screwed up. I wanted to fix the mess on my own."

"Pride goeth before a fall," said Joe. Seeing her jaw clench and her eyes narrow, he held up his hands. "I ought to know; pride is one of my specialties. I'd have done the same. I won't tell anybody how he got out," said Joe.

She gave him a surprised and grateful look. Then she turned back to the telcon and rang up the Ship. No diplomacy here—she pulled the rank of chief medical officer on them. Hoffmann had to go to the Ship. She did not have the capability to treat full-blown paranoid schizophrenia. And his continued presence in the Base constituted reckless endangerment of everyone there, which blatantly violated mission protocol.

Hoffmann's transfer to the Ship could be accomplished within the parameters of subquarantine procedure as specified in the Book, and anyone whose business it might be to set up subquarantine procedures was to be consulted, immediately, gotten up out of bed if necessary. She signed off to let the authorities on the Ship digest that.

The two of them waited in the conference room for reinforcements from the river. Neither wished to leave the maniac unguarded, and the electronic lock seemed more vulnerable than the bar. Hoffmann was an electrical engineer, however demented.

Hoffmann pounded on the walls with the pipe, making a din. He raved.

"If I heard things like that said about me I'd blow a gasket," Joe said.

"It's not music to my ears." She folded up in a chair, arms wrapped around her knees, shaking visibly. "My God, what a mistake. It was inexcusable for me to forget to bar the door to his quarters. And then to go after him on my own. Even with you helping me. I could have been killed, and you too." She shook her head. "You're so right about pride."

Hoffmann subsided into moans and mumblings.

"What you did," Catharin said, staring at the floor, "was not what I meant by 'act like a hero' but more than close enough. And you really wanted a fight."

"Not for long. I've got too much sense to tangle with a maniac."

She nodded. "I've never heard of schizophrenia developing so fast. But there's so much I don't know. I'm no psychiatrist." Wearily, she rubbed her forehead. "Who needs alien viruses? We brought our own maladies! God—it is all so complicated. And frightening."

Joe looked up through the skylight, saw a rift in the gray clouded sky, a streak of not quite Earth-sky blue. "The best way not to let bad feelings eat you is exorcise 'em with exercise," he said. "Not that it'd do much for somebody that far gone." He thumbed Hoffmann's direction.

She looked at him over her wrapped arms. "What's eating *you*?"

He started to turn away.

"Please?"

"Not your business."

"My fault, maybe?"

"Why do you say that?"

"Why not?" She shrugged wearily. Hoffmann's accusations, irrational or not, must ring in her ears.

"Not your fault," he said grudgingly. "Leaving Earth. That's what's eating me, if you have to know."

"Why did you?"

"Let's say I made an enemy."

"Just one?"

"The wrong one. Somebody who decided to ruin me and was in a position to do it." Even telling a highly edited version of the truth twisted his gut with remembered bile.

She looked interested.

Joe said, "He'd have made sure I couldn't do my work, not the work I wanted to do, not with the resources I needed. Like it or not, that kind of freedom is important to me."

Catharin nodded. "That figures."

"I had my mind on science, not politics."

"That I can believe."

"My mistake." As he thought about the predicament he'd found himself in at the apex of his career, anger swelled up inside of him. Joe found himself shaking with the fury that he had felt before he had to leave Earth, remembered but not felt since stasis, until now. With an effort, Joe contained the anger. There had been enough raving and ranting in this room tonight.

"You're not telling all."

"Do I have to?"

She shook her head. "My business stops at the point where I can be reasonably certain you won't crack up."

"What made you think that?"

"You've scared me," she answered. "With your temper. With no convincing reason for leaving Earth. And walking away from the others today."

Joe marveled at the fury he had just felt like a black wave. It had passed swiftly, but left him feeling closer in mood and memory to Earth than any time since stasis. "You could say I was being myself a little more than usual, today. I've always gone off by myself. Gone to swim for miles in a pool or across a lake, when there was a clean one. Sometimes I go—went—walking in city. For hours."

Hoffmann raved again. Catharin cringed. When the raving subsided, she said, more or less evenly, "I think I understand. Just remember it's not as safe here."

With a short laugh, he said, "I don't mean up and down the power towers, or in the residential islands. I walked in undertowns."

"Undertowns? Are you serious?"

"Yeah. Undertown LA, London, Manhattan. I wouldn't have taken any of those for a new surname, either. Not after having seen the underbelly of those cities at night. That's how I saw the Home Guard in action a few times," he added.

"At night?" she echoed, incredulous.

He shrugged. "People in undertowns don't recognize scientists. And that's the whole point. I like to be alone. It was easier to find a crowd to be alone in than a wilderness."

"You must have led a charmed life. You could have gotten killed."

"I did land in the emergency room twice. But I'd had practice taking care of myself in the neighborhood where I grew up. Wasn't the best district in Toronto."

"One more question. You changed your name. So did many in the Vanguard. But I don't believe that you share their dreams. So—?"

"The city of Toronto meant something to me." Being young and brilliant and in love, to be exact. But that was then. This was a thousand years later Ship time, and longer than that for Earth.

She jumped up. "I'll be right back." Joe got to listen to Hoffmann's ravings alone for a few minutes, and did his own brooding. He hadn't thought he'd end up like this on the other side of the stars. He hadn't done much thinking at all, just blindly scrabbled his way out of the trap that had been sprung on him on Earth.

It hadn't been pleasant to be in that trap. Joe felt a bizarre impulse to let Hoffmann out of his. But Hoffmann would use freedom to hurt people; Hoffmann belonged in a cage.

Catharin returned with a flash wand, which she handed Joe.

"What's this?"

"The extent of our problems."

"Statistics?"

"No, profile of one individual. Male, fifty-two years old. I think he—" Her voice broke. She had to struggle to keep talking. "He's really sick."

Joe had eidetic memory. Now he remembered with photographic clarity how he had seen her earlier. Lying on her stomach on the couch—a very attractive pose, but also the way somebody would have looked if she had cried herself into a brief sleep, and the cat had come to purr comfort and then bed itself down on the small of her back. When she had woken up and yelled at Joe her eyes had been red-rimmed. Even before Hoffmann made his escape—and part of what made her forget to bar his door?—she was worried to tears. "This patient is not hopeless yet, but heading that way, eh?" Joe asked.

She nodded. The corners of her lips quivered. "Keep the information on that disk to yourself. It would upset people."

Chapter Eighteen

WINTER

"It's okay now, Cat. It's *okay*!" Becca tried to reassure her, sitting with her on the edge of the bunk in Catharin's room.

Mutely Catharin shook her head.

"Go ahead and cry," Becca coaxed.

"I can't," Catharin whispered. She felt an ache deeper in her spirit than she could comprehend, locking tears and feelings into a block of agony. She doubled over, burying her face in arms folded on her knees.

"Oh, Cat!" Becca flung her arms around her.

"He's crazy. But he's right." The words came out with difficulty. "I cast my vote for the moon search. And the rule of my profession is 'First do no harm.' I betrayed that," she gasped.

"No, Cat, No! It was a good decision. Look what we found."

"*Look at the shape we're in!*"

"Something tells me what you know is worse than what you've told anybody else." Becca's voice sounded uneven, but her embrace did not falter. "Maybe you better tell me everything. You can't keep it to yourself."

Catharin let out a sharp, short cry, muffled in her hands.

"What hurts now? Cat?"

"I've already said too much. I may have made one more terrible mistake. I gave Joe a report that shows the score. How badly the molecules are hurt. As though I could trust him—"

"You can! We saw that today."

"I need him more than I ever imagined. If he can repair the human genome, many patients will be saved. I don't know how he'll react."

"He wouldn't turn his back on sick people, would he?"

"I don't know." Tears leaked out. "It wasn't supposed to be this way. Sickness and violence. Not this bad, not this soon, impossible to fix." With clinical detachment, a part of Catharin's mind noted that she was trembling uncontrollably. "I'm up against too much. Just like my parents." That broke the dam, and she started to cry. "What can I do?" she asked in a sob-strangled whisper.

"For starters, cry as much as you need to."

☽☾

The doctor got what she wanted from her colleagues on the Ship, and when the shuttleplane came booming out of the sky to collect Hoffmann, Joe watched from the observation deck along with most of the rest of the Base personnel. It was a good show. Hoffmann had been doused with disinfectant, stuffed into an environmental suit, and then deposited—drugged and sluggish—beside the runway. The shuttle remained on the ground only long enough for two men in environmental suits to drag Hoffmann aboard. One of the men threw out several large bundles of supplies, and the shuttleplane blasted away.

Climbing for outer space, the vehicle soared over a bank of clouds so gray that they were almost steel blue. "They cut it close," said Sam Berry. "That's a polar cold front coming."

Joe had always liked weather because it reminded him of his own moods: sometimes stormy, sometimes crystal blue. Now he wondered about that. He'd felt a brief black storm of anger yesterday. But what about all of his other feelings, the ones he'd once compared to brilliant sunsets or summer nights?

Had he left the best half of his heart on Earth?

When Joe returned to Medical, he found Becca watching Catharin finalize the instructions for Hoffmann's biolock on the Ship end. Hoffmann was scheduled for removal of epidermis and all bodily hair, prior to a full six weeks in strict quarantine and confinement in the hospital. When Catharin signed off, Joe remarked, "You're not unhappy to put him through that."

"I don't like him," she said bluntly. She still looked frayed around the edges.

Eddy trotted in with a parcel. Catharin took it from him and then smiled. "It's a care package from Lary! Joe, do you like scones?"

With fresh coffee, the scones tasted better than anything Joe had eaten while on the Ship. Somebody up there could work wonders with the mess machines.

"After you hit the sack last night," said Joe, "I looked through that wand you gave me."

She gave him a wary look that Joe interpreted as *please don't ruin my day yet.*

"I can help him."

Catharin exchanged a significant glance with Becca.

Joe got the idea that Becca knew more than he did. He felt a stab of jealousy. Disgruntled, he asked Becca, "Are we going to have weather today?"

"There's always weather, remember," Becca answered.

"I'm ready for something more dramatic than the usual."

"You might get it. A strong cold front is bearing down on us. When it collides with the moist air from the sea, there'll be some snow. Maybe even hail."

☽☾

To Joe's disappointment, no hail was forthcoming. Mount Unity's first winter storm arrived with weak gusts of wind, like the puffing of an overexerted old man. Then came a mild and steady snow. Joe turned to his work.

A couple of bacterial clones had failed badly, the worst of which put out monoclonal antibody contaminated with bacterial toxin. Numerous analyses, debates, and proposals for variations in procedure ensued. Joe did not have a high tolerance for the inevitable, dull, and inconvenient problems of turning theory into practical mass production. It doubly frustrated him to direct the process long distance through an off-and-on link to the Ship's Intelligence.

In the early Green-evening, 1700 PM, Joe decided to take a walk. Alone. He went to the conifers at the edge of the Base clearing. It had long since stopped snowing. With a half-Blue up, twilight was thinner than it had been the night of the crash. At half strength, the blue light made snowflakes dribbling off in the furry-pine branches look like pale plastic confetti.

Joe looked straight up at the moon, challenging. Half blue day with cloud swirls, half dark night with glimmers of lightning, the hurricane moon lorded it over the winter sky. A filmy cloud crossed the moon, and the light seeped into the cloud, like a streak of luminous paint across the night sky.

Spectacular as it might be, the moon didn't exert any tangible pull on his brain. No mysterious forces muddied Joe's logical thinking. Joe smiled thinly. The hurricane moon might motivate planetologists and inspire artists. Maybe it had triggered Hoffmann's psychosis, but Hoffmann had been so unbalanced as to tip at any trigger, or none. The blue moon would have no appreciable effect on a healthy mind.

His gaze drifted to the stars in the sky, faint flecks washed out by the moon. Under the starry sky the whole winter world lay still, glazed, gave his eyes and other senses no particular impression to latch onto. His mind phased to another winter sky over the city of Toronto. Freewheeling, his mind flashed through memories that had not visited him in such clarity since before he took to the Ship, since years before that. Eidetic, photographic, the memories were clear as glass. They were also emotionless. In stasis.

He turned back toward the dome. Under the jacket he broke into a cold sweat. He started running.

Entering the Medical wedge door in a hurry, Joe nearly collided with Catharin. With dignity, she pushed him away. "Well. Frustrations all worked out?"

"Just stepped out to take a look at the sky. Can we see the stars from here?"

"What do you mean?"

"The star Mira. Where is it? Can you ask your friends upstairs?"

"I can answer you myself. We came more than two thousand light-years. Ordinary stars are too faint to be visible that far without a telescope."

Disconcerted, and knowing that it showed, he threw off the jacket, hurling it a chair. The telcon windows were full of Catharin's business. "Reapportion. I've got work to do."

"So do I." She examined his jacket. "These flakes of snow didn't fly up off the ground onto your shoulders. They fell off the pines, didn't they? You were out in the forest alone. Why?"

"Experiment," he said with reluctance. "Wanted to see if the moonlight at half strength addled my brains."

"And?"

"Nothing."

"Not true. You dashed in here like something was after you."

"That's it. Nothing. Nothing to mesh with the brain. So the brain freewheels. Memory, fantasy, stream of consciousness overflowing, running out of its banks," he said, desperately glib. "But nothing tangible, nothing real comes from the moon."

"Thoughts affect biochemistry, just as much as biochemistry affects thoughts. The end results can be indistinguishable. If the moon simply provides a kind of ambiance for certain kinds of thought and feeling, that's enough for real effects."

"That sounds like pure superstition."

"Even superstition works if people think it does. And that is medical fact."

"I need to get some work done," he said flatly.

"Certainly." She started battening down her business on the telcon. Halfway through, she looked up. "When we left Earth, there were many women named Mira."

Joe shrugged away from her inquisitiveness. "That was then, and this is the day after forever. Mind your own business."

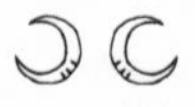

Joe was impossible. En route to the basement domain of Quartermaster Wimm Tucker, Catharin seethed with exasperation. Joe was arrogant but charming. Intrusive. But sometimes so unwittingly vulnerable that she felt a very inconvenient warmth of sympathy for him. Worst of all, from her point of view: he was unpredictable.

Catharin found Wimm in the warehouse, sorting the supplies included in today's drop from the Ship, with Eddy helping him. Wimm was a middle-aged man, pleasant-looking rather than handsome, with neat sand-blond hair. "One confidential item for you," he said, and handed her the wand she had been expecting.

Eddy said, "Can't they transmit information coded for your notebook?"

"Not with a snooper in my notebook."

"Joe?"

"Joe."

Wimm, Catharin, and Eddy looked at each other. Wimm said, "He's a bright, beautiful bastard, isn't he?"

She sighed. "Right on all three counts."

"Does he play chess?" Wimm asked.

"I doubt he has the temperament to be good at it."

"Well, I might just challenge him tonight. After I have my go at Aaron."

"Losing a game of chess might do him some good," Catharin said.

After supper and another hour of work in Medical, Catharin went to the mess hall, which doubled as recreation room, to find almost everyone else already there. At the wide end of the wedge-shaped mess hall, Aaron and Wimm were setting up their championship chess game. Boredom, thought Catharin, taking a seat near the door, was when this many people showed up to watch chess.

Unity Base resembled Antarctic or Martian or Lunar bases: an isolated community with long nights of winter outside and severe constraints on anyone's going outdoors. Not alone. Not in bad weather. Never in the twilight. By now, people were showing raw edges that hadn't been apparent months ago. Some tended toward irritability; others had assumed an artificial cheeriness even more grating to the nerves. Off in one corner sat Raj North, the man who had wandered off from Sam's survey team, which had led to Carlton Wing being added to the team and Raj being consigned to work in the greenhouse. Raj, visibly malcontented, cast a one-man pall over his corner of the room.

In another corner, Maya London flirted with Joe. She stood close to Joe with chin tilted up toward him, then made a half turn with a little flounce of her hips and a look over her shoulder with long eye contact, tossing her head so her hair rippled. Classic, textbook flirtatious behavior, Catharin thought with sharp displeasure. Worse, Joe seemed to encourage her. Everyone else covertly watched the little sideshow.

Fortunately, the chess match started, and attention turned to that. Maya departed from the mess hall while Joe, Catharin noticed with satisfaction, stayed.

Catharin's satisfaction lasted only until she realized that Joe, for the benefit of the people in his immediate vicinity, was imitating Maya. He pantomimed her flirtatiousness, including the flounce of the hips and the toss of imaginary long auburn hair. Shock waves and amusement went around the crowd, derailing the chess game.

Becca Fisher walked in through the door near Catharin. "Did I miss a joke?"

"Joe was ridiculing Maya behind her back."

Becca grinned. "That's safer than doing it to her face."

"It was extremely rude," said Catharin.

Becca sat down at Catharin's table. She worked hand cleaner around her fingertips, then pulled out a handkerchief to wipe them with. "If you come right down to it, I don't mind it one bit if some rudeness comes around back to her."

"Why?"

Becca fidgeted. "She wouldn't dare be rude to you. You're beautiful. She's no threat to you."

"Or to you," Catharin said quickly. "She's competent but shallow."

"She puts me down whenever she gets the chance. I can live with it, but I don't have to like it. Or her."

Catharin felt embarrassed. She had been oblivious to Maya's attitude toward Becca. Too busy looking for stasis sickness, for pathology like Hoffmann's, she had failed to notice something that hurt her friend.

After the disruption, the chess game got under way again. Eddy approached Catharin. "Did you see what Joe did?"

"Nobody in here didn't."

"Are you sure he's straight?"

"I'd swear it," Catharin said.

"I've never seen a straight man that good-looking who could imitate a vamp that good." Eddy sounded fascinated.

"I once had a stallion like him," Becca said. "That horse was a perfect gentleman with mares and nags. Full of himself and high-strung, but a gentleman. Except when it came to other studs. Then he was a prancing holy terror."

"What a fascinating image," said Eddy.

The Maya episode had evidently undermined Aaron's concentration. Wimm trounced him. Then Wimm invited Joe into a game. When Joe took him up on it, Wimm rubbed his hands. He was an understated, competent man, but the gesture said that he relished this challenge. The galvanized crowd clustered around the players.

Joe Toronto radiated intensity. With his attention fixed elsewhere, and all eyes on him and Wimm, Catharin could study his good shoulder bones and sculpted hands. She could hear him from here. "Your move." Without the all-too-typical sarcasm, his baritone voice was clipped, attractive, deep enough to be solidly masculine, high enough to be more interesting than a bass rumble. A chill shivered through her, a manifestation of pure physical attraction.

Catharin was living in the crucible of winter in Unity Base. Sexuality and jealousy, love and animosity, depression and aggression were crystallizing, cross-linking like a lattice of chemical reaction, affecting her as well as everyone else. She swore to herself that she would guard her dignity, unlike those who were finding various ways to lose theirs.

Muscles on the side of Joe's face bunched in frustration. Shortly thereafter, he lost his game.

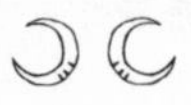

Sky brightly blue over his head, Joe followed a rough trail. It looked, even felt, like a winter morning. His breath condensed white. The cold kept down the alien smell of the pines. He set out to walk off the frustration of losing to Wimm Tucker last night.

To his surprise, Joe met Sam Berry stamping her way uphill. "I've got a jeep stuck on the road, and I need a big strong helper," Berry announced. "One who doesn't mind getting dirty. Most people can't stand the thought, but you've already been baptized in Green-mud once already. How about it?"

"Let me at it," Joe said cheerfully. The more exercise the better.

Berry was short and pear-shaped in middle age, but wore well-fitted field clothes and hiking boots and abundant gear attached to her belt. He had to press to keep up with her hiking pace. She veered off on a faint trail that twisted among rocks and furry pines. "On a clear day, there's a fine view over this way."

Sightseeing was fine with Joe. Threading across rough mountainside that was piebald with wet spots and shadowed, unmelted snow, the trail reached a promontory, a piece of solid mountain bone jutting out over the lower slopes. In the distance lay the hazy sea. A sliver of the sea thrust into the blue-green land.

Berry said, "Once Upstairs gets over their willies, I'm going to take the boat that way. Down the river into the estuary. That could be one of the richest veins of life on the planet, if this one is anything like Earth."

"A motherlode of sea bugs and slugs, sea-zucchinis, eh?" Joe would have liked a stormy, mysterious, dramatic seashore, preferably inhabited by seals, not just a broth incubator for overgrown invertebrates.

"There may be more to discover than we even dream. This *is* an alien world. Anything can happen here." Berry put her arms on her hips. "Except for one thing. I doubt we'll ever fill this world up with people like we did the last one. As much as the Vanguard is dead set on reproduction, it won't be as easy as it used to be. Right?"

Joe was fully aware that Catharin wanted to keep the truth a secret. But Berry had figured it out for herself. Joe saw no reason to lie. "Right. Sorry."

"I'm not sorry one bit. On Earth, humanity was a plague species, and I left because all my hard work in restoration ecology was going down the tubes. I'm glad that won't happen here."

Mother Nature with combat boots, Joe thought, and then she lobbed an artillery-grade question at him. "So, do you enjoy reproducing—or do your tastes in recreation sometimes run in nonreproductive directions? Do you sleep with girls, boys, or both?"

Questions like that didn't faze him; he'd fielded them all his life. But not every questioner deserved an answer. "Why do you want to know?"

She stood on the trail between him and the way back. Her chin jutted up at him. With the stern air of a judge, she said, "After last night, some people are wondering about you, and I'm one of them. I don't care how much romantic hell you raise around here except in just one regard. Eddy and Wimm are very good friends of mine, and I don't want to see a home wrecker in their future. In fact, I won't stand for it."

Joe smiled. "I can go either way, but my taste in men is very specific. It runs toward tall, blond, and striking. Not sweet little dark-haired guys like Eddy. I like Eddy and Wimm. They remind me of my dads."

Berry's expression changed to quizzical. "Let's go get my jeep out of the mud while you tell me more." She led the way back to the road with a spring in her step.

Joe said, "My mother was an artist. She had two friends, a gay couple, and all three shared a house. They helped her have me. Then they helped raise me. Two dads."

The jeep, a compact vehicle with massive batteries, was mired in muddy slush at a low spot in the rocky road. Joe shoved the jeep, straining against the weight of the batteries, while Berry revved the motor. Icy mud spattered on Joe, and the jeep crawled out of the mud.

"I don't usually care for whitecoats, but you seem all right," Berry told Joe. "Hop in!"

Berry drove with a lead foot and a carefree air, and the jeep lurched up the mountainside, careening on the muddy turns. Watching her hands on the steering wheel, Joe shouted, "Why are you wearing a wedding band?"

Berry smiled, deepening the elaborate wrinkles at the edges of her eyes, crow's-feet like an oriental fan. "She's my spouse, and she's up on the Ship, First Tier. Ten years from now, when she comes out, we'll be the same age."

Samantha Berry reminded Joe of Aunt Adrian—the old friend of the family who had been as sensible as Silke was not, and had done more than her share to give Joe the upbringing he needed. He'd been the fairies' child. In spite of occasional taunts from other kids, mainly American ones, he'd been happy as child of Silke and Mike and Jean-Claude and Adrian.

He could call up the memory of his home life then with as much eidetic clarity as anything else in his life. He could remember enjoying home, parents, holiday. Strangely, though, he didn't feel what he remembered. For that matter, he could remember lovers after Mira, mostly female, a few males. He could recall what he'd done in bed with each of them, too, but he couldn't remember feeling in love since Mira. What the hell had he been doing those years? Working. Walking. Inventing. Suddenly Joe thought about fairy tales, the ones about changelings who grow up to find that they have no soul. It was an uncomfortable thought.

Wait. There'd been a man in Toronto, Joe's last night on Earth. His name had been Tamas. A researcher in Joe's own field—a rival, in fact—but at the eleventh hour, in a maelstrom of fear and fury, Joe had been seized by a desire to leave several of his favorite discoveries somewhere other than the company he worked for. It had turned into more than that. Willowy for a male, shorter than Joe but not by much, blond and striking—and very bright—Tamas had given Joe a night that meant as much to Joe as the novel gene sequences that Joe had handed to Tamas.

For the first time since stasis, Joe remembered Tamas, with an aching alloy of loss and pleasure that he was glad to be able to feel.

Samantha Berry revved the jeep up the last grade to Unity Base and hit a shallow washout. Joe's stomach lurched from the washout and a thought that hit him out of the blue.

In more than one way, Tamas had resembled Catharin Gault.

☽☾

It was a long, hard afternoon for Catharin, work unbroken by the annoyance of Joe Toronto, who for once was not around. Finally Catharin retired to her bunk room. Afternoon sunlight flooded her small west-facing window, making the room as cozily warm as she wanted it nowadays. Which was warmer than she used to keep her room temperatures. Ever since stasis, Catharin had been oversensitive to cold.

In snug privacy, Catharin opened her personal notebook and read the wand that had been discreetly sent down to her from the Ship. Among other things, it detailed a thriving test-tube pregnancy implanted in a woman who had volunteered to carry it to term. If birth was premature, it could be sustained outside of the birth mother's womb now. But there was no sign of trouble. Joel had added a personal note: *Cat, we better think of a name.*

As agitated as she was tired, Catharin closed the reader and lay down under the blue blanket, dislodging Nunki to do so. Nunki regrouped and curled up beside her.

Catharin remembered vividly what she had told Joel months ago, before she came down to the planet. *Joel, our reproductive future is in jeopardy. I don't know if anyone is going to have a child the natural way ever again. Maybe it will only happen in test tubes, with a lot of material sifted down to a viable egg and sperm. Then in volunteer wombs, and probably most of those will miscarry, but we may be able to save some of them.*

Joel, I've tried an experiment. To learn what we can. It's in-vitro fertilization with some of the most damaged eggs and sperm. Both astronauts.

Uh, you and who else?

Mine and yours, Joel.

Joel had paced. She had thought that he was upset. And then Joel had walked over and put his hand on the nape of her neck. He whispered, "I'd rather do it the old-fashioned way," and his voice had the lilt that she loved to hear, and she had wished to God that he were not married. She'd distanced him and her own feelings by saying, *It won't live. But it will teach us something.*

Later, "*Joel. There's one woman in particular who would be a good choice to carry it. Your cousin. She has many of the same genes you do. She's volunteered.*"

And now it was Joel's turn.

We better think of a name.

Catharin tossed and tangled herself up in her blanket. A different remembered voice from a different man came back to haunt her. *Who do you want? God?*

I played God, she thought. Without having a god's wisdom.

Chapter Nineteen

BLUE TIME

Sam let Joe out before she went to garage the vehicle. Slapping his shoulder affectionately, she pointed him at the men's outside shower. "Hose down," she reminded him.

Emerging from the shower in a poorly fitting, generic coverall, Joe was attracted by a silvery thread of sound, conspicuous in the too-soundless outdoors. It came from behind the hangar, where he found Becca Fisher sitting cross-legged on a large rock under a furry pine. Playing a silver flute that gleamed in the midday sun, she acknowledged Joe's arrival with a nod between one note and the next. Joe did not recognize the song except as something Irish. It fascinated him. So did she, although he was not quite sure why. Becca was a small woman. She had a slight upper body relative to her hips. Her face looked androgynous, formed of delicate edges and planes rather than soft curves.

"This world seems incomplete. That's why I like to play my flute outdoors. This world needs bees and birds."

Joe was badly dressed, but it did not matter. Women had found him attractive ever since he was a young teenager. "You and I could fix the lack of birds and bees," he said.

The offhanded proposition made Becca turn bright pink. She said quickly, "I meant environmental sounds."

"You're right. Play some more."

She rearranged herself on her rock and played a new song. Her eyes flicked to him under long translucent lashes.

The metal must have been cool to her lips. Joe's wet hair was ice cold. But he did not mind. He felt warm—alive—inside. And true to his old form, the activity of his imagination matched that of his libido. The next time she paused, Joe said, "You're Pan in disguise, aren't you?"

"Pan?" A look of consternation crossed her face. "I thought Pan was male, with goat's horns and hoofs."

"That's the one."

Hopping to her feet on the rock, and therefore at Joe's eye level, she demanded, "Are you calling me a goat?"

"No. It's just that your music sounds like spring." *And you have strong legs and nimble feet. And goats can be pretty.*

"But Pan had a wooden panpipe."

"It wouldn't have to be made of wood nowadays. That's why you're here, isn't it? To bring spring to a dormant world?"

A smile tweaked the edges of her lips.

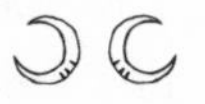

Joe put his supper dishes in the cleaning window just as Wimm hit the switch to roll the mess hall's shutters closed against the night. From the narrow end of the hall, Manhattan made a serious announcement, a variation of the usual one. "It is now twelve PM. Those who are taking walks, remember the rules. Buddy system. And the full moon rises at sunset. That means admire it, but stay close to home, and nobody leave the dome after full twilight begins at fourteen hundred."

Joe joined the unhurried exodus from the mess hall. He lifted his jacket from its peg in the mess hall's back wall and put it on, walking out the dome's main door by himself.

Becca Fisher veered toward him. "Planning to break a rule?" She hurried to match his stride.

Joe slowed down. "Got your flute under your jacket? Going out to sing up some crocuses?"

Becca gave him a little grin. "Too cold to play a metal instrument, Joe."

"In that case, I know a good place to watch the moon rise. Interested?"

"That isn't breaking the rule, but it's bending it."

"Game?"

"Game." Becca zipped up her jacket.

It wasn't far down the road to the trail to Sam's favorite outlook. From behind Becca, Joe enjoyed watching her walk. She moved energetically, with hands tucked in jacket pockets and an appealing, feminine sort of swagger. She said, "I like the way the light slants through the pines. It's like home if I squint. I mean Brightwood, Tennessee, in the Smoky Mountains. What's that, a trail? Does it lead to where you want to go?"

At the trail's end, Becca stopped on the brink of the promontory. A cold, wet wind from the sea knifed through the fabric of their jackets.

"Brr!" said Becca. "Great view, but I don't think I can stick around up here until moonrise."

"It'll be warmer just below here, and there's probably a spot nearly as good to watch the moon come up," Joe pointed out. They scrambled down the shoulder of the promontory. Below the promontory a stream ran swiftly, with an almost metallic clatter of small rocks. And the wind still felt cold.

"Brr. I can't stand still here either," Becca admitted.

"Then let's go downhill some more."

"This isn't the time to start a long hike," she reminded him.

"At the rate the sun moves, we've got an hour before twilight. See that grove of trees the stream flows into? They'll break the wind."

He was right; the whatever-kind of trees did break the wind and make it easier to linger in one place. Becca looked at the trees, her forehead furrowed in puzzlement. "These aren't furry pines. They look like another kind of tree that usually grows farther downhill. Smaller, but the leaves look the same, sort of like oaks."

Joe said, "According to Wing, there's nothing on Green as highly evolved as oaks. These are analogues to gingkos, which are much more primitive than oaks. They flourish at a lower elevation."

"We're in a sheltered valley here. Maybe the ginkgo-things like it farther down because it's warmer, but this little valley is right for them."

Joe felt comfortable here. Becca, on the other hand, still needed to move to stay warm. A heavy, wide mass of logs was lodged in the streambed. Debris from the blast that flattened the Mountain for Unity Base, Joe guessed. Becca pranced back and forth across the deadfall, surefooted, with small feet in neat boots. Joe thought about the graceful, wild, goat-footed god Pan.

Becca looked up at the crowns of the trees, where late light streamed between their slender, platted branches. "With sunlight behind the leaves, they look like thin, carved slices of turquoise." Wonder was written on her upturned face. Her lower lip glistened, as though she had absentmindedly moistened it with her tongue. "This was a great idea."

The stream ran wider and deeper. On impulse, Joe jumped to the opposite side.

"Here I come." Becca gathered herself for the leap.

"Isn't it kind of long for you?" Joe asked. Becca answered by launching herself across the water. She made it, but the stream bank started to crumble under her feet.

Joe caught Becca. Then he pulled her closer and kissed her. He felt her back stiffen in surprise, so he quickly let her go and pocketed his hands. They stared at each other.

"What's that?" she asked.

"What?"

"That sound." She took his wrist. The gesture pleased him, telling him that she had accepted his kiss or at least overlooked it.

Following the bright, burbling sound, they discovered an astonishingly green dell. Trees ringed the dell, thick with turquoise leaves. Dapples of late sunlight splashed on lush ferns growing in the dell's sides. The bottom of the dell was green and lush, with the stream running through the middle of it. Golden mist hung above the purling water. Most surprising of all, the air felt warm, like going from winter to spring in a few short steps.

Joe said, "It heard you, Becca. The Mountain heard you playing."

She knelt onto the green floor of the dell. "This is moss, not grass. Sweet clean moss." Joe crouched beside her on the moss. Too warm for a jacket, he took his off and dropped it in a heap. Becca unfastened hers. Under the jacket she wore a simple shirt, unbuttoned to the collarbone.

She flopped down beside the edge of the stream and dangled a finger into a pool with pieces of golden fog hanging over it. "There's snowmelt coming from upstream. But there's *warm* water bubbling up here. And look, colored pebbles." She held up a handful of glistening stones. Joe recognized Wing's amber.

Joe knelt beside her, and with an urge that he could not resist, placed his hands on the sides of her hips.

Becca quickly rolled out from under his hands and curled up between him and the edge of the water, knees against her chest. "What do you want?!"

Joe backed off. "I wanted to kiss you again. I'm sorry."

"Just don't take me by surprise."

"Okay." Joe sat down. Consumed with desire for her, he wrapped his arms around his knees. Lust or love or life itself—he wasn't sure how to identify the feeling, but it flared, driving out the stasis-cold that lurked in the depths of his being. Arms locked around his knees, Joe barely contained himself. "You might want to leave," he said, his voice rough.

"And I might not." She came to him, put her hand on his shoulders, and lightly kissed the side of his face.

Touching her chin with his fingertips, he brought her face closer to his, tracing the edge of her jaw, as delicate as porcelain under his fingertips. This time he kissed her longer than before; long enough to feel the soft, moist warmth of her lips against his. Laughter bubbling up, she wrapped her arms around his neck and kissed him back harder.

☽ ☾

Breaking off the kiss—third or tenth, Joe had lost count—she sat bolt upright. "Oh, no! It's *late*!"

Joe opened his eyes to see Becca profiled against pure blue twilight. "Don't go away," Joe said.

"I'm not. You're going with me. Rules are rules."

Joe touched her neck, which felt warm and moist. He tangled his fingers in her hair. "Don't make us go," he pleaded. "It's cold out there. A little while longer won't matter. We've already broken the rule."

"I'm enjoying this," she admitted. "But you're the one who got in trouble in twilight."

"I was hurt," he said quietly. "And scared."

She soothingly ran her fingers through his hair. Joe offered her another kiss. She accepted it, with warm soft lips. His hand slid onto the curve of her back. She breathed rapidly, and her back was supple, flexing into him.

With his fingertips, he traced the fine edge of her jaw, and the side of her neck, followed the edge of her shirt to where it was buttoned between her breasts. He curled his fingers around the material, marveling at how soft and warm she felt against his knuckles, under the shirt. He gently pushed her to lie down, and she let him, and the moss under them smelled like challah bread or patchouli, and felt as soft as bedding.

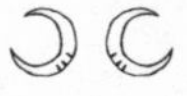

She pulled away from him abruptly. Joe moved to stay beside her, but the urgent tone of her voice brought him up short. "*Joe!* Where have we come to?"

Wondering what she wanted to know, Joe answered, "A world called Green?"

Bathed in blue light, her body language telegraphed alarm. She sat up straight, arms folded over her breasts. "Do right and wrong exist here like they did on Earth?"

Joe's body was riveted on pleasure, but he held himself back from the woman and tried to marshal some kind of intelligible thought for her. "Sure. Just like day and night exist here. It's the same universe."

"But there's Blue times too, and that's different from Earth. I wouldn't do this on Earth. Is what we're doing right or wrong?" she asked urgently.

"Neither. It's Blue," he said, as sure of the truth of that as he was unsure of what logic made it so.

"I don't understand."

Teased out by the sweet, ambiguous smell of the moss, old memories and feelings came to Joe's mind. "I loved a woman for the first time at the University in Toronto, when I was fourteen."

"Fourteen?!"

"But it was perfect. I was precocious. She was a small woman, but I was just the right size for her then, because I wasn't grown. We had pastry in cafes, made love in a park at night. She taught me. I loved her. Blue time is—" For once in his life, thought came no faster than words. "When what you do breaks the rules, but it makes a wonderful new pattern, even if only for an hour or a year. That's blue."

"This feels that way to me too," she whispered, and held her hands toward him.

☽☾

Like a little kid, her active playful phase was followed by falling sound asleep. She only partly came awake when he started putting her clothes back on, then murmured an objection when he picked her up and started carrying her uphill. It took fifteen minutes of blue winter air to wake her up completely.

"This is silly," Becca objected.

"You're lighter here than on Earth."

"What'll you say if somebody sees us coming back in like this?"

"I'll say you sprained your ankle, which is why we're a bit late. That should cover the forty-five minutes or so we'll have to explain away, eh?"

"Why don't we say *you* sprained your ankle?"

"Sure, if you carry me home."

She laughed, but stayed in his arms. Joe felt pleased. She wasn't the carry-me type of girl; she felt truly at ease, trusting him. She swung her feet and burrowed her cold chin into the warmth of his neck.

Joe did not feel cold at all. The exercise was enough to warm him on the outside. Afterglow warmed him inside.

Medical was reliably the least populated entrance into the Base. Joe entered quietly, operating the door one-handed with his arms full of Becca.

Catharin, standing not far from the door, dropped a clipboard she'd been holding. "*Where have you been all evening?*"

Behind Catharin, Eddy stood with his mouth agape.

The conspicuous chronometer on the Medical wall said 1800 PM. Becca yelped with dismay. They'd been in the dell for more than four hours. Joe's mind slipped out of gear while Becca clung to his neck, speechless. Vivid green smears showed up all over her clothes, with a matching streak across her nose. The sweet-smelling ground moss had left abundant stains.

Catharin saw the green too. She stepped in front of Joe. "*What did you do to her?*" The fiction of a sprained ankle fled from Joe's mind, because Catharin was clearly furious.

Becca blurted, "It wasn't his fault!"

Catharin arched an eyebrow.

Overcome by consternation, Joe shoved Becca into Catharin's arms. Catharin took a step back under the weight of the smaller woman, but did not drop her.

Joe fled from Medical. Catharin screamed after him, "Take a bath *immediately*!"

Chapter Twenty

MELTWATERS

Becca emerged from the Medical shower wrapped in a large towel, pink with hot water and embarrassment, as Catharin returned with clean clothes from Becca's bunk room. "Aaron called in the search party, and everybody's glad that you and Joe are accounted for," Catharin reported. "Unfortunately, the Base is buzzing about it."

Sitting down on the edge of a cot, Becca put her head in her hands. "Do people know we spent four hours fooling around with each other?"

"Yes, because Alvin guessed as much, and is busy spreading the news."

"Oh, *damn*. What am I going to tell Domino?" Becca whispered.

"I can't imagine. Are you sure Joe didn't coerce you?"

Becca shook her head energetically. "It was just as much my idea as his."

"In that case, do you mind if I ask how it came about?"

"I don't *know*!" Becca's voice shot up to an incredulous squeak. "I do *not* understand why I let this happen. Joe's too tall for my tastes, I have never in my life fallen for a guy who made me look like a midget standing next to him in public, and he's *way* too moody!" She looked at Catharin with wide blue eyes.

Catharin seated herself on the cot next to Becca. "You were out in the moonlight, and that's been known to cause perceptual problems, illusions, and even mood changes."

"Other people lost their minds, but the moonlight made me lose my *morals*!?" Becca threw up her hands. "It felt right at the time!"

"Sex usually does," Catharin pointed out.

"I forgot that Domino would mind!" Consternation was written across Becca's face. "Or that you would," she said in a small voice. "I'm sorry. I didn't mean to poach."

Feeling suddenly vindicated, somehow, Catharin murmured, "I haven't laid claim to him."

"You could be mad at me anyway and I wouldn't blame you," Becca murmured.

"I'm not mad at you. I was terrified for you because you had disappeared in the moonlight. I am vastly relieved that you aren't hurt." She thought, but didn't add, *And not changed*. Becca seemed completely herself, albeit badly rattled.

"Cat, moonlight wasn't all. There was this warm little place on the mountainside, a dell, and it was really pretty and cozy, and I think the place suggested what we did."

Catharin gave her an incredulous look.

"I think—no, it's not a thinking thing. It's pure intuition, if not an overactive imagination. But it felt to me like the place had the idea. It really did. Nothing and no one made me do it, not Joe. He was a gentleman. Um, there's something you ought to know, Cat. He's quite a lover."

"A Don Juan?" Catharin heard the edge of disapproval in her own voice.

Becca shook her head. She turned pink again but, candid as ever, went ahead with an explanation. "Those hands of his that you admire so much—he's really good with them."

☽☾

Sometime in the middle of the long, cold, unstructured darkness that the clock called day, Joe went to look for Becca. He found her in the hangar, following flute melody into the back corner where the pilots kept a kind of office. It was tolerably warm in the office because she had a small heating unit going.

She put her flute aside, looking small, unhappy, and not surprised to see him. "Damn it, Joe, every busybody in this base if not up on the Ship is talking about us."

"I'm sorry. I honestly didn't think we spent that long. When I climbed up the Mountain the first time, two hours seemed like all night. I don't know why four felt like forty minutes."

She nodded. "It was unreal there. Everything else felt like a dream. Now that does."

"It doesn't have to be a dream," Joe suggested.

"I think it does."

Her words hit him like cold water in the face. "Why?"

She abruptly left the office. Joe trailed after her into the hangar. She turned on the overhead lights, pulled on gloves that had been lying with an open toolbox on a small table in the hangar, picked up a tool, and turned toward her plane, her back to Joe. *Kite*'s engine cowling was open. Becca reached in and started adjusting something.

"God damn it, is she right?" Joe demanded.

"Who?"

"Catharin. Did I hurt you?"

Becca looked over her shoulder. "No. Not at all, Joe. As for all this gossip, well, I'll live." She shrugged.

Breath came out with white vapor in the chilly hangar, and words sounded hollow, like so much cold smoke. Joe wanted to touch Becca, persuade her with physical gestures. But her plane loomed over her like a stern guardian spirit. Seething in frustration, he kept his hands in his pockets. "Don't you think we ought to close ranks?"

"What do you mean?"

"Look smug about what happened. For the sake of the busybodies."

"I don't think that'll work for me."

"Why not, Becca?"

"One problem is, I've got a boyfriend. Or had one."

The copter hulked in its own corner of the hangar. Joe could guess the identity of the boyfriend. And he wanted Becca to be his, not Domino's. "So, you've got choices, eh?"

"Not really. I've decided to mend things with him."

Decided without asking Joe. He let out a short, sharp breath between his teeth. Becca flinched and hovered closer to the plane. Joe wanted to snap, *So, do you usually two-time?*

But Joe remembered his younger dad, gentle Jean-Claude, telling him, using his family nickname, *Jato, you must learn to hold your tongue. Don't be so sarcastic. It can hurt people terribly*. Joe said, "He's a better lover than me, eh?"

"Oh, Joe." Her low voice sent a chill of desire through Joe. "The thing is, I knew Domino on Earth. He was one reason I could bear to leave, knowing he'd be here as a friend, at least. We've been making up our minds to be more than friends."

Joe's sex drive was ready to put words into his mouth. Not sarcasm: sweet persuasion. Then he remembered his dad Mike—a pragmatic man doing his best to be a good father for an oversexed teenage boy—saying dryly, *Next time, don't let the little head think for the big one, son.* Joe just hunched his shoulders in the hangar's cold.

"You'll settle down with someone else, someone I care a lot about too."

Hearing a disconsolate note in her voice, Joe seized on it. "Don't think I was just making do with you until something better came along. You're beautiful."

She flared, "Don't you dare say that to me and not mean it."

"But I do." Joe wanted to touch her, to persuade her how much he meant what he had said. He slid his fingers over the plane's cold wing instead. "You're quite a woman."

"*You* think so?" He read vulnerability on her face, legible even in the harsh lighting.

"I know so."

"Just between us, I . . . did enjoy it." She turned her face half away from him, eyes closed, profile against the plane, a glint of a tear under her eyelashes.

Joe understood why she had left the warm office for the cold hangar. She wanted him as much as he wanted her. Therefore she had fled to where it was too cold to do anything about want like that. Joe could not stand the painful clarity of the moment anymore. He shrugged. "All right. We'll leave it at once and only once. Do you want me to say I pressured you?"

"Oh, no, Joe. You're right. It was as much my idea as yours. I'll tell Domino that. He can react however he sees fit. I think he'll get over it."

Joe felt hollow, as though he had just lost something important and irreplaceable. "You're sure there's nothing I can do for you to love me?"

"My mind's made up. But I do love you." Placing her hands on his chest to distance him, she kissed the edge of his lips. Then she turned her head aside and sighed, her regret a moment of faint smoke that vanished into the air. "I don't think we'll be the headline news around here too long. Sam's riverboat test flight is coming up."

To be so close yet light-years away from her made Joe ache. But he forced a grin. "Test float, you mean."

Becca laughed. "Yes, I do mean that."

☽ ☾

Becca was in the crowd that had come to watch the *Beagle* launched. But she avoided Joe and let Domino stick possessively by her side. At least she wasn't being a passive doll. She made some remark to Domino and jabbed his rib cage with her elbow, a joke with a bony point. Their laughter jolted him.

Only a dusting of snow lingered on the Mountain, whiteness around the feet of the trees. The slopes were lively with waters, melted snow. Wind flowed warm from the sea. Warm air met cold water, and cool fog filled the backwater like a gray blanket. The riverboat team unmoored *Beagle* and let it bob in the backwater for a checkup. By the time the checkout was done, the sun showed through the fog, pale orange like a piece of candy.

Joe remembered the candy-sweet, hours-long moment that he had spent playing with Becca. Lovely and lively really were close, just a vowel apart. Joe wanted Becca so much that it hurt just as much as his cracked shoulder bone had pained him, and deeper.

Domino noticed Joe watching Becca. Radiating hostility, Domino managed to block Joe's view of her. The *Beagle*'s crew was now running interminable calibrations of their scientific equipment. Eddy Pazmino drifted over to Joe's side. "I suppose they can't just hop in and roar away. But it's not terribly exciting."

Joe agreed.

"The people-watching is a bit more diverting. Isn't he pretty?" said Eddy. He cocked his head toward Domino.

"Pretty hostile too," said Joe.

"He's not the only one. I don't suppose you've heard Maya London's reaction?"

"Do I want to?"

"Oh, you'll appreciate this. Maya said, 'I can't believe that urchin beat me to him!'"

That made Joe grin. "The urchin's a sweetheart."

Eddy nodded wisely. "I know what you mean. It's why I stay with Wimm."

Beagle finally pulled out of its dock, engine churning the gray water. Cheers sounded all around. When the boat disappeared around the tributary's curve, the onlookers sorted themselves out to ride in the jeeps or hike back up the Mountain. Eddy plucked Wimm out of the crowd and pulled him in Joe's direction. Holding hands with Wimm, Eddy asked, "Catharin said that Becca mentioned something about a pretty dell, one that had aphrodisiac effects."

"Hadn't thought about it that way," said Joe. "And I'd be happier if you didn't spread it around." If he couldn't have Becca again, he felt jealously possessive of the memory of making love in the gold and green and blue place.

"Of course. But could you give us directions to get there?"

☽☾

Back in Medical, Joe split the telcon window. Half showed the picture from *Beagle*. The boat floated on blue-gray water as its occupants scanned for organisms under the glass bottom.

The other half of the window communicated with the gene center lab on the Ship. Mass production of his antibodies was under way. The bacterial clones had been culled, the most productive of them set up to grow en masse. Each bacterium was infected with the virus Joe had designed to introduce the catalytic antibody instructions into its genetic coding, and the viral material was diligent. The bacteria oozed antibody. It would be processed to administer to people with aching, wasted muscles.

Beagle chugged along with a blunt wake behind it. Great excitement ensued when something that looked like a dessert plate with eight jointed legs started up in a cloud of particles out of the slime on the bottom of the river.

A dark and slimy impulse lifted up out of the depths of Joe's mind. He wanted to confront Becca, to argue with her, and turn his sarcasm loose on her after all. Maybe she deserved it. She'd loved him and let him go.

Over the telcon Srivastava, with a harumph, had to repeat what he had just been saying. "Congratulations, Dr. Toronto. Our project is very successful so far, and the clinical trials commence today."

"Fine. Keep me apprised. I've got another project on my plate."

Joe left Srivastava to tend his bacterial garden. Trying to distract himself from Becca, Joe opened up the virtual notebook to review the molecular details of Patient Doe's stasis-racked body.

The man's blood wasn't working right. Worse than the existing hemoglobin being damaged, the blood stem cells hadn't made any good new stuff since the star flight. Too much DNA in the stem cells had been disarrayed—relatively few bases out of place, but in the intricate puzzle palace that was DNA, the few were too many.

Joe had believed that he could fix the patient's blood since the night Catharin handed him the summary. But today, pondering the damaged DNA that was causing the problem, Joe suddenly and very clearly knew *why* he could fix it. Not because he'd invented calico hair and sea dogs. Rather, because of the work he'd been forced into at the end of his life on Earth. Before he ran away from it, he'd learned a very great deal about the human genome and what parts of it were the keys to life and death.

With startling clarity, Joe recalled the initial excitement of that project. And how he'd eventually realized that he had been maneuvered into a job that would take all of his life and genius. And the final shock that had made him claw and lie his way out of the trap.

Joe felt prickly sweat break out on his skin. His eidetic memory was not only clear as glass, it was shot through with the emotional hell he'd gone through just before he left Earth. Patient Doe couldn't compete with these memories. Nor could the river expedition. Pacing, he stubbed his toe on the leg of Catharin's chair. Joe cursed. That had been happening to him ever since he came out of stasis, stubbed toes and stumbling into things. Maybe he just hadn't gotten used to the Ship's variable gravity, or the slightly-less-than-Earth gravity here. Or maybe stasis had inflicted subclinical nerve damage, he thought grimly, with the molecular wrack of Patient Doe still displayed in the telcon window.

The stubbed toes reminded him of his adolescent growth spurt, and the calamitous agonies and ecstasies of that time. Skinned elbows and barked shins. And his first lover: small, lively, lovely Mira. Joe remembered his anger and his pain when Mira's Old Catholic parents found out about the two of them, and forced them apart. His heart pounded out the quickened beat of old rage.

Catharin barged in to use the telcon. "May I?"

Joe shrugged, camouflaging the fact that he was relieved to have the wild train of his thought derailed by her interruption. Catharin shunted the telcon link from his lab in the research center to hers in the hospital. Joe watched over her shoulder. "Still trying to find the crazy button, eh?"

"We need to know why he cracked up." Catharin spoke with a head nurse, who reported that Hoffmann had been incoherent and incomprehensible except to the extent that he clearly believed that the psychiatric nurses were all virus-infested aliens in human shells.

Catharin set the telcon up to receive pure data from tests on Hoffmann's brain. She drew up a chair at the telcon, in case anything interesting came across with a flag on it. Relaxing, she stretched out her long legs, her knees only a few inches from Joe—a more companionable distance than usual.

Beyond a few words of business, they had not spoken since Joe had shoved Becca into Catharin's arms the other night. Feeling suddenly slightly disoriented, Joe asked, "Do tall girls have growth spurts?"

Catharin smiled. "I certainly did. My parents even took me to the doctor when I was twelve and shot up from five four to five eleven. They thought I was a mutant." Her mouth leveled, squeezing out the smile. "That ruffled my fragile self-image. Later, though, height helped me pass for older. I went to college somewhat early."

"I got dragged to the doctor on suspicion of being a mutant too."

"For your growth spurt?"

"Not that. When I was a kid, I only slept about three hours a night."

She looked at him thoughtfully. "You don't sleep very much now. I thought that was . . . recent."

"Hell, no."

"In fact, I thought you were bipolar," she admitted.

He snorted. "You're about the sixteenth doctor or guidance counselor to wonder about that. No, *non*, I'm not a mutant and not bipolar either, even if

I do have traits that make people start to wonder. Not needing much sleep is normal for me. So's moodiness. I don't go on spending sprees, but I do have a high sex drive. It's not manic, it's constant. So you won't get to practice psychopharmacology on me. Sorry," he bristled.

"I'm not sorry at all."

Her voice was pitched a shade lower and slower than he expected. The tone gave Joe pause. Had he admitted to more than what he'd intended? High sex drive, he'd blurted. He wondered what Becca had shared with Catharin. Joe felt his face heat up.

"Are you coming to Wimm's party tonight?"

Joe shrugged.

"Oh, do. We haven't had a party since Unity Base was founded, and it's about time."

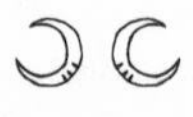

CONGRATULATIONS, SAM read a large, hand-lettered banner. The river explorers were being feted for getting their feet wet. Wimm had opened the patio roof despite a cold night outside: he had the heating units going full blast. Lights had been strung up around the patio. Clouds skidded across the night sky above, ice blue where they crossed the gibbous blob of a moon in the west.

Joe felt a brittle watchfulness centered on him as Domino shepherded Becca away. Catharin promptly walked up and handed Joe a drink. Wimm had hops plants growing in a corner of the greenhouse and claimed to have synthesized a reasonable approximation of fermented barley. But what Wimm called nearly beer was not, in Joe's opinion, near enough.

Catharin nudged Joe. "Look at the time."

"Where?" Then he saw the object suspended over the patio, a ridiculous thing: a dial clock, kludged together. "That?"

"Alvin made it. Go ahead and read it. What time does it say?"

"Twelve fifty—What?" The dial of the clock showed thirteen numbers, and the hour hand was pushing thirteen, thirteen o' clock.

Catharin laughed. "It's been up there the whole time, thirteen and all! You didn't notice."

Sinking, the moon behind the clouds reddened. The clouds went unearthly purple for an eerie moment, then back to gray normal. Joe breathed easier. With the moon out of sight, the party seemed more like a university mixer. Somebody put on bland but danceable music.

"You do dance?" Catharin put a hand on his arm. *Yeah, and trip on my own feet ever since I got here. Thanks for the opportunity to trip on yours in public.* Joe abandoned his not-too-near beer on the side table, and started off across the floor with Catharin.

He was surprised to find her a good dancer. She wore earrings that gleamed as she moved. Real gold, Joe thought, and a nice accent beside facial features that were regular and attractive. It dawned on Joe that if it had really been a university or lab mixer in his previous life, he would have singled this woman out of the crowd to start with.

Distracted, Joe stepped on Catharin's left foot. "Sorry," he muttered.

As a new song started up, Aaron materialized beside Catharin. "May I?"

Catharin glided away with Aaron. So Joe borrowed Eddy for the next dance. He started something. For the next hour nearly everybody tried a round with everybody else. Joe had Catharin one more time, and she pulled him close to whisper, "Thank you for coming."

☽☾

Late in the night, Joe went back to the Penthouse for a few hours of sleep. Wing was already sacked out, getting his well-earned night's rest after his participation in the successful field trip. Joe didn't sleep readily. His body wanted company in here other than the peaceably snoozing Wing. Joe tossed and turned, his mind full of Becca and Catharin, the women tangled together in a skein of arousal and consternation.

He'd thought that Catharin hated him. And that the feeling was mutual. And, finally, that she was inhibited. But he began to think that he had been wrong on all counts. Beyond a doubt, her self-control was intentional.

Joe slid sideways into an uneasy sleep and dreamed about the gibbous blue moon high in a strange sky in a shroud of purple cloud.

Chapter Twenty-One

HIGH TIDE

The telcon window showed images taken by Becca Fisher from *Kite* weeks earlier. Sitting in the conference room with Manhattan, Samantha Berry, Becca, and Catharin, Joe watched the window as raptly as the rest of them. The Ship's Intelligence had enhanced the images, originally blurred and distant, into a still imperfect but tantalizing clue to life on Green.

Cloud-diffused sunlight put a faint sheen on the river's estuary. In the water, for only a few moments, a dark oblong shape appeared. It might have been a submerged rock or shoal. Except it moved against the tide.

Joe wanted it to be a seal. It probably wasn't even close. The idea excited him anyway. When he was little, he'd been Silke's son. He'd imagined being a Selkie's son out of a myth. And he grew up fascinated by the transformation of living beings. Anything remotely resembling a seal would make Green far more interesting to Joe Toronto.

"Everybody seen enough?" asked Aaron.

"Not by a long shot," said Sam. "But we've looked at that picture enough."

The telcon window switched to the people Upstairs—Captain Bixby and the starship pilot, Atlanta, who asked, "Was that a sea monster?"

Sam said, "Maybe a single large bony fish, but more likely a school of smaller fishes."

Joe suppressed a skeptical grunt. To his eye, it hadn't moved like a swarm.

Sam continued, "On Earth, estuaries were rich breeding grounds for ocean life. Here, in spring, the river's mouth may harbor tendrils of the highest forms of life on Green. We should take *Beagle* into the estuary."

"That's the reward," said Aaron. "Now we've got to evaluate the risk, and—" he nodded toward the telcon "—ask for permission."

"We know the worst danger," said Sam immediately. "It's the moonlight. We know to curtail ambitious activities in proportion to the amount of moonlight at night. If we leave at Green-dawn, *Beagle* can make it to the estuary and back well before the sun sets. The sooner we go for it the better. The moon is new again. There's only a trace of moonlight mixed into the daylight. Captain, in space-faring terms, what I'm proposing is a modest little day trip."

The Captain nodded slowly, probably reflecting on his own role in the hazardous exploration of the Solar System. Smart move on Sam's part, to allude to that: by such a yardstick, her expedition did sound like a Sunday picnic.

"I've decided," Bixby said. "The quarantine will remain in effect for six weeks after the trip, until Cat sees if anybody develops strange fever. But you have my permission to go for the river. Wish I could come along."

Beside him, Joel Atlanta nodded too. With both men in the same picture, both in Ship's coveralls, the contrast between them was stark. Atlanta was a man in his prime, brown-skinned features regular and smooth. Bixby looked aged and sick. His face was laced with wrinkles; the skin had a pallor that made it look like crumpled paper.

Joe suddenly realized who Patient Doe was. Not a nobody and not an anonymous field of molecular wreckage.

A week ago, Joe had transmitted up to his staff the specifications for DNA repair of Patient Doe's blood. They created a retroviral package containing the material for functional hemoglobin and infected his blood marrow with it. Patient Doe had since reported feeling better and had been able to get up out of bed.

Joe could see with his own eyes how much more repair work Bixby needed to keep him alive. Joe forgot about fish in the gray river. He had more exciting work: wrecked DNA in a real man. If Joe could bring order out of that chaos, and make Bixby better, it would please Catharin—

Wanting to please Catharin? That impulse, a shadowy feeling flashing under the surface of his mind, quickly submerged again, and left Joe disturbed.

☽☾

A hand-lettered message appeared overnight on the mess hall's bulletin board: SAMANTHA (SAM) BERRY HEREAFTER WISHES TO BE KNOWN AS S. HOUSTON.

The name sounded like a good fit, Joe thought. Hadn't Sam Houston been a general somewhere? Mother Nature in combat boots.

For the big day of the expedition, breakfast was served alfresco, on the patio, the thin wedge of the dome with a roof that could be rolled back. Plenty of seating was provided by crates and rolls of supplies. The air outdoors felt cold and fresh, buffered by heating units on the patio, and the sky looked pretty: a predawn lapis lazuli, shading to violet, a rim of magenta on the horizon. Wimm had done his best with the synthetic-eggs Benedict. The food tasted good with general anticipation for sauce. Knives and forks clacked against plates. Wing came up with a plate in his hand. Joe made room for him to sit on the crate. "Launch still looks good?"

"According to the Ship, we expect clouds by late afternoon, but no rain."

Aaron and his assistant, Maya, clustered with Sam and her lieutenants, finishing up the plans for the expedition. There was no sign of Becca. But Catharin arrived looking better put-together than almost anyone else at this hour.

"Catharin is a cool customer," Joe said to Wing.

"She's like a violin. Quiet and tightly strung."

"D'you suppose she ever lets her hair down?"

Wing answered with a promptness suggesting he'd reflected on this topic before. "I think her nickname, Cat, is apt, Joe. I think she has the soul of a tiger."

Catharin swerved over to join them. Either she was being sociable or, more likely, sensed them talking about her and came to take control of the situation. Wing did not miss a beat. He chirped, "We have a difference of opinion, and you're on my side."

"I am?"

"When we left Earth, he took the new surname Toronto to honor his home city. Many others have done the same."

"Not home, favorite. People are still doing it," Joe contributed. "Seen the mess hall bulletin board?"

Catharin gave a quick smile. "That's her way of expressing confidence in everything we're doing."

"You believe in the same things, but you didn't change your surname," said Wing.

"I don't have to," she said pleasantly. "I have my middle name, which my parents gave me in honor of a city. One of the luminous cities of the Western world."

She said no more, so Joe guessed. "Los Angeles?"

"Certainly not. Did you ever study history?"

Wing offered, "Athens. Athena?"

Catharin smiled. "Close."

"Rome, Roma," said Joe.

"Even closer."

"Italy? Venice. Milan. Florence—"

"Right."

"You don't look like a Florence," Joe commented. "And the time I was there it didn't look like much of a city."

"Didn't you notice the old cathedrals and campaniles? The glory was cracked and faded in places, but it still showed, an echo of the Renaissance. As to your other remark, my parents used the Italian form."

"Firenze," said Joe.

Sam began rounding up her troops. Catharin said, "Take good care, Carl."

"No rain today," said Joe to Wing. "So make your own luck."

Wing hurried away. Catharin checked her watch. "I almost forgot, I've got a conference with the Ship in three minutes. No time for breakfast now. May I?" She helped herself to a triangle of toast from Joe's plate, giving him a sparkling little smile. Joe was left with the plate on his lap and the word "Firenze" echoing in his mind like a campanile chime.

☽☾

The riverboat had met its destiny, floating capably toward the sea. Unfortunately, the trip differed little from the uneventful maiden voyage. A few organisms turned up, scuttling aquatic bugs and slugs trailing in the bottom slime.

Joe sporadically listened in to the chatter between *Beagle* and Aaron and the biologists on the Ship. Joe knew those people, the xenobiologists, most of them scientists of the pedestrian type that he disliked. They had limitless interest in protozoa and slime. The prospect of mollusks sent them toward ecstasy.

Joe amused himself by hacking his way into Catharin's virtual notebook—her private one. Having the name of Bixby to go on, Joe found the man's medical records in full. And a highlighted note. *Joe, I'll tell you all you need to know. Just ask me. Please stay out of these files. Respect his privacy.*

Damn. She'd anticipated him, even while it was getting progressively clearer to him that he did not understand her at all.

Hearing footsteps, he quickly closed Catharin's notebook. But the steps belonged to Alvin Crawford. The shutters of the Medical section's skylight had developed a piercing squeal, evident as Alvin cycled them open and shut from the control panel. "Must be the squeak Snow White was complaining about," said Alvin, and laddered up into the ceiling.

Joe grinned at Alvin's turn of phrase. He wondered where the prim princess left off and the tiger began. It had to be an interesting boundary layer.

Shuttering the windows made the telcon picture more vivid. A high riverbank was lush and green with what looked like grass, an assumption that went unquestioned until Wing pointed out that the grasses of Earth had been very highly evolved plants. *Beagle* launched a canoe carrying Wing and the limnologist, Tezi Young, to investigate more closely.

Alvin clumped back down the ladder and tested the skylight, which now rolled back and forth with an efficient whir. Joe's opinion of the Vanguard went up a notch. They had the sense not to rely on engineers for maintenance work.

The riverboat team members aired concern about the rocks at the sides of the river. Fractures in the rocks evidenced the impact of violent water. The river originated in the highlands to the west. Someone speculated that floods of melted snow came down in the spring. It was spring now. And a warm day. Fortunately, automatic water level monitors were positioned upriver and would warn of sudden snowmelt in time for *Beagle* to retreat to the shelter of one backwater or another. No such signal had come yet, and the meteorologists on the Ship thought a flood unlikely. Proceed, said the Ship.

Sam, on *Beagle*, asked the Ship to repeat the anticipated time of high tide. The river should be rising already, she was told. "Your calculations are off. Run through 'em again," she replied. "We haven't seen the river rise an inch." Sam's voice sounded assured, the tone of a captain of her own ship.

Beagle veered toward one green bank. The image from a camera on the boat showed a steep slope covered by bright green tubes. Not grass: long worms, rear ends anchored in the rocks' cracks and crannies, bodies suffused with algae that soaked up the midday sun. The whole limp, slimy lot would be submerged at high tide.

The xenobiologists on the Ship sounded overjoyed.

Passing through Medical, Catharin reacted to the image in the window. "A colony of *worms* as extensive as that? Yuck!"

The image or Catharin's fastidiousness irritated Joe. He threw down a pencil. "Some Eden!"

Catharin stopped and crossed her arms. "Why the foul mood?"

"Why not?"

"Oh, come now."

"Maybe something's on my mind." Something other than the stew of sexual feeling that Catharin's presence stirred up. "I always get crabby on the brink of realizing something significant." He peered at his window on the telcon.

"I might also say, go sleep on it. Take a nap."

"What I really want is a good swim."

"Well, you can't have it. Stop grousing. Just try to *not* think about whatever it is and maybe it'll come to you."

Beagle asked the canoe about rising tide. No, the canoe hadn't noticed any rise of water either. Wing had been watching a certain rock with a long horizontal fracture, just above the waterline. The fracture had not been inundated.

"They're having a real field day out there," Joe grumbled.

"They're doing what they love—what they came for. We thought we'd find a planet with green veins. The primary exploration mode would be the riverboat."

"You too. You've got what you came for, what you're trained for," he said bitterly, holding his aching neck.

A fleeting hurt expression crossed her face, as though he'd hit a nerve, but she said, "What's wrong with your neck?" She stood behind him and probed his neck and shoulder, removing his hand to do so.

"Ow!"

"It's probably a muscle spasm." She massaged his neck. It felt good. He lowered a shoulder. Tall lady, long fingers, and she knew the spots to hit. She rested her hands firmly on his shoulders. "Joe, one of these days try taking an interest in our dream instead of just walking away from the rest of us."

His mind flashed back to the day he had walked away from the river party. The day was filed in his memory as a kaleidoscope of images, mostly too gloomy or lurid to be a pretty sight. But the pattern suddenly shifted in the vision of his mind's eye to one of galvanizing simplicity. "Does tide ever come in all at once?"

"I have no idea."

He described the single, river-wide, breaking wave that pushed a stick upstream, raising the water level as it did.

"That was tide?"

"I don't know, but if so it was a long way from the sea, and it had to be bigger when it started up the river. Canoes aren't made for wave action," he added. "They capsize."

"Wouldn't someone have thought about that?" She instantly answered her own question. "More obvious things have been overlooked. I know who'll know." She opened a new vocal link to the crew deck Upside, and got somebody named Lary to talk to her. She asked him if a tide could come into a river all at once.

Lary said, "Off the top of my head, I don't know. I'm from Mars, you know."

"Look it up! Joe, tell him what you saw."

Joe described his wave, his recall, as always, perfect.

From Upside, the reedy voice said, "Uh-huh. Yes. Tide sometimes comes in the form of a wave front, which nicely matches what you saw. It's called a bore."

"They've got people in a canoe," said Joe. "If that happens, how big could the bore be where they are right now?"

"That's a tough one. It's a complex function of hydrology and position of the moon. . . ."

"The moon how?"

"Bores are biggest at spring tide. Sometimes a river produces a bore *only* at spring tide, i.e., full moon or new moon. The spring tide at new moon is the heftier of the two—the sun is on the other side of the moon and they pull together. The blue moon's new now, of course—"

"Check the observatory. Can't you look this way?" Catharin asked.

"No can do, the Ship is a hundred degrees away from local zenith."

A different voice, male and gravelly, came over the link. Joe recognized Captain Bixby's voice. "Somebody in trouble down there?"

"Maybe, Bix," she replied.

Lary said, "Here, I'll review the old footage."

Bix said, "For a good reason, I can blast open the emergency channel."

"Stand by," Catharin replied.

Joe paced, thinking about Wing in the fragile canoe. Lary muttered over the footage. "The day the boat was christened was overcast, no pix. But we've got radar mapping images from then. Nobody's reviewed the radar for that, of course."

"Well, do it now," said Catharin, with an edge to her voice.

"I don't know enough about tides," said Joe.

"Nor do I," Catharin said.

"That's a high bank on both sides of the river—why's it so damned high?"

She understood what he meant. "Good Lord, I hope not."

The planetologist mumbled, "Your river is arranged for bores, all right. Its mouth is funnel-shaped. On Earth it'd produce a noticeable bore on occasion, a few inches high. Hang on, I'm visualizing the radar footage from the day Toronto saw the bore in the river."

"They're fifty or so yards behind the boat," said Joe. "Maybe they should just pull the canoe out of the water."

Catharin murmured, "One of the expedition protocols is to keep people out of the biological gunk on the edge of the water."

"The gunk might be safer than getting capsized."

Lary transmitted an image that showed the river in gray tones, a funnel-shaped estuary and thinning river-ribbon winding into the hills. At a glance, the picture told Joe nothing about a bore. But Lary crowed, "This is a radar image from about half an hour before Toronto saw his wave near Camp Darwin, and there's a bore all right! It's several miles inland. So is *Beagle* at present." Joe made out a thin, wavering line across the river, above the estuary. "Let me just calculate how high . . ."

"We're onto something," Joe muttered. He and Catharin traded tense looks.

They both jumped when Lary screeched, "*Five meters!* Something like that could—"

Bixby drowned him out, opening the emergency channel, starting with the shrill all-attention signal. "*Beagle*, Bixby, go to the 'Bravo' river tributary at top speed, you're in imminent danger."

☽☾

The river looked peaceful enough in its wide, smooth, blue-gray extent, but Wing steered the canoe prudently, not drifting too close to the ragged rocks below the bank except when they nosed into the bank to sample the worms. Careful not to touch the creatures or the rich black slime of the river's bottom, Tezi Young deftly scooped worms into collecting vials.

Wing heard the surf in the distance. It surprised him that the sound carried so far inland on the wind from the sea. High overhead he noticed the moon, a bright bent wire of a crescent. He spared only glances for the moon, keeping his main attention on safe travel as he steered the canoe. Tezi powered it with firm strokes. The sun glistened on the dark brown skin below her shirt sleeves.

Beagle maneuvered at one-quarter of its engine power, with depth soundings and water flow readings in all directions. The canoe kept up without difficulty, well to one side of the riverboat and behind its wake.

"Hey, look at the worms," said Tezi. The creatures were contracting themselves into chinks in the rock, an amazing act of strength for such gelatinous beings.

"Anticipating the tide?" Wing hazarded.

"Could be. These buggers are fragile. They might break in the turbulence as the water rises over them. Look, each worm has its own little home hole."

"We are falling behind. A bit more speed, please," Wing said politely.

But *Beagle* pulled away faster. Judging by the wake that spilled out from its tail, those on board had revved the engine up to full. The wake rolled back toward them. As the canoe bobbed, their two-way crackled to life. Sam's voice said with urgency, "Tezi and Carl, get out of the river! Abandon your craft if necessary, but get out, and go up the bank!"

Wing aimed the canoe for a niche among tumbled blocks and boulders. There would be no way to port a canoe up over those obstacles, so Tezi stuffed her pockets with samples as she prepared to spring out of the canoe. "What's the problem?" she asked through the two-way.

"The tide's coming in as one big wave!"

Shocked, Wing instantly recognized the concept. Old China had a river where sea-tides came in as one enormous wave. That was bookish knowledge; he had never seen the thing himself. Tezi hauled the canoe up onto the rocks with Wing still in the stern. He leaped out into shallow rocky water.

"I'm bigger. Go first," said Tezi.

Wing found the rocks slick with residue left by the worms. His feet slipped. He fell, painfully striking his shin on the rocks.

By dint of bruising scrambling, Wing got over the rocks and started up the smoother part of the slope. Here the worms grew thick as grass. And their secretions made the bank impossibly slippery. Wing could get no traction and find no handholds. He slithered down in a heap. Even when Tezi braced herself and pushed his feet, the effort failed. "We can't climb out," she transmitted back to *Beagle*, which had vanished around downriver. "The bank is too slimy!"

"You've got to!" Sam answered harshly. "The tide is coming in *one wave as high as the bank!* Forget the canoe! *Get out!*"

Their struggles only bruised and slimed them. Panting, tumbling down again onto the rocks, Wing heard the surf. It sounded louder. *Closer.* Not surf at all but an approaching tidal wave. Desperately he looked around at the piled rocks, too obviously tumbled and splintered. The wave and the rocks would pummel their bodies to pieces. "Back to the canoe!" Wing yelled.

"What?!" Tezi screamed back.

"It is about waves! Safer in middle of the river!"

Tezi had not lost her wits. She held the bow as Wing piled into the craft. Then she dove into the canoe herself and thrust it away from the shore. "Paddle like hell and we might make it!" she called out.

The river looked as calm as ever. But its banks were bare of green. The clever worms had all hidden themselves. That wire-thin moon watched everything from high in the sky, as implacable as the lidded eye of a dragon.

With all their strength, they stroked to midstream. Wing hastily cocked the canoe's bow toward the sea.

"Here goes." Tezi pulled the cord to inflate her life jacket. It puffed up into a carapace around her. "Keep the bow into the wave." She poised, paddle at the ready, muscles on her arm bunching under streaks of slime and blood.

Wing's own arms quivered with terror. He nearly overcorrected for the canoe's bow shifting in a vagary of the water. The bow *must* face the wave.

Kyrie eleison.

It came upon them, sudden and fearsome, twin mountains of water. At either side of the river a moving mountain erupted foam and stirred great rocks with a roar. Between the double peaks lay a saddleback ridge of clean wave with gleaming flanks and a crest of foam. The canoe, no more than a stick in the water, bravely pointed into the face of the great wave.

With an edge of panic on her voice, Tezi called, "Been nice knowing you!"

The great wave pushed air ahead of it like a gale. The canoe pitched up. For a transfixed instant, Wing looked up at the wave's curled peak, translucent water like glass, a crown of foam that blew and shook like fire. Then the canoe shuddered as foam poured down around his ears.

At the wave's crest the canoe slipped out of line with the wave. Foaming water overturned it. Thrown into the cold torrent, Wing tumbled like a leaf.

He struggled to swim up to the surface. At the end of his breath he reached the air.

The canoe wheeled by his head, upside down with its bow clear out of the wave, spilling water. He ducked to save his skull.

The whole mass of water moved with a mighty pull and turbulence that threatened to drown Wing for good. He seized the gunwale of the canoe. Floatable material, it would stay near the surface, swamped or not. And so he hung on. He felt the great wave's wake churning upstream, carrying him with it.

"Tezi!" Wing screamed. He thought he heard a strangled reply, but the voice or the lungs were drowned in the raging water. After a turbulent eternity the water smoothed and slowed. "Tezi! Tezandra!" he called out, uselessly.

The water was bitter tasting. Wing desperately wanted to get out of it. He let go of the canoe and swam to shore.

A battered-looking tree perched on the rim of the bank. The water had risen so high that Wing floated within reach of the tree's roots. He grabbed at the roots and sobbed with relief when his hand closed around the sturdy vegetable matter. He crawled up the roots, pulling himself out of the water, shivering as the air met his soaked clothing.

Dazedly Wing looked around. His eyes burned and watered. He rubbed them, blinking to force vision through them. He could see no sign of Tezi or of *Beagle*. In the river, the overturned canoe bobbed heavily, low in the water, floating away.

Sudden nausea wrenched Wing's stomach. He vomited up water. When the racking sickness passed, he stood up. He swayed. He meant to start walking downstream. He had to find Tezi.

He had walked up to Unity Base from the earlier disaster, the crash of the shuttle. This time, he could not walk away from ruin. He was too sick. Stripping off the life jacket, he hung it on the bare tree by the water. Then he collapsed onto the ground, convulsed by another bout of sickness.

Chapter Twenty-Two

NIGHTMARE

Joe outran everybody else and reached the hangar first. As Joe skidded in through the door, Domino Cady confronted him. "We need Becca, and she's not here. She told me she'd be in the moss dell, and you know how to get there." Cady's "you" had the force of a curse.

Taking the straightest course down the Mountain by leaps and bounds, Joe raced through the pines and jumped over the stream's crooks. He heard Becca's flute. Panting, Joe skidded to a stop on the brink of the dell. Becca was already scrambling to her feet, flute in hand and a startled look on her face. "We've got people missing in the river!" Joe held out his hand. She took it and he pulled her out of the dell.

The helicopter sat in front of the hangar with its main rotor circling slowly. Aaron and Catharin were climbing in. Over the rotor's *thump-thump*, Becca told Joe, "You're a swimmer. Get in!" Joe took a place on a bench against the bulkhead between cabin and cockpit beside Catharin, who was belting up.

"Got your black doctor bag?" Joe asked Catharin. She nodded curtly.

Wearing a headset, Becca had the copilot's seat. She leaned out of the cockpit toward Joe to hand him a headset of his own. "You do know that when a copter tips its nose down, that's what it has to do to fly *up*, and it's not going to crash?"

"Thanks for the warning," Joe said.

Lifting up off the ground, the Starhawk pitched forward so drastically that Joe was tossed against the bulkhead behind his back. He tightened his seat belt. The copter hurtled away from Unity Base. It was a big, powerful flying machine in a hurry. Alarm shot through Joe's nervous system, and old pain flared in his shoulder.

Aaron leaned toward the cockpit in anxiety, even though that didn't help Domino hear better through the headset. "The wave would carry the canoe *upstream* for some distance. Then the current reverts to normal, and they'd come back downstream."

"Is *Beagle* watching for them?" Domino asked.

"I'll ask," said Becca. The background noise in Joe's headset changed to open-line hiss. "*Beagle*, Starhawk. We're on the way. Are you where you can watch the river in case it carries Carl and Tezi past your position?"

The voice of Sam Houston answered. "Negative. We're stranded in a mess of weeds in shallow water." Her voice sounded ragged. "I can't send anybody through the muck to get closer to the river. There's a built-in homing signal in the life jackets, but we haven't received either of them since the wave."

"The usual frequency?"

"Yes!"

"Head zero eight seven," Becca said to Domino. "Directly toward *Beagle.*" The copter tilted. Joe sagged against his belt.

Catharin did not seem troubled by the copter's motion. She must have done some training in this kind of machine. Her mouth was a level line, her attention absorbed in her own thoughts, probably rehearsing medical procedures.

Becca said, "We better think about rescue tactics for somebody in the water. We've got a hoist, cable, and rescue collar on this bird. We can drop it down to anybody in the drink. They have to be able to put it on, though. Either that or somebody jumps in to help them, and I think that's Joe. And I think you better show him how to use it, Domino."

"I'm flying."

"I can fly a helicopter in a straight line."

Domino came out of the cockpit. With no headset, he didn't bother to talk. He quickly unstrapped a piece of gear from its rack on the back bulkhead and demonstrated it to Joe, pulling it on himself. Collar goes over the shoulders. Chest straps secure like this, tighten this clamp. Domino easily kept his balance even though the copter was tippier than it had been when he was flying. Crotch strap fastens like this, and make it good and tight. *Understand?*

Joe nodded. Domino rapidly unfastened the rescue collar and ducked back into the cockpit.

"If it comes to that, don't ingest any of the water," said Catharin. "There might be something toxic in it."

"There's *Beagle*!" Becca sang out. Catharin and Aaron leaned into the cockpit door to see ahead. Joe peered out of a little window on the Starhawk's side. As the copter swerved—Domino at the controls again, making a smooth and drastic turn parallel to the river—Joe glimpsed the riverboat wallowing in a backwater full of ropy water-weed, like noodle soup. He tried not to think about Wing and Tezi and the fragile canoe in the teeth of a monster wave.

Suddenly, voices clamored, Becca's higher than the rest. "We've got a homing signal!"

"Look, international orange!" Aaron pointed. "Ahead—out of the water—in a tree by the water! It's a life jacket hanging in a tree!"

"There's no sign of the canoe," said Becca.

"There's somebody! There's somebody by the tree!" Aaron almost yelled.

The helicopter tipped its nose up, and Joe felt his stomach lurch. The copter plummeted toward landing.

"He's not moving!" Aaron exclaimed.

Joe heard the dismayed intake of Catharin's voice. He jabbed her with his elbow. "Dead men don't hang their life jackets in trees."

The copter settled on the ground, its noise shutting down drastically as the rotor slowed. Aaron sprang out with Catharin on his heels, Joe behind them. Domino and Becca began unstowing equipment. For a moment, Joe stood under the copter's coasting rotor to get his balance and his stomach back. Domino had picked a relatively flat spot in otherwise rolling, shrubby terrain. Under a scrawny tree about a hundred feet away, Wing was curled up, looking small and still.

Aaron and Catharin reached Wing in moments. Joe, walking on unsteady legs, took longer to get there. Domino shoved past him, arms full.

Wing was alive. He had been sick, and stank of vomit. Heedless of that,

Catharin was checking his vital signs. Squeamish sometimes, Joe thought. Not now. She was totally focused. He doubted that a small explosion behind her would have distracted her from the patient.

Domino unfolded a collapsible stretcher. Catharin directing them, Domino and Aaron lifted Wing onto it. Wing's face was pale, the color of ivory.

"*Joe! Joe!*" Becca stood on the crest of a low hill beside the river, gesturing toward the river. "*I see her!*"

Joe sprinted to the nearest spot on the river's edge. At the foot of a long bank, the river stretched out light green and lazy to the other side. Out in the middle of the water bobbed the orange of a life jacket. Its wearer's head lolled, uncoordinated or unconscious, stiff black hair plastered over her face.

Joe calculated the distance and the speed of the woman's drift while he flung off shirt, pants, and shoes. He evaluated the contours of the water. No whirlpools, no rapids—current wide and steady—to his Earth-born eyes, it looked like an honest river. He slithered down the bank, slipped in over his head in the cool water, and started stroking hard.

The water surged around his shoulders. Joe found a bitter, salty taste on his lips. He spat.

Becca had spotted Tezi just in time—if Joe swam fast enough. He swam hard, demanding top speed of muscles that hadn't handled water for months. No, a millennium.

He couldn't make it with a side stroke. So he took his bearings on Tezi, plunged his face in the water, and closed the remaining distance with a crawl. Swiping river water off his face, he looked up to see her floating past almost beyond his reach.

He lunged toward her. His fingers curled around a strap on her life jacket, and he jerked her to him. Tezi cried out in pain: she was hurt but alive.

Joe found a better hold on her life jacket and aimed for shore. One of Tezi's hands clutched his upper arm. "Help kick," he gasped.

"Arm hurts." Pain edged her voice. Her left arm trailed crookedly in the water.

Current bore them both downstream. Joe angled for shore. With each thrust of Joe's feet and free arm, Tezi gasped. "Hang on!" Joe panted. "Catharin's here. She'll fix you up."

The grip on his upper arm tightened, and Tezi kicked harder.

Once out of the main current, he could make straight for the shore, and swim slower and smoother, easier on Tezi. Joe felt for the bottom under his feet. The bank sloped into the water at a steep angle. Green worms that had emerged from their hiding places glistened on the upper bank and waved below the water line.

The steep shore was too slick to stand on. It offered Joe nothing to seize with his hand, either. Fragments of grass-green worm came away in his fingers. His struggles to find a foot- or handhold jarred Tezi. She cried out.

Joe stopped thrashing. With Tezi in tow, he let himself drift beside the bank. His hand explored for a hold, slid over gelatinous worms as the margins of the current eased them both downstream. Finally his hand brushed a rougher patch of bank. He closed his fingers around a handful of wiry roots—too fragile to climb on, but strong enough to anchor Tezi and himself. Joe craned his neck to look upward. Scrubby bushes stood on top of the bank, probably sturdy enough to anchor a rope, if somebody had thought to bring one.

Aaron and Domino appeared among the bushes. "Got a rope?" Joe yelled at them.

"Here!" Domino flung a rope's end toward Joe.

Joe tied the rope under Tezi's armpits. "She's got a broken arm. Pull up slow."

Tezi whimpered with pain, but used her good hand to guide herself as they hauled her to the top of the bank. The rope snaked down again. Joe grabbed it with both hands and half climbed, half let himself be dragged up by Domino as Aaron tended Tezi. When Joe had crawled over the lip of the bank, Domino and Aaron formed a cradle of their arms. Joe placed Tezi in it. The other two men rushed her toward the helicopter and Catharin.

The greenish ground cover consisted of an abrasive, scratchy, almost glassy moss, hostile to bare feet. Shivering, Joe waited for it to occur to somebody to bring him his shoes.

He surveyed his skin and found himself fairly clean. Maybe they would let him ride in the same helicopter trip as Catharin's patients.

Becca came running between the low hills, her hands full of Joe's shoes and clothes. She stood for him to brace himself on her shoulder as he pulled on clothes and shoes. "Joe, you were great!"

Joe noted the absurd intimacy of the situation. He felt his mouth crook in an ironic smile. "You too."

She looked up at him, suddenly grave, her brow furrowed. "Are you still mad at me?"

"No."

"Can we be friends?"

"Friends," Joe said. Her forehead smoothed. But she looked pale, freckles showing up more than usual. "Feel okay?" he asked with concern.

"It's okay," she answered, and set out with him for the helicopter.

When they got into the copter, Wing lay there strapped on the stretcher, wide-eyed and solemn. Joe paused to grasp Wing's hand. "Your turn to convalesce, eh?"

"I'll be glad to," said Wing, faintly.

Tezi sat beside Catharin, belted in, eyes glazed, Catharin's painkiller already at work. "Let's get these people home," said Catharin.

The rotor noise burgeoned, and the copter surged toward Unity Base. This time Joe and Catharin sat on opposite sides of the cockpit door. Catharin leaned past the door toward Joe, removing her headset. She snatched off Joe's. Into his ear and audible only to him she said, "I didn't think even you were damned fool enough to jump into a strange river!"

"I know how to read water!" he retorted.

Her eyes flicked to Wing, assuring herself that he was not overly distressed by the helicopter's steep climb. Then she glared at Joe. "One day one of your stunts is going to give me a heart attack!"

"Do you care about me, Doctor?!"

She crossed her arms. "We need you. Personally, if you jump into the river—or the planet Blue—*I don't care!*"

Becca looked on, leaning closer to overhear—from the copilot's seat, where Catharin could not see her. Becca quickly shook her head, grinning. *Don't believe it.*

During the helicopter flight back to Unity Base disaster struck again on the river. With *Beagle* dead in the shallow backwater, its engine fouled with weeds, an eddy of the tide seized the stranded boat. The bottom of the backwater was seemingly bottomless, slick sediment. It provided nothing to tie a line to, no friction to keep the boat in place, and the weeds that clogged the engines broke off from the bottom so easily that they offered no resistance to the tug of the tide. *Beagle* slid back into the river and floated toward the sea.

Sam called Domino, frantic. But before they got the hoist rigged on the helicopter and flew it back to the boat, Sam and her crew had to abandon ship and swim for the shore. Sam stayed aboard as long as she dared, but the engine refused to turn over and the boat was carried like a leaf toward the open sea. Sam finally jumped off and swam to a tiny islet. Domino and Becca picked her up with the Starhawk's sling. So the day ended without loss of life. But the one and only riverboat was lost at sea—complete with its scientific equipment.

In Green's midafternoon—late evening by the twenty-six-hour clock—Joe visited Wing in the infirmary. Wing told what he had experienced in quiet, precise tones. But he shuddered now and again. He had ingested native organic matter along with the river water, material incomprehensible to the human metabolism. His body had begun getting rid of the foreign matter at once. So ill had he been on the riverbank that he had felt he surely must die; he had forgotten that those alive enough to feel deathly ill are seldom at death's door, where feeling wanes. Only when Wing had seen the helicopter landing had he realized that he would not die alone on a desolate river shore.

After the visit, Joe went to the Penthouse to turn in for the "night," the sleep period in the middle of the long Green-day. He still hated how much the apparently necessary sleep time in the daylight seemed like an unwelcome afternoon nap.

Dozing off amid the uncomfortable onset of muscular ache and strain, he had another of his recurring dreams about the blue moon. This time his subconscious had new material to work with. He dreamed about Wing's bore, the Mountain of water crowned with wildfire foam, the great wave looming over him as he struggled to swim a cold, wide, nameless river. He woke from the nightmare chilled with sweat and trembling.

When he was fully awake, he had one of the moments of lucid inspiration that can come in the middle of the night. There had been talk of naming the blue moon something other than Blue. Hurakan and Aeolus had been suggested. Earth gods. Pointless, Joe thought, and beside the point.

Call the thing Nightmare.

☽ ☾

Catharin rose before anyone else in Unity Base the next morning, a new day that began with the slow setting of the sun. She checked on Wing, who was soundly asleep, and Tezi, who was resting, though not comfortably—no one is comfortable with a freshly fractured bone.

Catharin was glad to be here and not on the Ship today. There would be unpleasant questions about how the entire cadre of mission controllers, planners, and planetary scientists had failed to anticipate a tidal bore in the river. That sort of inquiry had been no fun on Earth, where stasis-damaged brains were not a possible explanation. She did not envy Joel's responsibility to figure this one out and assign the blame.

Full of restless energy, Catharin left the dome to walk outdoors. She felt sorry that the boat had been lost. But everyone was alive and her patients would mend. So much worse could have happened that the outcome of yesterday came as a relief to her, as well as something of a revelation: as tension-racked as the day had turned out to be, she had enjoyed the unscheduled trip into the wilderness. She needed to get out more.

Catharin walked toward the edge of the clearing farthest from the dome. Long clouds lay in the western sky—gray forms, gilded and colored by the setting sun. Underfoot, the dirt crunched. Crunched? She stooped to inspect it. A thin, thready lichen had established itself in the dirt, gluing it down and muting the red color.

She meandered among the furry pines with their familiar strange smell—anything and everything but pine. Stroking a bole sheathed in plush fuzz, she appreciated why they had been nicknamed "furry."

After sunset, no one was supposed to be out alone. For once, Catharin resented that rule as she turned back toward the Base. The dome's lights had come on. Lit from within, it glowed golden in the early dusk, like a chrysalis.

So it was. Nestled in Green's mild spring, Unity Base held the promise of a colony on Green. For the first time in a long time, Catharin reflected on her original purpose in coming to the stars. Crises had kept her mind off that for a long time. And other voyagers who shared her vision were up on the Ship, most of them still in stasis.

The personnel in Unity Base were explorers and scientists, not humanists—and, considering their flaws and foibles, unlikely seed material for a better society than any before. And yet, seeing the chrysalis-look of the dome, Catharin could believe in her dream again.

The clouds in the sky had changed. In abrupt pattern recognition, Catharin saw a definite shape: a long, tangled gray cloud was a human form, reclining. The cloud bank looked remarkably solid, its illuminated contours as smooth and rounded as musculature, like a gilded Greek cloud-frieze of vast proportions.

No, not a figure reclining, one swimming. Catharin studied the cloud with fascination. Against a pale blue-green sky, the gray cloud was a tall man swimming over the sunset, one arm flung over his head, legs long and dynamic, a torso with rippled muscles highlighted by the sun.

She hadn't admitted it until now. *He's magnificent. I'm fascinated by him. I've never wanted anybody like this.* Catharin felt traces of tears start in her eyes—warm tears for the sheer intensity of feeling. She could no more change the feeling than speed up the sun or tell Blue to stand still in the sky.

Dream and desire were both alive. Alive. An old dream and a new desire, both compelling enough to change her life to the core: she wondered if fate would allow the fulfillment of only one or the other. Or neither.

☽☾

After breakfast, a small group gathered on the patio to debrief. Arriving with Samantha and Aaron, Catharin found Joe already there, slouching in a light folding chair. It was twilight, not quite night: they left the patio lights off and pulled chairs into a small enough circle to see each other's faces.

Sam Houston slumped in her chair. "Bores happen on Earth. Average a few inches high. This one was average for this world! Why didn't I anticipate that?"

"It wasn't your job or your fault, Sam," said Catharin.

"That and worse. My responsibility. And it took a couple of whitecoats to save the day. Thanks, whitecoats."

Wimm Tucker—cook, quartermaster, and sometime distiller—had provided Bloody Marys. Considering Sam's haggard face, Catharin poured some drink into a glass for her.

Sam said, "Thanks, honey, I need it." She took a swig.

Catharin sipped hers cautiously. The drink was laced with hot sauce, donated from Domino Cady's personal supply of Cajun seasonings. "The Ship should have foreseen what happened. They'll set up a review board on how so many people could sift the data we've got for this planet so thoroughly—and miss the probability of a tidal bore."

"Hell, I saw it with my own eyes weeks ago," said Joe. "If I'd had my mind in gear, I would have added it up sooner. Should have." Catharin had not known that Joe could even go that far in admitting he had made a mistake.

Sam said morosely, "I must be going senile. Freezer burn on the old meat."

"Don't say that," Catharin said quickly.

Sam shook her head. "We've all had lapses."

Catharin nodded sharply, silent, thinking of a purple pond, and of Hoffmann and a door not locked. Aaron stirred—not disagreeing, Catharin guessed, just anxious.

Someone appeared at the edge of the patio and stopped short, surprised to stumble into a party at this hour. Catharin called, "Carlton, what are you doing here?"

"I do not mean to interrupt," Wing's voice floated back across the gloom of twilight.

"No, come here. You shouldn't be out of bed." She touched his forehead. "You still have a fever."

"I woke up with a terrible taste in my mouth," he said meekly.

Joe took the pitcher of Bloody Mary. "Have some of this. It'll cauterize your taste buds."

Catharin wondered about the advisability of that. But Joe poured only a small amount of the dark red drink into the glass he handed to Wing.

"What is this?" Wing asked, settling into the chair Joe pulled up for him.

"Tomato juice, hot sauce, and moonshine." Joe answered. "Liquor manufactured under makeshift circumstances."

"Oh. Moonshine." It would be hours before the young night became chilly; but Wing shivered, chilled either by the breeze or by the thought of the moon that had casually pulled up a twenty-foot wall of water over his head.

"Hair of the dog that bit you," said Joe.

☽☾

Midway through the benighted day, Joe was working at the telcon when Catharin formally released Wing from the infirmary. Joe cocked an ear and was relieved to hear Catharin say lightly, "And since you're so much better, the best prescription I can offer is that you relax for a while. Feel free to borrow my cat. She's as good as a muscle relaxant."

"Thank you, Doctor." Wing paused near the telcon to notice the image. "What are you doing, Joe?"

"Curing stasis."

Wing was fascinated by the double helix of DNA in a multiplicity of colors. So Joe explained further. "The problem started with the weird stasis chemicals. Even in the dark at subfreezing temperatures, they reacted with each other and with our chemistry, made products such as hydroxyl radicals, resulting in molecular damage, breaks or changes in long complicated molecules such as proteins." He pointed to a highlighted spot.

"Nucleic acids?" Wing asked.

Joe simply said, "That too."

"I wondered," Wing said quietly. Catharin came to the telcon to stand beside Wing.

Joe continued, "There've been cases of borderline anemia, borderline diabetes, you name it, not life-threatening as long as there's medical treatment available. Eventually the body replaces the missing molecules, provided that the genes to do so are intact, more or less. There's margin and redundancy. Up to now, she's only had one hopeless case."

Catharin winced, then explained to Wing, "One of my patients was, well, borderline everything. He got replacement therapy for a great many of the substances the body needs to function. That technology isn't perfect, particularly when it is so multifarious. His body never began to produce the damaged proteins on its own."

"It won't ever," Joe said bluntly. "So it looked like highly multiple replacement therapy for life, with all of the complications. Who'd want to live like that? We're talking medical invalid even before he got cancer, which is highly probable. Prognosis, in short, was bad."

"Why was one person afflicted so severely?"

"Being over fifty years old and male went against him," Catharin said tersely.

Joe said, "He'd worked in space before, more radiation. And one or two more prejudicial factors." Such as, having been in stasis twice. He traded a somber look with Catharin.

"You both say 'was.' Has he perished?"

"No. I've begun fixing him." Joe pulled up images in the telcon window, double helixes in technicolor, dense diagrams that Catharin might understand if she studied them. Even Wing might get an impressionistic sense of what Joe could do. "DNA repair," he said.

"Post-stasis therapy does that already." Catharin corrected. "As do our bodies even by themselves."

"Careless choice of words. Sorry. I mean reconstruction. Creative rearrangement. To make the DNA work again. You see, even in the shape this one's in, somewhere in his body there's good intact genes for everything. Intact hemoglobin genes may be in his liver where they're suppressed and don't do him any good now. But we ferret out the good genes and put them in the right places, make sure they're expressed, and he gets better."

Catharin bent over the window, tense and eager. "Joe fixed the hemoglobin."

"That was trivial, compared to what still has to be done."

"Trivial?!"

"It was like fixing the hole in an old cathedral's roof, or maybe shoring up a broken buttress. But DNA that's damaged like his is starts to show holistic effects. Like a cathedral bombed in a war. Stresses and strains affect the whole structure, and sooner or later it falls down. Unless you get an architect and some contractors in to reconstruct it."

Forgetting Wing, she gave him a long look. "Can you really do that?"

"I'm capable of more than you know," Joe answered. "I can make the difference between life and death."

In his final—unfinished—project on Earth, precisely that had been the issue. Of course, the full meaning of what he'd said escaped Catharin, who looked relieved, and Wing, who said slowly, "What of the future? What of children?"

Catharin sighed. "The answer is, we don't know yet," she said.

"We're getting the picture, though." Joe touched the telcon window, and it switched to a new set of double helices, differently and more subtly damaged than the first. "Eight-month-old fetus," Joe said. "DNA's been analyzed in the standard ways, and it looks normal. But it isn't. Don't ask me exactly how I know. Just say something feels wrong."

Catharin stiffened, and color drained out of her face. She said, "Carl. Excuse us. Joe and I have to talk in private." When the door closed behind Wing, Catharin whirled toward Joe. "*How did you get that gene scan?*"

He was surprised by the intensity in her voice. "I asked around in the Ship's hypercomputer, followed one lead and another, offered one password and another, and voila. Did notice that it was pretty closely guarded. But I'm good at bending protocols without breaking them."

"I was going to ask you to look at it . . . later."

"Well, now you know what I think."

"Do you know my next question?"

"If there really is a problem with the DNA, which you're not admitting yet, your question is, could I repair this one too? Yes."

Catharin slumped into the chair and put her face in her hands. A conscientious doctor, she must be tremendously worried about the child on the Ship.

"Doctor, you should take some of your own medicine. Relax." He put his hands on her shoulders and gently massaged them.

She put her hands on top of his. "Let's go for a walk."

☽☾

When they were out of the dome into the night, she reached for his hand. Electrified, Joe laced his fingers through hers. In silence, they walked hand in hand toward the edge of the mountaintop.

The sky flamed with stars. They stopped in a clearing in the pines. A rock loomed behind her, dark under a wide piece of starry sky overhead and a circle of dark trees, a backdrop for Catharin with starlight shining on her fair hair and light-colored clothing. "I've never seen light like this on a woman," Joe murmured.

"You've never seen light like this," Catharin answered, "because Earth didn't have this many stars."

"Your hair catches the starlight. It's like nothing I've ever seen."

"I'll take your word for that."

He reached out to touch her hair, sought and found and pulled out a clip.

"What are you doing?"

"Taking down your hair, so you can see it."

To his surprise, she let him. He disassembled the coiled braids. Free, her hair fell to several different lengths, the longest reaching her hips, one ringlet lying on her breast, and wavy locks that framed her face. Joe stepped a half step back to look at her, "You look like an angel in a renaissance painting," he said.

Catharin laughed. "Very romantic, Joe."

"Why don't you wear your hair down more often?" he asked.

"Because it makes me look too pretty."

"Not just pretty. Beautiful." He heard how it came out, rough with unmasked feeling in his voice.

She put her hands on his shoulders and pulled him close.

Desire jolted Joe like an electric shock. With one hand curled behind her neck and the other on her hip, he kissed her, hard. And she held him hard and returned his kiss, force for force, passion for passion.

Chapter Twenty-Three

THE THIRTEENTH HOUR

Catharin went toward the Unity Base conference room in a startled daze. A single long braid hung over her shoulder. Joe had braided it for her before they came back inside, after holding a double handful up to show her that yes, the starlight did shine on it. Her skin tingled where he'd touched her, as if she'd dipped her hands and rinsed her face in starlight.

Wing hailed her in the corridor. "It's just beginning! We were wondering where you were."

Becca was testing the exploration drone from the conference room tonight. The drone was on the Ship, but its surroundings would simulate the upper atmosphere of Planet Blue. Catharin really didn't want to miss the drone sim, but she'd waited until the last possible second to come in from Joe and the starry night. "Lead the way."

Joe had gone back to Medical. He wanted to work, he said. He had an old cathedral to patch. *Go with my blessing!* she had answered fervently.

In the conference room, Aaron had settled into a chair to watch the telcon, his high forehead furrowed in concentration. Becca perched on a chair in front of the telcon.

Things happened fast for Becca with Joe too, Catharin thought. For the same reasons or different ones? Under the stars, it had seemed right to Catharin, and it still felt right, for an astronaut to fall in love under a night sky full of stars.

Not that she couldn't foresee problems in falling in love with that particular man.

The telcon window showed the wide curve of a white-streaked blue horizon. At the bottom of the window, a bank of icons glowed and flashed. In the bottom right-hand corner was a bright string of downward-pointing arrows. "Aha." Catharin pointed at the arrow-string. "Vertical speed," she said to Wing. "The drone is falling only slightly slower than a rock right now because it's where the atmosphere is high and thin."

Catharin recognized Becca's weather-flying mode: tense concentration on her face, relaxed but quick hand action. Instead of handling a control stick, she punched keys on the telcon to control the drone. "Is she flying the drone?" Wing asked Catharin.

"In part. There's a time delay between Green and Blue, and that is built into the simulation." Aaron moved his chair closer to Catharin to hear better. She said, "The drone flies itself—it's a self-directing robot—but the remote operator, Becca, can take over. It's a two-layer control scheme, autonomy and telepresence. Becca is nearly three seconds behind the conditions experienced by the drone, but she can anticipate and intervene at certain moments."

Becca nodded briefly in agreement. She hit a key and the window divided into three parts, all three full of wide high sky and the tops of clouds. "Views to the front and both sides of the drone," Catharin murmured. "It's down in weather. It's an aircraft now, not a rock."

All three views had spidery lines superimposed on them. Information about the drone's angle of attack, its attitude relative to the horizon, its heading, and so forth crowded the window. It would have been more legible with the information projected into the air around the telcon. "Doesn't the telcon have a holographic mode?" Catharin asked Aaron.

Aaron laughed. "Our technology is all antiques, remember. Sturdy, proven technology works better when you're far afield." The flying craft descended into a wide sky valley between two hurricanes.

Joe had recently made remarks such as *When's Manhattan going to activate the holo mode? How long's he going to tightwad with the holo?* Joe, too, was under the impression that the conference room telcon was holograph-capable. Catharin could imagine his ire when informed otherwise. She made a mental note not to be the one to inform him.

Surely Joe could work around not having a state-of-the-art telcon. Becca was doing just that with aplomb, manually keying in control directions. She gave Catharin a quick smile. "I'm teaching the drone to play tag with a hurricane."

A wall of cloud loomed ahead of the drone. This was file footage from Earth's hurricanes, no less mighty than Blue's, just fewer. The cloud barrier looked awesome, brilliant white on the crown, with a base of thick gray laced with lightning flashes.

"Here goes," said Becca.

The drone dove into swirling mist that rapidly thickened and grayed. The string of arrows at the bottom right of the window flashed dramatically, down-arrows illuminating in sequence, fading as a string of up-arrows above them lit up, then reversing. The drone bounced like a Ping-Pong ball in turbulence in the cloud. Becca punched keys with tense concentration. The picture darkened almost to black, with erratic pale flashes of lightning.

"How big is the drone?" Wing whispered in Catharin's ear.

"Fifteen feet long," she whispered back. "It's no antique, either. It's a custom-made modern flying machine."

The drone broke out of the black cloud into dazzling sun. Becca sat back. "It's a quick study too. By the third updraft, I didn't have to give it any orders. Luckily the wings weren't torn off in the first two. All make believe," she added.

"Is Bix going to authorize a real encounter with Blue?" Catharin asked.

Aaron answered her. "It depends on these trial runs. I strongly advised it. We need a success in exploration."

Becca spoke to the Ship. "*Aeon*, you've got a good little bird here. It can do the job."

"You think we ought to go for Blue?" came Joel's voice.

"Affirmative," said Becca.

Catharin moved to Becca's side to speak on the link. "Nothing would be better than scientific understanding now. More than ever, we need to understand Planet Blue," said Catharin. "As things stand, it's a blazing blue mystery that makes disasters happen."

"You prescribe scientific understanding?"

"I do."

"We'll take that under advisement," said Joel. "Becca, ready for the structural debrief?"

"Ready." The whole drone appeared in the window in wire-frame form, the grid shaded white and blue, yellow and red for different stresses on the aircraft's structure.

"Joel agrees with us," Catharin said to Aaron. "I can tell by the tone of voice. He wants to send it to Blue."

"What Lary Siroky-Scheidt has in mind is more ambitious," said Aaron.

Becca caught Catharin's eye. "Get *this*."

"He wants to send the drone down between hurricanes to land on one of Blue's islands."

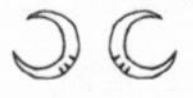

"That's it." Becca leaned back tiredly. "We've debriefed it to death and said good night, and we're still sure. It would have survived the flight. We can do it."

Wing unsuccessfully suppressed a yawn.

"My, it's late," said Aaron. "Not yet thirteen o'clock, but high time to hit the sack." He and Wing departed. Catharin felt no desire to follow suit. She still felt energetic, high on kissing Joe Toronto.

It was quiet and dark in the conference room, with only the sibilant murmur of an air blower and the telcon's blue window, Becca profiled against it, to impress the senses, until Becca said, "It may not be thirteen o'clock yet, but it's the thirteenth hour. You know that saying about the eleventh hour, meaning almost too late to change anything? Well, the thirteenth hour means it's way past deciding time. Some things can't be changed now."

Catharin nodded. "It's that way for Bix." *Not even Joe can make his DNA the way it was. But maybe close enough.*

"Not just for Bixby." Becca's voice sounded low and shaky.

"What's wrong?" Catharin asked in alarm.

"I felt awful yesterday when we went out in the Starhawk to find Wing and Tezi. After we landed at the river, I went behind the bushes to be sick, and that's how come I saw Tezi."

"Sick how?"

"Airsick. It's been happening a lot. I don't think I should fly anymore. Not alone."

What Catharin was hearing did not seem real. Her voice felt disconnected from her. She heard herself say, "Let's go to Medical. Now." She rose.

"Wait, it's not an emergency and won't last that much longer. Oh, Cat, you look like I told you I'm dying, and that's not what I mean." Becca took a deep breath. "I think it's morning sickness."

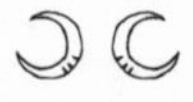

Catharin had hoped and all but prayed to have this test result in her hands. But she had not expected it so soon, and not under these circumstances. They huddled in Catharin's office. The doctor was not nearly as composed as she needed to be, not calmed by the ritual of steeping tea. "You're definitely pregnant."

"I'm sorry!"

"What for?"

"To do this to you!" Becca's voice slid up toward shrill frustration. "I didn't mean to!"

"I'm not mad at you."

"Why not? Please don't be too understanding, I can't stand it!"

"Honest, Becca, I'm just stunned."

With an inquiring meow, Nunki woke up from her nap in the corner. Catharin snapped her fingers. Nunki jumped up into her lap. Stroking the cat, Catharin listened without interrupting the torrent of feeling on Becca's part.

"Why me?? I know I'm healthier than many. So I intended to get together with Domino, and I thought we'd have a little one, but—! And I can't tell Domino because it's taken him this long to get to where he can say two words in a row about Joe without snarling!

"It wasn't my idea. At least, not that this would come out of it. But it was what the dell had in mind!" Becca blurted.

Catharin paused with her hand in midstroke on Nunki's back. "The dell?"

Becca nodded energetically. "I finally went back and had a word with it. In daylight. Words don't work, so I played my flute."

Catharin pursed her lips as she considered saying, *Were you out of your mind?* "Did you know that this is probably the first natural conception since we reached this star, certainly the first on Green? Unless you feel it wasn't natural so much as supernatural."

"No. I was ovulating; I know that because I was very interested in men that day. But I didn't think once about contraception."

"A number of couples have been trying very hard to conceive," said Catharin, "in addition to others who are mainly interested in each other and not bothering with contraception. No one else has gotten pregnant. I'd have said the chances of *any* given couple conceiving were not much better than for Wimm and Eddy."

Becca's face fell. "That slim?"

"That slim."

"That's a thin thread to hang the future on."

"I know. You've handed me hope on a silver platter tonight. So I'm certainly not angry."

"The future is one thing, the present is another. It wasn't fair, because Joe's yours, and I've got a good one of my own. How can I make it up to you?"

"Do you need to hear whether I'm jealous? No. Joe is mine if I want him. And I do."

Relieved, Becca rearranged herself to a less tight, tense position. "Did you know that Alvin's been taking bets the two of you would get together?"

"No, I did not know that." It did not improve Catharin's opinion of Alvin.

"What Joe and I did played hell with his odds, and he was cussing and fussing for a couple of days."

"I wouldn't count on logical odds around here," Catharin said flatly. "Whether or not there's anything supernatural going on—and I, for one, doubt it—the probable and the improbable are not what they were back home. For example—Becca, if you feel you want to make anything up to me, just let me confide in you. And don't tell anybody else."

Becca was wide-eyed with interest. "Sure."

"A series of in-vitro fertilizations have been done on the Ship. Most failed, which fueled my pessimism. One, however, is eight months along, gestating in a volunteer birth mother."

"What does that have to do with screwball odds?"

"Both parents were astronauts. In stasis twice."

Becca sucked in a breath. "You and who else?"

"Joel. I never imagined that it would work."

"Maybe it was what the stars had in mind?" Becca suggested with a twist of a smile.

"I'm not ready to believe in astrology. Out of curiosity, what did you play in the dell?"

"A Methodist church hymn. 'All Creatures of Our God and King.' It says, 'Thou flowing water pure and clear, make music for thy Lord to hear.' It was my way of . . . of telling the dell that I worship God and it should do likewise and not impose *its* ideas on *us*, and it listened to me."

When Catharin raised an eyebrow, Becca insisted, "Not when I talked out loud, which just made me feel silly. Words don't belong there and just scatter on the wind. The melody, though, sank in as though the ground was acoustical tile."

Catharin briefly wondered if pregnancy had made Becca irrational. But what she had said, though illogical, was perfectly in character. And Becca was quite rational enough to know how strange it sounded. She had turned pink.

Thoughtful, Catharin stroked the contented creature in her lap. "I don't understand. It would be hubris for me to say otherwise. It was hubris enough to experiment as I did with conception."

"You had to know the worst, right? And the worst wasn't as bad as you feared."

"One researcher suspects a problem." Catharin grimaced with the irony of expressing it that way. "I'll level with you—*Joe* thinks there's a problem. If that's so, it wasn't bad enough to prompt miscarriage. Perhaps it will show up only after birth, and the child will suffer, unless Joe can come up with a cure. Whatever your dell did was less blatant than what I've done, don't you think?"

"I'm not blaming you," Becca said. "Does the birth mother have any problems?"

"A violent disaffinity toward anything that smacks of peppermint. As long as she stays away from minty flavors and odors, she feels fine."

"And I get a disaffinity for flying! I was wondering," Becca ventured, "about medicine for nausea."

One word rang in Catharin's mind. *Thalidomide.* Catharin shuddered, recalling that piece of medical history, how a drug meant to ease morning sickness mangled the unborn child. "I don't know what effect known medicines have on our bodies, after the slight but pervasive changes caused by stasis. It might not work—or might harm you or the embryo."

Becca sighed. "I had a feeling you'd say that. That's why I pushed for going ahead with the drone. It's something useful I can do from the ground."

"You can do the job even better if you control the drone from the Ship."

Becca pointed out, "Quarantine's still on. Now Bix wants you to watch for odd illnesses in the people who got dosed with river water, and the people who rescued them. So I can't go back up."

"That has to change," Catharin said flatly.

☽☾

Walking quietly, she stopped just inside Medical, in the shadows around the door. Joe was on the telcon. She watched him, unobserved herself. He seemed to be scrolling through gene scans, one after another. Catharin shook her head in silent amazement. It took most trained medical professionals half a day to decipher one of those, so they relied on AI interpretations, which, post-stasis, were anywhere from inaccurate to misleading. But Joe could apprehend more about DNA at a glance than most researchers could see in an hour.

With him, everything was fast. Life. Love. Work. Moods. Especially moods. Kissing in starlight had been wonderful. She'd been pleasantly stunned by how romantic and gentle he could be. Unfortunately, she had every reason to think that his mood could easily morph into something less enjoyable for her. Maybe it already had. The set of his shoulders said something beyond concentration. His shoulders were slightly askew, and Catharin read bad mood in that.

It had been wonderful in the starlight. She wanted to hold on to the memory because everything later this evening had been so jarring. She didn't need to experience a foul mood of Joe's right now. She quietly backed out of Medical, and returned to the telcon in the conference room.

Chapter Twenty-Four

BLUE'S MOUNTAIN

No matter what the topic, Joel Atlanta enjoyed speaking to Catharin via telcon. He would have liked it even better to see her in person, but the quarantine precluded that for the time being. "So you think it's time to take Blue by the horns," Joel said.

"Yes, I do. That's not why I called you back, though." Her face was serious—more so than usual for her. Intense.

"Go ahead, Cat."

"The quarantine has outlived its usefulness. True, there may be biological hazards down here. But Joe needs computer holo-capability to do his best work. And I've now got a pregnancy on my hands. Never mind who. I'm not sure she or the fetus are safe here without the kind of prenatal care available only on the Ship."

"Whew! That's good news at a bad time." Joel rubbed his forehead in consternation. "I don't think we can put that in the balance against the safety of the Ship and have it come out anywhere near even."

"No. But that's not the way things are." She crossed her arms. Joel recognized Catharin's unyielding mode. She had made up her mind, and her resolve now consisted of steel. "The greatest danger lies in what we arrived here with—damaged genes and big brains that are susceptible to moonlight and madness. It was on Earth that nature in the form of germs was out to get us. That is not the case here."

"That's a change of tune for you, Cat."

"Yes," she admitted. "But you better think about it too, Commander."

"Acting Commander," Joel corrected.

"It's no act, Joel."

☽☾

"Hel-*lo, Joe*!" screamed the green parrot, flapping its wings excitedly.

"Jo-el," said Joel. "Hubert, say Jo-el."

Hubert ducked his head, signaling a desire to have his neck scratched. Joel complied absently, his mind on Catharin and her unexpected—unwelcome, he had to admit—advice.

Hubert swung upside down on his perch, hung by one leg, and pecked at the dangling, homemade bell, causing it to jingle merrily. Just like any other Amazon green parrot—just like one that hadn't been frozen for a thousand years—Hubert was a brassy clown of a bird. Not many people here knew why Hubert was so named, that the parrot's namesake was a guy who could be a brassy clown. Not often and never on the job. But Joel had seen the man clown around on more than one memorable occasion. But that had been before the star trip and stasis that went on so long that it was too near forever.

Joel held a finger out to the bird. "Hubert wanna go with Joel?"

"'Ubert go!" the bird screeched, climbing onto the finger. Joel transferred Hubert to his shoulder. Claws gripping the fabric of Joel's shirt, Hubert fluffed his feathers and leaned forward expectantly. "*Go!*"

"Hey, not so loud in my ear! Put on your bedside manner, you noisy bunch of feathers."

Responding to the affectionate tone Joel used, the parrot cooed, "Go bedside."

☽☾

Hubert Bixby grinned. "You look like a damn pirate with that parrot on your shoulder."

He'd been better for a while, up on his feet for most of a week. Now he was worse again. Flat on his back in the infirmary bed, Bix made less of a bulge under the sheets than ever, Joel noted with alarm. He was losing weight. Going downhill fast. Bix drew in a deep, ragged breath. "Gonna pirate my Ship?"

Joel was speechless for a moment. "No!" he sputtered.

"You ought to. I'm not up to it anymore." Another ragged breath.

Joel tried to sound calmer than he felt. "I want to ask you about something. Cat thinks we're in so deep that quarantine's pointless."

"I sure am." The gnarled arm lying outside of the sheet was tracked with needle punctures—the marks of the therapies that had to be delivered intravenously. "Sorry. I can't be much help anymore. I feel like I'm just waiting for something."

Joel sat down in the chair, overcome by implications in what Bix had said. Catharin had once told him that the terminally ill often wait for holidays and such.

Agitated, Joel crossed his ankle on his knee. Hubert promptly marched down Joel's chest and up the leg to the knee. That much closer to Bix, Hubert fluffed his feathers and regarded Bix with one beady eye. "Hel-*lo*, Bix! *Bix!* Bix!"

Bix grinned again. His mouth was crooked—not just a wry twist, it looked jagged. "I must have a parrot word for a name."

"I don't. He ignores the 'el' on the end and calls me Joe." *If Joe Canada is such a genius, such a miracle worker, it's high time for him to prove it. Do his molecular-biology thing before it's too late for Bix.* "We've got a little expedition coming up. You may want to tune in, starting tomorrow." Joel indicated the wall telcon window with his thumb.

"Downside?"

"Nope. This one's ours—the Ship's. It's time to check out *Lodestar*, and a trip to Blue and back ought to do it."

Bix nodded. Interest mitigated the pain inscribed on his face. "Couldn't ask for a better test distance. How'd *Lodestar* do in the static test?"

Joel made a circle of his thumb and forefinger. Sensing that Bix was more relaxed, Hubert Parrot preened, balancing on Joel's knee. Joel named the three-person crew he'd selected for *Lodestar*'s test run. Flight engineer, copilot. "And Kay Montana is pilot/commander."

"Good bunch."

"I'll look over their shoulder. And while they orbit Blue, they'll drop out the winged drone for a spin in Blue's atmosphere. And maybe land on one of the islands."

Bix grunted dubiously. "That drone's a valuable piece of hardware. Blue's hurricanes could turn it into titanium confetti. You want to risk it just for a show of flag-planting?"

"It's not just flag-planting. Ever since the riverboat got hit by the bore, morale has slipped, and Sisseton the psychologist is testing everything and everyone for altered human factors. I want to prove that the Ship can mastermind an exploration job and bring the people and the hardware back in one piece."

Bix just shrugged.

Joel let a deep sigh filter out inaudibly. *Bix wants me to make the decisions now. Fair enough. But when I need to ask somebody "What the hell do I do now?" who is there?*

Hubert Parrot looked up at Joel with one beady eye. Joel did not like what he read into the bird's look. *You're it.*

☽☾

On the Big Picture, the interplanetary exploration craft *Lodestar* maneuvered against a glittering star field. Sitting at *Aeon* Command, Joel watched as steering jets flashed on nose, tail, and stubby wings and the spacecraft pirouetted against the stars.

The Aeon Foundation had bought off-the-rack equipment when it could, and IEC *Lodestar* was a prime example. *Lodestar* was just aerodynamic enough to duck into a thick, low-gravity atmosphere like Titan's in the Solar System. Rockwell Mars Ltd. had designed it for speed, to be a fast courier between the colonies on Luna and Mars and the moons of the outer planets. It had taken *Lodestar* a bit under three days to reach its present low orbit around Blue. The winged drone was tucked into *Lodestar*'s cargo bay. All systems were go for the drone's big day on Planet Blue.

Lodestar yawed, its nose swinging past the point of view that *Aeon*'s Intelligence had fabricated for imaging this moment. Behind the spacecraft, a wide blue horizon entered the picture. The world looked deceptively like Earth from this initial oblique angle: you couldn't tell that there were no Earthlike continents. The stars faded, outshone. The planet rolled farther up, and the Picture revealed the hurricanes tattooed across its blue ocean skin.

Unlike tattoos, these marks moved. Fast. Joel turned toward the Planetology station. "Lary, you still think there'll be a window wide enough to take the drone down in?"

"Sure. The windows are high-pressure ridges between the lows that are the hurricanes. The touchy part is finding a window that will move over one of the islands at the right time."

The barren blue-gray islands were inconspicuous. Given the swirling cloud cover, Joel could not make out any of them in the big bright expanse of world on the Big Picture.

Kay Montana appeared in a window in the Picture. "*Lodestar* to *Aeon*. Maneuvers completed. All systems go." Her short hair and close-fitting coveralls were only slightly fluffed out in the zero gravity, her manner military crisp and a bit more deferential than it used to be.

Nobody questioned his right to sit in at Command station. Not Kay, not the control center folks. Nobody objected to the fact that it was Joel, not Bix, making decisions today. Maybe the time had come. That didn't mean he wanted it that way. "Let's go over the steps toward releasing the drone."

Due to the finite speed of signals crossing the void between the Ship and Blue, it was several seconds before he saw her nod in reply. "Opening payload bay doors."

"Let's talk com-con," said Joel to Planetology.

The man at Lary's left, a telecommunications coordinator monitoring the complicated link between Unity Base, *Aeon*, *Lodestar*, and the drone, opened the communication-configuration matrix on the Big Picture. The matrix showed times when starship, *Lodestar*, Unity Base, and—since they wanted to do the operation in local daylight—the sun happened to be in the right relative places: an array of times scattered over the next three days.

A seam appeared on *Lodestar*'s wide back. Clamshell doors eased open. Sunlight fell through the doors, shining on the drone inside, neatly bundled on its launching rack, wings folded back like the fins of a flying fish at rest. With the same slow grace, the clamshell closed again. "Payload bay doors check out operational," Kay reported.

"Okay, Lary," said Joel. "Match up your storm tracks with the com-con matrix. What do you get?"

"We have an alpha window." A fast-moving, storm-free high-pressure area would cross squarely over one of Blue's islands. "Sixteen hours from now."

Every head in the control center turned toward Joel, expectant. He thought about the drone—a priceless piece of equipment—about the depth and turbulence of that blue atmosphere, and how fast the windows moved. He felt the need to decide settle on his shoulders, digging claws of conscience into him, heavier and more onerous than a green parrot.

Joel made the inevitable conservative decision. "We won't land this time around. Just in and out. The drone's instruments can read what we need to know. Landing would be showing off—like planting the flag. It's not like some other nation is going to beat us to *this* moon."

Joel waited for an outburst from Lary. *If the guy was obstreperous with Bix, he's gonna be downright insubordinate with me.*

Lary said, "May I request a conference to discuss the risks and benefits of landing? A private talk, that is?"

Joel concealed his annoyance. "Sure."

☽☾

The fact that Lary offered coffee and scones lent the flavor of sweet-talking to the conference, held in Lary's office. Joel accepted a scone. But he resolved to judge the case on the strength—or lack of it—of Lary's reasoning.

Lary started off by explaining how he had come up with the window, what he expected in the way of wind speeds near the surface of the water, and a description of the geometry of the island he wanted the drone to land on. He produced a communiqué from Becca Fisher declaring the idea doable.

Joel pocketed a corner of his scone for Hubert. "But how do you justify the risk?"

Lary had barely nibbled on his scone. He pushed it from one side of his plate to the other. "I'm afraid I'm not very objective. There's a burning question I want to answer."

Joel wondered if Lary had grown bonier, his face thinner, in recent days. But he'd not had much jowl to start with. "What question?"

"What kind of rock are the islands made of? Whatever it is, it's ubiquitous on Blue. Every island falls into the same range of color and albedo. Basalt is an obvious guess, but woefully inexact. If we knew exactly what kind of basaltic rock, composition down to the microscopic and chemical level, and could guess what geological process formed it, maybe we'd be able to understand why the islands on Blue are arranged the way they are. The positions of the islands have a maddeningly geometrical aspect. Look." On the office telcon, Lary called up a model of Blue. False-color red dots represented the islands.

Joel saw what Lary meant. There was a pattern. It seemed incomplete, though.

"Mind you, we're talking about mountains. Each island is a mountain peak. Our theories of orogeny and plate tectonics can't explain the mountains being where they are!

"There are a million other questions, starting with life-forms, if any. Do algae live on the islands, or is anything else able to withstand the storms? Oceanic organisms? Are there extinct life-forms on Blue, fossils? But this one question—*what are the islands made of?*—that may have to do it for me. I really would like to know before *I'm* extinct. Which may be rather sooner than I might wish. You see? No objectivity."

Oh, no, damn, no. The scone sat heavily in Joel's stomach. *He's sick too, got sicker later but quicker than Bix. He would. He's a thin, birdlike guy, and birds get sick fast and hide it until they keel over.* Joel forced out a simple, rational question. "I see what you're saying, Lary. And I agree with you that this is important. But how will landing the drone prove what Blue's mountains are made of?"

Lary's eyes sparkled from fever or inspiration. "Let me explain, if I may, about weathering processes."

The control center hummed with excitement.

"Drone's away," Kay reported. The Big Picture showed it launched out of the shuttle's bay, arcing toward the blue world below.

Joel's fists clenched and unclenched with tension. Maybe he should not have okayed this. But it was a golden opportunity to check out the shuttle and its deployment operations. And visiting Blue was a wonderful adventure. Everybody on the Ship and in the Base, the sick and the well, had tuned in today, fascinated. *Maybe we can pull off an interplanetary, unmanned exploration better than we can muck around down on Green. If something goes awry, Becca can abort the landing. She will if there's any reason to.*

"Fisher's wired in now," said the telecommunications coordinator.

The Big Picture illustrated the drone from an imaginary viewpoint that stayed a certain distance above and behind it as the drone descended. Penetrating the thicker part of the atmosphere, the drone bucked and tossed in the gales of Blue, plummeting toward a small region less shiny than seawater: one of the bare islands of Blue.

"Jet engines on," Becca's voice reported. "Airfoil control looks good. Broken clouds at seven thousand feet."

Arrowing toward the island, the drone's cameras and instruments clicked away, and the Big Picture reproduced what the drone registered. One face of the island rose up from the sea abruptly, steep and featureless. The opposite face had a much more gradual slope. "It looks landable," Becca reported. "Moderate wind blowing down the sloping side. That slope's really smooth. I'm surprised. Most sea islands I've seen are craggier than this one."

It was one of the universe's least interesting islands. Monochromatic, barren, and almost symmetrical, it would have been a steep cone had not two hundred million years of hurricanes' onslaughts scoured one face to a shallow slope.

Approaching the island against the wind, the flying machine flared as it neared the dark rock slanting out of the water. The drone's nose pointed up at a thirty-degree angle, and its wheels reached for the surface.

A voice in the control center announced, "Touchdown!"

"We did it!" somebody else crowed.

Even in this interlude between hurricanes, the prevailing wind that spilled over the top of the island made the drone rock and dance as it taxied uphill. Planet Blue was never calm.

The Big Picture now came from a camera in the drone's nose. The island's crown was a smooth dark curve in the jumpy picture. *Most rocks in the wild aren't that smooth*, Joel thought. And most rock formations had soft spots for the weather to chisel away, resulting in interesting shapes. The stuff of this island was very homogenous indeed. . . .

The skin on the back of Joel's neck prickled as Lary's hints came together for Joel, into a mental Big Picture, one that jarred him. *Sick people wait for Christmas and such. But great-grandmama said they see other worlds. This isn't what the old lady meant, but . . .* Joel felt an impulse to panic, order the drone to blast away, out of there, now. But now he wanted to get a piece of Blue too. Besides which, sick people also hallucinate. He broke into a hot sweat.

Becca managed to taxi the drone into a slight fold of the rocky slope, out of the worst of the wind. "Brakes on. Here's hoping they hold," she said, her command flying on toward Blue at the speed of light.

Lary said excitedly, "We've got half an hour before the winds from the approaching hurricane get up to gale force."

"We'll be done by then." Suspense propelled Joel up out of the chair to pace around the Command station.

Becca's voice came from Unity Base. "It's up to our little friend now. Kay, I'm handing the link over to you."

"Got him," said Kay.

☽☾

The hatch in the drone's tail section opened. A canister fell out and tumbled toward the bottom of the slope, rolling faster the farther it went. When it reached the rim of rubble around the Base of the island, it hit a rock and took a dramatic bounce, spinning in the air. The canister landed amid fractured boulders beside the surging sea.

The bottom end was heavily weighted, so the canister settled with that end down. The top end popped open. Tango 21 extended the front half of its body from the canister with quick, constrained movements of its legs, then paused, like a hunting spider in its trapdoor, to survey the wet-streaked boulders all around it.

An urgent order from the orbiting *Lodestar* came to the spider, relayed from the drone. The spider quickly exited its canister and scurried uphill, up and over rocks, just before a wave boiled behind it, sweeping the empty canister away.

The robot spider paused in a field of pebbles uphill from the larger rocks beside the sea. Most of the stones were varied shades of gray similar to the broken boulders the spider had just clambered over. Some were a darker, monotonous bluish gray, just like the bulk of the island that loomed above the spider. The island was made of hard stuff. But the sea, chewing at it for eons with teeth of wind and water and stone, had nibbled off some small pieces.

Obeying directions relayed to it, the spider used its front legs to grasp an island-dark pebble. It stuffed the tiny rock into a pouch glued on its underbelly. The spider then extended its front legs to elevate itself an extra inch, raised its eyestalk like a periscope, and looked out to sea. Waves surged in from the dark ocean, ranks of white foam one behind the other. Beyond the surf, the horizon was clotted with gray cloud. Distant lightning stitched the juncture of sky and sea like strands of brilliant thread.

The spider pivoted to trek uphill on the storm-scoured flank of the island. Wind gusted. Almost blown away, the spider flattened itself to make a lower profile. At the top of the hill, the drone's wings were flexing even in its sheltered parking spot. The drone pirouetted around, its nose seeking the wind.

The wind dropped off for a few moments. In the lull, the spider scuttled uphill and dashed the length of the drone's fuselage, running between the wheels to where the cargo hatch door made a ramp. Skittering up the ramp into the drone, the spider packed itself into a waiting, empty canister and shut the canister door, ready for the ride home.

☽☾

Taking off was easy. Becca disengaged the brakes and let the drone weathervane around to face the wind off the sea, then let the wind lift it. Staying up was hard, because just above the boundary layer of air between the mounting winds and the sea, a strong wind shear almost pitched the craft into the waves. Jet engines blazed to full thrust, and the drone raised its nose toward Green: a huge, pale green ghost of a world-moon above the battlements of hurricane on the horizon. The image of Green silenced the chatter in the control center.

Becca's voice sounded loud, coming over the link from Unity Base. "Wow! The spider almost got drowned or blown away and I almost crashed the drone into the sea on takeoff, but we made it! We got the contingency sample! Wings coming in now."

The drone folded its wings back against its fuselage, its engines switched from air-breathing to rocketing, and the drone became a missile boring a hole in the storm-racked sky of Blue.

Kay and her copilot began maneuvering to rendezvous with the drone. It would be several days until *Lodestar* returned to *Aeon* and the canister was disinfected, transferred from the spacecraft's cargo bay to the laboratory in the Starship, and opened.

Joel had a word with Bix. Bix knew some geology; he'd pecked out rocks on the surfaces of moons from Jupiter's Callisto to Neptune's Triton, and had prospected with robots on Mercury. Brow in jagged furrows, mind off his problems, he told Joel what he thought about a rock formation like that island—uniform weathering, the dull blue albedo of the island under the bright sun, and the luster of the blue pebble. "Ever hear of goldstone?"

Joel left Bix's bedside with the universe on his mind—a more complicated and contradictory universe than he had previously believed. He went directly to the Captain's office and keyed into the Captain's telcon. It responded to his thumbprint. Bix had long since taken care of that.

They were all surprised when Joel summoned them to the telconference: Miguel Torres tuned in from the Life Support Systems office, and the microbiologist Srivastava from his lab. Marie Mike Sisseton looked up from her personnel files. Downside, Catharin, Carlton Wing, Sam Houston, and Aaron Manhattan crowded into the telcon-cam field of view in the Unity Base conference room. "What's up?" Catharin asked.

"We need a holiday," Joel answered. "Not a little bitty, glad-it's-Friday holiday. We need a real, honest, full-bore holiday."

"The occasion is the successful mission to Blue?" asked Sisseton.

"Yeah. But this holiday is more than that. It needs to be a religious holiday." Seven intelligent faces regarded him with different shades of surprise. Joel continued, "I'm Baptist. Miguel's Old Catholic, Wing New Catholic. Marie—?"

"Native American."

"Cat is humanist, Manhattan Jewish, Sam Houston's Neo-Pagan, Srivastava Hindu—did I get everybody's affiliation right?"

"I don't think of my philosophy as a religion," said Catharin.

"I need your opinion too."

Manhattan sounded bemused. "There are several more sorts of religion or philosophy held by people down here."

"And more up here!" said Srivastava.

"I know. You all have to speak for your friends and anybody else whose worldview you understand. Now, a holiday is a holy day, right?"

Wing and Manhattan nodded. Catharin conceded, "That must be the etymology."

"I'm thinking about holidays like Easter, like Christmas in country churches. Passover. Lunar New Year. I don't know what you other folks do. Anyway, celebration of important things in the past. Such as, that we came here to these worlds after a long journey that killed some of us—"

"That's not to celebrate," said Cat.

"Oh, but it is," said Wing.

"Remember the Day of the Dead," said Miguel across the telcon link to Catharin.

Joel continued, "Holy days are about the present too. How the present is a critical time, a mixture of things known and things unknown to us."

"Mysteries, yes," said Wing.

Mysteries. One of which looks like it's gonna get bigger and brighter real soon. "People aren't cut out to stare a big mystery in the face and say 'Oh, how cute' and go about our business."

"I *think* I see what you mean," said Catharin. "We won't understand everything about Green and Blue, even after today. It will do no harm to . . . publicly acknowledge? . . . as much."

Carlton Wing nodded. "You envision a collective gesture, above what each individual is feeling and fearing. A corporate action."

"Yeah. That's it. Not compulsory for anybody—but available for everybody."

"What a difficult idea," said Srivastava. "It might be better to—"

"I'm not taking a poll on this. I'm announcing it and I'm asking you all to help me make it work."

Catharin asked, "Is that an order?"

He hesitated, then took the plunge. "Yes, Cat."

"As you wish. I'll cooperate," she said. He sensed the rest of it, unspoken. *You're the commander.*

Sam Houston and Manhattan whispered together out of the telcon's pickup range. Sam announced, "We're with you."

"So how are we to call this holiday of yours?" asked Srivastava.

"What's day after tomorrow the anniversary of, in Green time, one revolution around the sun?" Joel countered. He got blank looks from everybody but Catharin.

"Oh," she said. "So it is. One Green-year ago, the Ship stopped here."

"Starfall," said Joel.

It was well past midnight when the urgent call came to Joel from the planetology center. They had received the rock sample only two hours before. The geologist who made the call, a man named Yandell, wore a rumpled white coat and a grave expression. "Analysis of the sample is yielding impossible results."

Joel called Lary, who had chosen to spend the evening modeling Blue in the control center. "Come meet me in Planetology," Joel told him. "The other shoe's about to drop."

A bit had been sliced off one end of the pebble. The trimmed pebble and the spider rested inside the white-lighted clean box, behind a contamination barrier.

Yandell displayed a thin, translucent section of the end of the pebble, magnified hundreds of times. Pointing at the image, the geologist explained in an agitated tone, "This is not a natural rock." He rattled off telltale technicalities of microcrystalline structure, chemical composition, and hardness.

Lary seemed calmer than usual, rather than excited. Joel's aged great-grandmama would have sat in her favorite recliner and said, *I told you, boy. The dying have second sight.*

Yandell finished, "I assure you, that is material from Blue. It's not possible that anyone substituted anything by accident or by way of a joke. But there is no adequate explanation for it!"

"If it's not natural, it must be artificial," Joel supplied.

He could see the geologist's mind lock up like a braked train wheel, throwing sparks, at the word "artificial." "But—but it's the predominant rock in the island—and apparently every island—on Planet Blue!"

Under magnification the specimen was sapphire blue, with an elaborate, sparkling crystalline structure. Joel's eyes ached. He'd been up late tonight researching rocks and minerals on his own. Including nomenclature. "It's Scheiderite."

Startled out of his reverie, Lary flashed a sweet grin.

Yandell said, "Commander, let me try to explain more clearly. If I weren't certain it came from that world, I'd tell you it was man-made, without a doubt. But every island on the world!"

"Definitely Scheiderite," said Joel.

Chapter Twenty-Five

COMMEMORATION

Joe heard it from the edge of the clearing on top of Unity Mountain: the shuttle booming toward Unity Base for a landing. The boom marked the end of the seemingly endless quarantine, the day he'd awaited for months. Now it was not what he wanted to hear.

Out here in the open, he'd first kissed Catharin at night, held her, and she'd tasted sweeter than anything he could remember. They'd tried it a few more times and it was even better. And last night, he'd slipped into her bunk room, and she'd spent the night in his arms, exhausted into a weary haze, but clinging to him, and he'd been happy to hold her and cuddle her when she roused. But then somewhere in the long hours of the night, he'd realized how much he was afraid of her.

Wheeling, Joe faced a lopsided furry pine tree, half its branches blown off when the mountaintop had been blasted flat nearly a year ago. Joe struck the tree's bole with his fist. The pain gave him something to feel other than the feelings that seethed in his gut like acid.

"Good afternoon!" Joe instantly recognized the cheery voice from one of the few throats he wouldn't have wanted to strangle for interrupting him in this mood. Wing emerged at a brisk pace from the pines, decked out in field clothes and gear, returning from a hike downhill. "Let's go greet the—" He broke off, looking closely at Joe. "Has there been bad news?"

"Don't know, don't care. I'm having a bad day."

Joe heard the shuttle again, loud enough to jerk his head up to look.

From out over the lowlands, it roared in, startlingly big and blazing, heavy iron compared to Becca's *Kite*.

Wing said, "I made a discovery for you today. Albeit a belated discovery, since the quarantine is over and you will return to the Ship on the shuttle."

"Maybe." Joe ground the word out.

"On the north side of the Mountain, below that romantic dell of yours, the stream flows into a deep, clear pool. It's the size of a swimming pool—and deeper, like a rock quarry—and very clear. Eddy can test the water, but it looks clean enough for swimming."

"Thanks for the thought. I may not go back up after all."

Wing raised his eyebrows. "I thought you looked forward to that above all else, Joe!"

"Carl, what I want is to do *my* work. Not what Catharin wants me to."

"I see." Wing seated himself on a rock with a fractured edge where the blast that flattened the mountaintop had split it off the parent stone nearby. Both rocks had sheets of new, blue-gray lichen already skeined over the raw faces.

Joe said savagely. "I've sampled DNA scans from the whole population. It's the same story. I'm certain the whole germ line is damaged—mostly in places on the DNA that won't be expressed in this generation but will show up in the next generation or so. Carl, I never wanted to be a doctor because people bore me, and now I don't see any end to the work she'll have me doing!" He ground the knuckles that he'd bruised on the furry pine into his other palm.

"You don't have the right facilities down here, such as the virtual arena on the Ship. That will make the work better."

"Yeah, and I feel at loose ends without a virtual arena to work in. But that's not it. I don't want to throw all of the rest of my life into this." Joe paced. "Not even to save the human race."

Anybody else in the Base would have sputtered and contradicted Joe. Wing just asked, "Then why would you?"

"What are you, the devil's advocate?"

"Sometimes. Why would you try to save the human race?"

"Because that's what she wants me to do. And I don't think I can live or love without her!"

If that surprised Wing, he hid it well. "Ah. I know sleeping on your problems won't do you much good. You might try swimming on it."

"I can't swim back to Earth!"

"The rest of us can't either," Wing said dryly. "Or we'd join you. We're sad and afraid. And homesick, even if most of us thought Earth was a sad home."

"On Earth I dreamed up weird and wonderful creatures, and they worked, they came to life. I could have done unspeakable things too, and I didn't. Don't I get any cosmic credit for that?" The words spilled out, surprising Joe. What was this, he asked himself, confession?

A mechanical roar swept across the mountaintop. Shuttle coming back to land, having dumped off the speed of its atmospheric descent. Joe jerked his head up at the late-afternoon sky. A ribbon of vapor twisted across the air, the smoke of the shuttle's first pass. It looked like DNA on a blue field only slightly paler than virtual reality. The contrail dissolved in the winds aloft, like a dying dream, and the sight twisted in Joe's stomach like a knife.

Wing seemed to read Joes's pained expression. "I don't know any way for you to square the circle either," he said. "That may change. Sometimes life is more gracious than we expect, or have a right to expect. Magic happens."

"Or doesn't."

"Or doesn't," Wing agreed. "Let's meet the shuttle. News was supposed to be coming down with it."

"Good idea." Joe still felt rotten, but the pressure inside was less unbearable, as though caustic steam had been vented. It was going to build back up, though.

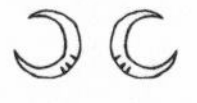

Parked on the runway, the big flying machine loomed over the clustered base people. A lanky woman in a flight suit stood on the shuttle's steps as if addressing the crowd. But she wasn't speaking at the moment. Everybody else was. Aaron gestured animatedly. His hand clipped Maya on the side of her head, followed by an agitated apology in her direction. "Something tells me the news was a bombshell," said Joe.

Aaron saw Joe and Wing arriving, and turned toward them with consternation written on his bony features. "The sample from the moon was artifi-

cial, not the result of natural processes! All of the mountains on Blue are the same stuff and—"

"Somebody manufactured it. Two hundred million years ago!" interrupted Becca. "Another intelligent race—"

"At least that explains—," Sam Houston began.

"Planeformed, it was planeformed!" shouted Aaron over everybody else.

Joe's mind reeled to the single most important question. "Where are they? Was anybody home?"

The woman on the shuttle's steps answered him. "The Commander asked me to personally bring the news down, rather than transmit it, as a courtesy to you folks down here, and I was briefed in full. The answer, I can assure you, is *no*. We've got a planeformed world up there with not a single sign of life on it. Does everybody copy that?" Her crisp alto carried over the crowd. "No life. The water vapor in the air tells us that the seas are acidic. There were no traces of microbes or algae in the sample. And the *planeforming* isn't two hundred million years old. The *weathering* is. We already had reason to think that Blue was a rogue planet, captured by this sun and this world only a couple of hundred million years ago. It could have wandered between the stars, frozen solid, for ages and ages before that."

A world in stasis? Joe thought. The crowd buzzed. Catharin turned to Aaron. "Aaron, this is truly momentous. Can we postpone your ritual until after we've done all the debriefing we need to about Blue?"

Aaron folded his hands and drew himself up to his full, spare height. "No. It must begin at sunset, and I have the Commander's full support on that."

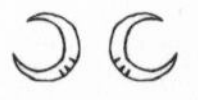

Of all times and places, Catharin thought, *this is the last time and place I want to be dragged through a religious ritual.* The news from Blue had unsettled everyone. More personally, last night had unsettled her. Joe had stayed with her all night, holding her in bed, helping her sleep a full seven hours while he seemed to have slept his usual four. She would not have expected that kind of patience from him.

But in the early hours of the morning, something had gone very wrong.

He had tensed up. By the time she came fully awake, almost well rested, he was strung tight, muscles corded in his arms. And he wouldn't say why.

A breeze cooled Catharin's face and hands as she climbed to the observation deck. Green's air was moving, its weather changing. The sky was tinged pale orange in the west, with the sun setting in a tangle of red and purple clouds. Aaron greeted Catharin as cordially as though she had not expressed strong reservations about the timing. "Good holiday." He smiled. Behind him was a large table set with thirteen place settings of plates and cups. The rest of the observation deck was jammed with chairs and small tables enough for a dozen more people, the number of those in Unity Base who'd elected to attend the ritual. Catharin had a place at the head table. *What a privilege.*

Most of the attendees arrived within the next five minutes. So did a platter, which Eddy ceremoniously placed on the table. Around the edge of the platter were arranged a neatly diced tomato, a small pile of mint leaves, and a larger, paler leaf that might have been endive, except that all the greenhouse had produced to date was plain lettuce. "I hope there's more chow than that," said Sam, taking a place to Catharin's right with a loud rattle of the chair.

Wimm came carrying a white pitcher and a plate piled with vat crackers. Joe abruptly seated himself to Catharin's left. He had been taciturn all day, and nowhere to be found for three solid hours in the afternoon. Whatever he had been up to hadn't helped, Catharin thought in dismay.

Aaron stood up. The cloud-reddened light of sunset fell onto the planes of his face and made him look rosier and less scholarly than usual. "This is the first of three ceremonies scheduled for this evening, then again at Green's midnight, then at sunrise. So Starfall lies across evening, night, and dawn for the planet—twenty-four hours in Earth time."

And not long after Green-dawn, the shuttle would return to the Ship with Becca and Joe. Becca could start having sophisticated prenatal care. Joe could start working in the genetic laboratory, with the virtual computer arena he seemed to need. Getting the two of them Upstairs would happen none too soon. Maybe Catharin could begin to sort out her troubled feelings and her sexual needs then.

Aaron was saying, "This is loosely modeled after the Jewish Passover Seder, may my grandfather Rabbi Perlmutter and my grandmother the Rebbitzin forgive me for just how loose it is. A full meal will be forthcoming shortly—a good one. Wimm has outdone himself in the kitchen tonight." A scattering of applause faltered as the applauders wondered if they'd done something improper, but Aaron made a gracious gesture with his hands.

On the Ship, Joel had taken charge of the first phase of his holiday. It was supposed to be about remembering the history that had brought them here. What they were getting Upside was more like a Baptist revival than a Jewish Passover. Joel had picked a truly bizarre point at which to decide to exercise command—ordering the Ship and the Base to concoct a religious holiday. But he'd also ended the quarantine, a right move. People had odd ways of expiating their mixed feelings about claiming authority.

Ignoring the fact that one place setting was still unoccupied, Aaron went on. "The Jewish Passover has much to do with springtime, but more than that, it is a historical story which, in the Seder meal, is symbolized by food."

"Ritual hors d'oeuvres?" Domino asked skeptically. Across the table from Catharin, he sat close to Becca, with an arm flung around her shoulders.

"I invite you all to consider the fact that the platter on our table symbolizes *our* exodus—from Earth to this place."

"Does your idea of food include native plants?" said Sam. "That green leaf is swampcress. Totally inedible."

"Spoken in the true spirit of the evening," Aaron said cheerfully. "Passover is a time for questions and observant attention. The children present at a Seder meal ask ritual questions about the meaning and elements of the holiday. The children take the roles of wise, simple, wicked, and ignorant. The wise one asks intelligent questions. The wicked one asks questions as if they concern others only and not himself—he is considered wicked because he refuses to consider his personal involvement in his people's history. Tellingly, he phrases his questions in terms of 'what does it mean to *you*?'"

Next to Catharin, Joe jerked in his chair, which clanged against hers.

"The simple child knows the appropriate question but doesn't ask, and the ignorant one does not know the question and is therefore unable to ask. So I invite all of you to ask questions. Just stick to the history of our flight from Earth. Let us not discuss the moon now. That will be debriefed—" he chose the word with an ironic curl at the edge of his mouth "—later tonight, under different leadership." He inclined his head toward Sam and again, with dignity, toward Eddy.

"The vat crackers symbolize the food on the Ship, right?" said Becca, eagerly. "Because that's our manna in the desert, what we ate in the trip."

"So what does that tomato signify?" asked Tezi Young.

"The first fruits of this world," Aaron answered solemnly.

Maya asked, "And the boiled kernel corn?"

I must be the simple child, Catharin thought. I know Aaron wants us to ask about these things, but I honestly can't care. *Damn Joel's timing.*

Aaron steepled his hands. "On Earth, corn was one of several widely grown food grains. Corn fed billions. When monoculture led to plant plagues and enormous crop failures, millions died for want of corn. I thought we should remember that tonight."

Catharin had come this far to help build a world where the lessons of the Green Revolution were applied, rather than learned the hard way. She had imagined a human world with enough wisdom to make hunger and sustenance balance out, with margin to spare for the vagaries of nature.

"Okay," said Sam. "What about those mint leaves?"

Aaron answered, "The Jewish Seder uses bitter herbs to symbolize the bitterness of the Israelites' bondage in Egypt."

An unwelcome, spontaneous reflection came to Catharin. Maybe this new world would not be better than Earth. Maybe it would be bitter in its own way. She thought about chromosomal damage from stasis, children who might be doomed before they were ever conceived. She thought about Chase Scanlan and Fredrik Hoffmann. The breeze of sunset coiled into the observation deck. Catharin shivered.

Aaron continued, "Mint and basil are the only greenhouse herbs we've got. I opted for the mint."

"Sweetness of Earth," said Sam, "and the wild plants that Earth gave us on its own." An approving murmur swept around the table.

Joe said, "So one child should say what does it all mean to *you*? I doubt anybody else here wants that role. I'll take it." He had hardly spoken three words to Catharin all day. Now he was in a mood to speak in public. "What does that inedible swampcress mean to you?"

Aaron intoned, "Carl, you discovered swampcress. Would you answer that?"

"This world offers us no sustenance," said Wing. "Even to swallow small amounts of organic matter here turns the stomach—I should know. It is not Earth, and its abundance of green plants is not ours to eat."

Catharin could usually reject any morbid speculation that entered her mind, discard it as not useful at the moment. Not tonight. From the beginning, the human race had struggled against sickness, death, and disaster in a dangerous and cryptic universe. Peoples had filled in their gaps in knowledge with speculation and ritual, but had, in the long run, learned enough about the physical universe to cross the stars. And disease was insurmountable as before, and the genes as selfish as ever, and in Blue and Green humanity confronted a new facet of nature as mysterious and threatening as the old world had been. Catharin's stomach, empty except for acid from frustration and anxiety, dully ached.

Aaron picked up the pitcher. He sniffed the contents. "Is this drinkable?"

"Could be smoother, but it'll do," Wimm replied.

Aaron poured amber liquid from the pitcher into the cups around the table. When he had portioned out the beer, Aaron gestured over the platter. "At Seder, we do not eat the symbolic food. Here, we will, because food is not to be taken for granted on this world. Worse than doing it differently from Seder would be to waste a single crumb." The edges of his lips quirked up. "What my grandmother the rabbi's wife would have said about this would take the peel off an apple. She was very strict about religious observances. But here goes. Everybody take a cracker, and put a bit of tomato and mint and a kernel or so of corn on it, and eat it. Take a shred of swampcress too, but as Catharin would say, do not ingest that. Just let it remain on your plate for the duration of the meal."

It was a strange and barely palatable hors d'oeuvre. Catharin suddenly remembered Miranda Blum and her dinners. No rabbi's wife: a brilliant, highly educated woman, Jewish by culture, agnostic in outlook, and an accomplished hostess whose hors d'oeuvres were legendary in medical school. Catharin felt tears prickle the corners of her eyes.

"Who's the thirteenth cup for?" Becca asked. "Isn't there a cup at Passover Seder for somebody who isn't there?"

"Elijah, the prophet, at a Jewish Seder" said Aaron. "Perhaps there is another prophet to be remembered."

Catharin surprised herself by saying aloud, "There were people who told us to go to the stars, and showed us how."

A murmur of agreement went around the table. Becca said, "How about the engineers, the technicians, the miners, and all of the people who made *Aeon*?" To that, there was a chorus of assent. The memory of Chief Gerald Donovan came to Catharin's mind.

"Do we toast 'em or what?" asked Sam.

"Not yet. At Seder, one drop of wine is taken from the cups for each plague that was visited on Egypt before the Israelites escaped, to signify compassion for what the Egyptians suffered. Tonight, we should remember those who suffered and died from everything that we escaped. There are twelve of us at this table. We ought to be able to come up with one plague each." Standing, he dipped a finger into his cup, and flicked a droplet of beer onto the table. "Pollution."

Sam stood with a rasp of her chair. "Overpopulation," she declared.

Tezi Young said, "Extinctions."

"Acid rain," offered Raj North.

Catharin reluctantly rose. "Antibiotic-resistant bacteria and savage viruses." Then there was silence as people remembered the drastic medical plagues of the early twenty-first century. No one seemed game to top that.

"The greenhouse effect had several disastrous aspects," Aaron prompted.

"The oceans rose." Maya London gracefully flicked a drop out of her cup onto her napkin.

"The ozone layer thinned," said Wimm.

"Desertification," Eddy offered.

Wing stood up, offering, "War."

"Pestilence," said Becca. She rapped Domino's shoulder. "You went to Sunday school."

"Famine?"

Now only Joe remained seated. The world's abundant silence flowed over the observation deck. Catharin could hear Joe breathing—short hard breaths, as though he had been exercising. Joe stood abruptly. "Death."

Aaron said, "Thank you. In the first Exodus, the death angel passed over, taking the lives of the firstborn sons of Egypt, and that was the last of the plagues. In this new Exodus of ours, we have certainly been delivered into a new land. Not the one we expected." Aaron picked up his expedition-issue white cup, wrapping his long fingers as gracefully around it as though it were a crystal goblet. He began to chant in a different language with an exotic cadence. Hebrew. A human tongue older than old. Even Catharin, not in a receptive mood, felt the hair on the back of her neck rise with awe. On this quiet, voiceless world, with a quiet breeze blowing, Aaron's words could carry all the way to the alien forest. Then he said, "Everybody take a sip of your beer."

The beer tasted strong, laced with the flavor of hops. A little sputter came from Maya on the other end of the table.

Wimm and Eddy took the empty platter, plate, and pitcher away, returning with serving dishes. Aaron was right; Wimm had outdone himself with aromatic tomato salad, eggplant parmesan, and sweet-smelling bread pudding. The bit of shiny swampcress isolated on the very edge of Catharin's plate looked unnatural next to terrestrial food, as inedible as plastic.

Becca asked, "Is it kosher if the milk stuff, the egg stuff, and the meat stuff come out of the same vat—but none of it is real meat or milk, and there's no blood at all?"

How appropriate that she should ask the child's questions, Catharin thought. *She has the child—and no one here but she and I know that.*

"Given a strict old rabbi like my grandfather, the setup you have accurately described would curl the edges of his beard," Aaron answered. "More progressive rabbis might say kosher is not the question; here, there are a different set of distinctions to be made, to make us mindful of God's purpose in our history."

"What makes you think there's purpose, much less God?" asked Joe abruptly.

"We made it here," Becca said.

"Speak for yourself," Joe retorted. "Remember, I'm the wicked child."

Beside Becca, Domino put down his fork with a bang. "Why in hell did you come?" Becca put a cautionary hand on his arm.

"It's a long story," Joe answered in a drawling tone that made Catharin's nerves knot up in tension. Joe's voice usually sounded that way when he meant to devastate somebody with remarks to follow. He turned toward Aaron. "Want to hear it?"

Aaron's shrug flowed into his outspread hands. "The purpose of this evening is history."

Catharin almost let a bitter chuckle escape from her. *Mistake, Aaron. You have just let your ritual be upstaged by Joe's mood show.*

"Remember how Earth was?" Joe began. "Anything you wanted to eat you had, anywhere you wanted to go you could, most of the aging processes had been conquered by medical science." He gave Catharin a sarcastic little salute. "Then there were the toys. Virtual reality playgrounds in which anything was possible because nothing was real. Of course, some people's taste runs toward real things to play with, like flying machines." He smiled at Domino with too many teeth showing for the smile to convey friendliness. Domino bristled.

Aaron was not going to let his show be upstaged without some effort to keep the symbolism intact. "You have just described the fleshpots of Egypt," he said. "Many of us thought that decadence was rampant, offensive, and incurable, and that's part of why we left."

"Fleshpots? Good word for it. Hell, *I* enjoyed stirring the pots. I told you I was the wicked child. I redesigned DNA theoretically; and my flunkies in the company, and whatever outside scientists we released the rights to, actually made the novelties."

"Look, why don't you keep this short and sweet," Domino interrupted. Becca's fingers tightened on his arm.

"It's short and sour." There were tense muscles bunched at Joe's jaw.

"Passover recognizes life can be very sour indeed," said Aaron, still trying to get things back on track.

Domino said in a harsh tone, "You meddled with people. Made some nontherapeutic, nontrivial modifications. And one of them died. Federal felony. So you had to run. Right?"

Becca hissed at Domino to shut up.

Joe's laugh had a razor edge. "Guess again. I was the theoretician. *I* wasn't liable if somebody else made something illegal, and yeah, the company sacrificed a few."

Catharin felt her stomach lurch, as if she'd just tripped. "A few what?"

"Scientists who did the mods and got caught. And mods. Not all of them were viable."

Anger hit Catharin so suddenly, and so hard, that it made her gasp. "You designed illegal modifications of human beings, knowing that what you proposed would be brought to life?"

"DNA doesn't want to stay the same!" Joe flung back at her. "It wants change even if changed organisms die. Don't you see that by now?"

She struggled to find words to frame her fury. "You wouldn't feel that way if *you* were the one changed!"

"Hold it!" said Aaron. He put one of his hands on Joe's shoulder and the other on Catharin's. They had been leaning toward each other, and Aaron pushed them apart. The dozen Unity Base personnel not at the head table were transfixed, as though they were at a dinner theater with an enthralling play. Catharin felt her face flame with embarrassment. Aaron said, "Go on, Joe. Why did you leave?"

"Guilty conscience can't be it," Sam commented.

"The CEO of my company was Vladimir Pang-Park. Heard of him?" Joe looked around Aaron at Catharin, with a challenge flashing in his eyes. Even in a cloud of anger and embarrassment, Catharin realized that she had.

"Oooh. I remember reading about him," said Eddy. "Powerful and rich, influential in politics."

"Had his pockets full of pet politicians. And scientists," Joe said curtly. "He offered me the project of a lifetime." Joe's phrases came out short and hot, like steam vented from a boiling kettle. "He wasn't going to take no for an answer, not from me."

Catharin was dazzled with comprehension. "Not only did you lie in the assessment interview—you picked the wrong enemy, didn't you?"

Joe's face twisted. "I saw my future on Earth, and it was working as a slave scientist."

Faces around the table looked stunned or amazed. "Oh, my gosh!" said Becca, ignoring the wrathful expression on Domino's face. "You ran away to the stars to be free?"

"You'd respect me if I said yes, wouldn't you?"

Catharin could hear naked need for her respect in his voice. Becca could hear it too. Her eyes widened with compassion. Catharin trembled with anger. "You told *me* that a few months ago—and I did respect you for it!"

The cup Joe held shook in his grip. "I accepted the deal because Pang-Park offered me a playground just to keep me fresh. There's a lot in life that didn't bother me, Doctor, as long as I could make interesting things."

A sudden gust of wind blew napkins and swampcress shreds around. Nobody moved to chase the napkins. Catharin felt hot anger and icy dismay at the same time, and her fists clenched.

"But the thing he wanted me to do made me sick. After a while I couldn't stand it any more. Simple as that. That's why I'm here." Joe jerked his head toward Domino. "Short enough?"

The door from the Base to the observation deck suddenly opened. Kay Montana stood there. "Done yet?"

Aaron expelled a deep breath and ran a hand though his hair. "I had nothing else planned but a final toast."

"There's a storm blowing in. You're all about to get drenched, and I need people to help push the shuttle into the lee of the Base."

"Of course." Aaron hastily lifted his cup, by the handle, like an ordinary cup.

"Hold it!" said Sam. "A little rain isn't going to hurt us, and we're not finished. Kay, use horsepower, not people. Dig our man Alvin Crawford out of the machine shop in the hangar. He can tow the shuttle with a jeep." Kay departed. "We're not going to be a bunch of ignorant children—" Sam put her hands on her hips. "—who don't know what to ask! That man just said a project horrified him. He's not squeamish. Meddling with the germ line was fine by him—lost no sleep over that—no matter the life expectancy of the finished product, right?"

"That did matter to me," Joe insisted. "But when I altered the germ line, I enjoyed it." He shot Catharin a daggery blue glance.

Catharin had not known it was possible to feel this angry. And Joe was barely two feet away from her. She held the edge of the table to keep from yielding to an impulse to hit him.

"If nobody else is going to ask the question, I will," said Sam. "What would have taken you the rest of your life and mind, but made you sick to the bottom of your soul, Joseph Devreze?"

Joe looked up at the approaching storm made of clotted dark clouds with sunset-stained, bloody edges. His jaw was clenched so hard that muscles corded on his neck.

Wing walked around the table to put a hand on Joe's shoulder. "The unspeakable? But in the end you did not do it—and you do get cosmic credit for that, Joe. What was it?"

Joe said in a low voice, "To get death out of the human genome."

Catharin groped for meaning. There had been two kinds of old, powerful people. Miranda and Pang-Park. One kind imagined a better future, trained a younger generation to attain it, built *Aeon*. Pang-Park—

"He was an old man who didn't want to die? How selfish!" said Maya.

Joe said, "Selfish as hell, but not in the way you mean. He already had the benefit of every rejuvenation therapy and every single-gene-replacement longevity treatment ever devised. What he wanted from me was germ line alteration so humans wouldn't have to die. But it was all wrong."

Catharin's voice came out with a sharp, out-of-control edge. "*Wrong?* How could you think saving lives is wrong?"

"You don't understand, *Doctor!*" His voice was thick with feeling. "It would have violated something basic. Raped nature." He stumbled like a bull in a china shop of words. "The genes want change and chimeras and disease, not fixity. The human genome wants to change, and I helped it. But to make it not die, I would have had to kill it. Death is a part of life."

Only now did what Joe was saying sink in for Catharin. Humans who didn't die—at all?

Would such beings still be human?

Sam nodded emphatically. "Good man!"

Catharin felt stunned. The desires of human *genes* felt important to him, but not the welfare of human beings?

"The death angel passed over," said Wing, "and the image of death is an angel, though a terrible one."

It began to rain. Aaron said emphatically, "Drink! *L'chaim!* To life!"

Catharin gulped her beer as rain spattered on the deck and on the table.

And the taste of the beer reminded her not of beer at all but of hospitals, of the critical care ward where the victims of savage viruses writhed and bled and festered to death. Then rain poured down. Aaron's guests rushed toward the door to the conference room. Sam, however, stood there like a rock in a stream, looking up into the rain and letting it puddle in her cupped hands.

Becca veered to Joe's side and spoke to him. Domino ran over to pull her away from him. Becca shook Domino off as Joe stalked away toward the outside stairs down to the ground. Becca hurried to Catharin. "At first I thought it was rain on Joe's face, but it's tears! You better go talk to him!"

"He can jump into the river," Catharin snapped.

"Didn't you hear me? He's crying. He's hurt, and you're the doctor!" Becca shoved Catharin with surprising force toward the stairs.

☽ ☾

But I'm not that kind of doctor! She was already soaked to the skin, and thunder rumbled in the sky, and she had never felt so close to hating Joe, but she followed him down the stairs and across the open ground. He cornered around the hangar. She did too. *Why am I doing this?*

Joe stumbled into the little valley behind the hangar. He seemed uncoordinated, or not to be seeing clearly, and stopped between the flat rock and the furry pine that grew there. In the patter of rain he did not hear her approach. She was about to rap his shoulder to get his attention when he drew his hand back in a fist, aiming an all-out blow at the tree's bole. Without thinking, Catharin caught his hand. Joe's force caused her to skid toward the tree. Her shoulder banged into the bole. They both gasped. Joe grabbed her upper arms. "Did I hurt you?!"

"That would have broken your hand!"

He shook her. "What else could I have done??"

"Hit something softer, or throw things, but don't hurt yourself!"

"That isn't what I mean!" he shouted.

"Then tell me what you do mean!" she yelled back.

"What else could I have done but leave Earth?" he demanded, face close to hers.

She put her hands on his chest and shoved him back. "You need to know right now?"

"Yes!"

It rained harder. A sodden wisp of hair fell in her eyes. "Didn't you have friends in the industry, other places where you could have worked?"

Joe shook his head so hard that water flew off his hair. "It's a competitive business, Doctor. And I was a competitive SOB. Didn't have a lot of allies in the industry and at work. And Pang-Park was one of the most powerful men on Earth." He turned away, making fists.

"Joe, no!" She flung her arms around him from behind, grabbing his wrists, afraid that he would strike the tree or the rock.

He threw himself into a crouch, covering his face with his hands. Since she didn't let go of his wrists, she was dragged down too, her feet slid out from under her, and she ended up sitting on the ground behind him, dazed at his sheer physical power.

"Mike didn't like the idea of genetic engineering. But Mike was a cop. Jean-Claude was a poet. They didn't know science. Oh, God, I miss them! *How could I have shut them out?*"

His voice rose while Catharin thought, *Who is he talking about?* There was a flash of lightning; thunder crackled almost immediately. And Joe screamed in raw despair. Twice. Without the thunder masking his screams, they would have brought people running out of Unity Base in alarm.

"Oh dear God!" Catharin whispered through clenched teeth.

"What else *could* I have done?" His voice was hoarse. "Tell me! Tell me!"

She felt surrounded by a minefield. "You know the easy answer. You could have found freedom in the work. But you couldn't do that."

His shoulders shook. She moved her hands onto his, tried to unclench his mud-streaked fingers, and when she did, his hands clamped around hers and drew them to his chest. With her face pressed between his shoulder blades, she felt grief racking him.

Mud streamed around their knees. "Doctor, I never thought you'd join me in the dirt," he said.

She swallowed hard. "Me either."

"Do you care about me?" The voice was hoarse—strained by the screams he'd let out.

Catharin still wanted to slap him for his arrogance, his cavalier attitude toward human well-being. Yet: not when he was this miserable. She nodded against his back.

"Pang-Park used a beautiful woman to tempt me to stay and work for him," Joe whispered. "I thought she liked me. A lab tech tipped me off that Pang-Park had set it up."

She knew the next question was going to be loaded. And it was.

"Would you make love to me in order to use me?"

"No! That idea is abhorrent to me."

"How about the obverse? Love me without using me?"

Something inside her had known that it would come to this. *In our hour of need, he won't cooperate.* Damn his impossible—pathological—arrogance. But that didn't change the fact of attraction, or the overwhelming intensity of it. Catharin gritted her teeth.

"Long silence, Doctor. The answer is no, eh?"

"The answer is *yes*, I would love you without using you, but not in the dirt. Get up!" He let her pull him up and shove him down to sit on the edge of the rock. She sat beside him, wrapping her arms around him. In his ear, she snapped, "I will not let you be less of a hero, less sane, than you can."

"Won't let me be less than you want me to be?"

"Don't put words in my mouth. I said what I mean. I've had lovers too. Never has a lover done all for me that I wanted, because I don't pick spineless ones." She paused to catch her breath. "But if I have to be the voice of your conscience, and it does sound like you need one, I will!"

Incredibly, under that tongue-lashing, the knotted muscles in his back and shoulders relaxed. She rubbed her chin against him, feeling the softening. His hair hung in dark damp ringlets. Her lips brushed a cool wet lock on his warm neck.

"When would you like to start reforming me?"

"Not now."

He turned her hand over and kissed her palm.

Catharin's mind reeled. There couldn't have been enough alcohol in the beer to cause that. It was him, her physical attraction to him. She wanted him like nothing and no one she'd ever known before. She released a sharp sigh, then wrapped her hand around his neck and kissed him on the side of his face.

A shudder ran through him. Then she realized that he was crying, sobs tumbling out of him. Appalled that he sounded so brokenhearted, she rocked him back and forth.

It got darker. Her adrenaline ebbed. She simmered with desire, anger, and hurt on the inside, but felt chilled on the outside. The skin of Joe's neck was warm where she put her cheek against it.

Parts of the evening replayed in her mind. She remembered boiling over at Aaron's table. Joe's collar was near her lips; she closed her teeth on the soft material in mortification, remembering how everybody, including Joe, had been more in tune, less incoherent, or had at least asked good questions.

Suddenly Catharin knew her own question, unasked, not even imagined until this moment.

Joe had said he refused to undo death in the genome.

Did that mean he had seen how to do that?

Chapter Twenty-Six

NIGHT CIRCLES

Catharin disliked the long dark "days" of Green: even in summer, they got cold and seemed endless. This one was more hateful than usual. The rain made the air cool, and having been chilled to the bone in the rain with Joe, Catharin never really warmed up.

She worked on a report to encrypt for transmission up to the Ship. The report consisted of medical information about Becca's pregnancy. Listening to the endless, soft night wind, Catharin toyed with the idea of going up to the Ship herself. But she could not leave the Base without a physician. It would take an astoundingly good reason to have someone else substituted for her. A better reason than the amalgam of: *I embarrassed myself with the crowd down here and I'm tired of long dark nights and I want to personally care for Becca and be Joe's conscience.*

In the deep darkness of midday, she received an encrypted transmission back from the Ship. It came from Joel.

Ours is going to be born in less than a month, and the birth mother's agreed to give him the name I suggested. He'll be named John, after John the Baptist, who was born to parents who were too old bear children.

Still no medical reason to suspect a problem, Catharin surmised. Maybe Joe had been imagining things. Did he really know the difference between life and death at that level? Could he really feel a trace of deadly change somewhere in a human chromosome?

She did not ask. Joe seemed to be himself today, sarcasm and all. "Sam'll probably have you stand in a circle and chant at the moon," Joe informed her.

Catharin had only the vaguest idea of what Sam had in mind for the women, and did not look forward to it. She had no idea at all what Eddy had planned for the men. "And perhaps the rest of you will be howling at the moon."

"I doubt it. Eddy's no alpha male."

☽☾

After supper, the Ship transmitted a conference on Blue, new findings about the artificial islands. Catharin slipped in at the last minute, when the lights were already out and Blue on a black field shone on the back wall of the conference room, the Base's own Little Picture.

As she glided into a chair in the last row, Catharin heard a scratchy voice slightly too loud to qualify as discreet. "Sounds like last night turned into quite a shindig. So Snow White has a temper after all?"

Raj North's voice replied, "Remember, Alvin, she's the doc. That means scalpels. If you value your balls, better watch your tongue." Both men snickered.

Catharin crossed her arms, glad that the gloom hid her blush.

Lary and Joel were windowed into the picture to provide commentary. Lary said, "This is an artificial, cloudless image of Blue. Note the islands, and the vaguely geometrical way they seem to be arrayed on the globe. Now, I've done a historical reconstruction given so many millions of years of weathering. The storms are worse in Blue's temperate latitudes, in fact, severe enough to have worn some islands completely down below the waves. So, with radar scanning from *Lodestar*, I looked for submerged seamounts in certain places."

Catharin's attention strayed to Joel. The dignity of command sat well on his even, coffee-and-cream-complected features. Catharin briefly closed her eyes in tired amazement. Her attraction to Joe was more intense than ever, yet had done absolutely nothing to make Joel less attractive. In fact, the now-Commander's emotional stability struck her as extremely desirable.

Catharin was jarred back to the here and now by surprised murmurs around her. On the picture, Blue looked dramatically different, exquisitely patterned with gray dots. Lary said, "As you can see, two hundred million years ago Blue's mountains were as geometrical as the segments of an orange—though not quite that simple."

Joel made a low whistle of amazement. "It's neat as a Christmas tree ornament."

"No plate tectonics or planetary processes known to us—or guessed at, for that matter—would have given that result. At some point in the distant past, Blue was planeformed on a massive scale according to a rather elaborate master plan." Lary beamed at them. "Questions?"

"Lots," said Sam. "But the big one is why?"

Lary shrugged. "That's for our archaeologists, of which I imagine we have one or two in the freezer, despite the fact that it was not assessed as a mission-useful vocation. . . . But we think this was done elsewhere in the galaxy, and that Blue wandered between the stars for ages. So your answer may be lost in the mists of time and interstellar space."

"How can you be sure it wasn't terraformed in situ? Right here?" said Sam.

"That raises more questions than it answers. If Blue has been here all along, it's spinning too fast and orbiting too close. Planetary evolution should have left it phase-locked with Green and located considerably farther away than it is, long before life reached the point of development we see on Green."

Catharin's attention had been riveted to Joel before, but now she listened raptly to Lary along with everyone else. Then it dawned on her that his color did not look right. Nor did the loose texture of his skin.

"We haven't seen even an infinitesimal trace of life down there, much less civilization," said Joel. "We've detected no radio signals from Blue except from lightning noise and the magnetosphere. Nobody interfered with the drone when it flew down either. Nobody's home."

"My friends, the absolute most recent date for Blue's remodeling is two hundred million years ago. That happens to be a short time for a planet," said Lary. "But rather long for a sentient species. On Earth, *our* species came into existence one hundred thousand years ago. A couple of hundred million years ago, the first mammals were scuttling around the feet of the dinosaurs!" Lary waved his hands and laughed. Midlaugh, he lapsed into a coughing fit.

Catharin quietly left, going back to Medical, intent on contacting the hospital Upstairs, asking them if Lary Siroky-Scheidt had fallen ill. In the hallway in front of Medical, Joe stepped in front of her. Startled, she jumped.

He put a hand on her arm, not circling it, so she could shake him off if she wanted to. "I didn't mean to startle you."

"I've got something on my mind. I think a friend of mine Upstairs is sick, and I didn't know about it."

His face hardened. "Were you coming to discuss that with me?"

"No. Honest. I just had to know more from the Ship. Please don't blame me for hoping!" Tears sprang up in the corners of her eyes.

He sighed and then leaned close to kiss her forehead. Shaken, she moved close, into his embrace. "This reminds me," he said into her hair. "I wanted to say good-bye in relative privacy. This is as good a chance as any, eh?"

"It won't be forever. Quarantine's over, and there will be coming and going."

"Will you miss me when I'm gone?" he asked.

On impulse, she kissed him. Feeling warm for the first time in hours, she wrapped herself as close to him as clothing would allow, and wished she could have been closer still.

"Hot damn!"

Catharin whirled to see Alvin leaning on the nearest corner, grinning wickedly. She remembered what Becca had said about Alvin's odds-making activities, and her voice came out hard as cold-soaked metal. "*Why don't you mind your own business?*"

Alvin actually took a step back. "I am. Sam and Eddy sent me to look for you two."

"Then go tell them you found us and we're coming. I emphasize, *go*!"

Thanks to Alvin, the passionate and vulnerable moment had evaporated. Catharin told Joe, "We better go our separate ways before they send that hobgoblin after us again."

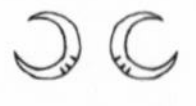

It was very late, nearly Green-midnight, at Camp Darwin, where the river ran flat and tranquil under the dark night sky. Half of the women from Unity

Base, plus Kay Montana, wandered around Camp Darwin looking at the stars or the river while waiting for Sam to return with the last jeep-load of attendees. Off to one side, Becca sat by the water alone.

Catharin went toward Becca and knelt in front of her. "I'm sorry I snapped at you after the meal. I did need to talk to Joe. You were completely right."

Becca patted the rock she was sitting on.

Catharin accepted the invitation and sat. "Furthermore, I am profoundly sorry that I made a fool of myself."

"In a weird way, it all fit together. Even your arguing with Joe. Did you make peace?"

"Yes." She was relieved that so much of what had come loose last night was mended now. Feeling the weariness that she had been fending off all day, Catharin would have been glad to sit here indefinitely.

"I told Domino I'm going up to the Ship. And why. That's why he was so ill-tempered with Joe."

"Can he accept what's happened?"

"He'll come around," Becca said. "It'll do us good to be apart for a while so the upset on both sides can cool off. But I'm probably going to feel sick as a dog on the shuttle. I don't look forward to it."

"Morning sickness never killed anybody. It has a purpose—to keep you from ingesting toxins. I was wondering how to signal you not to drink the beer."

Becca nodded. "I only took a symbolic sip."

They heard a vehicle motor, increasingly loud on the quiet air. "Here they come!" Tezi announced. "Everybody look religious."

With the last jeep-load of women trailing behind her, Sam strode into Camp Darwin. "Let's take off our shoes, sisters."

Catharin complied. This felt sillier than Aaron's feast, which had been a dignified if odd affair. On the Ship, it was Srivastava and Lary attempting to cooperate in some kind of Hindu/Unitarian ritual, complete with incense: Part Two of Joel's folly, Upstairs edition.

"Thisaway, sisters," Sam called. "A short walk to the main river."

"In bare feet?" Maya objected.

"The ground is mossy and soft."

"And presumably nontoxic," Catharin murmured.

Single file, the women wound their way between the trees at the edge of the fern forest beside the water. The moss underfoot felt so fuzzy that it almost tickled Catharin's bare feet.

Where the canopy thinned, the stars threw down just enough light to see everyone else as shining shapes. "We walk in moonlight and starlight—" Sam intoned.

From Becca came, "*Yipe!* I stepped on a zucchini slug!"

The line of women reshuffled into a circle around the slug.

"I hope I didn't hurt it!"

Sam bent over the slug. "It's fine."

"That's one of the slug things?" asked Kay. "They have shiny dots on their hides?"

The slug moved with a shivering motion across the moss toward the water. "What'd it feel like?" asked Tezi, jumping out of the slug's way. "Nasty?"

"Like suede," said Becca. "I just wasn't expecting it."

The slug vanished into a stand of swampcress beside the water. Continuing, the women came to a peninsula between tributary and river. A crescent Blue shone over the river, blurred by cloud. The rest of the sky blazed with stars, and the water gleamed blue and silver.

Maya asked, "Are we going to have a ritual?"

Sam answered, "Not the way I think you mean. No bell, book, and candle. Ritual is when the magic goes away. To begin with, let's just listen to the night."

Catharin soon realized that she had never experienced a silence like this. Even in Earth's cities sparrows and crickets could be heard. This land was silent as a library.

Sam finally said, "Let's all sit down in a circle. Let's introduce ourselves. We have names here that mean something important, names from women's history."

Catharin nodded to herself, a private guess confirmed: Sam practiced a womanist flavor of paganism.

"For example, Samantha is an old English and New England name. Several of the witches executed in Salem were named Samantha."

The group rustled.

"Go around the circle counterclockwise; leave out surnames—which are male inventions."

"Well—I'm Maya."

"The power of the Hindu gods for illusion and dream. As powers go, that's a high feminine one."

Maya trilled, "So many girls are named Maya—I never thought of it that way!"

"I'm Sheryn, which doesn't mean anything."

"It means you," Sam answered. "The heroine of your own story."

"I'm Tezandra Matsuko," said Tezi. "Grandma Tezandra was a community organizer. Grandmother Matsuko was a dentist."

Sam approved. "Strong foremothers."

"Kay. Arthurian hero. Male." Kay sounded unapologetic.

"It's good to steal the thunder of their names," said Sam.

"Catharin, a saint, spelled differently," Catharin murmured.

"I think we should call you by another name here. A circle name."

"Well, my middle name is Firenze, the city Florence. Flowers."

"How nice," said Maya.

Sam said, "I mean Medicine Woman."

Catharin objected. "I do not pretend to cure people with herbs and chants."

"Medicine people put people in harmony with the powers of life and death. You might try it someday." Sam gestured at Becca.

"Rebecca is from the Bible, and so is my middle name, Marie, it's a form of Mary."

"Now, that's quite a name," said Sam. "By some lights, Mary was the ultimate male-dominated woman, pious, barefoot, and pregnant."

Becca curled into a little ball.

Sam continued, "Yet she was the Mother of God. And in Mexico, she became the Virgin of Guadalupe—the dark-skinned Maria standing on a crescent moon; a new image of an old moon goddess."

Catharin felt an urgent need for the topic to be changed. "Are you going to introduce us to a moon goddess here, Sam?"

"No. Kay is."

Becca caught Catharin's eye. In the bright darkness, Catharin could read her body language. *Does Sam know?* Catharin shrugged, a tense motion to telegraph back, *I don't know how she could.*

Kay produced a glass vial that gleamed in the moon- and starlight.

"If we were all pagans, she'd be Woman Who Drew Down the Moon," said Sam, her voice capitalizing the phrase.

Kay snorted.

"Pass it around."

Catharin's night vision had improved. She could see the vial passing from hand to hand. Her night hearing had improved too, detecting purls from the river, and the audible breathing of Kay and Becca on each side of her. Then there was a muffled giggle from Becca. Maya asked, "Whatever is funny?"

"I had a really irreverent idea. I should keep it to myself."

"Don't bother. I don't stand on reverence," said Sam.

"I just imagined the people up on the Ship having a religious procession and carrying Tango 21 on a liturgical silk pillow. The spider that brought the sample back. With its little eyestalks looking around—"

Laughter overflowed from the circle as Catharin received the vial from Becca, who, though still giggling, carefully placed it in her hand. Catharin felt the contents slide from one end of the vial to the other. The vial held half of a pebble.

Blue rode in the sky over the plateau to the west. Framed by a sapphire crescent, its dark side glimmered with ceaseless storms.

The human race once more for the first time beheld a bright, changeable globe in the night sky. And reacted with fascination. And fear. And worship. *Have we crossed the stars just to fall back to superstitious square one?* Catharin handed the moon vial back to Kay abruptly, like a hot potato.

"It was planeformed, so what do you do with that?" Kay asked Sam. "That moon doesn't seem like a goddess to me."

"I do hope you realize that Wiccans and New Pagans didn't make pilgrimages to Earth's Moon," Sam said dryly. "It was scientists and museum curators who made shrines for Moon rocks. The Moon was holy because it was a mirror of our lives. It showed us the reality of change, by its phases, and imperfection, by its cratered appearance." Catharin caught an overtone of lecture. Sam had, after all, been a university professor on Earth, and old work habits die hard. "Medieval thinkers made it the lowest sphere of heaven—downgraded it on the same grounds that pagans worshiped it. It changes."

"And so does Blue," said Catharin, anticipating where Sam was going.

"But it's decorated," said Maya.

"Those islands aren't painted on. They're the peaks of undersea mountain ranges. That world was *changed*!"

A muffled sniffle was audible in the silent night.

"Sheryn?" Sam said.

"I miss Luna. I was born there. I'm sorry I left."

"Luna is hundreds of light-years away, but her influence is woven throughout our evolution, our bodies," said Sam. "We women are joined to the powers of life and change and birth. Birth scares the men. That's why *we* scare them. But change doesn't have to scare *us*. It's the power of the Goddess."

Maya said, "I've never thought of that. But it feels true somehow."

"The ultimate change is death," Sam went on. "Joe is right. It's a part of life."

It did not feel true to Catharin. *Death is my enemy and I'm so afraid it won. We were too close to death for too long.*

Sam saw her shaking her head. "Don't you agree, Medicine Woman?"

Catharin crossed her arms, refusing to answer to that name.

Maya said, "Oh, no, the moon's gone!"

"Set behind the plateau," said Tezi.

"So is this the end of the show?" asked Kay.

"There's magic *here*," said Sam. "Sometimes I can feel it when I'm out here in the field."

"How?" asked Maya.

"Turn around. Each of you pretend to be alone here."

It was not the cloud-shrouded moon that Catharin faced, but rather the Mountain. The Mountain was a molehill on this green world from space. But from here it stood as a huge shape against the stars. A wind blew. The fern trees on the lower slopes of the Mountain quivered like the fur of a great beast. It wore its name lightly—Unity Mountain, a tag applied only a year ago, a minute of the Mountain's ancient life, ago.

Becca edged closer until she bumped into Catharin. The Mountain's presence was so monumental, and so nameless, that Catharin intuitively knew how Becca felt: daunted and, because of the fragile embryo within her, vulnerable. Instinctively Catharin put her arms around the smaller woman, as if to protect her from the Mountain's nameless and unhuman presence. With a relieved gasp, Becca clung like a small child.

Sam made her way around the circle whispering. Catharin froze, wondering if Sam was going to scold both of them for not playing her game correctly.

Sam had to reach around Catharin to put her hands on Becca's shoulder. "Blessing to you and the child within," she breathed, almost too softly to hear. Becca quivered.

Then the hands moved to Catharin's shoulder. Sam whispered into her ear. "Healer—if you don't like being called Medicine Woman—for you my blessing is a question. Are you against death, or for life?"

☽☾

Going out into the night with the other men, Joe felt like he was coming down with something drastic. He ached, he felt dizzy, he had a chill that shivered into hot fever and back again. Maybe he would get sick. Maybe Catharin would take care of him.

Eddy and Wimm led the procession of men away from the dome. They held hands, which evidently bothered Domino, who muttered loudly enough for most of the group to hear, "I don't know why I'm going along with this."

"I do," said Joe. "Becca asked you to."

Domino turned with an expression of dislike clearly visible in the dim light of the dome. Alvin sniggered.

At the edge of the bare mountaintop near the furry pines, Eddy chirped, "Didn't we all used to flop down on the ground and look at the sky when we were kids? Spread your blankets—in a circle—and let's look up at the stars."

Joe was glad enough to lie down. He felt terrible. Wing neatly unfurled a blanket beside Joe's.

"You don't mind doing a pagan thing?" Alvin asked Wing.

"God is one," Wing replied.

"Have you thought about the Goddess?" Eddy asked brightly.

"The goddess Kuan-Lin was worshiped by my ancestors in China, and my heart has not abandoned that face of God."

Domino jerked on his blanket, which rasped against the lichen on the ground. "I thought you were a priest!"

"I am."

"Don't argue. Let's free-associate," said Eddy. "What does the sky make everyone think about?"

Aaron responded, "Blessed are you, Lord our God, King of the Universe."

"Hail Mary, Queen of Heaven," said Domino. It came out sounding like a rejoinder to Aaron.

"Speaking of goddesses." Wimm sounded pleasant.

"Mary is not a goddess!" Domino sat up, indignant.

"This is fun," said Alvin.

"It might be religious, if some of the religious types would get over their differences," said Wimm, sounding testy.

Lazlo Tulsa, the shuttle pilot, said, "I'm not a religious man. My granddad was a backyard astronomer who showed me the stars from the time I learned to walk. And that's what led me here." The stars were brilliant and legion, diamond dust strewn across the sky.

Joe fidgeted. "The stars don't make me think of gods or goddesses or granddads. There are galaxies of galaxies of them, and black holes that we can't see. How the hell can anybody be happy with that?"

"God created it," Aaron said.

"But we're less than nothing in this cosmos. Not even just insignificant and temporary, less than that." *And this is what I ran to when I left Earth!* The stars that he so carelessly aimed himself toward burned his soul with their incalculable immensity and indifference. Joe's heart thudded. He wondered if he was going to have a heart attack.

Eddy seemed at a loss for a quick answer. Wing offered, "Before the thought of God, the Creator of this universe, can delight me, I have to meet the Christ or the Goddess or some other manifestation of God in a form close to me in kind and form. Otherwise the love of God is not real to me, and I am stricken by the magnitude of the universe and by my smallness and mortality."

Domino contradicted him. "There's only one Christ."

Wing persisted pleasantly, "One Jesus, but more than one compassionate human face of God. Mary, for example. And Buddha. And Kuan-Lin."

"You're a polytheist!" Domino sounded aghast. "Next you'll say Christ is anybody!"

"Sometimes," Wing agreed.

"I think we Jews found God's close and compassionate face in our history," said Aaron, sounding meditative.

"For pagans it's nature," said Wimm. "Especially trees."

"Is the nature of DNA more close and comforting to you than the stars?" Wing asked Joe softy.

Joe knew what he would have said a year or a star flight ago. *Yes, when I move genes and bring new life into being.*

But Catharin wanted him to take up the challenge of a blasted human genome. And *that* was too much like these stars: a remote and implacable cosmos of possibility, in which the hidden black holes of critical damage were many and incalculable. Joe's throat constricted. Allergic reaction? What the hell was wrong with him tonight? He managed to whisper to Wing, "Not anymore. I've realized it can be as terrible as it is fascinating."

"Ah, Joe, you have the soul of an unconverted saint," said Wing. "Your European ancestors said that God is the mystery that terrifies and fascinates."

"But I can't stand it!" Joe rasped through his tight throat.

"Of course not—not until you recognize your Christ or goddess and take comfort in her."

Joe tried to swallow, and found he couldn't. Wing was wrong. He wasn't having a religious crisis. He was sick. And it had come on as fast as any of Earth's savage viruses. Maybe he would be dead by morning.

"Look at Blue," said Eddy, sounding excited.

The crescent moon stood just above the horizon. Beneath it, a silvery-blue radiance covered the plateau that lay to the west of Unity Mountain.

"There's fog on the plateau, and the moon's illuminated it," said Wimm.

"It looks like blue silk," Aaron murmured.

Joe discovered a new symptom in himself. A ringing in his ears. It reminded him of how his ears rang the day Catharin brought him out of stasis. Inner-ear nerve damage—audible evidence of more extensive damage to his nervous system? Was stumbling into things, and stepping on Catharin's foot while dancing that night, just stasis-muddled coordination, or would it be more like Lou Gehrig's disease?

Joe shook his head to clear his ears of the ringing, his head of insane thoughts. This parade of symptoms was psychosomatic. The psyche part was running wild and giving the soma part fits.

"Oh, my, fog is pouring off the plateau, there on top of the saddleback," said Wimm.

"It looks like water from a chalice," Eddy breathed.

"Great show," commented Raj North. Alvin emitted rasping snores. Idiots, Joe thought. They wouldn't know the difference between a holozoo and a tiger at close range in the wild, didn't understand they were on the blue moon's territory, where it had the power to create sensory illusions, lift up tidal bores as big as a small mountain, and plant compelling ideas in a human community. A starship full of people was no match for that moon. Joe was no match for it.

His symptoms were adrenaline-related, Joe realized. His body was saturated with adrenaline because the blue moon intimidated him.

And knowing that made it even worse.

Chapter Twenty-Seven

MORNING PRAYER

The predawn air felt cold but fresh to Catharin as she and Becca climbed the outside stairs to the observation deck. "This is my favorite time of day here," Becca commented. "It reminds me of being on the farm when I was little, but there's even more time to enjoy the dawn while you do the chores."

Catharin stumbled.

Becca quickly reached for Catharin's elbow with her free hand. She had her flute in the other. "You okay?"

"Just clumsy. There was so much on my mind, I didn't sleep well." That was an understatement. Catharin had had a bad dream, one that transmogrified the Ship into a hollow, awful place, with everyone dying around her. She had been helpless to halt the ravages of stasis. Terrifyingly, she had lacked the medicines and the machines to save her friends. After that nightmare, she had lain on her bunk too tired to be fully awake, too horrified to sleep.

They found the observation deck swept clean and appointed with chairs and a table neatly draped in cloth. Among others—nearly everybody in the Base had decided to come—Maya and Sam sat together in earnest conversation. "Other people had a thought-provoking night too," said Becca. "I think Maya's getting interested in Sam's religion."

Catharin located the shuttleplane parked on the runway below, ready to take its passengers up, and make her job easier. She had thought the morning would never come. She felt frayed to the breaking point. There was no sign of Joe either down there or on the deck.

Becca veered toward Kay Montana. "Nice to see you here."

"I'm enjoying watching people trying rituals on for size like a crowd in a clothing store," said Kay.

"The Acting Commander was right about how much we all needed this, wasn't he?"

Kay shrugged.

"I don't know either," said Catharin. Joel's experiment in comparative religion had certainly hit nerves in Unity Base. Hers included.

A short procession emerged from the conference room. Aaron, Alvin, and Wing each carried an object with which they approached the draped table serving as altar. Aaron set down a raw red rock. Alvin, an unlikely acolyte, placed a battered piece of metal on the tabletop with an audible clang, which had the effect of galvanizing everyone's attention like a rapped gavel. What Wing carefully positioned on his altar was a potted plant blooming with delicate purple trumpets.

"Morning glory," Becca whispered to Catharin. "I spent days weeding that species out of cornfields when I was little."

Alvin passed out printouts with the words people would be expected to sing or say.

"Ha," Sam said. "Only Christians think worship means getting together to read something!"

Wing stood in front of his altar. "Welcome to the last ceremony of Starfall. On the Ship, they will join in a Native American ceremony. Here, I offer the New Catholic matins, or morning prayer, a service which celebrates resurrection, day coming after night, life after death, hope renewed after doubt. And grace following after sin and error. After much struggle to find the best words to say, I decided that there are things here that speak in silent words better than any homily of mine! I invite us all to listen to these. The red rock is debris from where we blasted the mountaintop, destroying what existed here before us."

Leveling the mountaintop had been a necessity, Catharin thought, when they had no idea what level of biological hazard existed here. But just now, Wing had only said that the blasting destroyed what existed before, which was true enough.

"This—" His hand hovered over the crumpled metal.

Catharin heard a sharp intake of breath from Becca. "It's wreckage from the crash," Becca blurted. "What are you saying about Chase?"

"I think this bit of wreckage accuses all of us. We misunderstood how different this world is from Earth. Jason was a victim of our overconfidence."

Down on the runway, pilot Lazlo Tulsa circled around his shuttle, preflighting the big machine. Kay would be his able copilot. They had all learned how to be smarter; there wouldn't be another shuttle crash, Catharin thought, but her conscience immediately added, *Unless.*

"And this."

"Not even I think morning glories are essentially bad," Becca murmured.

Wing smiled. "I have grave doubts about introducing our flowers, much less crops, to this world where they do not belong." He stroked a leaf. He had a green thumb; nobody else in the Base had any luck with flowers. "Yet God brings beauty out of morally dubious success."

Still no Joe, not even arriving late. Being Wing's roommate in the Penthouse, he must have gotten wind of the sin-and-error drift of this, and stayed away on principle.

With a gesture, Wing brought everyone to their feet. "The service of matins begins with the Psalmody." He chanted with a pleasant tenor voice, sentiments that Catharin did not believe, words that rang with twenty centuries of poetry and piety in the Western world. "'In his hand are the caverns of the earth; the heights of the hills are also his.'" The dawn breeze carried the phrases across the Mountain's sheared-off crown.

Next came a psalm. Catharin discovered that she remembered the words from childhood, from the years between six and twelve when New Catholicism had worked for her, before she discovered the extent to which humanity could, and should, forge its own fate. Next to Catharin, Becca's voice rang out clear. Her family had raised sheep on their Tennessee farm. She identified with what the psalm said. Catharin's own voice faltered on "though I walk through the valley of the shadow of death—" The dream last night had been exactly that. And *she*, the one who should have been able to dispel death, had failed.

At the last word, "forever," Becca stood beside Wing with her flute. Raising the instrument to her lips, she played a tune in a minor key. The dozen or so voices present here sang the words off the printout in ragged unison. Catharin recognized the old hymn used by the Navy for generations at the burial of the dead at sea. In the twentieth century a new verse had been added for aviators. Last came a verse for those lost in the line of duty in deep space. It sent a shiver through Catharin.

Next Wing sang alone. It was a canticle, and he had chosen to sing it in Mandarin Chinese. Familiar melody and unintelligible words let Catharin's mind skid back to her nightmare. The dream had ended on a weirdly positive note like the melody of Wing's canticle—solemn but not mournful. Sober victory. Had another dream—a more optimistic one—overlain itself on her memory of the first?

"Let us pray." There was an anticipatory rustle. "For the ill in body, mind, or spirit, we pray to the Lord. We name them aloud and in our hearts."

Catharin did not believe in prayer, except as a mental focusing tool. And today she was focused already, on her responsibility. For which reason names came to her automatically.

Bix. Lary. Wing named Frederick Hoffmann. *We can't just pray. We've got to fix them. I've got to fix them.* Catharin felt an intolerable sense of burden, and wanted this to be over.

"And for those who have died in this past year of this new world, the several on the Ship, and the completed life of Jason Scanlan." Becca sniffled. Surviving the crash, Wing had first pulled Joe out and then gone back into the wreckage looking for Jason. The pilot had died in Wing's arms. Wing sounded serene as he referred to it now.

With a mental jolt, Catharin felt her nightmare fall into focus. *Without medicine, she had known what to do.* The awful dream had ended on a grace note of sorts. But she had forgotten exactly what it was that she had done to make it so.

Wing invited silent meditation. The endless silence of Green followed, in which Catharin groped for the content of the conclusion of her dream. It seemed terribly important.

Footsteps resounded as somebody ascended the outside stairs. He—sounding weightier than most of the women—was in a hurry. Expecting Joe, Catharin automatically turned.

"Is it over?" asked shuttle pilot Lazlo Tulsa.

"No," said Wing. "Must you leave sooner than scheduled?"

"Where's my other passenger?"

"Joe Toronto?"

"Since he was in the earlier crash, I want to sound him out on how he feels about riding another shuttle. But he hasn't showed, and this is the last place I know to look."

Catharin felt a flash of anger. Trust Joe to take a last rebellious walk alone and thereby disrupt Wing's lovingly crafted ceremony.

Wing did not look angry, but rather gravely concerned. "Aaron, we should mount search parties. Joe has been very troubled lately."

☽☾

The hangar bustled with the activity of mounting a search. Unlike the night of the crash, there was no hesitation about searching, no delay in starting out. But what Wing was saying did not bode well. "I left him in the Penthouse when I got up at three AM to work on the matins, and so I don't know when he left. But he'd been restless the whole night, moaning in his sleep."

Aaron groaned. "Three hours unaccounted for."

"I'll take a party to the river," said Sam.

"Good," said Catharin, fully furious at Joe now. He was troubled, but why did he have to deal with it in his usual solitary way, upsetting everyone and risking his irreplaceable talent yet again? "He's attracted to water."

"There's another place too," said Wing. "I found a lovely pool on the mountainside and told him about it, but whether he could find it in the dark of the night, I don't know."

Becca said, "After that rain we had, the dirt's still soft. I can track, not that I'm an expert, but I served on a national park rescue squad one summer. Carl, let's head out for that pool of yours and I'll look for his tracks."

Aaron said, "There's only one doctor. Which party should Catharin go with?"

"I've got paramedic training," Kay said.

"Excellent," said Catharin. "Go with Sam's group, Kay. I'll go with Carl."

"So will I," said Aaron. "Wimm, you're in charge of searching the Base. Domino, stand by the copter in case you get a call."

Sam's search party—including Raj North, Alvin, and Kay—piled into the jeep and roared off toward Camp Darwin. Wing led his small group across the clearing toward the furry pines. The sun was finally coming up, pouring thick pink light across the ground.

"The lichen doesn't take our tracks," said Becca. "I'd have to study it long and hard to find a sign, and I still wouldn't be sure it was his."

Wing ducked under the pines. "There's bare earth—I mean dirt—here."

Becca quartered back and forth under the trees. "Somebody did come this way. Somebody with long legs and running like something was after him."

"Something was," said Catharin. Her anger ebbed at the sight of the faint scuffs in the dirt under the trees. She remembered the man sobbing in the rain. "He has excruciatingly painful memories nipping at his heels."

Aaron asked, "Did my Seder trigger that?"

"Yes, but they were already on the verge of coming out," Catharin said. "He'll be better than ever if he comes to terms with his memories. If he doesn't do something foolish."

Wing looked at her with worried eyes.

☽☾

Bands of mist lay draped over the Mountain's sides. "This is radiation fog, coming up off the ground," said Becca. She and Wing held hands as they forged ahead. He knew the way better in and out of the shrouds of mist; she needed to look for clues; neither wished to make a dangerous misstep without being anchored to someone else. Catharin and Aaron followed.

This fog felt warmer than Catharin would have expected. The Mountain seemed just as alive now as it had last night when she looked at it from Camp Darwin. And here the impression was closer and more immediate, as though the fog were a long, long slow exhalation of living breath of a vast being under her feet. Her skin goosefleshed. It had been a long time since anybody in Unity Base called Green the World Wide Park. By now, they all understood too well that it was no park at all. "How well do we understand this mountain geologically?"

Aaron answered, "We don't. Just yesterday, our seismometers picked up traces of activity, as though rocks shifted under the surface. We don't know whether it did that before we came, or if it's still settling down from the blast. We do know that the Mountain is not solid. It has hollow places, possibly a cave network."

Catharin absurdly free-associated. *Lungs?*

Becca suddenly pulled Wing toward a fern tree in the mist. "Look at this broken frond branch. "There aren't any animals here. None but him. He went straight downhill here."

Aaron put a hand on his two-way. "Are you sure enough for us to call everyone else?"

"Well—no. We did have a few gusts of wind during the night."

Wing said, "If he walked directly downhill from here, he would have discovered the pool. Unless he veered to the left in the dark and fog. Upstream of the pool, there's a ravine."

"He's got too much sense not to have had a flashlight and watched where he's going," Becca said quickly.

Does he? There were moods in which he'd jump into an alien river or break his hand on a tree. The young Green-day suddenly congealed around Catharin into a mass of dread. *We can't afford to lose him. I can't bear to lose him.* Years of medical training took over, enabling her to put feelings to one side and react decisively in an emergency. "You two go downhill to that pool. Aaron and I will check the ravine."

☽☾

Catharin and Aaron picked their way through a narrow, fern-walled rock valley. The stream hissed and muttered around rocks large and numerous enough to constitute a precarious path of stepping-stones. The air smelled damp and stuffy.

In deep shade under the ravine wall, bunched pale fungi looked like corpses, like the body parts of bloated drowning victims. They were unspeakably ugly. Aaron discovered greenish and yellowish puddles of algae on the floor of the ravine. The algal ooze reminded Catharin of the ugly fluids discharged by diseased, dying patients.

This is the valley of the shadow of death, Catharin thought. I will fear no evil, said the psalm. But Catharin was terrified. She felt the walls of death closing in on her. For the first time, she calculated the odds of fixing the damages of stasis with no genius to help. The odds were very bad. Catharin felt cold, even though her skin bore a sheen of sweat.

A rock had fallen on one fungus, crushing it, near the ravine's wall, which was heavily matted with roots. A zucchini slug appeared to be devouring the remains of the fungus. Catharin paused, watching in distasteful fascination. A slight, cool, weird-smelling breeze blew into her face. She shrank back from it.

"Catharin!" Aaron waved for her to hurry. She waded across a shallow, pebble-floored widening of the stream to join Aaron where the ravine ended in a narrow rocky slot where the stream spilled out into a deep, rock-rimmed pool. Mist hovered over the pool, pearly pink in the early sun.

Crouching at the water's edge, Becca looked up. "I can't tell if he was here. It's all rock."

Shaking his head in disappointment, Aaron exited the ravine through the slot to make his way down and across the blocky rock wall beside the waterfall. Catharin followed him, gingerly finding footholds between the clumps of fern on the rocks.

Wing suddenly surfaced in the pool. "Cold!" he gasped. He dove back under again. His shirt and shoes were piled beside the water.

With one last long step, Aaron made it to the flat rocks on the rim of the water. He held out a hand to Catharin to help her join him there. Wing reappeared to shake his head. No sign of Joe.

"We must be on the wrong track," Becca said unhappily.

"Maybe Sam found him," said Aaron.

"She'd have called," Becca said.

"If he got this far, he would have flung himself in and had his swim," said Catharin.

"I c-could explore the bottom more," Wing said through chattering teeth. "It has dark fissures. Deep springs."

Catharin suddenly remembered the weird, cool breeze in the humid ravine, and what Aaron had said about the Mountain having hollow spaces. "I think we've overshot. There's a cave opening up there in the ravine."

They looked at her uncertainly.

"He's not crazy enough to swim into an underground fissure, but I think he'd go into a cave." She didn't know Joe all that well. But an intuition that felt certain spurred her back toward the rocky slot, back up into the ravine.

☽ ☾

"Something skidded down the ravine wall," Becca said. "Look at these mossy rocks. The moss only grows on the top side, but the rocks were dislodged and now they're willy-nilly."

"Here's the cave," Wing said. "Behind these roots. They're loose enough to push to one side."

"Which he did!" Becca said excitedly. "See the rootlets torn loose?"

Wing called into the dark opening. "Joe! Jooooe!" His voice seemed to fall into a long, empty place. Catharin would not have ventured in there if her life depended on it. But she was convinced that Joe, in his fey mood, had. After a long listening minute, Wing shook his head.

Aaron groaned. "Did anybody bring a flashlight?"

Wing took a thin flashlight out of the pouch on his belt and pulled the skein of roots back like a curtain.

"Don't go too far—you don't have the equipment for a cave search," Becca said.

Aaron nodded. "We'll simply check it out. The two of you wait."

"Not here," said Catharin. "We'll be at the pool. If you call out, we can hear you from there."

☽ ☾

"You think it's as clean as it looks?"

"I'm sure it's cleaner than the fungus in the ravine."

Becca washed her hands in the pool as directed.

"I'm worried about you being exposed to some kind of environmental toxin. Right now, you're more vulnerable than anyone else."

"I'm glad I went to church this morning." Becca sat down beside the water.

The slow sun had climbed high enough to send a beam slanting toward the water's surface, from which it reflected, dazzling to the eye. This might be the prettiest place on the Mountain, with clear blue water and ferns frilling the wall near the waterfall, a shining ribbon of water. Trees with fan-shaped leaves surrounded the pool. On the other side of the pool lay a scalloped bank of land, grass-green in the sunlight, which looked sensuously inviting, a perfect place to make love. Catharin shuddered with unmet, maybe hopeless, physical need.

Becca sat bunched up and anxious. She pressed her clenched fist against her lips. "I know they've got more sense than to go too far in and get lost themselves. . . ." Her voice trailed off. "Should we look for them?"

"No. I will not let you expose yourself to a cave where there might be toxic slime. It's only been ten minutes." Catharin felt deeply fatigued. She leaned against a big rock, closing her eyes. The purl of the water sounded like a serene, sibilant voice. Catharin found herself listening to it, imagining words.

Chapter Twenty-Eight

LOST SOUL

Joe blundered into a small fern tree and heard the soft snap of a frond breaking off. The forest was murky in the starlight, and he had been running like a madman. His chest heaved for breath. His legs ached.

The fern forest fragmented the world beyond it. The fragments showed him what he expected: a rocky edge like the rim of a pool. He pushed his way out of the fern trees, eager to find the water. At the last instant he realized that he'd stepped onto a steep slope. He tried to catch himself by grabbing a fern trunk. The trunk bent over and he lost his grip on it as he fell. Feet first, he skidded downward. He scrabbled for handholds but only dislodged stones. Landing hard on rocks and softer things, he shook with the adrenaline fired during the fall.

Joe picked himself up, wincing at bruised flesh and bone. He looked around at the ravine. Maybe this was Wing's pool after all—it did have high curved rock walls—but if so, the water had drained out of it. Joe was vaguely aware that some bodies of water in cave country alternately filled and drained, or siphoned, their water disappearing into the bowels of the earth. So much for a swim, Joe thought bitterly.

He flashed his light on damp rock walls, across which crawled two, make that three, zucchini slugs—small green ones with shiny dots on their skin and bristly, sticky feet. Near the slugs a black patch of wall resisted his flashlight. Joe finally realized that it was a recess partially screened by roots. The flashlight didn't find a back wall in the recess. So make that a cave.

What kind of cave? Large, small, shallow, deep, flooded—? He yanked the roots to one side and flashed the beam of his flashlight deeper into the cave. A long passageway slanted down like a mouth with a deep gullet. Joe forced his way in, making the roots emit a strange bruised smell. He proceeded twenty or so feet into the cave, stumbling once or twice on roots underfoot.

Joe stopped at a low rib in the cave roof. The cave went on and down. Shivering, he zipped up his jacket and remembered the warm bedclothes in the Penthouse. He also remembered the terrible stars and the baleful moon and suddenly couldn't stand the thought of turning his face toward them again. He ducked under the low spot and went down, driven by an impulse he didn't understand.

The cave turned into a passageway laced and rimmed with roots. The fern forest trees above here looked too small to send roots down this far—but there they were. Large and small roots wound around bumpy irregularities in the rocks. The bumps were fossils, stone seashells by the look of them. Ancient shells with elaborate frills and whorls that made them resemble flowers.

Finally Joe stopped, breath sawing in his chest. *Far enough?* He snapped off his flashlight. Sure enough, no light of moon or stars came this far. It was as smoothly dark as black velvet down here.

But—

The hair stood up on Joe's head as his brain registered dim green patches of light in the corner of his eye. Nerves jangling, Joe glanced around. The faint lights vanished when he stared at them, reappeared in his peripheral vision, and had familiar shapes. They were roots, coated with goo, and the goo glowed in the dark: more of the phosphorescent, parasitic lower life of Green.

It was just phosphorescence, not quite bright enough to register on the cone cells in the center of his retinas. Maybe he'd better stand still a few minutes and get his physical, and especially mental, balance back.

So this was the nasty insides of this world that never got anywhere. Flowerlike shells must have filled clean blue seas in the past; there must have been oceanic meadows of those shells to lay down this many fossils, between climatic catastrophes when the then-lonely world's axis toppled over. Roots, limned with stinking slime that glowed in the dark, fingered the seashells.

But here, as above, there was no evidence of intelligent life. Evolution whipsawed by climatic change had never made it up that far.

Joe grew aware of a weak breeze and odor in his face, not the sharp smell of broken roots at the cave entrance. Fainter and more puzzling to the nose, it wafted from the depths of the cave. He felt a sick curiosity about how far down into worldwide futility the cave went. He turned his flashlight back on and continued downward. The descent of the passageway was ridged with thick roots. Goo lined the roots, stood up in ripples on the top edges. Joe's upper lip curled in disgust.

Suddenly, and for no good reason, the faint odor in the air reminded Joe of Aunt Adrian's chow-chow relish, supper in the fall, being in school and so much brighter than everyone else that it was an agony and glory, all of the young days Mom and Dad and Daddy knew that he'd be a scientist and were proud of him—

Joe staggered forward under the unexpected weight and the immediacy of memory. His feet splashed into water deeper than his shoes. Water, dark and shiny, spread out in front of him as far as his flashlight beam went. Wavelets lapped his shoes and licked the shore beside him. He thought he smelled salt in the air. On a whim, he stooped to trail a finger into the water, and tasted it. Salty! This was the sea.

The world's tide engine could probably drive the sea way, way inland, given a favorable geometry of whatever underground channels connected this water to the sea. Joe felt dazzled with understanding. He backed out of the water, noticing that his feet splashed without the echo he would have expected in a narrow cave. Wrapped up in the incredibly vivid recollection of his childhood, he'd walked out of the passageway, into a much wider space without realizing it. The sea came up into the darkness under the Mountain in a lightless bay.

He couldn't see walls in any direction, just a ridge of stone on his left. It looked as solid as a harbor rock, and as sea-scoured, with scalloped edges. Hoping for a better view, Joe climbed the ridge.

His new vantage point suggested a huge cavern looming beyond the limits of his feeble light. The rock he stood on reached out into the wide dark water like a finger. Dimly visible were other ridges like this one, fingers of rock interlaced with fingers of water, rock cavern and sea holding hands in the dark.

The sample on his fingertip had tasted like clean seawater, but something down here wasn't so fresh. The air hinted of rotten fish soup and then some. The complex smell reminded him of Mike's aftershave before he and Jean-Claude went out for the night—

And his own ten-year-old words: *Why couldn't I have had a normal dad, not two queers?* The hurt of that remark had lingered a long time in their house. But they forgave him because they loved him—

A fragment of Joe's consciousness railed at him for standing here on top of a skinny ridge underground, crying like a ten-year-old boy. He sat down and turned off the flashlight, wrapped his arms around his knees, and stared across the blackness of the water. He felt the dark weight of the Mountain above him.

After a few moments it dawned on him that a dim canopy of light stretched over the subterranean water. Joe jumped up, almost losing his balance. If that was the roof, glowing in great wide swaths, it was vast. The shining swaths looked like roots, rounded and knobby. But by the size they should have been the roots of a tree as big as a hill.

It probably wasn't against the laws of nature to have a high ratio of root to tree trunk. Or a high ratio of frill to snail house in a seashell. No more than it was against the same laws to have highly stable nucleic acids, so that the mutability of organisms was strikingly low compared to life on Earth. But he wondered what it meant. Nature everywhere he'd studied it had a fractal aspect, patterned chaos, with patterns tending to repeat.

Then Joe saw the stars.

Stars, *below*, a constellation of them. The sight jolted him. No. No. That couldn't be. Had the stars hunted him down? More likely, was he hallucinating? Morbidly compelled to find out, he turned his flashlight on and went looking for the fallen stars. He skidded down the opposite side of the ridge from the side he'd climbed up. Along the scalloped, scoured-looking base of the ridge, his feet crunched in shingle until he entered a dry depression littered with debris spilled from a great pile of rock and root further out into the cavern. The debris didn't look like the rest of the smooth-edged, cleanly curved, rock shapes in this place, and there were some pieces of root tangled in it too. None of the mess resembled stars.

He turned the flashlight off. When he let his eyes adjust, the stars had come back. They were in the debris in the depression.

Of course, the stars really had come down from the cosmos in the form of *Aeon*'s shuttleplane with its bomb that blasted the mountaintop, and shook the Mountain to its roots. The bomb had caused rockfalls in this underground cavern. Joe's skin crawled. He snapped the light back on.

He almost dropped the flashlight in the shock of seeing long, white bones right in front of him.

☽☾

The bones in the dry bowl added up to something that wasn't remotely human. The long tangle of bone was half buried in debris. A wide flat beak or snout gaped open in a soundless agony full of fine teeth.

Teeth?! But this was Green. There weren't supposed to be animals here. This didn't make sense to his rational mind. It made perfect sense to Joe's crocodile brain, which screamed a red alert. If there was a skeletal monster with sharp teeth, there could be live ones stalking him in the darkness—

Joe swept the flashlight in all directions. Nothing lurked behind his back; his flashlight beam swept over barren rock and shingle. But the beam was puny in this cavern, and his imagination could populate the dark with monsters.

With gooseflesh on the back of his neck, Joe turned back to examine the skeleton. He noted the delicate fanfold of bones of a flipper. It was a swimmer, a sea-thing—its kind would not pounce on him from the rocks. Relieved, the crocodile brain downgraded the alert to yellow.

Dry, white stuff that looked like salt ringed the depression. At some point in the past, it had been a shallow pool with a creature in it. Maybe at a very specific point in the past, Joe thought, with a sense of dismay thickening in the pit of his stomach. Maybe it happened when the Vanguard had blasted the mountaintop. Loosened rock cascaded from the roof of the cavern and cut the pool off from the water. The creature died. Its pool evaporated.

Joe crept closer. He found the bones covered with busy little insects feeding on the dry scraps of flesh clinging to the bones. Things happen slowly on Green; it might take a year to decompose a large creature. On the other hand, maybe it took the creature months to die, trapped on the wrong side of the rocks. Joe felt a horrible sense of empathy knifing through him, a convulsive shudder.

In the end, it was a bioenergy windfall for the sarcophagal insects. Their phosphorescent lights were turned up bright and visible even in the flashlight beam. These were his stars.

Alongside the star-spangled bones of the skeleton lay several strings of dodecahedral beads. As fascinated as he was horrified, Joe crouched to see better, closer. He'd seen a beaded string of dodecahedrons not long before. Maybe one of Maya London's India necklaces—? Joe shook his head: that wasn't it.

The skeleton's long, curved spine consisted of big blocks of the same shape, dodecahedral. That made the bead strings—

Little ones. The creature had been pregnant, or whatever equivalent its alien metabolism entailed, when it was trapped behind the rockfall.

The skeleton reminded him of a seal. The braincase, if that was what it was, was large. Here was a higher form of life than they'd known was on Green, maybe one with real brains, and the first thing they'd done had made it suffer and die. With its several young.

Wing had had moral qualms about blasting the Mountain all along. Joe owed Wing an apology. As a representative of *Homo sapiens*, maybe he owed the bony skeleton of the Green-seal an apology too. "I'm sorry," Joe said.

Joe suddenly became aware of a faint rushing sound. He stiffened, remembering that Wing said the tidal bore had been audible in the river before it came upon him. It had sounded like distant surf, according to Wing.

Joe felt numb. He sat down on a lumpy, raw-faced rock and turned off his light to wait for the tide.

The rush of water got louder, slowly. In the darkness, Joe studied the shape of the roof, vaulted by the glowing roots. He also gradually discerned the damage on this end of the cavern. The roof had broken; vast roots dangled down, pointed accusingly at more rockfalls, three or four that Joe could see from here. Blasting the Mountain had damaged the cavern and torn holes in the fabric of a weird, un-Earthlike and unparklike ecology.

The peculiar smell in the air was much stronger here than it had been up on the rocks. Maybe it came from the decomposing Green-seal. It coated Joe's tongue.

Suddenly the smell tasted exactly like the fruit-fly breeding room at the university. He had been sixteen years old when he learned how to do recombinant DNA, changing fruit flies into interesting little monsters, creating novel organisms and an unprecedented argument at home. *It's immoral!* Aunt Adrian snapped.

I'm good at it!

Mike crossed his arms. *With your brains, you could be a doctor. Something useful to society.*

After that Joe had spent more time on the World Net, using the Net nickname of Changer. He spent more time with women, too. Their scents came back to him now.

Like they were a monkey on his back, he couldn't shake the odor-triggered memories off his mind. He doubled over with misery.

The rush turned into an unmistakable wave sound, sharp breaking surf that jolted Joe back to the present. Belatedly Joe realized that this was not the place to wait to meet the tide. The skeleton was high and dry. He'd stay that way too. Feeling foolish, Joe stood up.

The breeze of the tide blew into Joe's face. With it came a new gust of smell. Less cloying than the stink of the dead creature, this one was neither pleasant nor rotten so much as indescribable.

Joe felt his way toward the sea and the odd odor, clambering up another curve-edged rock ridge. On the far side of the ridge lay another depression, but this one contained water in a rounded shore. Joe cautiously waded in, finding the shore sloping gently under the water. In the middle of the pool, the water came up to his knees. He was ironically aware that he'd finally found a pool of sorts, but not the idyllic one described by Wing. This one was shallow and unsatisfactory. And it had a smell like nothing his nose had ever met. His brain threw out olfactory identifications like cards dealt from a deck. Pineapple! Cat box! Liniment!

The beam of his light danced on the far side of the pool—a barricade of rocks and roots. More rock- and root-fall. Water seethed through the barrier, but it had blocked the tide's wave. As Joe looked, a small cascade of broken rocks trickled into the water.

He had overheard Raj and Aaron talking yesterday about some seismic activity in the Mountain, maybe subterranean rockfall. So this rockfall might be considerably fresher than the others. For that matter, it might not be over.

Before he could process that thought and decide whether to retreat before rocks fell on his head, Joe's leg struck something soft. He shone the light down. He recoiled from two huge dark eyes.

☽☾

The large, flat-snouted head flinched from the light. The rest of the big dark shape lurched away from Joe as fast as he jumped away from it.

Standing well back on the shore, he pointed the light at the creature in the pool. It cowered in the deepest part of the pool, shaking so hard that the water rippled. Longer than Joe was tall, thicker than his shoulders were wide, it watched him fixedly, eyes barely up out of the water, blinking.

Joe put the flashlight behind his back. That way enough light bounced off the rock ridge for him to see the creature without blinding it.

With a flick of membrane, a huge third eye opened on the creature's forehead, a wide moist orb. It shut immediately. Even indirect, the flashlight was too bright for it.

A third eye adapted to the faintly luminescent darkness under the world? Maybe the other two eyes were for daylight, maybe it usually lived at sea. He remembered the image from *Kite* that didn't act like a school of fish and could have been an animal swimming in the river from the sea. Would a creature like this swim in here from the sea to give birth? There might be advantages to a sea creature of birthing young in an inland cavern. It depended on how many predators there were out in the open water.

The glistening dark green hide had shiny dots on it. Part of the riddle suddenly fell into place.

Manhattan had a string of dodecahedrons coiled like a necklace on a shelf in the planetology lab. It was the spinal cord of a zucchini slug. Zucchini slugs had shiny dots on their skins. "Did you just give the Mountain a new crop of slugs?" His grin faded as he thought more. "Did you come in to give birth in this sweet shallow pool and get trapped when rocks fell from the roof yesterday?"

It turned away from him and shuffled toward the barricade. Joe's sympathy for the creature took an immediate nosedive, because in the flesh—if it was the same kind of animal as the fleshless skeleton he'd seen—it did not resemble a seal in the slightest. It was as ugly as sin. Its body had a wide, quivering flange around the edges. Its mouth opened and closed, and Joe could tell that gauzy flesh veiled the teeth. It might be a filter feeder. Then there was the lurid color scheme: green with purple spots.

It could creep around the pool, but not make it over the rockfall that the tide had boiled through. And the tide had stopped streaming in. This was as high as it got. The tide was already leaking out through the barrier.

The size of the braincase probably had more to do with the third eye than with intellect. But it displayed a modest amount of intelligence. It was trapped and it knew it. It investigated the barricade with apparent agitation, like a prisoner who'd just seen the prison door slam shut in his face for the *n*th time.

A new wave of smells wafted at Joe. It came from this thing. A living Green-seal had even more smell than a dead one, a pointed, tickling smell that activated old memories in Joe's brain even as he willed it not to happen. This time Joe smelled a brand-new laboratory dedicated to turning his theories into organism. Or maybe it was acrylic paint, because when he went to his parents' home from that laboratory for the first time, it was the last night he ever went home and Silke had been painting in her studio. *Change a dog into a seal?* Her face—with spots of acrylic paint on her cheek and chin—had reflected pure dismay. *But Jato, that's not right.*

Aunt Adrian hadn't liked the news either. *When are you going to change into a human?* she had demanded.

Jean-Claude, as ever, tried to mediate. *He's got to express his creativity, his own way.*

But Mike was furious. *If you thought more about what's right and wrong and less about doing what you damn well please, you'd never have taken that job. You sold your soul. Get out of here. I never want to see you again!*

Vladimir Pang-Park had helped Joe disown his family. In the national Net database, an altered version of Joe's background unobtrusively replaced the real one. Joseph Devreze's unorthodox parents turned into a respectable couple deceased in the Pantoxia virus that swept Chicago in 2085. He changed the Labrador into the sea dog in a fiery burst of creativity that helped him forget his parents. The same creative rush that also saw the first human mod. It died.

You wouldn't feel the same if it were you being changed!

Joe staggered back as if he'd taken a blow to the face.

He sucked in cleaner air, farther away from the Green-seal, his brain reeling. He regained his sanity by clutching scientific truth, like a life preserver in a maelstrom of feeling. The Green-seal communicated by odors. Complicated, maybe grammatical ones—smells that struck the human brain as compelling, unidentifiable, and evocative.

Unable to resist communicating back, Joe went back toward the Green-seal. He crouched beside its prison-pond. "I could give you a human offspring, I think. Might take no more than a needleful of your cells, and splice in an interesting assortment of ours."

The Green-seal vibrated its flange, stirring the water, and emitted a new aromatic outburst, instantly evoking lab and hospital smells, Continental dinners, and the gene splice that had undermined a human mod's metabolism.

It was an accident. Joe had not known that one of the genes he'd spliced in would have that effect, and not until afterward did he understand why. The boy had smelled like honey and died before he was five years old. The Green-seal smelled like guilt. Shaken, Joe murmured to it, "But humanizing your genetic material wouldn't do *you* any good, would it? You just want out."

He waded toward the rockfall and explored it. The Green-seal slithered out of the way to watch him with wide eyes.

The news wasn't good. The rockfall wasn't solid, because water sieved through it; but it wasn't going anywhere, regardless of how he pushed and shoved at it. The fall consisted of big raw chunks of rock netted in slippery roots.

The Green-seal bumped Joe's knees with its soft, quivering flange. Anxious to get out, it pushed at the rock as high as it could reach up with its beak. The water was shallow enough for Joe to see the flipperlike extremities under the flange, and how the flange was ragged around the edges from scraping against the rim and bottom of this tide pool.

The Green-seal radiated smells. Fending off a new array of guilty memories attached to gene-lab smells, Joe said, "I get the message. You're screaming *help me!* Why the hell not?" Joe squatted in the water and put his arms around the Green-seal. It quivered and flicked its head. Joe glimpsed the numerous pointed teeth in their fleshy veil. "Please don't bite. My doctor would be very upset."

He hefted the Green-seal, and it went limp. Joe grunted. "Either you understand I want to help or you've got a fainting reflex like opossums. Hope it lasts." Weighted down, Joe found first one foothold, then another, up the rockfall with his arms full of limp, slippery beast.

Joe stopped to pant. The Green-seal in his arms quivered, making its slippery weight harder than ever to hold. He desperately found a better grip. "Please stay calm. Look, it's the least I can do. We wrecked your maternity ward, or cathedral or whatever it is down here, eh?"

Joe reached the top and teetered there. He had the flashlight clipped to his belt. The dangling beam told him that he was looking down at deep water. The tide's waves had more or less scoured out the rockfall on this side. Joe gathered himself and heaved mightily.

The Green-seal flung itself toward the water at the same instant. Joe took a balancing step onto a slippery root and his foot slid out from under him. He struggled for balance. As he heard the seal splash, Joe fell off the rocks.

He tumbled into water over his head. The water embraced him greedily. It refused to let him surface. Shocked, Joe recognized an undertow pulling him down.

Joe fought the water. He could not let the undertow have him. If it pulled him to the sea he would drown long before he met air again. Fired by panic, he clawed at the surface of the water.

Something bumped Joe in the stomach, then in the back. He was desperate for air now, kicking against the undertow. False lights from anoxia danced in his eyes. His lungs burned.

Then something shoved him upward. Joe's head broke out of the water. He gasped, filling his air-starved lungs.

Something pressed against his back. Flailing, his hands hit a slick form behind him.

The Green-seal had his jacket clamped in its filter-teeth.

In its element, the creature was more than strong enough to push Joe through the water. He craned his neck and took greedy lungfuls of air. With stinging salt in his eyes, Joe couldn't see where they were going, whether it was across the cavern or out to sea. Then his chin scraped something rough. He flung his arms forward to embrace a solid shore.

Joe felt the salt water drain away from his legs. A splashing behind him might have been the Green-seal flinging itself into the tide toward the sea. Then there was nothing but silence and darkness, broken only by several racking coughs and wheezes from Joe.

Finally, with his lungs cleared of salt water and full of sweet air, Joe rolled over and lay on his back, exhausted. He studied the faint contours of the roof for a while. The glow varied. It pulsed. Long slow waves of light crossed from one end of the vast cavern to the other, and back, and met, and doubled on the thoroughfares of massive roots.

He thought about aspen-clones on Earth. Groves of trees were all the same individual, reproducing by sending up shoots. Some of Earth's aspen clones had been very old. Here, the entire forest of fern trees could be just the cloned hair of an ancient root system.

Next, Joe considered the flippers of the Green-seal. If it was analogous to marine mammals on Earth, its ancestors had roamed on the land before they sloughed off their feet and returned to the mother sea.

Both ancient roots and flippered seals implied longer periods of climatic stability than was supposed to be the case here on Green. If it had been solitary for billions of years, before the new blue moon dropped in to stabilize the climate, how could such trees and such a beast as the Green-seal evolve?

Joe felt a surge of excitement, nearly sexual in nature and intensity, familiar. He always felt like this on the trail of an original idea.

The idea that had been crystallizing in his mind hit Joe like a blue bolt in the darkness. *Blue isn't new*. Green had had eons of life with a moon in the sky, and produced animals, and intelligence: an intelligent species that *moved*

Blue back in and then remodeled it in the sky. Finally—and still hundreds of millions of years before the present day—they died out.

But maybe they didn't die out. The cells of zucchini slugs harbored six million times more genetic material than should have been necessary to code the biology of the organism, even considering that the slugs were a stage in the life cycle of Green-seals. Hidden in the Green-seal genome might be an entire evolutionary history that included the morphology and mentality of a tool-using, space-faring, planet-moving race. For that matter, there was enough genetic material to encipher racial memory. Maybe even an explanation for why they evolved back into Green's sea.

Ferns and slugs veiled a planetary history far longer than Earth's and with vast uncharted convolutions. Green was ancient, but more than a case of failed evolution on a planetary scale: incalculably more than that. Joe sat up. His mood felt better, like a storm-battered, becalmed sailboat feeling a fresh light wind. He wanted to go back to Unity Base.

But Joe could see nothing besides the roof. He had no idea where in the immense cavern the Green-seal had deposited him. The flashlight was missing from his belt, snatched away by the undertow, leaving only a broken belt loop. Joe was soaked, cold, shivering, and weak. Too shaky to walk, he dragged himself farther up the shore, hoping for drier air.

Brightness puddled under his hands and knees, startling him.

The dense sand that he was crawling on had living creatures in it, and when agitated, they glowed.

He traced his name in the sand. *Joe.* He'd been Joseph on Earth, Jato to his family. He was Joe here. A name as plain and elementary as most of the technology used for the star expedition. But it looked too short. He added + *Cat*, and liked it a lot better

Joe's eyes made out dim, oblong spots higher on the shore. He closed his eyes; the spots went away. Not retina lights. When he opened his eyes, the spots were still there. And the oblong, indented shape was unmistakable. Joe got up on his wobbly legs and went closer.

The glowing patches were footprints. His. Right size. The toes pointed toward the water. The Green-seal had brought him to the place where he had first discovered this underworld sea.

Chapter Twenty-Nine

ECLIPSE

"Cat!" Somebody shaking her by the shoulders brought Catharin awake, disoriented.

Becca excitedly pointed toward the ravine's exit window. At the crest of the waterfall, Aaron held Joe by the collar like a truant schoolboy. "We found him!"

Catharin's spirits surged at the sight of Joe. She sprang to her feet.

"What took you guys so long?" Becca called up to Aaron.

"There was a steep passageway—"

"We had to help him climb back up," Wing amplified.

"Is he hurt?" Catharin started toward them.

But Joe held up a warning hand. "Stay away. I've been exposed to alien glop." His voice sounded rough.

Turning to Becca, Catharin commanded, "Go around to the other side of the pool!" She called up to Joe. "Come down here and wash up. Right now."

Catharin followed Becca around to the other side of the pool, retreating away from Joe as she watched him clamber down the rock wall. His hair was damp and disarrayed, strikingly black against the pallor of his face. His khaki clothes were wet all over and stained with the bright pink of water-wet blood. "What happened?" Catharin demanded in growing alarm.

"I was looking for this." He talked slowly and with effort, gesturing toward the pool. "Found something else." Bruises showed on his arms as he dipped his hands in the clear water.

"What, Joe?"

"There's an arm of the sea under the Mountain and a dead alien sea animal. Remember the picture from *Kite*? Decayed. And a lot of saprophytes feeding on it. I got pretty close."

Catharin steered Becca to the hill of smooth moss, uphill from the pool, even farther away from Joe. Becca muttered, "Are you sure he's not imagining things?"

Catharin could not begin to judge Joe's state of mind. "I will not take chances with you."

Wing and Aaron briskly washed their hands in the waterfall at a distance from Joe.

"A live one too," Joe announced.

"A live sea animal? You saw one?" Becca asked across the pool.

"Saw it. Touched it. Helped it. Then I fell in the sea. Almost drowned. I'm thirsty!" Joe drank deeply from his cupped hands while everyone else was stunned silent. "You were right, Carl, we shouldn't have blasted the Mountain. It caused rockfalls inside. Killed the first one. Destabilized the cavern. Last night's tremor trapped the other one in a shallow pond. But I helped it out. That's where zucchini slugs come from."

The rest of them stared at him.

Joe sat back cross-legged with his hands wet. "I fell in and the current was dragging me toward the sea. I would have drowned. It dragged me back to shore. Saved my life."

"Hallucinations??" Becca hissed in Catharin's ear.

Suddenly Catharin couldn't swallow for the cold lump of anxiety in her throat. Joe needed to be up on the Ship where they could heal his mind.

Behind Joe, Wing stretched closer to examine Joe's clothing. "There are punctures in the back of his shirt. It looks like the imprint of a long jaw full of teeth!"

Galvanized, Catharin ordered Becca, "Start up. Now."

Becca started to object, "But he's—"

Catharin herded Becca uphill. "He's hurt, but he may be carrying germs that are dangerous, especially to you." Over her shoulder she said, "You three follow us. But stay away from us. Downhill. Downwind. Whatever. All three of you are possibly contaminated."

Joe seemed weak, his pace slow. Wing dropped back and slipped under his arm to help Joe uphill. "Catharin!" Joe called.

She held her breath expecting, *Help me.*

He pointed toward Becca. "Boy or girl?"

Catharin let out her breath in a gasp. "Girl."

"Becca," the battered man called up. "Will you name her Silke? For me?"

For a moment, Becca's face was a study in puzzlement and embarrassment. Only she could have recovered her wits enough to answer under circumstances like these. "Sure, Joe, it's a very pretty name."

His face lit with a grin.

Catharin took Becca by the shoulders and turned her to go up. "What are we going to do when we get to the Base?" Becca asked.

"You're going up on the shuttle and so am I."

Aaron heard that. "How will we manage without a doctor?"

"Kay will have to assume medical duties down here."

Sounds carried on the damp, still air. Catharin heard the two-way as Aaron turned it on to notify Sam to call off the search. He asked Tulsa to prepare to take off without his copilot. "Tulsa objects and so does Kay and so does the Ship."

"It's a calm morning. There's no extraordinary danger in the air. I'm still the Ship's medical officer, and in that capacity, I need to be up there. Tell the Commander I said that." She added, "In other words, Joe, I go. You stay."

He answered, "I'll miss you. But I'll work hard while you're away. I promise."

That startled her. Enormous problem unexpectedly solved. With that thought, she forcibly moved her attention to her other looming problem.

When she had dozed off beside the pool, listening to the semblance of words in the water, Catharin had finally remembered the end of her dream: she'd told someone—she wasn't sure who—*you will die and I will help you get ready.* She'd distinctly heard those words, spoken in a woman's voice in the dream. Forgotten, that imperative had tantalized her. Now that it had risen into her conscious mind, it was simplistic, no panacea at all. Just her own subconscious telling her that she had an unfinished job on the other side of the sky.

The thunder of the ascending shuttle dwindled in the high distance over Unity Base. Joe, now scrubbed clean and decorated with bandages and carrying a bright disinfectant smell with him, dropped onto his bunk in the Penthouse. Wing sat down on his own bunk with a deep sigh. "What an interesting morning. I am quite tired."

"Sorry I disrupted your prayer service."

Wing pulled off his shoes. "From what you've told me, you completed it, I think. And now what, Joe? You must stay here instead of going back up."

"I'll grab some sleep. Then do what she wants. Work on the medical problems, starting with the old guy."

Wing raised his eyebrows. "Have you not been working already?"

Joe told Wing what he'd held back from Aaron. "Yes, but I couldn't concentrate, because I didn't want to do it for the rest of my life."

Wing gave him a puzzled look. "Have you had a change of heart now?"

"Hell, no. I'm just ashamed of being always the changer, but never the changed. I'd still damn well rather keep being the way I've always been, though."

Cross-legged on the bunk, Wing folded his hands in his lap. "Welcome to the human race."

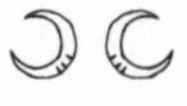

A distinctive blend of smells and sounds, gravity and light constituted the familiar environment of the Ship, but with a patina of unfamiliarity from her long absence. Catharin privately noted this and put it aside to think about later, focusing on Becca, who lay in a bed in the Ship's hospital in Outtown. Becca had just recovered wavering consciousness. Pale, her skin drawn tightly over the bones of her face, she looked up at Catharin. "Did I get sick? On the shuttle up?"

"Yes," Catharin said, and spared her the details.

It had looked like anaphylactic shock—out of the blue, at the maximum acceleration of the shuttle. Becca had lapsed into unconsciousness. Her vital signs had quickly faded. Catharin risked an injection of atropine. Which probably saved Becca's life, even as it triggered a cascade of unintended consequences. By the time they got to the Ship, Becca was violently ill.

Becca closed her eyes. Tears trickled out. "I lost it, didn't I?"

"Not the way you mean."

Becca's eyelids snapped open. She touched her abdomen under the blanket. "I don't feel right."

"What happened to you was something like Rh incompatibility—a violent allergy to the fetus. The onset may have been triggered by the stress of the shuttle's acceleration." *Redheads tend to have allergies—but not like this. One of a potentially vast number of unpleasant medical surprises in store for us. In store for me.* "The fetus was successfully transferred to another woman. At three months, that's not a difficult procedure with modern medicine. But she will be the birth mother, not you."

Slight, conflicting expressions shifted across Becca's face. "I need to think about that."

Catharin pulled the covers up to Becca's chin. It was cooler in the Ship than daytime in Unity Base. "Do that. I have a couple of other visits to make here."

For temporary relief from grim medical matters, Catharin stepped out onto the balcony at the end of the hall. The balcony overlooked Outtown. After more than a thousand years of changeless preservation in a nitrogen atmosphere, Outtown had been pressurized with Earthlike air while Catharin was away. Water flowed in a fountain. Plants fringed some of the sidewalks, looking scanty. Catharin wondered if the plants were failing to thrive, or simply new-planted seedlings.

Since the hospital had been operational long before Outtown had oxygen in its air, the balcony was glassed in. A wall of glass stood between Catharin and the promise of a city. She wondered if it ever would be a city in the fullest sense: well ordered but lively, grounded on democracy and tolerance, with a populace healthy and long-lived enough to systematically explore both the cosmos and the inner universe of the human soul. Catharin sighed. This future city had been easier for her to imagine while the Ship was in Earth orbit, before its journey took it to unexpected and disastrous ends.

Changing into clean paper coveralls before going into the pediatric unit, Catharin thought, *How self-indulgent of me to come here; this is not a patient of mine.*

But she wanted to see this one for herself.

It had been a bad twenty-four hours since the shuttle docked at the Ship. She'd lain awake during the Ship's quiet night, shaking with the feelings that had had to be suppressed while she was fending death away from her best female friend. Never had she had a critically ill patient who was so close to her personally. There was, of course, a first time for everything.

In the middle of the same distressed night, John Mark had been born. Catharin had yet to find time to talk to Joel. She wanted to ask him, *You told me you wanted him named John. But why Mark? That was my father's name!*

The baby boy was dwarfed by the pediatric unit, which had accommodations for ten to twelve babies, and badly outnumbered by doctors, nurses, and technicians. Evangelina—Miguel's Leni—came to Catharin when she saw her enter.

"How is he?"

"A little bit small. A little bit weak," said Leni. "But still a miracle."

Looking through the glass bubble, Catharin saw a normal-looking newborn with ten fingers and ten toes and wrinkled brown skin. Too good to be true?

"Dr. Pei wants to keep him in the isolation bubble for a while to be sure there are no problems," Leni said.

Catharin nodded. Immune function was exactly what Catharin would have scrutinized first, keeping the infant in the isolation bubble to protect him from germs in the meantime.

She had one more visit to make. The worst one.

He wasn't very far away, just a corridor or two, but those two corridors seemed longer than the way across the stars. Her feet dragged in exhaustion and dread.

Joel stood outside Bix's door with the green parrot perched on his shoulder, ruffled and unhappy. Joel said, "He's in terrible shape, Cat."

This was not a good time for this. Visiting Becca and seeing John Mark had taken a lot out of her. She remembered feeling this ragged when she had been a medical resident. But not this sad at the same time. She had never lost a patient who was also a dear friend. "I had a bad dream last night, and it made me realize that it's too late for Joe or anybody else to help Bix, and I've got to tell him that."

Joel's reaction surprised her. With alacrity, he put his hand on the door to open it for her. "Thank you for coming."

Bix was awake. She inwardly cringed at seeing him in person. He was hideously ill, reminding her of her failure to heal him in the first place, and let him go in the second place. She wanted to make him better with some last, desperate magic. Instead, she embraced him and wept.

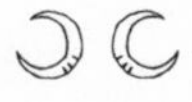

The Captain's private dining room echoed the era of sailing ships on the seas of Earth. It was furnished with a long table and seven comfortable chairs, and the *Aeon* emblem on the dark wall. The head chair stayed empty as Joel, Catharin, Lary, and Miguel took places around the table. "Don't look at me," said Joel. "He isn't gone yet, and I'm not taking his chair."

Over a casserole in which the vegetable was unidentifiable, Miguel asked Lary, "Can Joe Toronto be right about Green and Blue?"

Lary's Adam's apple moved as he swallowed with difficulty. "You mean his idea that whoever remodeled Blue also moved it back in—and that they evolved here in the first place? I'm starting to think he is."

Joel's attention jerked toward Lary. "Why? That world down there has nothing but plants and slugs, even if some of 'em are giant live-bearing sea slugs."

"Evidence is trickling in that Green's ecosystem might be five or six billions of years old. Older than Earth itself. On Earth, the cockroaches and coelacanths were hundreds of millions of years old, some of the sulfur-metabolizing bacteria more like a billion. You see, Joel, in the long run, evolution has a bias toward the durable rather than the spectacular species." With a wry smile, Lary added, "Oh, but it can be fun to be one of the less durable forms of life."

His words twisted like a knife in Catharin's heart. She knew he was hanging onto the health he had left by a thread.

"You're not mad at us, are you?" asked Joel. He was more abrupt, more blunt these days than Catharin had ever known him to be before.

"Not at all. I came to the stars because I dreamed of another Earthlike world to study." Lary included her in a wave of his hand. "And you've given me two. I don't regret what's come to pass, my friends."

What Catharin had dreamed about on Earth seemed like a dry pressed flower now. Faded color, frozen form, it had found no way to take root in the alien soil of this changed future.

"But how could a body of such immensity—a whole world—be moved?" asked Miguel.

"Let Lary eat," said Catharin.

Joel said, "You could do it if you built big enough mass drivers on both worlds. I do mean *big*. But there's no sign of the machines—no sign of the race that did it—"

"Perhaps under the deep sands and seas of time," said Miguel, "we would find some evidence of them."

It was no wonder they wanted to talk about the hurricane moon. That distracted them from a dying Captain, and the other people who were hospitalized with stasis-caused illnesses, and the hospital bed waiting for Lary. And the hundred casualties of Seventeen Wedge T still in stasis.

Lary forced down another bite. "There's a more obvious place to look for your evidence, namely, the double planet's geometry. There's an eclipse coming up—a total eclipse of the sun by Blue as seen from Green. It so happens that this event occurs almost precisely every six of Green and Blue's years, due to their distance from each other and inclination of their mutual orbit with respect to the plane of the ecliptic."

Joel looked at Lary narrowly. "You used to say that inclination was evidence that Blue was a stray world that fell in out of the void."

"So I thought, but its inclination facilitates the peculiarly regular eclipse cycle. I calculated the effects of two hundred million years of tidal drag on both worlds, and when I did, the 'almost' I just mentioned came out exact. To the *hour*. I think the worlds were positioned for regular eclipses with timing of some ceremonial or religious significance."

"Good Lord," said Joel, putting a fork full of food back down on his plate. "You think Blue's a sacred astronomical monument like Stonehenge?"

Radiating bizarre good cheer, Lary nodded. "And there's Blue's spin." To

Catharin's dismay, Lary stopped eating, abandoning his knife and fork to gesture with his hands while explaining. "Blue's spin has the effect of making hurricanes. Who knows what symbolic significance the hurricanes might have had?"

Miguel looked intently interested. "Kamikaze, divine wind for the Japanese," he murmured. "Hurakan for Caribbean Indians."

"On the other hand, maybe Blue spins to keep infidels out of the temple."

"Say what?" Joel said.

"The hurricanes rather effectively prevent itinerant life-forms like ourselves from colonizing Blue. Perhaps those who moved it and reshaped it wanted it that way. I'm not sure about the religious or philosophical thinking that goes into keeping cathedrals holy, as there are no cathedrals on Mars."

"There are in Mexico," said Miguel, looking thoughtful. "With gates that can be locked."

"I'd like to think that the auroras are a sacred sideshow," Lary continued. "Auroral displays, such as the one last summer, are another result of Blue's inclination."

"I didn't like the aurora. It seemed too weird for words," said Catharin. "Will the eclipse be beautiful, like solar eclipses on Earth?"

Miguel said, "Those were not beautiful to peoples who thought a demon devoured the sun."

"Surely any race capable of moving worlds would not be superstitious."

"But they might be philosophical," said Miguel.

"Remember how much bigger Blue is than Luna," said Lary. "It's going to be more spectacular than any eclipse you've ever seen."

☽☾

"I need to sit for a while."

Miguel took one look at her face and proffered her his own desk chair here in the Life Support Ops office. Catharin sat down and put her face in her hands. In the silence of the interval between breezes from the air-conditioning vents, she heard Miguel's slow breathing. Long minutes later, she said, "Bix is gone."

"Ah. Better so."

"Better still if I had given my permission earlier." She shuddered as she remembered the changed expression on his ravaged face when she had talked to him two days ago, just after seeing John Mark for the first time. The expression had been one of relief.

"Permission?"

"He didn't want to disappoint me, I think. I should have known it's my job to let people die. I had a dream just before I came back up here. It was horrible. Everybody was dying and I didn't have any medical science anymore."

"A nightmare," said Miguel.

"But the end of the dream wasn't as bad as the rest. I told someone they were dying and that I'd help them get ready. And it had a very powerful feeling in the dream. It doesn't feel so powerful in life."

"The power is truth," he said. "To say aloud what the dying man knows in his heart of hearts. Then to stop fighting for life, and let there be some peace."

Miranda Blum had known as much. *Think of it as rehearsing for death. It comes to us all sooner or later.*

Catharin recalled something Miranda had said years before, in a lecture, when Catharin was a medical student. *You must distinguish the battle from the battlefield.*

Bix had been a battlefield for much too long, because the doctors up here would not give up on him, because he would not ask them to, because he did not want to disappoint her. Catharin felt tears coming on again. She had already cried enough on Joel's shoulder. She pressed her thumb and forefinger to the inner corners of her eyes.

Miguel handed her a glass. So pure that it was tasteless, the water eased the lump in her throat. "For an astronaut," she said, "I'm a slow learner."

"The heart learns slower than the head."

"Before Bix died, I asked him about burial. He said, 'Some spacemen wanted burial at space. Not me. Too alone. Next time the Ship adjusts its orbit, just throw me in the engines and let me go out in a blaze of glory.'"

Bix had grinned at that turn of phrase, and the parched edges of his lips had cracked and oozed blood. "I think we should honor his wish. I came to ask you about it."

"Of course. We can keep his body for a little while and then fulfill his last wish."

"He's truly not alone. The people who died in stasis—Wedge Seventeen, plus the isolated casualties—do you need them?"

"The biomass is relatively little. No. It is not needed for our closed life-support system. Besides, I am not sure that people, myself included, are prepared to drink water and eat food knowing that our deceased comrades have been injected into the loop. Are you suggesting that we honor all of them that way?"

"Yes." Fidgeting, she held up the glass in front of Miguel's bank of plant specimens in climate-controlled containers. The water caught and reflected the monitor lights on the plant bank. "We tried an assortment of old rituals in Joel's Starfall. That wasn't enough. We need a new one, for here and now. Listen to what I have in mind and tell me if it will work."

☽☾

Joel woke Catharin up in the middle of the night, buzzing her on the Ship intercom. "I'm awake." Barely, and by dint of fighting her way out of a deep blanket of exhaustion. "What's wrong?"

"Toronto is right. John Mark is sick." Joel's voice was toneless and flat.

Catharin sagged back into the covers. "How?"

Joel struggled through an explanation, his words alternately faltering and spilling out. The tiny child had developed fever and respiratory distress with signs of a metabolic disorder. It might have been a single deranged gene that controlled a cellular process so basic that it was involved in healthy tissue in a hundred ways; or it might have been a set of malfunctioning genes in a subtle and unholy alliance. In other words, they did not even know what was wrong, much less how to fix it.

Catharin went to her office with its telcon and called Joe. "You were right about the baby," she said bluntly.

His haggard appearance jolted her. So did his reply. "I'll do everything I can."

Not good enough. I want you to tell me you will perform a miracle. Aloud, she only said, "Thank you."

Ever since his excursion into the cavern, Joe had been working too hard, in Wing's opinion. Joe's work was surely best approached as a long and arduous trek, not as a mad dash. He should at least take an occasional break. "Joe, come out to watch the eclipse with everyone else."

"I'm not in a social mood."

"Then come with me into the woods to experience the eclipse in peace and quiet."

Joe turned away from the telcon. His skin was strikingly pale, even for a Caucasian.

Rather than join the crowd at the promontory, they went the opposite way through the furry pines, Wing leading Joe to a wide rock outcrop that broke the forest. They gingerly sat on top of the rock heated by the sun of the long day. High in the noon sky, Blue confronted the glory of the sun. Sunlight falling through the interstices in the pine's foliage dappled the ground. The dapples were imperfectly round: each had a small notch in the side. The eclipse had begun, Blue sliding between Green and the sun.

Already the air seemed somewhat dimmer. Wing had heard that eclipses on Earth caused a hush to fall on the land. Today the silence of Green seemed unnervingly appropriate, as though Green always waited for the darkness at noontime.

"Is this a good time for bad news?" Joe asked. He sounded bitterly serious.

Dismayed, Wing answered, "Eclipses were once thought to portend ill. What is it?"

"You know how scientists sometimes lose their edge after forty?"

As Joe's words sank in, the silence of Green rang in Wing's ears like a funeral toll. Wing struggled to keep his voice even. "As far as I know, that does not inevitably happen."

"I think it did this time. Age or stasis. I've lost my touch, Carl. The inspiration won't come. And we're all in big trouble." Joe's breath sounded ragged and loud.

Wing, for his part, found it hard to breathe at all for the dread closing in on him. "Have you given up, then?"

"I'll die trying before I give up."

The breeze began to blow, a long soughing from the west—the air of Green rushing into the cool shadow of Blue. Wing knew eclipses on Earth had been accompanied by winds. But this was a bigger eclipse and a longer wind.

By unspoken consent, they started back to the Base, at first walking slowly, then—unnerved by the wind's constant whisper in the pines—almost running.

"I can't explain this to her," Joe panted. "I'll botch it if I try. But she needs to know now. Atlanta better know the score too, but I can't bring myself to tell him. Carl, I never thought I'd need a priest for anything, but—"

"I will speak for you," Wing said.

☽☾

Working in her laboratory in Level Seven, Catharin followed the progress of the eclipse in a telcon window with audio feed from the control center. She was numb with fatigue and continual anxiety. The catalog of medical problems displayed on her workstation seemed like a labyrinth that led to the minotaur of early, evil death. Who was the Greek hero who had killed the minotaur? Catharin hoped for a Canadian hero. *Joe, hurry.*

The Ship had orbited over the boundary between night and day. Half of the sunlit side of Green was stained dark red by the penumbra of the shadow of Blue. And the umbra, which on Earth would have been a bullet hole of black, was more like a cannonball's hole on the eastern limb of the world.

"Unity Base has a light westerly breeze," reported one of the stations. Another issued a Downside weather report: the eclipse was likely to have an effect on already unstable atmospheric conditions Downside, and thunderstorms were in the forecast. On impulse, Catharin paid a quick visit to Becca.

Well on the way to recovery, Becca had been moved to the infirmary in the Medical section. She sat up in bed, alertly watching the telcon window in her room.

The cannonball's hole had crawled over the still-nameless continent and covered it with darkness. Catharin could barely find the spot on its southeastern coast where Unity Base was. Becca said, "You know, if Lary's right about the orbital geometry having been constructed to make eclipses, it sure wasn't done for beauty's sake. Not what humans can call beauty, anyway."

Around the umbra, the blood-red penumbra enveloped the planet like a huge wound in the world. Catharin shuddered. "It looks awful from space. Why would any intelligent race make this happen?"

"Maybe they didn't care what it looked like from space," said Becca. "But if they remodeled Blue and moved it and Green to where they had just the right geometry for this, they had to have been out in space. And if it was meant to be a show seen from here, maybe they knew to expect the downfall of their civilization. Or the extinction of their species. In other words, I think it's about the end of the world."

☽☾

An hour later, the shadow moved far enough for the bright eastern limb of Green to shine again. Catharin breathed easier in unexpected relief. The eclipse had disfigured the green world to an astounding degree.

Then a knock brought her to the door of her laboratory to find Joel standing there with his arms crossed. "Drop whatever you're doing," he said. "You need to talk to somebody in the Base. In Bix's office." He was in a harsh, abrupt mood that Catharin had never seen before.

"Why?"

"Just go." Joel turned away. His voice sounded choked. That unnerved Catharin as much as the eclipse had.

The Captain's office had a holographic telcon display. So although Wing, in Unity Base, had only Catharin's two-dimensional picture on the window before him, he seemed fully present to her. Except when he suddenly faded and returned, which jarred her frayed nerves. "Carlton, your image is unstable!"

"It's the lightning. We have bad weather."

"We can see it from up here. Why did you need to talk to me? Is somebody hurt? Is Joe there?"

Wing seemed to stand right in front of her as he told her that Joe had lost his genius, that he could not make breakthroughs like he had done on Earth, and not for lack of trying. Wing spoke with his empty palms turned up.

So that was what Joe had meant when he'd said, "I'll do everything I can."

A lightning strike near Unity Base obliterated Wing's image. Catharin was left staring at the wall behind where he had been, shaking uncontrollably.

Chapter Thirty

IONBOW

"As you've guessed, I can't help John Mark. Not much, anyway. I'm sorry."

So am I! She held her tongue. It had cost Joe something to say that. She remembered when she'd first met him in a telcon window, how different he'd seemed then, incorrigibly arrogant and self-centered.

"I know who his genetic parents are now. I want to help him more than ever, because part of him is you." His voice was rough with pain.

Jolted, Catharin felt a hot-and-cold wash of feeling, and found it hard to answer him. "I believe you," she whispered.

Joe seemed to need to think aloud. "Simple repair won't do it. The shortest jump from where he is to where he'd be healthy isn't restoring normality, it's *more* change toward something more elegant." He didn't give her time to digest that statement, immediately adding, "I used to have the Net-name 'Changer.' I was too young then to realize change is a two-edged sword and the changer sometimes has to be changed. But now I've lost my edge."

Joe sat very still. Not like that assessment interview: now, he wasn't fidgeting at all, as if all he had been through had shocked him into physical calm.

As much as she was grateful for the privacy and the holography of the telcon in the Captain's office, Catharin hated the separation between herself and Joe—the new quarantine that his most recent, and most extreme, immersion in alien glop had dictated. It was hard to have him here, as three-dimensional as life, and not be able touch him. "Don't blame yourself. You've been working like a demon on basic research, and it's helping some people."

"Maybe if your psychiatrists took some kind of chemical can opener to my brain, the genie would come out again?"

She shuddered. They had no way to predict how the brain would react, after stasis, to any kind of invasion. "No, Joe, it might kill the genie. As a researcher, you're good, and desperately needed."

"You've got me, then. For what it's worth."

"You're worth everything in the world to me."

He reacted instantly, with a pained smile. "I wish we were in the same world."

"So do I," she murmured. "How are things in yours?"

"Kay hates being grounded. She's doing a decent job with the little doctor duties. But she's joined Raj and Domino in a gripe club. Oh, and Sam's back in business." Nunki lay stretched across Joe's lap. Joe stroked the cat with his strong, elegant fingers, at which Nunki shivered and stretched luxuriously. "Building a new boat—more like a raft—with Alvin's help. She calls it the *Dauntless*, and they had a river trial yesterday. At least it didn't sink."

"What's it made of? They aren't cannibalizing the Base, are they?"

"They salvaged wreckage from the crashed shuttle. Alvin's a first-class welder and fixer-upper. He grew up somewhere in Alabama where the largest body of water was a catfish pond, but he's gung-ho for a new career as able-bodied sailor."

"He does talk like one." Catharin found it a relief to resort to simple gossip in an overwhelmingly charged conversation.

"The boat's keeping people from tearing out each others' throats—or taking razor blades to their wrists, depending on personality type. Too much has gone wrong, and it's too damn clear how little we can do about it. But at least there's the boat for people to invest interest in. How's Becca?"

"She's recovering slowly but steadily, as though her body is finding its way back to its natural balances."

"Silke?"

Vested interest. "Fine, as far as we can tell, but don't count on too much, Joe. Remember—" Who was she reminding, Joe or herself, about Silke or about John Mark? "Another woman is bearing her. If she lives, she won't be really be Becca's and yours."

Joe let his hand close lightly on Nunki's side. Catharin could tell he was taking the pulse of the cat's soothing purr. "A group of people can think of a kid as everybody's. There were families like that even on Earth. I told you about my dads and mom and aunt."

He had revealed his atypical family background in a private telcon conversation soon after Catharin's return to the Ship. At the time, it had startled her. Today it made Catharin think. "Given our precarious state of genetic affairs, it will take the love and labor of many people to bring a child into the world. At best very few of our children will belong to just one couple." *At worst, few children will survive by any means. And in three or four generations there will be none. The end of the world.*

"Ironic, isn't it? *Stasis*, supposed suspension of life processes, caused runaway changes in the human organism." Wheels seemed to turn in his mind. "It's almost certain to cause a changed society."

"Does that appeal to you?"

He gave her an engaging grin. "I like change for the hell of it. But human society, the way it played out on Earth, needed some big changes."

"You had your big chance. You turned it down."

"Engineering the end of death was the wrong kind of change," he said emphatically.

Finally, she asked him the question that had haunted her for weeks. "Could you have done it, Joe?"

"Yes. DNA always repairs itself, because accidents always happen, but the mechanisms put in place by evolution only fix a high percentage of the ongoing damages. The accumulated balance accounts for aging and eventual death. I could have gotten it vanishingly close to one hundred percent. Not immortality, but centuries. But it would have shut out mutation and evolution as well. It wouldn't have been life. More like dynamic stasis at the cellular level, continually counteracting the changefulness that's intrinsic to the genome. The change to end all changes."

Then Joe made the kind of connection he was good at doing, closed the circle of his reasoning like a falcon swooping down on its prey. "Rigid, repressive, stagnant societies have to work damn hard at it. Our colony will never have the resources of time and energy to do that. The new biological situation will make the social order mutable. It'll end up different from how any society on Earth was—or could have been."

"I wanted better," Catharin said sadly. "Not different."

He looked away from the telcon and might have been replaying their first conversation in his memory. The side of his face glowed with light flowing in through Medical's door, which had been flung open for ventilation as the sun set on Unity Mountain. "The kind of better you want is more different than you realize. I wish you could have talked to my Aunt Adrian about the black roots of the human condition—about sexual inequality and social sexual patterns. The only way I can imagine a rosy human future is if the being is seriously changed."

"But to imagine a future at all may be optimistic," Catharin said in a low voice.

He nodded. "The more I study what we've got now, the more disastrous it looks for reproduction. And you're getting a new case of cancer or autoimmune disorder or diabetes every week."

She loved his honesty, and knew that she could be honest with him. "Bix will have more company when the time comes."

"I could have made that different."

Aching to hold him, she had to settle for sending words across space to him, which seemed like clumsy, blunt instruments for her feeling. "What would you do if the end of the world was near?"

His eyes held her gaze for a long moment. "Make love to you."

A surge of sexual feeling made Catharin shiver. How strange that sexuality could thrive even in the long shadow of death. Strange but true. "So would I. Damn the distance."

"I lose track of time. Is it five more weeks of official quarantine until you can come down or I can go up?"

"Yes, unless somebody turns green with shiny spots."

The corners of his mouth twitched. "I'll make a point of not turning green with spots if you'll make sure the world doesn't end in the next five weeks."

"It's a deal."

☽☾

It almost felt like the good old days, to be wearing blue coveralls with red piping and working in zero g with Joel and others. But Bix was not with them, and rather than a training exercise it was something that *Aeon*'s designers had never dreamed of, in response to a need that no one had foreseen except maybe in their nightmares.

The Axis flared as it neared the engines. Bundles of pipe and knots of instrumentation congregated on the inner surface of the Axis. The new pipe had been laid on the surface of all that, retrofitted, with elbowroom to spare. Catharin tightened connections between segments of the pipe, using a zero-g wrench, with Miguel working not far away. Joel and Chief Engineer Orlov and a couple of junior engineers clustered at the junction where the pipe went into the engine chambers, conferring. Shut down, the huge engines were cool and still.

With the slow, fluid motion of familiarity with microgravity, Miguel slid up along the pipe to Catharin's side. "The interior of these joints will not be thoroughly smooth. Though the vacuum will pull most of it through, some small amount may adhere."

While she'd been at Unity Base she had let her hair get longer than ever. A strand had nonetheless worked itself loose from the braid and was floating in front of her eyes. She blew it away. "Then we either flush the pipe or cauterize it. Do you suppose we can arrange some backflow from the ionizing realm—enough to clean the pipe but not reach all the way back into the stasis vaults?"

"Maybe an engine-rated valve could be installed close to the vaults." Miguel signaled Joel to come over. Stretching his arms out, Joel soared, rather than sliding along the pipe. Joel loved flying in microgravity. Today, the work on hand had temporarily relieved him of the burden of his wider responsibilities, and freed him to fly.

Miguel explained the need for backflow and the possible usefulness of a valve. Joel nodded. "Makes sense. I'll suggest that somebody—I mean, I'll put somebody to work on it." Then he said, "Mama had some idea what I'd be when I grew up. Space pilot, she saw that one coming. But not Ship commander. And not undertaker."

☽☾

The control center hummed with activity, with every station manned and the gallery packed. Yet a respectful relative quiet prevailed. Subdued voices called out status checks.

The chief engineer's place was occupied by Orlov when Becca entered the center. Catharin stood to let Becca sit in her own chair at Life Support Systems.

The Big Picture framed the double planet. In the light of the sun, Blue was half-bright, half-dark; Green was half-dark, half-bright. They looked huge and stately, but Planets Blue and Green were dancing with each other. Each trailed a long banner of light as the Ship's Intelligence visualized the magnetotails blown back by the wind from the sun. Blue's dangled toward Green like a dancer's veil, an intimation of touch across millions of miles of space.

Orbiting Green and approaching the edge of the veil was the small, bright dot that signified the Ship.

In the direction of Catharin and Becca, Lary remarked, "Last time, the auroral display looked almost uniformly pale green."

Catharin replied, "From Downside, it was brilliant enough to wake up anybody sleeping near a window. How's their weather?"

"Partly cloudy, but better than it's been since the eclipse," Lary replied cheerily. *He* was better than he had been in weeks. Joe was succeeding in helping Lary, at least, not with a tour-de-force of scientific genius, but with hard research. Lary's health had responded positively to a barrage of modified conventional therapies.

Green's magnetic field appeared on the Picture as white lines that curved from pole to pole. The veil-like magnetotail of Blue brushed the magnetic lines of Green. The magnetotail channeled streams of particles from Blue into Green's magnetosphere. The particles looped around the magnetic lines, rapidly corkscrewing toward the north and south polar regions of Green.

"There it goes!" somebody sang out.

"Already?" Lary asked. "Three seconds early. It'll be a big show, all right."

In the Picture, the north pole developed a faint, flickering circlet of light.

As the aurora flared into an emerald crown, Joel ordered the engines on at ninety percent of full power. A star flared inside the engines, briefly. The Ship ponderously lifted toward a slightly higher orbit aimed through the magnetotail of Blue.

"Maybe I'm hypersensitive because I was sick," Becca whispered. "But not only can I feel the engine vibration, I can feel patterns in it. I can tell what kind of shape the engine is in. It's talking to me."

Orlov sat at Engineering, rigid with concentration as he reviewed the information on his console. Orlov had been one of the anomalies in the stasis-aftermath pattern. He was as old as Bix and had been in space nearly as long, yet his health had turned out to be good. Had Catharin revived him, as per the Mission plan, rather than Becca, his health would not have been an issue. He had not forgiven either woman for the decision Catharin had made. But she did not regret it.

"We're crossing the magnetotail," Lary said. "It's a very impressive particle stream. Little of the radiation can get past the Ship's insulation, but we've lost our normal wavelengths of communication to Unity Base."

"That's okay. They're all outside watching the sky," Becca said.

"The engine chambers are hot," Orlov reported.

Joel nodded. "Open the valves. Everybody observe silence for the next minute or so."

Even informative audio signals were squelched. The control center had not been so silent since the day Catharin and Bix and Joel had gone in to turn it on just after Starfall, slightly more than a year ago. Becca closed her eyes, as if listening to the engines describe their work of ionizing the dead.

The Big Picture showed the Ship cutting through the lines of the magnetotail. The charged particles streaming through the magnetotail from Blue to Green poured around the Ship, flowing against the pool of ions released from the engines. The ions glowed. The Ship left a wake of light.

The Picture wavered with tears in Catharin's eyes. *Blaze of glory.*

"The, ah, special reaction mass is one hundred percent expended," reported Flight station.

"Shut down the engines," said Joel.

Murmurs echoed around the center as others registered what the Picture showed. The glowing ionic wake of the Ship was seized and sculpted by the magnetotail of Blue. The radiance took the shape of a shock wave in the magnetotail, stretching toward Green, where it eddied in the magnetic field lines of the green planet and poured toward both of Green's poles, creating a world-encompassing bow of faint light.

"Will you look at that," Joel said softly. "It's like a rainbow."

"An ionbow," said Becca.

The bow made contact with Green's auroral crown of fire. And at that spot, traces of other colors—pink, yellow, blue—swirled inside the green expanse.

"Is that a false-color picture?" asked Becca.

"No. We made a difference in the composition of the aurora," Miguel answered. "Oxygen ions produce the aurora's usual green. We injected ionized carbon, nitrogen, hydrogen, and trace elements in smaller quantities. The atoms that human beings are made of."

Joel's face shone in the colorful soft light. In a quiet but confident voice, he said, "And God made the rainbow for a sign that the flood was over and the waters of destruction would recede, and life would go on."

☽☾

Although broken clouds filled the night sky, Wing elected to go to the promontory an hour before dawn. The first green auroral light appeared in the northern half of the celestial sphere like a thin, gauzy curtain behind the clouds. It brightened into distinct ripples. The clouds developed sharp green edges.

"I can't believe this. It gives out enough light to read by," said Kay.

"But don't read. Watch. No camera is going to catch that like the eye can," Aaron murmured, gazing up at the sky.

The brilliant green sky had darker green clots of cloud in it. That sky all too well symbolized the mood of the Base for these last days, Wing thought: a pall of electric fear overshadowed everyone, with uglier curdles of animosity, despair, bitterness. His own mood had been as frightened as everyone else's. He knew how grim the medical situation was turning out to be. Joe had shared that with him in private, in anguish, and in detail.

Tezi said, "It looks to me like one of those clouds has a tinge of pink."

Moved aside by a high-altitude wind, the cloud unveiled a faint blot of pink, blue, and yellow halfway between horizon and zenith, blurred like watercolors. A star shone through the colors. "That's it!" said Aaron excitedly. "The footprint of the ion release from the Ship!"

The colors intensified, rippling like a thin silk scarf.

Alvin declared, "Fucking good light show!"

"Can't you be even a little reverent?" Kay snapped.

"Hell no."

The testy exchange hardly touched Wing's inner thoughts. He was mesmerized by the sky, the colors breaking the expanse of ominous auroral green, beautiful and benign light appearing in a haunted sky. Had inhabitants of ancient China ever seen a sight like this, surely they might have called it the Phoenix of lovely colors, the celestial embodiment of benevolence and harmony. Wing, a Christian, saw the ion-rainbow swirl in the green aurora and called it the promise of resurrection.

Chapter Thirty-One

THE HELICES OF CRISIS

It pleased Wing that Joe had asked for his company on this excursion. Wing was as fascinated as ever by Green's eerie twilights. The rules still forbade anyone to venture out during twilight, with or without a companion—but despair over broken genes and shattered futures had loomed so large in Unity Base for so long that no one heeded such rules anymore. Joe and Wing reached the rock-edged pool just at the twilight's beginning. A red-gold sunset still illuminated the tops of the trees, while the first shafts of blue moonlight shivered in the air.

"Clear as a bell tonight," Joe said. "Unlike the last full Blue." Three weeks ago, at the last full moon, it had rained torrentially, thanks to the weather precipitated by the eclipse. Then Joe said, "Remember the night we walked uphill?"

"I'll never forget that."

"When we were in the bog full of swampcress—the wok bog—my brain went into a fugue of wild ideas of creatures I wanted to invent. I thought I could see DNA I've worked with in the past, hanging in the blue air like a virtual arena. And I thought I could manipulate it."

"Without data?"

"I had my notebook. I checked what I'd entered into it later, though, and none of it made sense. It was a fever dream from being hurt and on painkillers and smelling the bog. But the blue air was just like a virtual arena. When Kay came down in all her glory to give us the news about Blue's mountains, the shuttle's contrail looked like DNA on the sky. That made me finally remember the molecules in the blue. I want to see if it happens again."

"And if it does?"

Joe crouched beside the water, looking down but seeming to be looking within himself. "On Earth, I did some of my best work when I was dreaming or walking, then went back to a workstation and fed in the figures. I haven't felt that kind of inspiration in months. Since the night we crashed. Maybe the ground rules have changed, but the game can still be played. Worth a try, eh?"

So this was not a simple hour's leisure, but Joe challenging the demon of his lost creativity. "Of course," said Wing.

The pool was flat and bright as a mirror. Wing thought of the beneficent effects of mirrors in Asian folklore; it had been thought that mirrors drive away demons. He fervently hoped that it would be so tonight. Then, in the back of his mind, he prayed about it.

Joe paced back and forth. "Good thing it's not overcast. I've got my nerves all worked up for this. If I had to put it off, I'd get cold feet."

"Yes. The twilight can be dangerous."

"That and part of me still doesn't want this to work, because if it does, I'm committed to work on medical problems the rest of my life. Same old quandary. I don't want to lose my life as I know it, don't want to change that much," Joe said dourly. "Not even if the alternatives are even worse for everybody else."

Wing sympathized. If someone had asked him, more than a year ago, whether he would volunteer to devote himself to study alien plants, and be torn away from his family, his faith community, and his religious calling in the Sixth Tier, he would have politely but firmly declined.

Joe alternately tinkered with the notebook and watched for the moon to rise over the fern trees. He radiated tension. Yet, he wasn't as self-absorbed as Wing might have expected. He stopped to look over Wing's shoulder as Wing examined small plants in crannies in the rocks, misted by the waterfall.

"I'm looking for flowers," Wing explained. "If flowering plants arose and declined in the long life of Green, some flowers might linger as small relic populations, like Catharin's purple-footed drakeflies."

The dusk evolved into a magenta mixture of blue moonlight and red setting sunlight, making it impossible to discern the small parts of the plants. Wing stretched out on the mossy hillside beside the pool. He jumped up when he found it surprisingly warm. More gingerly, he settled down again.

Joe drew into himself, working with his notebook. Wing saw a calmer and more pleasant man than he had first met on the Starship. Joe was facing the most painful question of his life with a kind of ragged grace. Wing approved.

The sun set, and its red light withdrew from the sky. The blue around them intensified. Joe stayed motionless and silent save for his stylus tapping the touch-window of his notebook.

The hurricane moon rose above the fern trees, pouring abundant blue light onto the pool. It made the hard shapes of the rocks soft and indistinct to the eye, and gave the soft form of water an uncanny hard luster.

Wing felt strangely close to God, *mysterium tremendum et fascinans*, the frightening and fascinating mystery. On this green world with that blue one in the night sky, there was plentiful and potent mystery to contemplate. For the first time since stasis, Wing did not regret having been revived for this place and time. Even if Joe failed, disaster unfolded, and humanity died out with Wing's own generation, Wing would still be glad that he had met the wonder of these worlds.

"I can visualize what I need to," Joe said suddenly. "I just think about it and then let my mind wander, and it's there. *There.* A double helix." Joe pointed at thin blue air. "The Ship sent me an analysis of Silke's DNA. That was a small mountain of data. But I must have somehow memorized it. Now I can see it. And—Carl—"

Joe's voice was so fraught with feeling that Wing sat up, alarmed.

"It took me days to realize that there was something wrong with John Mark. Now—"

Dismay knotted itself like a cold, tangled wire in the pit of Wing's stomach. "Do you see something wrong?"

"No. Everything's right. She'll be tall and slender, with dark hair and blue eyes. Carl, part of her is me! I know my own genome pretty well. I can tell the difference between Becca's genes and mine in Silke! It's almost like seeing myself in a magic mirror. Not completely me. But not a stranger either."

Wing sensed that it was a moment for the right word or none. He chose to say, "It is not always terrible to be changed, Joe."

Joe's intake of breath told Wing that he'd gotten the point.

"Can you see John Mark?" Wing suggested, aware that twilight would not last indefinitely.

Joe physically turned around, as though the other child's genome occupied its own place in the blue air. Joe's face took on a frown: the expression of a man evaluating a subtle and thorny problem.

Joe alone could see the molecules of the boy's life and death arrayed in the twilight. To Wing's amazement, Joe reached up to pluck something invisible out of the thin air; he moved it a few inches to the side, with an air of infinite precision.

☽ ☾

It was the earliest hours of the Ship's morning, and Joel lay in bed sleeping badly when he got the call he dreaded. "Commander, please come to the hospital."

Joel dressed in a haze of sick dread and had his hand on the door before it penetrated the haze the caller had not been Dr. Pei. It had been the clipped voice of Srivastava.

The molecular biology center chief met Joel in the hospital lobby. Srivastava had on the crisp white coat that he always wore—Joel could imagine him stone-cold dead and just as immaculate—but part of his black hair stuck out as though he'd slept on it. "What's up?" Joel asked.

Srivastava waved Joel into the hospital elevator. "The Ship has enormous computing power, and as much of it as could be spared has been used in the effort to find the cause and cure of the boy's illness. The Medical Intelligence ran through gene substitutions, modeling the outcomes in the patient."

The elevator glided past the floor where the pediatric unit was located. Joel realized that he had been holding his breath. Since the door wasn't opening on the pediatric unit after all, he let it out.

Srivastava went on, "If we change this allele to that, will the boy get better? If not this one, the next? Express this gene? Suppress that one? But the human genome is complex beyond even artificial intelligence like we have here. It has been like the earliest computers programmed to play chess, which did poorly because they examined every possible move after every possible move, an impossible number of considerations. We lacked a heuristic way to expedite the process. All of our existing heurisms are based on the genetic mistakes known to medicine on Earth, and what we have here is an unprecedented set."

"Has somebody come up with new heuristic code?"

"No. It seems that the Intelligence is being guided by a master."

"Joe Toronto?"

"He rang up four hours ago and interrupted the substitution routine. He has been sending up a set of exactly defined specifications for gene therapy, and having the Intelligence model the results." Srivastava pushed open the door to the Molecular Biology Center.

Joel did a double take: at three o'clock in the Ship's morning, the center swarmed with people, and every workstation window in the place was alight with imagery, with holovisuals in the air all over the place. "So the gene genius thinks he's gotten his knack back?"

"There." Srivastava pointed to a window displaying a geodesic framework of lines, with a complex array of colored dots packed within the frame. "It is a virus being designed to infect cells with a cure. My people are so convinced that Toronto is onto something that they have started to produce the virus."

It finally sank in that this might be good news. Joel demanded, "Are you telling me there's a cure for John Mark?"

"The Intelligence is modeling the outcome of the genes to be delivered by the viral couriers. Changes in the patient's metabolism and other cellular activities are played out. See?" Medical diagrams and figures unintelligible to Joel scrolled down the window. All of a sudden, Srivastava abandoned his factual rundown to exclaim, "My God, the AI thinks it will really work!"

Joel had been too beleaguered by dire problems for too long to believe it. Joel said flatly, "It can't be true that he's that good again. If he ever was."

Srivastava waved his hands in a gesture that matched the state of his hair: sprung loose from the usual composure. "I heard about that guy on Earth. Inside the scientific community, he had a reputation as a tinkerer. One who would undertake first this showy project and then that one, whatever caught his fancy. A genius, yes, but one without much staying power. I would have expected less from him than this, even if he had been still at the peak of his ability."

In the hubbub of voices in the center, one got Joel's attention. "Maturation modeling—" Joel turned automatically.

He'd seen the Intelligence's maturation modeling of John Mark before. It had bleakly fascinated him. The Intelligence had aged the sick baby to a sicker child, one with patchy skin, a misshapen head, and slack jaw. Thus the Intelligence had unsparingly predicted ongoing illness and developmental problems, followed by death in late childhood.

The boy visualized in the window stood with his back to Joel. He might have been six years old. Naked, he was well formed, his skin the color of well-stirred cafe au lait with none of the sick patchiness in the images Joel had seen before.

Joel walked closer. Two technicians quickly moved out of his way.

The boy turned around. The Intelligence must have been modeling this age of the boy with these new genes for the very first time; the image moved slowly. Slow motion gave the boy an uncanny gracefulness.

The face that turned toward Joel transfixed him. Brown eyes. Regular features. Something about the contour of his eyes and cheekbones, and the alert cast of the boy's expression, was familiar. Joel felt goosebumps form on his skin.

The boy resembled Catharin.

When Joel woke Catharin up, he was struck by how much her intent face resembled the boy's, until he told her the news. Then she broke down, crying on his shoulder, shaking so hard that he had to brace himself as he held her.

Joel found himself remembering the ionbow painted on the Big Picture a few weeks before, improbable and marvelous. "It'll be all right," he murmured to Catharin. "Death isn't the end. Life is."

Wing discovered Joe in the Penthouse, sleeping the sound sleep of the innocent, or the redeemed.

A gleeful commotion from the patio was faintly audible even from here. Everyone whom Eddy had fended off from distracting Joe at his vital work, all of whom Aaron had finally ordered out of Medical, had congregated on the patio to celebrate. With water, beer, and Wimm's new vintage of wine, they had toasted Joe as well as the moon, sun, stars, Silke, the Ship, Green, and assorted indigenous fauna. Then they started dancing, and most were still at it.

What Joe had done was received by Unity Base as a miracle.

Relaxing on his own bunk, Wing pondered this. He felt inclined to see Joe's astounding achievement as less of a marvel and more of a natural outcome of Joe's labors of the past few months. Inspiration, perspiration, and consummation were the natural order of human success. Gifted people might skip the second term, perspiration. The naturally brilliant can find ways to avoid having to labor as long and hard as their fellows. That was similar to how the beautiful often fail to cultivate their personalities. In either case they were impoverished in the midst of their abundance.

Not Joe's scientific breakthrough, but rather his change of heart, Wing found miraculous. From being a man who shied away from perspiration, and disavowed commitment to the common good, Joe had become a man who threw himself into the fiery furnace of labor for the good of others for weeks on end. And at the last, even Joe's wild genius had willed good. For that, Wing thanked a slender blue-eyed girl who had yet to be born. Silke had shown Joe change with a human face. She, unborn child and woman yet to be, had convinced Joe that change, even change reaching into the core of his being, did not have to be alien and awful.

Chapter Thirty-Two

SPRING TIDE

Speaking to Catharin and Joel over a private telcon link to the molecular biology center, Joe sounded less brusque than he had just fifteen minutes earlier while addressing the conference. Of course: he didn't need to assert his rank, as had been the case with his fellow scientists.

He wasn't editing his remarks as much, either. "John Mark is human. Same species as us. But a new variety. He's got traits that no human ever had before."

He had given Catharin fair warning about this, but put in straightforward words, it still stunned her. She managed to say, "Subtle ones, I hope."

"Very subtle. I wasn't showing off. But I didn't point the fine details out to Srivastava and company because it might rattle some cages."

"Mine included," Catharin murmured.

"Why did you do it?" Joel asked.

"The natural genome is jerry-rigged, improvised by natural selection rather than built by logical design. Restoring the jerry-rigging scrambled by stasis was impossible in practice. I had to find more elegant mechanisms than some of the ones evolution cobbled together in the first place. I know it's his humanity we're talking about. And he's your child," he added, addressing both of them with more empathy than Catharin would have thought conceivable a year or a thousand light-years ago. Her throat tightened. *Our child. He cares.* Strange that such simple facts could be devastatingly moving.

Joel sat with his chin propped on his fist, keeping his emotions to himself. "Sometimes life says change or die."

"Captain, may I give you some advice about the situation we're in?"

It was the first time Catharin had heard Joe call Joel anything other than Atlanta.

"I'd welcome it," Joel said.

They sounded like a captain and a chief scientist with guarded but genuine respect for each other.

"John Mark won't be unique for long. Reproductive roulette is the name of the game now. A rare couple may go off in the woods and conceive a child—" the corner of Joe's mouth twitched ironically. "But it's still likely to take medical and scientific intervention to bring the child to term. Any child from here on out. God only knows what the social ripple effects will be. I'm glad dealing with that isn't my job." *It's yours, Captain*, was implied. Joe went on, "That day on the river, Carlton Wing survived the tidal wave only because he knew to point the bow of the canoe into it, and he and Tezi had the nerve to stay in position. I'm a scientist, not a prophet—but I think the situation we're in is similar. I advise you to steer our colony accurately and unflinchingly." *Or see it wrecked.*

Joel evidently understood. A sheen of sweat had appeared on his brow. "Can I count on you to help with the science?"

Joe nodded, with the somber air of a man reenlisting in the armed forces in time of war. His image was holographic, an illusion that made him look close enough to touch, his mood tangible enough to feel. On impulse, with a surge of empathy for Joe, Catharin said, "But it's different in an important way from facing the tidal wave. The time frame is much longer. There will be time to rest. And play. Joe has damn well earned the right to play—and I might add, that's a well-known way to keep scientific creativity fresh—but he might need some of the Ship's research facilities."

"I don't have a problem with that." Joel asked Joe, "What do you have in mind?"

For a moment, Joe looked flummoxed at the unexpected turn of topic—or at the fact that it was Catharin who had turned the topic that way. Then wheels in his mind started turning. "I've always wanted to make a unicorn."

Aside, Joel asked Catharin, "Could he do that?"

"Safe bet. But how would the horse feel about it, Joe?"

To Catharin's joy, he took the question seriously. "Metabolic adjustments are dangerously tricky, but a horn is a lot more foolproof. The animal would be very unlikely to end up sick. A delicate physique is even easier. It's not genetic at all. Horses conceived and raised on the Moon ended up small and delicate. The trickiest part would be integrating appropriate behavior into the beast, so it didn't have reflexes that cause it to hurt itself, or inappropriately injure its friends. But I know a lot about the plasticity of behavior at the genetic level. It's important for horses to have a herd to feel all's right with the world, though. So how about a unicorn garden in the lower-gravity realms near the Axis?"

Amazing how Joe had upped the ante from unicorn, singular, somewhere, to a whole herd of them in the prize real estate in *Aeon.*

Joel's chin lifted, and he stirred in his chair. "Could you figure out a way to give people radiation-proof skin? Eyes that see into the infrared?"

"We could have done it on Earth, and it would have facilitated deep-space exploration," Joe answered immediately. "Unfortunately, that wasn't economically rewarding enough."

"I wondered about that." Joel had always been a man with imagination, and now he was thinking ahead into their new future. "We've got the whole rest of a solar system to explore here. And old-world economics don't matter."

A blue outline flashed around the monitor. The research center's Intelligence wanted the communications link back for uploading data from Unity Base.

Joel told Joe, "Earlier, I thanked you on behalf of the hope you've given everybody. I thank you personally too. For what you've done for John Mark. For what you've given me."

When Joe's image faded, Catharin and Joel were left in private. And Joel's façade of equanimity melted. He put his head in his hands. "I didn't expect this."

"I didn't expect any of this. None of what happened since we left Earth. Not the bad, and not the good." She rubbed his back.

"Did I do okay?"

"Yes, Captain." Patting his back, she took her hand away.

Joel smiled at her. "Don't miss your shuttle down to the Base. You've earned a chance to play too."

"I will. They're going to watch for migrating Green-seals, and I'm invited to be one of the observers."

"Lady, watching fish wasn't what I meant."

☽☾

To his surprise, Joe had just gotten what he had always wanted: permission to play. Ideas bubbled in his brain. For the next generation of space explorers, practical, radiation-resistant skin would be an inarguable plus—and the properties could be designed as decorative tiger stripes. He didn't know what Catharin thought about his resurgent itch to play with human genes. She'd gone inscrutable on the telcon after Joel brought up making modifications to people. In all likelihood, she was saving her opinion for their first hour of privacy.

He went outside. In the loading dock of Unity Base, Sam Houston was loading bulky equipment into three jeeps. "Need a hand?"

"Have at it! Is she coming back?"

"On the shuttle later this morning."

As Joe hefted an instrument package onto an already high pile of equipment in the back of one of the jeeps, he remembered meeting Catharin for the first time, and her well-honed determination to reconstruct civilization in the sunlight of another star. On one hand, there would be a future. On the other hand, the foreseeable future was fraught with genetic damage and painstaking repair, with incalculable societal ramifications. And there were no more hands than that. The human race at Green would not escape sea-change. Catharin's hopes had been dead on arrival, whether or not she'd admitted that to herself yet.

Nobody—not the scientists, not the Vanguard, not the colonists still in stasis—had gotten what they bargained for. Some got much worse, others far better, and some a very different prize than what they'd expected on the other side of the stars.

Joe was starting to feel like one of the lucky ones.

Sam noticed. As she meticulously secured Joe's contributions to the jeep's cargo, Sam chortled and told him, "Tall, blonde, and striking really is the type you go for!"

☽☾

Wildly mixed feelings would be easier to sort out while she was still on the Ship than while being welcomed back to Unity Base. Catharin detoured to Outtown's plaza.

As a doctor, it unnerved her that John Mark had subtle changes from the human norm. The sick boy had been a dismaying mirror for her. The well child was an uncanny one.

Shrubs framed wide white sidewalks. Water danced in a fountain, spurting up from the mouth of a fantastic brass fish. The fish reminded her of Joe. He could make fantasies real. He still had a streak of unruly wild genius, along with a new capability for hard work and taking responsibility. The combination was more compelling to Catharin than she would have thought possible.

Joe didn't know it, but she was planning to up the ante on him. She reached into the jacket pocket, checking to make sure Miranda's ring was still there. It felt smooth, heavy, and cool.

Unexpectedly and soberingly, the ring reminded Catharin of her original purpose. She had meant to help carry the forged, completed wisdom of civilization to the stars. For a long time, she'd been too busy beating death back to worry about that. Now she realized why she'd made a beeline to the plaza to do her thinking. It reflected her old dream—and told her that it was still just a dream. Even with a breathable atmosphere and landscaping, the plaza was strikingly clean and empty. And the longest stretches of sidewalks revealed a disconcerting upward curvature to match *Aeon*'s artificial gravity. The plaza wasn't so much the heart of a living city as a template for a future inspired by the past.

The ancient European Renaissance had segued into the chaos of Reformation. But people in Earth's twenty-first century had revived Renaissance ideals. Two of those idealists were the parents who had given Catharin *Firenze* for a middle name and instilled in her the hope of a new golden age, civilization re-created with perfection it had never had in the past.

Any such hope would almost certainly be wagered away in the crap shoot of a wildly unpredictable future on Green. Catharin's personal mission was a lost cause. It had been ever since she was revived for the first time at Planet Zero. She wondered if she could live happily with that failure boxed up and stored away deep inside of her.

The gardeners had succeeded in making healthy-looking marigolds grow beside the walkway in a rough ribbon of green and gold. But one of the dewy, new-budded marigolds was blue, obviously a mutant. Startled, Catharin kneeled to study it. The petals looked normal, a bit filmy for a marigold, but symmetrical. But as blue as sky.

Some of the fringes of stasis-induced change were tiny and harmless. But they could turn up anywhere, like omens, lest anyone forget the grim truth. Catharin bowed her head, nearly brought to tears by the little flower.

A gardener appeared at her side, looking concerned. "Doctor, are you all right?"

"Fine." She got to her feet. "I was admiring your sport."

His face fell when he saw the mutant marigold. Those on gardening duty were sensitized to the genetic debacle; it manifested itself in their hands every day.

Something clicked in Catharin's mind. People weren't marigolds, or horses, who had to accept being changed and uncomprehendingly live with it. Humans could embrace life even without arms—and make a society work even if the biological fibers that tied one generation to the next were unpredictable and brittle. People didn't have to be blind to the unexpected, or bound by fear of it. "It's pretty. With any luck, you might develop a whole new kind of marigold from this one," she said to the gardener.

On her way out of the plaza, she paused beside the fish fountain. The basin contained clear water, plus a few coins—souvenirs of Earth that had turned up in the recesses of pockets and boxes, useless as currency in a city-ship without money, tossed into the water for luck. They were in for luck, all right—a tidal wave of it, and not preferentially *good* luck, either. Yet, the human race here might face the wave of change and survive. It all depended on how well and how wisely they steered. And that would be Catharin's goal from now on. She would do her best. And Joe would help, and not reluctantly, not anymore.

She wanted to see Joe again, touch him, hold him, so urgently that the yearning was a pleasurable pain.

☽☾

The *thump-thump-thump* of the Starhawk's rotors echoed off the riverbanks, fading as the helicopter departed toward the drop-off points for the other three teams of spotters, farther downriver. Joe and Catharin checked to be sure they'd debarked with everything they needed: binoculars, two-way, ground blanket, hats to ward off the noon sun. And each other. Catharin said, "Well, we're alone at last."

She looked extraordinarily good this morning in her well-fitting field clothes. Joe felt more than ready to make love at this very moment. But not here on the river's scratchy banks and not with spotters positioned on land, water, and in the air. "Not alone enough."

They climbed the nearby hill. The river rolled by below within steep banks thirty feet high, vivid green with worms that didn't think the time had come to duck.

"Everybody in position?" came the voice of Sam on the two-way, blaring with enthusiasm.

Teams One, Two, and Three—which was Catharin and Joe—and Four, consisting of Domino and Aaron beside the Starhawk, which had landed on a bluff, reported in. *Kite* was aloft; Becca's voice was clear on the two-way as she reported her position, flying up the coastline toward the estuary. It was the same route she had taken the day she took Joe up. Wing rode in the airplane with Becca today, intent on viewing his old nemesis, the wave, from a safer perspective.

"Alvin just cast off the bow line. We're going out into the current," Sam informed them all. She and Alvin were aboard the *Dauntless*, well up the river, where the wave should crest at less than a foot high. Their homemade instruments and meters dangled off the sides of the raft like so many fishing lines. "Ten minutes and counting until the tide rolls off the sea."

"We'll be there," said the soprano voice of *Kite*.

Catharin and Joe spread a cloth on the ground and settled down for a comfortable wait. Catharin turned off the two-way transmitter to speak without being overheard. "Joe, I brought something for you." She placed something small and heavy in his palm.

It was a man's wedding ring, plain but lustrous, old gold. Startled, Joe said, "You came from Earth prepared."

"Yes, but not that prepared. It was a last-minute gift from a friend." She smiled slightly, the corners of her mouth curving up, but her face had a cast of fierce seriousness. "It's yours if you want it. So am I."

For weeks, Joe had wondered if a moment like this would come up. And if it did, whether he would run for his life—or give up the relentless independence he'd prized ever since he left home, like a snake sloughing its old skin. He lobbed the decision back to her. "Are you sure you know what you're doing, Catharin Gault?"

With a flick of her head, she said, "I'm finally changing my name. From here on out, I'll be Catharin Firenze."

Ever since she'd told him about her middle name, it had secretly fascinated him. Now, it tipped Joe out of indecision. He closed his hand around the ring. "I traveled lighter than you did. What was in my heart and head was all I brought. I could invent a nice plasmid ring for you, to specify an interesting genetic trait in future generations." He waited for her to explode.

She said, "Deal." The syllable resonated in a vast and unexpected space of permission. Joe was so astonished that words failed him. Laughing, she leaned closer to him and stroked the bridge of his nose with her finger. Joe took her hand and kissed her palm.

The two-way said, "Team Three, you're supposed to be paying attention to the *river*." Domino's tone was barbed. Catharin blushed an attractive shade of shell-pink.

"The worm clock says it's soon," Tezi Young reported on the two-way. The banks of the river had begun to turn pale, from the waterline up.

The hurricane moon rode high in the sky, almost new, a thin curved blue wire. It was a world that somebody had remade after their idea of grandeur. Maybe the blue world hadn't minded being remodeled. Joe suspected that worlds, like DNA, wanted to change.

Blue and the new sun pulled together, exerting the full force of spring tide on Green. The waters of Green flared up in response. Becca's voice came over the two-way. "People, you've got a tidal bore coming."

Wing said, "I can see it folding out of the water in the mouth of the river. From here, it is magnificent."

"Plain as day. We're following it," Becca said.

"Look for beasties," Sam reminded on the two-way.

"There's *Kite*." Catharin pointed. In the distance, the plane circled, the sun glancing off its long wings.

Becca said, "We see something. Five, six—no? You're right, Carl. Make it two or three, the water's so clear we can see their shadows on the bottom of the river. Elongated shapes. Maybe they're Joe's seals. They seem to be riding the surge about a hundred yards behind the crest. I won't fly lower and scare 'em, but the cameras are on telephoto. We've got an image on the monitor in the cockpit."

"Do they look like aliens?" asked the scratchy voice of Alvin, first mate on the *Dauntless*.

"I can see five aliens from here," Aaron said dryly.

"He's right," Catharin murmured. "We really are the aliens."

"Our children won't be," Joe said.

Catharin gave him an intent look with her green eyes, then nodded. "So be it."

"That flange Joe described is wider than I thought, and undulating," Wing reported. "They swim like manta rays."

Kite flew along the river, chasing the tidal bore. Layered under the drone of its engine, Joe heard a sound like distant surf, a sigh that grew louder and louder. He took Catharin's hand and pulled her up beside him to watch the river. Its steep banks glistened greenish gray. The worms had all taken refuge in their holes.

Catharin squeezed Joe's hand. The feel of her fingers, slender but strong, laced with his, gave him a shock of delight.

The big wave was not as ugly as Joe had seen in his nightmares. It looked stately as it approached, a graceful mountain of clear, light blue water. The wave passed by, raising the whole river in one mighty surge. Its voice swelled into a resounding hiss, with a clatter of rocks at the wave's skirts. Cheering and applause sounded from the nearest other spotting position. Catharin waved her hat. The wind from the sea blew a few loose strands of her long hair across her face, which was lit with an expression of delight. Joe had the ring in his free hand, holding it tightly. It meant *her*, he thought. She wanted to be his in a way no woman ever had been, and he was going to be hers. Scary thought. But attractive too, like the wave.

In the wave's wake, the river ran twenty feet higher, deep green in color, fringed with rich foam. The river's surface tossed and shimmered.

Tezi yelped over the two-way, "I see the seals! They're all on my side!"

The Green-seals had elected to migrate on the far side of the river, and it would be impossible to see them from across the turbulent water. So Joe flung his arms around Catharin, pulling her into an embrace. They staggered a giddy step, holding each other tightly and laughing.

ABOUT THE AUTHOR

Alexis Glynn Latner writes speculative fiction as well as nonfiction, teaches creative writing, works at Rice University's Fondren Library in Houston, Texas, and for fun and real-life adventure is a sailplane pilot. Her science fiction novelettes and short stories have appeared in *Analog Science Fiction and Fact* and *Amazing Stories.* Her short story "Kindred," in the anthology *Bending the Landscape: Horror*, won the 2002 Spectrum Award for best short fiction. In addition to fiction, she writes magazine articles about aviation, education, and technology. She teaches a creative writing course in the Rice University School of Continuing Studies.

Like many other writers, she has done an interesting variety of paid and volunteer work, including information technology support specialist, glider maintenance coordinator for the Soaring Club of Houston, and South/Central Regional Director of the Science Fiction and Fantasy Writers of America. In the past, she did stints as an oil-field services company clerk, a maintenance electrician, and a hospital chaplain. She has a BA in linguistics from Rice and an MA in systematic theology from the Graduate Theological Union in Berkeley, California.